COMPEL

Rae Wilder, Volume Two

CHAPTER ONE

The path to contentment should be clear to someone with a purpose, yet I diminished into the realm of the lost.

Grief smothered me until I gasped for air. I hummed with passion. Hate. I wanted the High Lord's head on a pike. I wanted to dance manically around his corpse and give in to the dark whispers in the corners of my heart. Nothing less would appease the burning ache in my chest or the carnivorous sense of loss that threatened to consume me.

Shivering, I glanced around. I sat by a pool of cool water with the most beautiful lush flowers I had ever seen blooming in the morning sunrays. The air was fresh and scented with a zesty bouquet. I breathed in deeply, letting the cool air chill my lungs even as my mind fought for clarity. The air tasted sweet and earthy and every noise, no matter how low or loud, washed over me like raindrops, like music. Colour was intense, and everything seemed to shimmer and glow. As the dawn passed and the sun climbed higher in the sky, the soft radiance emitted by the flora intensified. Never had I experienced a dawn like it. When I was at Temple the sun always retreated behind low and dark clouds, covering the land in a perpetual twilight. Here everything was made of light and shone brightly.

When I first arrived in this fairy Wyld, I had gotten a vague sense of being surrounded, and a low intense hum of feelings pressed on me from above like whisperings of the gods calling from the heavens. I had looked up, dazed, and gasped at the fallen stars scattered across the forest canopy. The twinkling I had glimpsed among the rich green leaves was the fairies and their auras. An immediate kinship bloomed in my heart and it petrified me because I had looked into their shining faces and seen exactly what my arrival meant to them.

The fairies stood on the porches and outer steps of tree houses seemingly growing from the thick bark that coated the broad tree boughs. The males and females both wore long tunics with dark trousers beneath, similar to what I had seen in the Grove, but these people seemed softer somehow. These were not warriors, but families with young children and elderly folk, who peeked down at me with expressions of awe. The elderly fairies, faces wrinkled and hair shades of pure white and grey, boggled my mind. How many centuries could have to pass for a fairy's skin to wrinkle and their back become curved with age? Two thousand? Three? Not that I had forgotten, but it brought my own age into question. I had eighteen years of memories as a human. I was ... *had* been a Sect Disciple found on a Priest's doorstep and given to the Clerics to become a protector of humanity.

Yet Breandan, the fairy-boy who had found me, claimed I was born before him. Two hundred years before him. That was when my mother had split the key to the grimoire - a powerful book of spells - into three amulets and hidden them with magical guardians. One, the amulet of protection, had been given to my older brother Conall. The second, the amulet of wisdom, had been given to me. The last, the amulet of power, had been given to her nephew, and the heir to the fairy Wylds, Devlin.

Had the protection of the key been my whole purpose, maybe I would not feel the need to run away. Perhaps I could have adjusted into my new life as a demon; a kind of being I had been raised to hunt down and kill if it threatened the safety of my human home. But what came with the amulets I'd nearly died for was a responsibility to use their power to protect and guide the fairy people, the cornerstone of demonkind.

Stricken with grief, I found myself in the midst of the people I was destined to protect. They intuitively looked to me for reassurance. Shaken and frightened after the sensational and violent departure of their High Lord they turned their faces down toward me, and I felt the weight of every gaze – a thick swelling of anxious consciousnesses pleading for me to soothe them. But I had nothing to give. Nothing. I was a girl, angry and full of anguish. What did they expect from me? I had watched their Lord abuse and murder my best friend. I was forced to watch her suffer, unable to help her as iron chains drained my power. Alex had been chosen for being nothing more than a source of purity, and as a twisted way for Devlin to get back at me. How could they have expected anything from me after that? I saw nothing but monsters. Pointy-eared and fanged monsters in a myriad of colours and creeds reaching out their talon-tipped fingers to trap and torture me.

Sensing my panic, Conall had clasped my elbow and brought me here to the sparkling pool and left me to go and do whatever fairy lords do after such a night as we had suffered.

But I was not alone in this magical place.

The two fairies he left me with took one long look at me then coaxed me to the pool's edge. Slowly, they approached. And when I did not move or speak, they began their careful grooming of me. Each touch was feather light and they clearly had a deep appreciation of my personal space for never once did I feel like hissing at either of them. Wrapping my arms around my legs, and resting my chin on my knees, I let them tend to me. They dressed me in a sheath of dark muslin and tied flowers into my hair. They were attentive and respectful, so I sat quietly and let them do what they wanted. In honesty, I didn't know what to do or think, and getting upset over a gentle rubbing down with a soft cloth and flower scented water seemed silly.

"I sense you have had healing magic, Lady Priestess," the older fairy-woman said in a tinkling voice. "It is not wise to indulge in healing magic too often, but would you let me sing to you? You will find it soothes your mind and revives your body."

I eyed her distrustfully, but even maintaining that seemed too much effort and I shrugged lifelessly. She smiled, her eyes crinkling at the edges, and she sung to me in a soft, lilting voice. I let the words wash over me and was surprised when I did begin to feel better. Finishing, she peered into my face and I gave her a genuine smile, even if it was a bit small. She beamed back at me and gave the other fairy– who I realised was her apprentice – a short order to tidy up.

They stood but I remained seated, glancing at them in vague interest. The elder fairy paused. "Should you have need of me again, my name is Lily." She motioned elegantly to her apprentice who stared at me in awe, her chubby face pinky-purple. "And this is Grace."

The fairy-girl sank into such a low curtsey the ends of her red hair scraped the forest floor. "An honour, Lady Priestess," she greeted breathlessly, remaining bent over.

"Hai," I blurted uncomfortably, my voice cracking from lack of use.

Lily winced delicately, her papery features wrinkling. "I served your mother and I know the burdens can be many. Should you ever have need of me do not hesitate to seek me out."

With a small nod of her head Lily left me at the pool's edge with my thoughts, gliding away with her hands clasped in front of her. Grace trailed behind her; the woven basket of oils and cloths clutched in her hands, shooting me an amazed look over her rounded, green shoulder.

Liking the peace and quiet, I enjoyed the sight of the sun climbing higher in the sky, edging toward the dense cloud cover I knew would smother its radiance until the next dawn. I suspected outside of the Wyld the bright yellow sunshine would become pale.

I heard the crunching of leaves behind me. It was not Breandan for I could sense when he was near. My brother?

I frowned when feet too big to be Conall's stepped into view. "We must talk," a gruff voice commanded. And it was a command. I doubted this fairy knew how to address others in a casual manner.

My eyes drifted closed. "Right now, Lochlann?"

He exhaled loudly. "I can bring myself to understand how this may be hard for you, but I do not have the luxury of time. Nor do you."

"Devlin will still be there in a few days from now. He'll die by my hand, and it doesn't matter if it is today or tomorrow."

"You know I cannot allow that."

My eyes opened and I shrugged, peering at nothing. "At what point did I give the impression I give a damn what you say?"

He crouched down on his haunches beside me. "I need your loyalty, Rae. I need your respect and," he grabbed my chin and yanked my head round, "at the very least, I need your full attention."

I jerked from his grasp and glared at him, my body recoiling at his touch.

His handsome face was stony, unimpressed, and his eyes narrowed at the same time as mine.

Lochlann was a fine fairy male. He was bulkier than Breandan, rugged, and from what I gathered, much older. His ears had the point of fairy and his skin had the faintest of green tinges. He had no tail or wings, but what he did have was a powerful and commanding presence that I had to fight not to feel intimidated by. His hair brushed his shoulders in golden blonde waves, and his jaw was square. The most striking thing about this fairy lord was that he had one green eye and one blue, both cold and beautiful. I saw much of Breandan reflected through that gaze and it made me uncomfortable.

"Why do you, Breandan, and Maeve look so different?" I asked. "Conall and I have the same colouring even though my fairy form is like this." I looked down at my tail, flicking on the ground by my leg. "Not that I understand why I'm shaped differently either."

Lochlann watched me for a while before he said, "Truly, you know nothing of what you are?"

I flushed. "Just what I've learned from the Clerics."

He snorted. "Then you know nothing. Fairies conceive like humankind but our bodies do not work the same."

He frowned. "The genetic markers do not behave the same. We are all born with a purpose and a destiny. We all used to have green skin, red or light-coloured hair, wings and tails, but as we evolved and mixed with other races our blood diluted. You and Conall come from an ancient bloodline, and there is strength in your blood that defies time. You have wings and a tail, proof of this. We have not seen a form so pure in a long time, Rae. It is a great honour."

He hadn't answered my question. "And your family?"

His upper lip twitched. "Breandan and Maeve were birthed by different mothers to my own."

"And may the gods keep them warm in their embrace for an eternity," said a high trill from behind me.

Maeve, the first fairy I had ever laid eyes on, skipped up to us and curtsied, clasping her hands behind her back and giving me a sheepish look. Her fiery hair drifted over her shoulders, and the damp, darkened tips slid across her pale green collarbones. She was slender, and moved with an innate poise gifted to our kind.

"Grace fell over herself telling me you were here, and that she had tended to you. I thought I would check to make sure you were alright." Maeve's scarlet irises darted between Lochlann and me. The tension between us was evident by the way her eyebrow climbed. "You are alright?"

My eyes went from narrowed to slitted.

"I will be," I replied flatly, and rested my head back on my knees to watch a dragonfly flit across the water's surface.

Maeve came to sit cross-legged on my other side, and sighed. "You know I had no choice. And I did do all I could to help. I made sure the chains didn't...." She cut off guiltily.

Lochlann chuckled. "I know you helped her, sister. I am not mad."

She gathered herself up and nodded. "Good. Breandan is always so grumpy and serious, but he smiles when Rae is around. Can you believe it? Breandan smiling. We need to keep her happy so she doesn't up and leave him." Maeve giggled and played with the tufts of weeds and flowers by her wriggling toes. "I'm glad to help you if it means I get to see one of my grouchy brothers content once in a while."

"Says one in a constant fit of giggles." There was a deep affection in Lochlann's voice when he spoke to her and I peeked at his face.

It had softened as he watched his baby sister. The affectionate expression was one I'd not seen on his face before, and it warmed my heart. All I had ever seen was him scowling at Breandan. I'd assumed he was cold to everybody, even his own kin. Possibly this fairy lord was worth following? It wasn't like I had many options.

Lochlann needed me, my blessing, to become High Lord of the fairy race, and I needed to decide sooner rather than later if I was going to give it to him. The least I could do was make sure if I did follow him that he was truly as dedicated to his people as Breandan and Conall professed him to be.

Maybe if it didn't feel like the morning was a massive inhalation of breath waiting to exhale, I would stay and learn about him. Possibly, if I didn't feel a pressing need to be gone from this place, I would come to understand him much better. But as it was I felt a sudden and urgent need to be gone.

"I'm going after Devlin," I said quietly. Lochlann and Maeve's attention shifted to me. Straightening my legs, I flexed my wings and rolled my head around my shoulders. "I'll get the grimoire back and we'll take it from there."

"It would be better if you stayed," Lochlann said in a measured voice. From the tone I could tell he was being mindful to not sound like he was ordering me about. "I have already tasked Conall with the retrieval of the spell book. He is my best warrior and tracker by far."

"Then I'll go with him," I said simply.

As far as I was concerned, the conversation was over and I reached through my bond to Breandan to discover where he was. It didn't take me long to find him, and it took even less time for him to find me, making me think he'd been closer than I had known. Breandan knew how to mask the bond, and at some point I had to get him to teach me how.

He stepped from the shadows of a tree and paused for half a beat when Lochlann abruptly stood.

As he approached, a hot flush spread over my limbs and my wings fluttered.

His body was tall, his face unspeakably beautiful, and his countenance fierce. Breandan glowed with a silver light that pulsed beneath his skin and made the black tattoos covering his lean body from head to toe shift and move. The marks on his torso were stunning; swirling lines and intricate patterns that weaved around runes of power and incantations of magic. As always, his eyes ensnared my attention first and kept my attention the longest. They were mesmerising, and more often than not trained on me. His silver-blue gaze was a prison I would readily endure for an eternity. Drooling in the company of his family was probably not good manners, so I let my gaze drift to the left and enjoyed tracing the shape of his ear, which curved from a slender ellipse to a sharp point.

He wore dark segmented trousers, rigid across his

thighs and shins but flexible about his waist, groin, and knee joints. Fairy males did not wear tops so their chests were always temptingly bare. Breandan's smooth and hard chest was more tempting than most.

Heart thumping - worked up from my bold and intimate stare - immediately I stood and waited patiently for him to come hold me, when what I wanted was to run headlong into his arms and rub myself over him.

He stopped a few paces away, wrapped his hands round my upper arms, and pulled me into him. I went willingly, my nature crowing in joy at the pleasure rippling from where his skin touched mine. I was unable to drum up resistance despite my inner turmoil at how easy enduring his touch had become. Sighing, he brushed his lips across mine. My heart skipped a thump. Warmth. Sunlight. My mouth parted when he paused a hairsbreadth away from kissing me again and I breathed him in, melting in his arms.

The power of our bond flared and settled around us like a comforting cloak.

Oh gods, it was true that I belonged to him.

"Brother." Lochlann's voice cracked like whip and shattered the sweetness of our reunion.

Breandan tensed and his face smoothed into a blank canvas. I blinked up at him, seeing much in his silver eyes and wondering how it was possible to read so much from the way they watched me. He tried to disentangle himself, but I placed my hands on his broad shoulders and rested my cheek on his chest. I couldn't help it, and the steady boom of his heartbeat was grounding.

He breathed out, the sound almost a chuckle, and wrapped his arms around me, resting his chin on the crown of my head and swaying me gently in comfort. I made a small noise of contentment. Had he truly expected me to push him away?

I had not seen my fairy since I'd saved Tomas from the sun and then climbed out of our hastily created tomb. Breandan had defended me and given me time to get my vampire safely into the cool ground to rest until he could protect himself again, regardless of his feelings toward Tomas.

"You understand I would do anything to keep you safe, to keep you with me?"

Brow crumpling in confusion as to what he referred to exactly, I nodded once. I was slowly coming to understand Breandan's need to have me with him. I felt it too.

"Say-so," I murmured and leaned back.

Breandan ran his finger down the bridge of my nose, "Good," he concluded.

Breandan's voice was something indescribable. To my ears every syllable was silkily profound. I was sure no one else could hear the raw beauty of his voice; and in some strange way, I was glad as it meant I could covet it for my own.

Over his shoulder, I saw Conall join us and I wiggled my fingers in a wave at him. Already I felt better simply for having my fairy close and touching me.

"The bond is ancient and powerful," Lochlann's voice had my shoulders hunching like he'd poked me with a stick. It took a great deal of will for me to not want to supplicate myself to him when he spoke like that, but Breandan no longer seemed affected and his hold on me tightened. "I would never go against the will of the gods and of magic," he continued as he moved closer to us, "but we must observe that fairykind expects ... certain customs to be observed and revealing this connection has been forged between the Priestess and the Wyld Guardian would not be wise."

Lochlann stopped so close to my back I could feel the heat of his chest. I shifted in Breandan's arms, pushing forward, not liking how close he was.

Over my head Breandan locked eyes with his Elder and held his gaze in a lengthy silence. There was a sudden and palpable pressure in the air.

Maeve skipped forward, her gaze flitting between her two brothers. "Brother...." Both turned to her, like me, unsure to which she spoke.

Conall appeared at my elbow and I blinked at his protective stance, his hand on my shoulder as if prepared to rip me away from Breandan. He watched both of the fairies with a careful eye, his long fingers flexing on my skin.

I held my breath, not wanting them to fight, but too afraid to say anything lest it start them arguing.

After a beat, Lochlann backed two steps away and continued smoothly with, "Rae, you must be discreet about your attachment to Breandan. The people are frightened and confused. They have much to concern themselves with. And the last thing we need is for them to lose all faith in their new leader before he has even acceded to the throne."

Conall bowed his head slightly and released me, but did not step away, keeping his stance defensive.

I arched an eyebrow. "Throne?"

"We have not used the term King or Queen in many millennia, but the High Lord and High Lady are effectively royalty," Conall explained, his glare fixed on Breandan.

I pursed my lips. "So what is the Priestess? Where does she fit into that arrangement?"

Lochlann breathed out hard from his nose in

impatience.

"Traditionally the High Lady was the Priestess," Breandan said quietly.

"Oh, right," I said cordially, running that through my mind a few times. It took a few beats for it to click and make sense what that meant for me personally. My eyes widened and though I was nowhere near him I took another step away from Lochlann into Breandan; the idea of being his making me feel ill.

"I'm not thrilled either," Lochlann said, surly. "Not only does my future Queen not dote on me, she also was not raised as a lady but as a human warrior. She is bonded to my younger brother, is willful, reckless, and has a blood tie to a vampire." He crossed his arms over his chest and scowled darkly. "The gods laugh at me."

"But I can't ... I mean, you know that I would never–"

"Choose me over him?" Lochlann motioned to Breandan with a bold swipe of his hand. "I am aware but it changes nothing. Until then we must give the people a united front to gather courage from. I will not ask you to mate with me until you are ready, or unless there is no other choice."

I spluttered and quivered as I tried to come up with a semi-polite way to tell him he had a better chance of mating with a high goddess than with me. Seeing the horror on my face and my furious rebuttal on my lips, Conall jumped in and argued, "The mating of the fairy Priestess with the High Lord is tradition." His gaze bounced between the three of us, unsure of whom to target.

Lochlann held up his hand for him to be silent. "Our mating will not be discussed at this time, but I will not let you make a fool of me in front of all demonkind. Can you be discreet?"

He asked the last not just of me as his gaze fell on
Breandan who flinched as if it was a physical slap.
Meeting his brother's contemptuous gaze his own eyes
filled with anger and went wild. He looked away, jaw
working manically, before he clenched his fists, and
swallowed whatever it was he wanted to say.

There would be no swallowing on my part that was for
sure. "We can try to be discreet," I agreed. "But for our
safety, not your pride."

I looked back at my fairy, who had regained control of
himself and gifted me with a long, heated stare that slid
up one side of me and rubbed down the other. My wings
fluttered and my breathing deepened as I sank into him.
The air between us warmed and buzzed with tension.

Conall cleared his throat and Breandan tore his gaze
away, a light flush across his cheeks. My own face burned
and I dragged in a shaky breath. I removed myself from
his arms, took a large step backward, and hugged my
stomach to make my trembling less pronounced.

Discreet. Right.

"You'll have to do better than that," Lochlann said in
a tight voice whilst holding out his hand to me. "Walk
with me around the tree bases before you leave. I will
announce we agreed you will seek out the grimoire once
you have left."

Maeve – whom I had all but forgotten, she was so
quiet – snorted then coughed daintily behind her hand.
She batted her reddish-purple eyelashes at her brother's
scowl. "Can I go with them?" she asked in her high trill.

"No," Lochlann replied.

Her face crumpled and she pouted. "But I–"

"No!" Breandan and Lochlann barked.

Maeve and I shared a long-suffering look.

Plainly irritated, Lochlann held out his hand again and didn't bother to disguise his dislike of me. Not that I cared. I thought he was repressed and boorish, but whatever. I gingerly placed my palm on his, cringing when his big hand engulfed mine and locked my fingers in an overly tight grip. A shudder wracked its way up his frame and mine.

Conall frowned at us. "You both look uncomfortable."

Lochlann forced his shoulders down from his ears, but I couldn't help leaning away from him until he practically held me upright.

Sighing, Breandan brushed his fingers across my cheek. The comfort was instant and my body unlocked allowing Lochlann to pull me upright. Breandan let his hand trail down my neck and across my shoulder blade before giving me a gentle shove forward.

Lochlann started off at a brisk walk and I stumbled to keep up with him. He was pretty huge, and two of his strides equalled three of my steps. Soon the three gigantic tree trunks came into view and the auras began to press on me again.

Lochlann slowed and pulled me closer to his side. "Smile," he ordered through his teeth.

Coming to a stop, he raised our joined fists high nearly yanking my arm out of my socket and forcing me to stand on my tip-toes. The move was met with a cry of jubilation from the crowds above. Happy voices singing praise and lower baritones bellowing greetings. I pulled the corners of my mouth up even as I clenched my throat muscles, moments away from emptying my stomach onto the ground in panic.

I did not like this habit of mine, the need to vomit when I got stressed, anxious, or scared. All emotions I experienced with worrying frequency since these demons came trampling into my life ... or did I stumble back into theirs?

Breandan was close by my side, silent, his eyes locked on his brother's hand engulfing mine. A wild desperation simmered beneath the surface of his calm that even I could see, and Conall kept half his attention on him and the other on me. He looked pleased and joined the salute with much enthusiasm, pride oozing from every pore of his being.

Lochlann let our hands drop. Before I could scurry away from all the eyes he yanked me closer to his side and leaned to murmur intensely in my ear, "You lead my brother into danger and I do not like it."

Instinctively, my head hung before I jerked it straight. I narrowed my eyes at him, annoyed he continued to use the power of his voice to try and intimidate me. "You need the grimoire and you need me. Don't forget it," I whispered in reply. "I'm doing the best I can. I'm thinking all things considered I'm doing well. I'm pretending I enjoy your touch aren't I?"

"You have no idea what we must face in the days to come as a people. I beg the gods you do not shatter both my brother's spirit with whatever perversion you have with that vampire, and the spirit of my people as you shirk your responsibilities," he scoffed in derision. "To think when I learned you had been found I was excited to meet my future mate. But now I see you are exactly like your mother, selfish."

I swallowed hard and forced down tears I refused to let him see. I was not weak. He would not see me cry. Was I selfish? Well, yes. I had been raised to look for my own safety first; to take care of myself so that I could in turn take care of those who depended on me. I couldn't change who I was in the space of a few days and become an altruistic leader no matter how many times I was told it was my true nature. I knew who I was to these people and what they expected of me. I was too aware of it.

"You think you know me," I said in a voice just as cold as his. "You don't."

"I can only judge on what I see. And what I see in you, Rae, is fear, mistrust, and confusion. Do I see evil? No, but I do not see the purity I expect of the Priestess."

"It's not like I asked for this. You all came looking for me, remember?"

My tongue thickened with the words. That was not exactly true. It had been me who had ventured beyond the Wall. I was the one who had been drawn to the forest and disobeyed the Sect Doctrine: the rules set down by the Priests that kept us safe.

The fairies had looked for me, but deep down inside I had been looking for them too.

Lochlann's gaze darted over my shoulder. "And look what happened when the most vulnerable of us found you." His gaze turned hard as steel, condemning me with the power at his command. "You will be the end of him, and it breaks my heart."

His will crushed upon my own and I grunted. Pushing my own influence up as a barrier was the only thing that stopped my knees from giving out beneath me, so sudden and intense was the attack. I pulled my hand from his grasp and spun on my heel, letting my tail flick behind me and punch him in the gut. Cursing, Lochlann stumbled at my unexpected jab. I sniffed at him over my shoulder before stomping off, ignoring Conall's plea to stay and Breandan's curious stare.

When I knew I was no longer in view of the fairies, I breathed out. Shaking, I rubbed my sweaty palms on my hips. This friction between Lochlann and I wasn't good. Nor was the deception by omission to the people. Did they truly believe I would mate with Lochlann now that Devlin was gone? How would they react when they learnt I had a bond to Breandan and a blood tie to a vampire?

Reaching the sacred ground Devlin had used to sacrifice Alex, I let the energy of the place soak into my pores. The vibration of magic was strongest here and I shivered. It was just a place. Nothing to be afraid of, right?

My eyes landed on the altar and the body wrapped in green vines and flowers that lay atop it. Standing before what was left of Alex, guilt and loss flooded my heart. Gathering my courage I placed my palms on her chest. There was a dim hum of energy from the body that was unexpected and I started, my hand lifting off her in shock. My brows furrowed and I cocked my head. Focusing, I pushed my influence out and sent it down into the cold flesh, not sure what I was expecting to find.

"Rae." The sharp call snapped me back into my own mind and I jumped, the connection and sense of consciousness lost.

I swallowed and looked down at my hands then the body. "I think ... it felt like she—"

"You should not play with the dead." Breandan took my hand and pulled me away from Lex's body.

Letting myself be pulled away I shook my head in confusion. "But I felt her."

"We are all connected to the Source on some level or another. As fairy we can tap into this energy and seek out minds that are not our own. That is how Lochlann keeps track of my, and Maeve's state. That is why you can feel Alex when you touch her body. It takes time for the energy to fade after the life has ended, more so when the death is sudden." He sighed. "Rae, what in the heavens did you think you were doing before using your magics to craft such perversion?"

Damn. All of a sudden my toes were the most interesting thing to stare at. "I– I don't know what–t you … m–mean…." My tongue tied into a knot, and my stomach cramped uncomfortably. I avoided his eyes as yet again I tried to lie.

"You tried to make a zombie."

My mouth fell open. It was out there, the word I had not even said to myself. "That's not possible. It's a legend told by Vodoun to scare witches and other demons."

"Yet that is what you tried to do to as she lay awash in blood at the altar. I felt it in the air. You called on the Loa, Rae, and they were answering you. You defied natural order and that is not your purpose."

I bit my lip, hard. "It was you? You stopped me?"

"If you had truly wanted to tie her to such a repugnant fate I would have let you finish." He held up his palm to stop me from speaking. "But I think I stopped you in time."

I grabbed his hand. "You think? I saw her twitch, but I thought it was her body being zapped with magic." I looked back to the body and thought of the energy I could feel within her. Was it possible? Was there a way to bring her back to me?

A shadow of a nameless emotion passed his face, like clouds over the sun, but it was gone in an instant, smothered by that expressionless mask he hid behind. "To complete the resurrection you needed to lock her soul in her body. She did not awaken, she was set free."

My excitement died and I loosened my grip on his hand. Tears welled in my eyes to run down my face. "I miss her," I confessed, scrubbing at my cheeks. "She's only been gone a few hours and I– I'm struggling to accept it. She doesn't feel gone to me." I tried to make him understand that her loss was not something I could rationalise. "She should never have been dragged into this. She suffered. They humiliated her and abused her body. I want … wanted to give her something back."

"You tried to give her life but it was not for her wellbeing."

I jerked like he had backhanded me and stared at him. "How could you say that to me?"

"You tried to reanimate her for yourself. No one would want to live such a wretched existence, least of all someone as vibrant as I sensed your friend to be. She would have become a killer, Rae, consumed with thoughts of flesh and pain. A slave to the urges and whims of the dark magic she was reborn from. Her flesh would be cold and dead. She would never change nor grow. You would have given her life, but lost the friend you knew."

"You don't know her. She would have been fine. I would have helped her, zapped her with good energy or something."

I looked inward, seeking answers to my own questions and complicated thoughts. In truth, I'd not thought of the repercussions when I had tried to reanimate Lex. How would she have felt becoming a zombie; kept alive by dark magic pumping through her body? The knowledge of how to create zombies had supposedly died out alongside the Bokors and Mambos who practiced voodoo a decade before. Lex's own mother was the last voodoo sorceress known to humankind – hunted down by the Clerics and executed. Her mother's power was the reason why I thought calling on the voodoo deity would save her from death. But would Lex have forgiven me? Could she have ever been happy?

"It was selfish," I admitted and my shoulders slumped. "But it doesn't matter. It didn't work. I swear to never try it again."

As I said the words, magic crackled and a heavy constraint wrapped around my neck and settled. Then the collar of air disappeared. I blinked, placing my hands around my neck.

"Uh, what happened?"

Breandan stared at me like I was mad. "You made an oath."

I rubbed my neck. "By saying I swear?"

"Our words are bound by magic. If you swear to do something, you must keep the promise." He pulled my rubbing hands down from my throat and placed them at my sides.

I shifted, still fidgety. I plucked at my bottom lip instead, knowing that yanking on my hair or rubbing my nose would be too big a giveaway to how uncomfortable I was feeling. "This goes hand in hand with the whole speaking the truth thing, right?" He nodded. "So if I break an oath—"

"You die."

I gaped at him then spluttered; "You didn't think to tell me this before?"

His shoulders lifted and fell. "You would not break an oath lightly." His eyes darted to the shadowed mound to the side of us then back to me. "You're finished?"

I grunted my disagreement and stepped away from him, wanting to get this next part over with quickly.

The thing I turned towards was a living crypt of trees and leaves. The great oak trunks had twisted down and their roots had reached up to entwine together tightly. It was stunning and I could not believe I had connected my power to that of the fairy Wyld and created this.

Breandan said it was because on this sacred ground my power was absolute. I rubbed my chest to soothe the ache the thought brought to my heart. Had I known that mere hours ago, so much might have happened differently.

I had left my vampire-boy, Tomas, slumbering in the earthen tomb I had made to keep him safe. He was dead and would not rise until sunset. I was pleased, because it meant I could focus on the grimoire and Devlin. From the moment I had met him, Tomas had been a complicated being I could not understand. He was always there on the fringes of my attention, but never the focus. When he had made me stop – by searing me with a kiss to leave me shaken and dazed – he had snapped into focus. It had been enough to sway my loyalty when faced with the choice of losing him or risking Breandan's affection.

Thinking of my vampire always made me confused and wary. He had a numbing, drug-like effect on my senses that I was beginning to love and hate equally. I needed to be sharp and definite not fuzzy and indecisive. I snorted at myself. I would think on my blood tie with Tomas and my promise to help him later. I didn't even know what it meant … and if I did know, what difference would it make? Could I break it? I knew my bond with Breandan was thrown into doubt because of my tie with Tomas. Devlin had made that perfectly clear when he had tried to claim me.

I glanced overhead, past the dense tree canopy, and saw we had nine hours of sunlight at best. When night fell he would come after me. I knew this like I knew the hammering of my heart when he was near was taboo.

Tomas was no fool, and so I knew not to worry too much about what would happen when he woke.

He would have to spend most of the night catching us up, and even if he did manage to gain on us – and catch us before the sun rose – he would hang back. He was wary of Breandan and for good reason. Breandan would tear him apart the moment he had a chance.

Distance from Tomas was good. I would have time to decide what was best for him and me. Please, gods, let me find an answer.

As I had lain beside Tomas in the earthen tomb, I'd wrapped my arms around him and wallowed, slipping deeper into despair, until my heart had called for its other half. My heart, despite its anguish, had told me what to do and who could help me. And he had been there waiting for me when I crawled out. Breandan's touch was as soothing as the sun's virgin light on my skin. He had held me in his arms – when I would let him – and let me wander around the fairy Wyld when I had needed space to move.

In my heart, I knew who was right for me despite the fact I craved the love of another.

Crouching, I rested my temple on a root and dragged my fingers, tipped with talons, along the bumpy surface.

"I have to go. I know you'll follow me when you wake, so be careful. Just ... don't do anything foolish, okay?" I knew Tomas couldn't hear me, but saying the words out loud made me feel better. "I will help you, Tomas. Give me time and I'll find a way to help you and your Nest."

Breandan came up behind me and pressed his legs into my back. "We must go if we are to have any chance of catching Devlin."

Standing, I patted the tomb once before turning my back on it. "Conall?"

"I am here, little sister."

My brother stepped into the clearing, geared up and

ready. He glowed brighter than any other I had seen; except when Breandan and I suffered the effects of our bond. Conall was beautiful, a face of hard angles and smooth planes. His eyes were gold, a family trait it seemed since mine were the same only lighter. His long hair was pulled into a low ponytail that reached the middle of his broad back. In leather pants and soft-soled boots, like Breandan he was always topless and bore a sword latched to his back by a thick leather strap that ran across his torso.

"Devlin will not make this hunt easy," he rumbled. "The High Lord is cunning and most dangerous when prepared. Devlin will head to the sea fairies at the tip of the region. They have always been sympathetic to his cause. We must reach him before he reaches them. We must travel well out of the way of the Temple and slip through the shifter Pride. I do not think he will be foolish enough but he may try to cut through the outskirts of the vampire city. Pray he does not." Conall focused solely on me. "Rae, if you become tired tell me. If you think you hear, see, or feel something wrong, tell me. If you need to eat or drink, tell me. If—"

"If I breathe too loud, tell you," I said cheekily and rolled my eyes at him. "I get it. Tell you everything."

He nodded once. "And try to keep up." Moving around me he touched my shoulder briefly then broke out into a swift run, blurring into the distance, forcing me to use my fairy sight to see him before Breandan nudged me and I took off behind him.

For most of the day there was the gloomy, damp forest, my ragged inhalation as I struggled for breath, and the footfalls of the one who called himself my life-mate as he raced beside me. The forest was teeming with life, yet all hushed reverently as we blazed past, in awe of us, in fear. Shaking my head at how my life had changed, I sped up, leaving Breandan a pace behind. We ran single file, Conall in the lead. The air was overly crisp on my skin signalling the coming winter and the last of the sun's rays were sluggish.

Devlin was less than half a day ahead and his trail was erratic: appearing unexpectedly then becoming deceptively faint, or weaving in odd directions. He was trying to throw us off course and used magics to slow us down so he could escape. Each time I was sure he had changed course Conall had disagreed and pointed out the way. At times we stopped for him to read the trails, listen to the wind, and press his ear to the earth.

It did not take us long to pass out of fairy territory, and I knew the moment we did. There was a subtle change in the air as we ran, a cool ripple rolling over my skin and a bubble of pressure popping as if we had broken through a containment of some kind. Rather than a crisp sweetness, the scents of the forest became harsh and syrupy. My nature sulked at the loss of connection with Wyld land. And while the forest close to the human Temple side of fairyland was bright and spacious with an orgy of vivid evergreen flowers and shrubs, we now passed through the other side of fairy territory where the plant life dulled, became mundane, and the thick glossy leaves withered into spindly brown spokes. The evergreen trees – bases covered in bright yellow lichen – were twisted into tortured formations. Bark lice and rotten fungi spiralled up devouring the dead bark. Silken webbing from the lice hung from the tree branches in wispy clumps, and when I batted some out of my way the secretion stuck to my fingertips. The dense canopy swooped lower, blocking out the light until everything took on the electric blue tinge my fairy sight used to see in the dark. This part of the forest had not seen care in some time, and when I sent a nauseated look at Breandan his responding look was sad.

The decayed smells of the trees faded. The wild, spicy smell of animal reached me before it became clear we had passed into the shifters' Pride lands. The air was heavy with hints of hay and soil. The trees thinned, became clumps of bushy shrubbery, then the tree line disappeared entirely and my eyebrows vanished into my hairline. Grass swelled up to my chest and flowed outward, rippling, causing the land to undulate in the wind. Grey clouds with black underbellies drifted sluggishly across the dusky blue sky.

As my feet took their first steps into the meadow, the grass blades bent and fanned down, crushed beneath the soles of my feet. Cool mud squelched between my toes and made a horrible sucking sound when I pulled them free.

The absence of other footfalls beside me had me abruptly aware that the other two had stopped running and I was blazing ahead alone. Cursing the gods, I slowed to a speed a human could follow, and curved around to double back.

I stopped dead as a feeling of foreboding ran across the crown of my head in prickly tingles. Was someone close? I reached out with my developing sixth sense to see if any auras were nearby as a large shadow engulfed my own.

Rough, calloused hands closed around my neck.

Instinctively, my wings spread, but were hindered by a pair of muscled arms. I tried to use my tail to beat at whoever had a hold on me, but I could not get a proper swipe in. The meaty fingers locked around my neck tightened. I could not breathe. I opened my mouth and tried to inhale. My lungs burned and blood rushed to my brain. Feeling pressure building behind my eyeballs, I did the one thing you should never do; I panicked and tried to scream. The remainder of air left my lungs and my attacker squeezed my throat tighter. My vision blinkered and impulsively I reached for the Source: the silo of energy that was nowhere and everywhere, and mine to command. The power I called to me in a panic slipped through my grasping fingers.

The next time my eyes fluttered open, I was disorientated, and I was on my back when a moment ago I had been upright.

My eyelids fought to lower. I caught flashes of a bushy beard, a large chin, a chunky neck and huge shoulders. A heavy hand held my shoulder down. I pushed against it and the mouth above the bushy chin cursed.

I dragged my eyes fully open and tried to scream. Nothing but hoarse squeak came out. I struggled and kicked my legs. He was so heavy. I tried to reach for the Source again, but my terror was too great. It filled me but I could not think what to do with it. All I could think was 'help'! The man above me smelled like stale sweat and bog water … and warm animal. A shifter? His breath was bitter, like rotting flesh. He grinned when I struggled. He leaned over and licked from the base of my neck to my temple. His tongue was rough, like sand had been pressed into it, and I squirmed at the saliva that burned my skin as it trickled down my neck into my hair.

I bucked, twisted, and clawed at him. I would fight my way out of this. I knew soon I would become too tired to move but I could not just lie there. Behind my closed lids I saw Lex bound and tortured, watching helpless as Devlin and his fairy mate abused her body. The horrific memory gave me a last surge of strength to fight harder.

There was a loud crack and the body on top of me went limp, crushing me. His heavy weight lifted off me and I heard a loud crash as if a tree had snapped in half and fallen. I blinked up into the darkening sky. Shaken. There was a horrible crunching sound nearby and a short, sharp wail of pain.

I rolled onto all fours and crawled away through the grass, the mud slicking my palms and knees as I quietly scrambled forward.

Something grabbed my ankle.

The touch was like a wave of peace over my entire body, and I scuttled around to launch myself into his arms. Breandan held me close to him, arms tight around my waist, burying his head in my neck, his breath ragged.

My eyes skipped over the tips the grass, looking for the bearded man. Two bounds away he lay in broken mess. His hands and feet had changed into tawny coloured paws with brown claws, and his face had elongated. Two dark triangles, ears, had moved to the top of his head with wispy tufts of hair sticking off the edges. A stumpy tail peeked out from his bottom. It was a grotesque blend of man and beast.

Conall stood over the dead shifter, looking down impassively. Blood was smeared over his hands. He glanced over at me, frowning when he saw me cowering in Breandan's arms. "He will never hurt you again," he said bluntly.

That was an understatement, but I nodded once in thanks. He missed it since he looked away from us, expression unhappy.

Breandan leaned away to run his hands over my neck. I winced. It hurt, a lot. We healed fast and I could guess the bruising was already a rainbow of colour. When after a few seconds it did not feel any better I rasped, "Why is it not healing?"

"Bruising is not a fatal wound, and the skin is not broken. This is new to you so you will not feel the difference, but your body can become exhausted to the point of death if you are not careful. Using magic is stressful on your mind and body, as is healing. Where it can, your body will conserve its resources. Since the—" His jaw clenched. "Since the shifter's attack, your body is still preparing you for a fight, or to run away. And you have been running all day. Your reserves are not replete."

"You need to become much more aware of your surroundings," Conall said chidingly, nudging the mangled body on the ground with his toe.

Really? He was trying to turn this into a lecture? I made a rude noise. "Honestly, is now the time for a lesson?"

All day he had been throwing confusing sentences and scenarios my way, expecting me to 'learn' something from them. He was taking his role as my protector and Elder seriously. I forced myself to feel loved and appreciated rather than smothered and overprotected.

Conall said nothing in response to me, too busy looking the dead shifter over, and the look Breandan gifted me with soon had me shutting up.

The grass surrounding me was primarily shades of green, peppered with greys and browns, and the occasional wild flower with spongy orange petals. The shading of late autumn had swept over the shifters' territory, and it was pretty. As far as I could see there was nothing but rolling terrain. The beauty of my surroundings was lost on me, however, as I inhaled slowly and swallowed, my face contorting into a grimace at how much it hurt.

I leaned my head against Breandan's shoulder then

rubbed my cheek into his neck seeking comfort. "I can't believe he attacked me. Why? And why did you kill him?" I asked Conall who inclined his head at Breandan.

My fairy looked uncomfortable. "Conall did not kill him. I did." I looked back at my brother who literally had blood on his hands. "Your brother was bitten so I snapped his neck. He was Changing, and not submitting to my will."

The unsaid was that this shifter had hurt me, and it was clear a transgression so great it could not go unpunished in Breandan's eyes. If the situation had been reversed, I had no doubt I would do the same thing in a heartbeat … if it meant his protection.

"This does not bode well," Conall said his voice dark and mad. "He was clearly a sentry watching for intruders. We will need to make reparation to the Pride he hails from."

"Another time," Breandan said.

My trembling had stopped and I forced myself to unclamp my hand from around Breandan's waist and stand. My wings slammed out behind me and my tail cracked from side to side. What had happened that morning had made me moody and short of temper, but this latest experience left me jittery. I plucked leaves from the mess of inky-black that was my hair and caught Breandan's scent before he touched me. Sunlight, earth, and rain. He came up behind me and his hands gently rested on my shoulders, squeezed, and then slid down my bared back to pass over my wings. They twitched and fluttered at his touch and I dragged in a shaky breath.

Gods, to fall for someone so hard surely meant you were bound to break apart; to unravel at the seams because you were undone by how they make you feel.

He continued, hands lazily wandering to my waist then

lower, gripping my hips. I shifted, but instead of backing off he pulled me into him. My heart thumped doubly hard and I sighed when his hands left my hips to gently feel my neck again.

"I'm fine," I rasped and thumped him lightly on the back of his thigh with my tail.

His fingertips brushed my hair back from my neck then he pressed a kiss to my pulse point. He let me go. "I believe you, but I want you to relax. You're too tense."

I slanted a pained look over my shoulder at him, not sure if admitting he was the main cause of my erratic heartbeat would be sensible. Gods knew what he would do.

"I want this over with," I mumbled. "I want Devlin dead and I want the book back. No shifter with grabby hands is going to distract me from that. The bruises will heal, eventually."

He sighed and muttered, "This is not going to end well."

My brows came together and I twisted round to look him in the face – unsure of what he meant. He glanced at Conall, truly unhappy, and his lips pressed into a thin line. Breandan was unbelievably skilled at controlling his expression. I had to watch him closely to see if he was mad, pissed, or upset. Judging by how his jaw worked, I was going for mad.

"What?" I asked, because it became apparent he had realised something before I had. "What are you not saying?" I tried and failed to keep the impatience from my tone.

I looked to Conall; the mighty warrior strong enough to massacre a small army of his kind. He said nothing at first and I knew it would be a mistake to push him – no one pushed him.

Irritated and grumpy I waited, hand on hip, for my bother to tell us which direction to take. He and Breandan sent each other a series of coded looks and signalled to each other with their hands.

My gaze darted back to the rigid body of the dead shifter, blood pooling beneath his twisted form, and I shuddered at how effortlessly they had ended his life.

"If you two wanted, you could grind me into a pulp," I said thoughtfully. "You're both warriors yet here you are babysitting me… I'm slowing you down aren't I?"

They stilled. Abandoning whatever silent conversation they were having, they turned to face me. Conall's face was perplexed. Breandan's was smooth, emotionless, telling me he was experiencing an intense feeling he did not want me to see.

"Rae," Conall said slowly. "Do you still not understand who you are?"

"I'm a fairy Priestess." I said it shyly, knowing he was after more but not wanting to insinuate I was more important than I was. How embarrassing that would be!

My brother shot a look at Breandan who inclined his head then came to stand before me. His heat muddled my brain, making me weak in the knees. I peeked at his face and saw a small smile of the corner of his lips.

"Who am I to you?" he asked.

"Uh, my boyfriend," I said with conviction, and cleared my throat since my voice was still raspy. "I mean, my steady." I was proud of myself for I had never said those words before, but when I looked up the smile gathering at the edges of my mouth dropped into a scowl.

Breandan looked horrified. "You are my life mate," he corrected, "and you belong to me." Conall made a small noise of protest, but apart from a tightening of the jaw, Breandan did not acknowledge it. "I am your protector. I am faster, stronger, and more resilient to physical injury. More than this, we are bonded, so our connection is fundamental to who we are. You cannot overpower me and I cannot overcome you, because you too are stronger, faster, and more resilient to physical injury than I."

I frowned, screwing up my face. "That makes no sense."

He seemed to be struggling with something. He leaned forward compelling me to do the same. Just shy of our lips touching he paused and hovered there, easing back when I carried on, mindlessly seeking the touch of his skin on mine. Sliding our hands together, he squeezed my fingers and held me still. I could barely breathe and lost brain function to sensation. A tingle ran down my body to the ends of my hair. It collided with a similar disturbance radiating from him. Seeing that I had picked up on this oddity he swayed forward, and my own vibration lessened, became weaker. Feeling too submissive I pushed back and felt my vibration grow as his shrank back.

"What one lacks, the other grows to fill," I murmured.

I was determined not to appear freaked out by what Breandan and I meant to each other anymore, so I smiled then ducked my head down so my hair covered my face as I balked inwardly.

Breandan's head bobbed from side to side in thought before he nodded. "That is how you stand in relation to me. What you do not seem to realise is that others not connected to you by blood or magic are far less powerful. Many of our kind cannot touch the Source, though they know it is there and they can feel it. Magic is to us as air is to breath—"

"And water to drink," I finished, catching up mentally. Bloody fairies and their bloody jumpy thought patterns.

A finger slid under my chin to tip my head up. Breandan's gaze darted to Conall who looked away, face stony.

The kiss he pressed to my lips was chaste, soothing, and ended with a wicked nip. Leaning back he hungrily drank me in with his eyes. I trembled.

Conall, however, had a frown of disapproval stamped across his features. In honesty, he was starting to get on my nerves with all the scowling and edgy looks.

"What?" I asked my voice still thick with lust. I cleared my throat, lifted my chin then lowered it again when I figured I probably should be trying for meekness not defiance. "Conall, what is it?"

His expression named him thoroughly not impressed. "I think I need to discuss something with you." No other explanation was forthcoming.

In the heat of my mortification I snapped, "We're busy."

"Yes. That is why I need to talk to you. There are certain customs that need observing."

"I have every intention of showing Rae some of our more pleasurable customs," Breandan said evenly, but the look he levelled at me had me all but panting.

I inhaled deeply and as I exhaled I said, "I'm ready for a lesson on customs now."

Breandan cocked an eyebrow. "You wish to learn?"

"Uh, yeah, if you're the one teaching."

Conall hissed and strode forward to grab my arm and yank me back. "It is understandable your natures would get the better of you, but Breandan has been raised by the laws of our people and I know he does not wish to continue dishonouring you so blatantly."

My fairy-boy winced as if Conall had struck him a blow. Lowering his head, he broke our mutual get-over-here-and-touch-me stare, and avoided meeting my gaze.

"Forgive me," he said softly. "Your Elder is right; I shame myself and the beauty of our bond by behaving so."

My back straightened. Instead of telling Conall to take a hike, my fairy stood there with his eyes on the bloody floor like he would keel over dead if he looked at me.

Conall cleared his throat. "You say you are a fairy Priestess, and you are wrong. You are *the* fairy Priestess. There can only be one of you. And though you think the powers you have seen are commonplace, many of our kind are simple folk who will never touch the Source, or be able to move as fast, or be as strong. In time, you will learn our ways. Who we are as a people."

"They're normal," I said feeling a pang of jealousy. "They all get to live normal lives and look to you to keep them safe."

"They will look to you," Conall said solemnly. "As we all will."

If my spine got any stiffer it would snap in half. The pressure and responsibility just kept building and I was sick of it. I did not want any of this. Hearing it laid out in black and white didn't make it more real for me, or prepare me for what was expected of me. If anything it felt more like a dream, no, a nightmare from which I could not wake.

A swell of peace I was sure was not my own calmed me. I sighed. Breandan would not be here if this was a nightmare.

"All of that does not change the fact the two of you could wipe the floor with me." I gave them both pointed looks, daring them to deny it. They knew it was true. Sure, I could fight, but I had seen the way they moved, and there was no way my Disciple training could match it.

Breandan snorted, his head lifting. "You have not been taught to use your body as it was designed. We shall teach you how to harness your power, and no one shall be able to challenge you." He grinned, dazzling me. "Oh, no one but me."

"Not even the High Lord," Conall murmured. "For the first time, we have a Priestess not mated to him."

"All will be well," Breandan snapped and shot the older fairy a look of malevolence. "Rae can control herself and she does not need you to smother her."

I stared at him, wide eyed at the harshness of his tone. Conall did not look too perturbed or offended, simply disinterested.

I narrowed my eyes. I was not the most perceptive of people, but I was not blind either. The undercurrents these two failed so miserably to hide flowed deep, and would have swept up even the strongest of the disinterested. I knew they had to be feeling the strain of the day before too, after all, so much had changed. Breandan had broken away from his brother and was considered an outcast. Conall had butchered several of his kind to give me retribution for Lex's life. We all had much to shoulder and deal with. I guess I could understand if they were both feeling wound up and were taking it out on each other, but gods did they have to be so rude?

Grumping to myself about bad manners, I moved away and heard them follow me. When I could no longer smell the shifter, I plopped down on the ground figuring the spot was as good as any.

"Let's get on with it," I grumped. "Clearly you're warming up to a lecture and the sooner we do it the sooner we can get moving again."

We did not have all the time in the world. Devlin

would have to stop too, but the fairy High Lord was powerful and tricky. He probably knew I would be slowing his adversaries down, and would use the time to take as far a lead as possible.

Breandan sank down behind me and I studied his face since the corner of his mouth looked suspiciously curved, like he was fighting a smile. I watched out for them since his smiles were so rare and stunning. His laughter was rarer, but when he did express amusement it was more than worth the wait.

Conall stepped lightly to seat himself cross-legged in front of me.

Over the silence was the sound of crickets, and a strong wind that blew through the tall grass, bringing me the earthy scents and smallest sounds of life on the Pride.

I waited patiently for Conall to begin, idly wondering why Breandan was not touching me and why he seemed painfully aware of how much distance there was between us.

"Our birth mother was Sorcha," my brother began. "Priestess and mate of Nyall the High Lord of all fairykind."

Already I had to interrupt him. "Don't we have a family name? I mean, I was given the name Wilder because the Priest who found me thought I was a wild thing."

My heart squeezed when I thought of the Priests, for then I thought of Temple, and everything I had left behind. I felt like a leaf that was once part of a great oak, captured by the wind and carried away into the unknown. I knew I was destined to go far, but I missed being unseen amongst others like me. I frowned. Was that the problem? That there was no other like me, yet I kept seeing myself as ordinary. I was unable to understand that

I could not think or act as others did because I was supposed to be the one others followed?

"We are fairy," Conall said as if that would explain everything. "We recognise no other names."

"But why? I understand there are few of us, but only having a first name seems … incomplete." I shrugged.

Conall tilted his head thoughtfully. "That is a good way to describe it. Incomplete." He sighed, something I was beginning to notice he did a lot, like he had the weight of the world on his shoulders. "Family names have power so we stopped using them many years ago. We are powerful yet vulnerable in many trivial ways. Nick us with an iron blade and we bleed for days. Feed us the rowan berry and we become violently ill. Too much and we die, unless healed under the full moon. Force an oath of suicide and we'll cut our own throats or drop dead if we do not comply." He frowned. "We must be fierce to protect ourselves from those who would hurt us for our trusting nature."

"It still seems extreme. Why should we feel incomplete in fear of power?"

"There was a time when our family names were secret, and known only to the kin. It was a way to bind us together and keep us strong. In that strength was our greatest weakness."

Fascinated by the fairy culture – my culture – I leaned forward and urged him on.

"You know there has been a bonding before?"

I bobbed my head. "Ana told me, yeah. She said that it didn't end well."

At the time I had sensed that was a massive understatement, but had not pressed the issue as it had made the white witch agitated. Then again, everything made Ana agitated. The term 'highly strung' came to mind when I thought of the petite blonde Seer. How she handled her Sight without going completely nuts was beyond me.

Conall looked away, face tightening. "They were consumed by each other and out of control. They were born into two of the larger and more powerful families. They broke with tradition, with sanity, and they...." He was unable to go on.

Breandan stiffened beside me and tension radiated across the space between us. I glanced at him under my lashes and saw his face, plainly upset.

My brother cleared his throat and squared his shoulders. "They gave each other their family names."

My lips twitched but I managed to remain quiet. That was the monstrous thing these two lovers did? For the love of gods, these fairies had melodrama down to a fine art. I tried to keep the laughter from my voice. "And?"

Both boys' heads snapped up. The twin expressions of astonishment told me my reaction was way off. I looked between them and shrugged sheepishly.

"She does not understand," Breandan murmured.

Resting his hands on his knees, Conall opened his mouth then closed it again.

At times, there was a language barrier between these fairies and I. They said things and expected me to simply grasp the significance. There seemed to be two meanings in every sentence, a thousand ways to interpret what was spoken.

It hurt my head.

I focused and tried to work through it, use logic.

Family names held power and were secret. Histrionic and strange, if they'd ask me, but voicing such a thought would only get me in trouble and I kept it as my own. Fairies breathed tradition. Every five seconds it was tradition this and tradition that. I guess it helped them retain their sense of purpose, or meaning. Just like the belief that every being has a destiny – that our lives are set, and it is only a matter of time before fate has its way. I wondered what that meant in isolation. Was Lex never meant to die, and was Maeve supposed to be dead in her grave? Was Tomas trying to save a Nest that needed to die out for a greater purpose? Was it time for the human race to fade away into legend?

I could not believe it. I knew the notion of having a purpose made sense, as it attributed to how the Wylds were structured and the royal family determined. Combine that with bloodlines, and surely you would create a sovereignty that would stand the test of time.

But I just ... it seemed so ... coincidental. They let their lives and decisions be based on small happenings and signs that could mean and pertain to nothing.

I rubbed my head, becoming aware mentally I was off track. Conall was still stumped, and Breandan stared at me in that intense, blink-less way he did when he was trying to see inside my head. He smiled; a small thing that passed over his lips.

I eyed him whilst rubbing my nose absentmindedly. How odd. It was like he knew I thought of him.

Cocking his head, he grinned broadly.

Frowning at him, I went back to mentally taking apart what I had learned and translating it into something I could understand. The fairies believed names had a physical power, a contextual hold over them. So… giving someone your family name meant they had your power? Was that it? Was Conall saying that by giving each other their family name…? "They relinquished complete control to each other," I said and looked up, ready to be praised for figuring it out by myself. "They gave each other something sacred to prove their love." Well, by the blank look on their faces I would be waiting a while for all that praise. I sighed. "That would not go down well with their families, I'm guessing."

"It was seen as punishable by death," Conall explained.

My eyes got wide. "They were put to death?"

He shook his head again. "They ran, and were found, of course. They, too, were young and like I said, consumed in each other, unable to think straight or function properly. They were brought back for judgment, after all their bond was clear." His eyes flicked over Breandan and me. "It is something anyone deeply attuned to magic can sense and feel, unique. There is no faking it." He sighed heavily, and muttered something to himself too low for me to hear despite my acute hearing. "A bonding is sacred, since you become a living embodiment of the Source. It was agreed it was not up to the High Lord to decide their fate, and so they turned to the spiritual leader. The Priestess. She ordered them separated and kept apart until nature took its course."

My heart became heavy with grief. "They died alone?"

The wind whipped through the grass as if in lament.

"They took many lives with them, in the end," Breandan said. "When bonded ones are kept apart the power builds between them. It grows with each passing moment building momentum and force. It is believed if they are kept apart and unable to come together to release the build-up of power that eventually the bond will simply consume them." He stopped, checking I was following him, measuring my reaction.

I thought on what they were saying and a chilling realisation passed over me. "They came together," I said and wrapped my arms around myself. "Somehow, they managed to come together and the nexus opened."

Conall nodded sadly. "There were once three Wylds in this region, not two. The Golden Glades was where the royal family reigned. It was destroyed the last time a bonded pair came together and it shook the foundations of what defined us as a people. That love could cause such pain and destruction … it was a reality many struggled to come to terms with."

I remembered the intense light that had blasted from Breandan's body and mine when we had finished healing. Conall and Lochlann had fought to save us yet forgotten to ensure that we touched skin to skin. The light that erupted as we did touch had burned Tomas as if his skin had been touched by sunlight.

What would happen to a bonded couple separated for a long time – say days – across a vast distance who came together in a passionate reunion?

The thought was terrifying and exhilarating.

"How?" I whispered. "How could that have happened?"

"It is said the male was guarded by her family and she guarded by his. The Priestess was more concerned with showing mercy than dwelling on the cause of their situation. Such a simple mistake can cause devastation. The bonded female commanded the guard to set her free. And they did – they had no choice."

My mind boggled at the intricacy of it. How such a small action rocked the foundation of a species and altered a fundamental way of life. The lovers had given each other their family names as a token of devotion, and in one selfish act they shattered the faith of so many. "That's why you stopped giving them?"

"It was considered best. It was not the only reason, but the beginning of the end. We let the old names of power die and the bonding became seen as forbidden. There are many who would try to hurt you in fear of what you and Breandan share." The warning in his voice was clear. "Long lost Priestess or not, they will try to harm you. If I had known … if the white witch had warned me of what might happen if you were to meet and touch I would never have—"

"Enough," Breandan said flatly.

My head swung back and forth between them, more than concerned now. They were being openly disrespectful to each other. Breandan ran a hand down my arm and I shuddered. Who knew how many he had killed with those hands. How many he would kill to get back to me if ever we were separated? I knew he was trying to distract me from what had passed between him and my brother, but it would not work. I could not ask them what was wrong, somehow I knew they would not tell me and would have a mutual agreement to keep it between them. But I would figure it out, oh yes; I would work it all out.

Leaning back on my elbows, I kicked my legs out in front of me to cross them at the ankles. "I understand."

"This is a good thing. We are beginning to hear each other clearly, little sister." He looked so proud I swallowed a disagreeing snort. Conall slapped his knees, face lightening, and becoming fair with a beauty I had not known a male could possess. "And now you learn our family history. Our mother was Sorcha. A fairy of such beauty and grace there was nothing she could not have or command from anyone. When I was a boy, I watched our father rule our people when the forests covered the earth. As a young man I watched him keep us safe when the humans built their cities and destroyed our forests." His voice became thick with emotion. "We learned to blend.

To glamour ourselves to look and move like them so we could be safe. We would convene in parks and woodlands to frolic and tend to the nature that was left. Our numbers dwindled and we became myth and legend to a race that once lived with us in harmony." Conall's face was tight, strained. "The other races spawned from us were not so amenable to change. They were not content to hide."

I sat up and blinked. "Wait. Spawned?"

Conall shook himself and focused on my face rather than the middle distance. "I am sorry. I forgot you do not know the history of such things. Rae, we all came from one Source." He cupped his hands together. "At the beginning of all things there were fairies. From them the species diversified. Over the years, genetic quirks and mutations created other whole species to walk the earth. We loved and guided them, loved them despite the differences, and their lines flourished."

"That's why the Priestess guards the balance. Fairies were the first beings."

Conall nodded. "We are honour – and magic – bound to take care of this world. It is why we feel so connected to it. To nature."

I slumped. "Ana told me Sorcha broke the balance. I had hoped she was overreacting."

Conall bowed his head. "Our family is … we are the only purebloods left from our line. We must fix this."

He sounded so tired when he said that I crawled forward and placed a hand on his knee. "Must? It's our choice. We can choose to leave this region. Find a new home."

He gave me a small smile. "If we do not make our stand here, where in the world could we hide? This is our purpose and we shall meet it with pride and courage."

I leaned back on my heels, plucking at the shorter grass by my sides. "It's not fair you're dumping all this responsibility on me. I understand that by blood this Priestess thing was unavoidable, but why can't I pass my title on to someone more worthy? More ... responsible and suitable. Like, abdicate, or something."

"It does not work that way," Breandan said. He stared at his hands as if they held answers to all questions. "We are chosen, and we do the best we can with what we are given."

"I don't want this," I said firmly. Biting my lip, I fisted my hands on my knees. Screw it. "What I'm asking is for you both to leave this region with me."

I did not look at either of them. Yes, I was ashamed, but I was more afraid of not asking. The power and strength I had felt when I had used the amulet of power that morning was gone. And though I now knew what my purpose was, I was terrified of it. How could I do this? I barely knew how I was feeling half the time. I did not think five minutes past my own nose, and more often than not concluded that running away was the best way to resolve my problems. Okay, yes, I was getting better at standing and fighting. No doubt if Breandan or Conall was in danger I would give everything I was to save them. It was everything else that worried me. Could I stand and fight on behalf of a race I had yet to come to love?

A finger tapped my chin up. I tried not to cry, and looked away from Breandan's knowing gaze. I did not want to feel comforted.

"We will be with you," he said softly.

"To the end," Conall added.

Their words held so much love yet they gave little comfort.

"Tell me what to do. Please. Point me on the right

direction because I'm lost, Conall. I'm sinking and I can't pull myself out. Something inside me is dead, festering. I can't reach that place where everything is okay. All I see darkness and it kills me." I closed my eyes. "Lex is dead; she is dead because of me. Maeve nearly died because of me. Breandan nearly died because of me. Why aren't you seeing a pattern yet?" My voice became angry at the end. "I'm no good at this. I'll fail."

Breandan said something in a low voice to my brother. He replied curtly and stood, patted me twice on the head lightly. The gesture was so joyous you would think I'd told him a storm was blowing in.

"All will be well," he said. He seemed to consider something for a long time then his muscled chest heaved with a sigh. "Rae, the trail has gone cold."

The abrupt switch in conversation topic had me scrambling around for a moment before my anger bubbled and churned. "You're lying." Even as I said the words I flushed, but kept my stare defiant.

Fairies could not lie – except for me, and I had been told eventually even I would be bound to speak nothing but the truth. A fairy's word once given was law. So my previous statement had been churlish at best.

Conall ignored the comment, flicking his hand through the air as if brushing his hurt aside. "Give me time." He speared Breandan with a warning glare. "She needs sleep." Then he was gone.

CHAPTER TWO

I stared after Conall and pressed my lips together.

"He will find the trail if it is to be found," Breandan said after a terse pause. "We have had so little time to talk and to be together … will you not look at me?"

I exhaled through my nose and fisted my hands on my knees. Turning so I faced him I nodded once. This was true. We had had no time to get to know one another, and surely it would do no harm to forget about Devlin and focus solely on the boy in front of me.

With a hot flush creeping up my neck and a too-hard thump of my heart, I realised this might be harder than I first thought. I was … shy. He was intimidating. And though I should feel comfortable with him, when I tried to meet his gaze my eyes fell to his lap, making me suddenly more uncomfortable because I was staring at his crotch.

Breandan said and did nothing. He watched me quietly, and was seemingly content to just sit with me.

I could not fathom why I wanted to rub myself all over him. The urge was starkly primitive and astounded me even as I acknowledged how absurd such a thought was. Wasn't I supposed to want him to kiss and caress me tenderly? What I wanted could in no way be considered tender.

I was not brave enough to stroke him so boldly – yet – still gripped in the vice of my own embarrassment. Scooting close, jerkily, I placed my fisted my hands on his shoulders and waited for him to take the lead.

He noted my silence and hesitation with the briefest of smiles. He trailed his fingers over the base of my wing pinions making me gasp and arch into him. I trembled. My face hovered in front of his, so close his eyelashes brushed the curve of my cheek. I trembled again.

He blinked and asked, "Are you frightened?"

I gulped and found myself unable to hold his gaze, liquid silver and shimmering with amusement. I was a whole lot of things, but frightened was not one of them.

"You're going to have to work for me," I said breathless, and backed up until I was half crouched. My lungs filled properly and I felt light headed. I lifted my chin. "You want me? Come get me."

There was a beat where he withdrew from me completely; my awareness of him winked into nothing and his face clouded over. I felt a split second of panic that swiftly became wariness. Breandan stood, uncoiling from his seat oh so slowly, and paced forward. His nature exploded in a gush of heat and fierce possession to suffocate my own into obedience. Still not willing to bend, panting, I stepped back and held up a hand in warning. He took another measured step and grabbed my hand.

"Are you sure you want to play this game?" he asked in a rough voice that had my eyes widening and my stomach clenching tight.

He had a feral way about him I'd not seen before and I felt his nature caress mine in such a way it would have been indecent if he decided to mirror the touch as a physical manifestation. He brought my hand to his mouth and kissed each of my fingertips before bringing my baby finger into his mouth and biting it gently.

"You are most beautiful to me Rae," he murmured and did it again, harder this time.

Dazed, I tried to catch his eye. "Say-say?" The high chime of my voice had taken on a new quality. It was throaty, husky even.

His expression was intense and he cupped my face in his hands like I was delicate, but he did not repeat himself, and I was more interested in touching than talking. I moved forward, pushing him back down so I could straddle his lap. My face felt hot, but I was determined to see this through. Leaning into him, I rubbed my cheek against his and made a soft hum at the back of my throat. The sensation of his firmer skin stroking against mine felt good. I shuddered and leaned forward farther to rub my entire torso against him, highly aware of the soft curves of my body as they glided against the rigidity of his. He pushed back and I made a noise – my thigh muscles tightening around his – acting purely on instinct. Enthralled by the sight of his skin pulsing faintly, the tip of my tongue flicked out to slide over his earlobe.

His body froze and he choked on his own air mid-breath. I swear even his heart skipped a beat under my palm.

Pulling back slightly so I could look down on his rigid profile, I waited; worried I had pushed it too far.

With maddening slowness, he placed a hand on my waist and another on the nape of my neck. He pulled my head down and my lips met his. I moaned, a sound that reflected the ache I had heard about – but never felt before – spreading across my hips. We kissed softly – lips barely touching – almost as if he was sampling me. Then suddenly Breandan pushed me down on the yellowed grass and grazed his teeth along my neck and shoulders, running his hands all over me. I arched into him, loving his weight over me. He was hot, skin ablaze, and when he touched me the fire licked from his fingertips. I pulled him closer, wanting not the slightest space between us. It was natural for my legs to lock around his back by the ankles, hands tugging at the waistband of his trousers. I sent up a silent prayer of thanks to the gods that all this boy wore was jeans. Breandan's hand pushed my dress up and he stroked my navel, then lower. I made a noise and bit his lip. I was inexperienced and my caresses were little more than an enthusiastic fumble, but I did not care. Gods, I did not care.

Then he was gone and I was groping the air, legs dangling upwards. I must have looked like an upturned beetle. I looked around for him and found him sitting up, a few steps away, his face a dull shade of red and body strung tight like a bowstring.

"I apologise," he said quietly. "I should not have let things get so out of hand."

Annoyed, I rolled onto my stomach and snatched up a twig. I scratched sharp, jagged shapes into the dirt, stabbing and prodding the earth in front of me with my hand balled into a fist.

"Rae...."

"Just don't, Breandan."

The ache was still there. Was there an off switch? Why did I still feel all squirmy and warm?

Sighing, I threw the twig away and twisted into my back so I could see the sky. A few birds zipped past and something furry clambered its way up an isolated tree trunk. I closed my eyes and rubbed my face on the grass, wishing it were something else ... rather someone else.

The grasses prickled my skin making me itchy and releasing a nutty fragrance as they did so. I stretched, enjoying the feeling of the muscles in my lower back and arms popping. I had been scrunched up so tight against him, locked in a bubble of breathy moans and hushed whispers, that lying there felt ungainly.

Already the niggle I felt whenever he was not touching me became uncomfortable. Ana the white witch had warned what could happen if we were separated for too long. I was not sure I was ready to put her words to the test. That and the story of the couple that had bonded before us had scared the crap out of me. The last time the nexus had opened between Breandan and I, there had been intense light. We had only been apart a matter of minutes. Only the gods knew what would happen if it was to open when we had been apart for hours. Surely we needed to practice being apart to gain some kind of control over this connection between us.

I inhaled through my nose and exhaled through my mouth. I remained still and focused on being calm. This was a new feeling – the want – but I had spent years controlling my nature without knowing that was what I was doing – that I was repressing the fairy in me. This was just another urge to control.

Breandan touched my ankle lightly. The ache lessened and the annoying niggles telling me to seek him out faded. Gritting my teeth I ignored him.

I blinked slowly and my lids took a long time to lift back up. The second time, my lids closed and stayed closed. I forced them open slowly. I was tired and with this admission, I felt disgruntled. Breandan did not look tired at all and I was sure he'd been up much longer than I had. And he'd expended more energy. My eyes felt heavy and I pinched my leg but it did nothing but leave a pain dulled by sleepiness. Then I noticed that the sun was winking out of sight, and that my sudden sleepiness may not be entirely natural. Was the dark calling to me? I shot up and swayed when my body fought for me to lie my heavy head back down. I did not want to sleep. I wanted to stay awake, but the dark called, I was certain of it. With a small sense of shock, I realised I was frightened. I immediately reached to place my hands on Breandan's shoulders and held on tightly, my past resolve to not touch him forgotten.

With a soft sigh of relief, he pulled me onto his lap and held me close. "Let your body rest," he murmured.

"I don't want to. The last time I slept I dreamed of," I paused briefly, "I dreamed of Tomas then when I woke he was there." I was not afraid of my vampire, but of what happened to me whenever he was near. He confused me, spun me about, and it was easier if he was elsewhere.

"That will not happen again. I have you, rest."

Pressing a kiss to my temple, Breandan gathered me closer in his arms, happy to openly show his affection now we were alone. I noticed that he did not like to be all over me in the company of others. I wondered if that was a fairy thing or a Breandan thing.

Resting my head on his warm, bare shoulder my eyes fluttered closed. I listened to his steady breathing, felt the solid pounding of his heart under my palm. Weariness wrapped round my limbs and tugged. Tentacles slithered into my mind and a wave of fatigue pulled me under, tumbling, tumbling into the inky depths of sleep.

I was racing through the forest, feeling nothing. Not the wind on my face or the earth beneath my feet. That was the trouble with being dead; you could not feel anything anymore. How had she managed to warm my heart when it had been cold for over a century?

My stomach clenched painfully. I was hungry, starving. My throat burned and my mouth was dry as ash. Without thinking, I honed in on a strong heartbeat, pumping thick hot blood through veins.

I breathed in deeply and scented the trail.

Then I saw her, picking some berries. I laughed darkly to myself. One so young and pretty should not be left to gather food by herself.

I quickly and quietly trod closer, so careful. She was not human and would be able to hear or smell me if I made too sudden a movement.

Closer still I moved.

Her heartbeat sounded like thunder. She smelled delicious and my mouth watered. My stomach cramped, squeezing tighter. The hunger was so acute I thought it would drive me mad.

My fangs ran out and I licked the sharp points. I hummed with anticipation of burying my teeth into her neck and ripping away the flesh. Drinking, slurping, and licking until the burning ache was satisfied. My hands shook.

I needed to feed.

Hand poised to pick another berry she paused, stiffened.

I stood still and silent. She would not hear me, I did not breathe, nor did I sweat. I carried no scent apart from an earthy-mineral fragrance she would attribute to a plant in the forest.

She sniffed deeply then shrugged, and went back to her gathering.

Slinking forward, I made no sound. I clasped a hand over her mouth to cover her scream and spun her round. I held her terrified gaze with my own. She stilled. I felt her relax under my grip and I let her go. "You are safe," I thought into her head. Her body trembled and her mind shifted, fighting to break from my hold. I controlled it and pushed away her free will. "You are safe," I thought again and pulled her closer. I did not waste time in lulling her into a deeper calm. Fairies were strong and compulsion never held their minds for long.

She went willingly into my arms and sighed as I bit into her.

The blood was wet, thick, and tasted rich with earthy undertones. I drank it greedily, already feeling warmth spread through my entire body. I fed from her and gently moved down with her as her body went lax. Her heartbeat stared to fail. I held on, wanting to savour every drop.

She was pure-blooded fairy. Rare Delicious.

Lost in the peace of the moment, I felt something, someone. A familiar presence I would know for the rest of my days. Rae? Was she here, with me? No. I pushed the feeling away. She had left me, gone with the fairy male. I did not want her, and I did not care if I would die. Just being with her had nearly cost me my life.

She was supposed to be salvation.

And that was what made my heart bleed. So pure a girl would turn her back on everything to save me. A murderer, a true demon bound to his bloodlust, a slave to pain and desire. How she could want a thing like me was not something I understood ... yet I did understand the incomprehensible need to have her near me, as I was sure she felt it too. I needed to see her, feel her beneath me. I wanted to own her, to take her, and reveal in the beauty of the darkness we could share.

I would go to her. I would take her away and make her mine. I could still make it work; it need not be the end of her if she came with me.

The girl went still beneath my hands.

Her heart stopped beating.

My eyes opened, and I stared into Breandan's face. From my position, I could see his jaw clenched, his lips pressed together in concentration. He shifted and looked down at me, aware I was now awake.

"You left your body," he said, voice strained. "I tried to wake you, but you would not return. Where did you go?"

"I– I'm not sure," I lied.

I had to swallow hard, for my tongue seemed to thicken as I said the words. I knew exactly where I had been and what I had seen, but surely, a lie to soothe is better than hurting with the truth.

"For a time, I couldn't even feel you. Our bond was smothered by darkness."

The words tore at my heart and I clutched him to me. "You'll n–n...." I struggled with the lie. "... never lose me, Breandan."

He stiffened. "You're finding it harder to lie now."

I buried my head in his shoulder. "I don't want to hurt you," I said. "I want you to feel like you can trust me. But I don't understand all of this."

"It'll take time for you to get used to being truthful." He paused. "Of course soon you will have no choice. It would be better for you if you tried to speak only the truth. Alright?" I nodded. "Besides," he continued in a light voice. "You are older than me. You should be setting a good example."

I snorted. "Yeah, two hundred years senior. How does that work again?"

His brows mashed together. "This upsets you."

Hell yes. I slid off his lap onto the soft grass. "You

don't have to declare my mood to the world each time you figure me out."

His head cocked. "Now you're mad." I gritted my teeth. Breandan ran a finger down the bridge of my nose, over my pressed lips and tense jaw. "So angry," he murmured.

He let his touch wander down the side my neck, brush lightly over my collarbone. A brief hesitation before his hand stroked the swell of my breast. I gasped. He chuckled and clamped his big hands over my upper arms to pull me closer. His eyes – two pools of iridescent light – flicked over my features as if he could not chose which to settle upon. My heart thumped in my chest as his head lowered and his tongue shot out to lick my bottom lip. He made a humming noise at the back of his throat, like the one I made, but his was almost questioning. Before I could dwell on how odd it was, he pressed his lips to mine. Most might have been gentle or tried to go in softly so as not to scare me, but Breandan was a force all of his own and he had decided he wanted to kiss me. His mouth latched onto mine tongue entwined around my own with enough skill and finesse to have me groaning into his mouth. Instinct. The more it guided me the more I gave it free rein – especially if the payoff was going to feel so damn good each time.

I tried to move closer but his hands clamped down on my arms kept me still. He pulled away to kiss the side of my neck. His attention had diverted from passion to something else.

He said, "You seem tense."

I held still and waited and when no further explanation was forth coming I replied, "It doesn't matter, please, don't stop."

"Tell the truth. Of whom did you dream?" His eyes

sparked, daring me to lie.

Flushing, I shifted and my head drooped, but he did not release his hold. Instead of feeling protected, I felt smothered, but I explained my dream in a reluctant mutter as truthfully as I could. As I spoke, he became increasingly tense. His grip on my arms hurt, but I did not want him to let go of me, so I kept that to myself. When I told him of the last thought – that Tomas wanted me and intended to claim me – his entire body quaked and his grip became so painful I could not hide it. When he realised, he relaxed, rubbed my arms, and there was an apology in the touch.

"That thing will never have you," he grated. "His time grows short."

The thought of my two boys clashing had my heart shrinking to the size of a raisin – all shrivelled up and black. I still disliked the idea of Tomas being closed off to me forever. It seemed wrong, final.

"I would rather you didn't say things like that," I said quietly. "Can't you see that as much as our bonding was unplanned so is this connection Tomas and I share?"

Gaze locked on the middle distance, Breandan was not listening to me. "I only have myself to blame," he murmured. He was frowning again, and I sighed as I used the pad of my forefinger to smooth the furrows. A tingle from the contact ran down my body and my eyes closed briefly as I savoured the feeling. "I was so anxious to get away from you I didn't pay attention." He looked at me, apologetic. "Had I simply waited a moment more and focused on you rather than how inconvenient my feelings were I would have known he was there. Had I taken you back to Temple he never would have had his chance to…." His eyes drifted closed and he whispered, "Sometimes I wish he had been overcome and bitten you from the first moment he saw you. Had he spilt your blood I would have known it and returned. Instead of seeking him out you would now be afraid. But our bond was still so new, and my head was in turmoil–"

I cut in, waving my hand to bat away his words. "You were protecting the amulet of protection. I understand. No harm done."

The despair in his eyes was heart breaking. How could he blame himself for something that was not even an issue? I understood there was bad blood between the vampires and the fairies, but Tomas had helped us – helped him. I leaned forward. "I know you think you failed me." I placed my palm to his cheek and made sure I held his gaze. "You didn't. You never have and I fear you never will. That's what makes your feelings for me so unbelievable, y'know. I don't deserve you and I'm worried no matter how hard I try that I never will."

"Every day I like what and who I am less and less," he whispered more quietly than before, "because I know you wish for a different life. And I cannot give it to you."

"You can't change our destiny. I know that."

His hand covered mine and he leaned into my palm. His silvery lashes gleamed against his creamy skin. "But you also know that I cannot run from it. It is not in my nature though I know it is in yours."

I swallowed. As much as I wanted to, I could not run from it; my destiny was a sphere of knowing I could never outrun. I was the Priestess and had to bring my kind back from the abyss lest the rest of demonkind spiral out of control. Always did I panic and tell anyone who would listen that I could not, would not do it. Never did I sit up and take the control offered to me from all those who would pledge to follow me. My fear was a blanket I hid behind to mask the truth. I had no motivation to help anyone unless it directly meant it would make Breandan happy. How sick was that? The only reason I did anything was to impress him ... to make him proud of me.

How could I be this legendary being if I thought solely about my own happiness, and that of my mate?

Breandan was strong. He faced all challenges with grim determination and did not stop until he was victorious. He went into every confrontation on his own terms, certain that he would succeed. I was dragged into situations kicking and screaming like a child. Lochlann himself had said I bawled like one. I flushed at the memory. Why had I not been ready to fight and avenge my friend? It should not have been Conall exacting payment for Lex's life it should have been me. So now, to make myself feel better, I was attaching myself to Conall's heels as he chased Devlin across the region, using the Tribe's need for the grimoire as an excuse to outrun my real responsibilities. How shameful and self absorbed. Worse, I still could not find it in my heart to feel bad about feeling and thinking in such a way.

"Is that is why you saved him?"

"Say-say?" I asked trying to pick up the conversational thread I'd dropped.

Breandan watched me with a curious expression. "You saved the vampire because you think his destiny is entwined with yours?" He no longer sounded angry or disgusted, merely confused, suspicious even.

I tilted my head slightly, my hair falling over my shoulder and into my eyes. "I saved him because I care about him." I thought hard on how I felt, what I felt. "He feels different to you." A faint shudder rippled through me. "I won't lie, he does scare me. He is ... dangerous, I think. But there is something that I can't help but like about him. Even if my nature shivers at what he is, who he is appeals to me in a way you can't." I looked guiltily down at my lap. The honesty was good, but it was embarrassing.

"The darkness," Breandan said matter of fact. "Compulsion."

I pushed at my hair and blew out a short breath through my nose. "It doesn't work on us." I was firm in this conviction. "He can't manipulate me that way."

"The blood tie makes you vulnerable to him in a way none of our kind has been to one of his. I cannot assure you what you feel is genuine. Only the gods know how he can bend or invade your mind." His lips twisted. "Even if I could lie to make you feel better I wouldn't."

"Does feeling drawn to his darkness make me bad?" I asked quietly, terrified of his answer. "I mean, Devlin is evil, but I'm not evil just for wanting to be close to the dark. I'm not evil." There was that heavy silence again. "Am I?"

Breandan said nothing.

I jerked up out of his hold, and marched away from him. Pacing a small circle, I yanked at my hair a few times. What? Had I expected him to cuddle me, and tell me I was perfect, and as innocent as new born babe? Of course, he would not say anything. He could not lie. And why should he comfort or give confidence for me to explore the blood tie. What self-respecting male would?

I stopped my pacing and stood over him. He shifted up and crossed his legs, resting his arms loosely on his knees.

Instead of conceding that he was within his right to fight for me I said, "I wish you could lie."

"No," he replied. "You wish you could lie to yourself."

"Can't you say something to make me feel better?" I brushed my hands over my arms, as if wiping dirt.

"Cleaner?"

"It is my purpose to keep order. I won't encourage a delusion, even if it pains me not to do so."

"I'm not a bad person," I said crossly. "I deserve to have you make me feel better when I'm feeling insecure. I've lost my best friend. Can't you bend a little?"

He sighed. "What could I possibly say that would make you feel better after what happened to your friend?"

I looked down at my hands, fisted on my knees. "You should know what to say. Then again, that is not the real problem, is it? The truth is you don't know me well enough to know what to say to make me feel better." I frowned. "And I know nothing about you. Not really."

How could I feel such emotion toward a person I knew nothing of? I had met him two days ago, and I could not look forward and not see him. If I looked back there was nothing before him. In my mind's eye the world was surrounded by darkness and he was shimmering silver light guiding me home, keeping me safe until I could see again.

"What do you want to know?"

There was no impatience or mockery in his tone, simply the need to please and reassure me. It made the idea of asking him about himself seem okay.

"I don't know. Stuff," I said and waved my hands.

He cocked his head. "No. I don't know. You have to tell me."

I resisted the urge to shrug. I was drawing a blank. "You could offer some information. Like...." Finally, Breandan and I were alone, and had time to talk yet I could not think of one single question to ask him. I looked at his face and thought of his lips. I looked in his eyes and marvelled at how they matched the silvery grey of the moon. So I looked down at his stomach, let my gaze drift lower over the pale, smooth skin and delineated muscle until it hovered around the tie of his trousers.

"Rae-love?"

I jumped and pressed my eyes shut. He called me love. I giggled and flushed in pleasure. Peeking at him, I took in his amused expression. "Have you ever been with a girl before?" Once I heard the words and realised how they may be interpreted, I blushed yet again, worried the blood rushing to my head was the reason I felt light headed. "I mean, have you ever had a steady?"

His lips twitched, eyes twinkled. "I do not understand."

Like hell he did not. "A girl who you found special. Who you wanted to ... you know?"

He made a small noise. "Ah, a lover?" The words were spoken full of wonder and magic. They coiled around me and stroked me silly. "No, I never found a female." Ah, a lover? The way he spoke was self assured and confident. Always so sure of himself and what he was doing, what he had done.

My eyes darted to and from his. "Did you look?"

A dull bronze bloomed across his cheekbones. I watched the colour heighten, captivated by him.

"For a while, but I was not suited to anyone." He met my eyes. "The reason why I never was is clear."

My fingers danced across his shoulder. I was dying to know all the gory details about any past relationships, but reluctant to push too far in case he asked about mine. Rather, the lack of mine.

"You didn't like them?" I asked.

"They did not like me. They found me ugly."

My mouth hit the floor. "Ugly?" I smacked my palm on his forehead, scowling. "I know the rules, but you have to be telling a lie."

At first he was stumped, face blank with shock. Then slowly a look of pure mischief stole across his expression. "You like the way I look?"

No way was I answering that bloody question. Turning away from him slightly, I played with the skin on my leg where the slash in my jeans used to be and was happy for the change of direction it allowed my thoughts to grab onto. The dress I wore was pretty, but I missed my own clothes. Where would I get clothes from now? There was a factory behind the Wall that produced clothes, of course, but I could hardly walk up to the hand-out booth, smile toothily, and collect clothes any more. Not that I smiled much before I met Breandan.

Said boy had become stiff beneath me, and it was uncomfortable to sit on someone who was as relaxed as a plank of wood.

His eyes were fixated on my hand. I realised then that my dress had ridden up to pool at the top of my thighs, and my legs were completely bare. His hand had rested on my thigh innocently, but now it flexed and tightened its hold on me. I said nothing. His warm palm moved slowly up my leg, gently kneading. I moaned, surprising myself with the urgency of my own voice and buried my head in the crook of his neck, breathed in the scent of him. I was sure it had imprinted itself on my brain. Sunlight, rain, and green things mixed with a spicy masculine smell that was all his own. Touching was so much more revealing than talking. Emotion flickered in my gut as I reached to trawl my fingers over his scalp, loving the feel of the thick dark hair that grew there. It seemed his hair grew as fast as mine, and I could not wait to see it longer. Would it be jet black like his eyebrows or be shot through with streaks so dark they absorbed the light entirely and glowed silver?

Yes. Yes, I wanted this. I was unsure of everything else but this. I wanted to lie in his arms and to love him. I wanted him to hold onto me and to love me.

My fingertips traced the lines of his nose and mouth. I kissed him. His eyes were open and bored into mine as he kissed me back. Then my mouth parted and his tongue slipped out to slide across the seam of my lips. I tingled all over and my eyes drifted closed. His tongue was slow, explorative and tasted sweet. Running his hands down the length of my body, he sighed, and I gripped his shoulders. I waited for the next kiss … but nothing happened. Opening my eyes – drunk on lust – reality filtered through my happy haze. Breandan was looking at me strangely, his mouth pulled into a thin line. Sliding me away from him, he jumped up gracefully, turning away so I got a tantalising view of his bare shoulders and broad back.

The marks on this side of his body were bolder, more ominous in design. If I had to sum them up in a word, I would have chosen 'nefarious'. I shivered slightly, and not from the sensations he ignited under my skin with his touch. Why did Breandan – the one person in the entire world I was sure had no darkness – have tattoos like that?

Confused as to why we were no longer touching I surged up, stood on my tail, and then sunk to my knees rubbing it, tears pricking the corner of my eyes, and a faint echo of the pain shooting up my spine.

Breandan spared me a glance and shook his head. He paced the floor in front of me. Eventually, after pondering gods knows what, he settled for stalking back over and yanking my head back. The pressure of his mouth crushing mine almost hurt.

"Let's go see if we can help Conall pick up the trail," he said and left me there, already a silvery blur in the distance.

Watching his retreating back, irrational rage replaced desire.

Was I supposed to understand what had just happened?

I jumped up and stumbled after him. He sprinted across the Pride green, the waist-length grass getting crushed beneath his boots. I chased him, as fast as he, and my rage was powerful. I sped up until he was at arm's length. Before I had the thought, I was pushing off the ground and soaring, latching myself onto his back. I dug my fingers into his bare shoulders, dragging my nails across his skin until I drew blood. He snagged one of my legs and hauled me off him, throwing me to the mossy ground. He pinned me and leaned his weight into me. He loomed over me; skin pulsing and eyes sparking like an avenging angel. I would have felt the need to prostrate myself on the ground before him if I did not feel so pissed off. Too angry to be shocked at my feral actions I bared my teeth.

Face a mask of rage he leaned down further. "Behave!"

"If you're disgusted with the way I behave why don't you just say it?" I tried to push him off. "I'm not proud of how I react when I'm with you but I can't help it."

He let go of my wrists and paced away, his hands clasped behind his head. I sat up – my knees bent – and wiped the leaves and dirt from my hair and clothes in forceful sweeps. It ground into my dress, and the rubbing made it worse. I was a bloody mess.

Breandan spun, fists clenched. "Why can't you see how I feel?" His voice drifted over to me soft-as-ash and filled with longing. "I have left my home and turned my back on my family. Everything I have done I've done for you." Stunned I stared at him. My eyes were wide and my mouth open. He half smiled at the look on my face. "The moment I revealed myself to you I made peace with what I was to do, of what I would be giving up. I belong to you. I choose you, I always will, but you have to understand that everything is not what it seems. And when I pull away from you it's because I want nothing more than to be close to you. You know how your family and mine feel about us. Why do you continue to doubt me?"

The feeling that overflowed in my chest was euphoric, but tinged with shame. I did not feel good enough for him and it was frustrating. It was like I wore big boots but my feet were pitifully small, and no matter how hard I tried to run in them without tripping over, they were simply too big for me. Tears trickled down the side of my nose. Why was I not brave, honest, and selfless? Maybe there was something broken inside making me selfish and devious.

Breandan dropped to his knees, taking my head in his hands. Disgruntled I tried to pull away, but he held fast and sighed, brushing my tears away. "I do not like to see you cry. Be calm, Rae-love, we will be together. We are together. Alright?"

"I don't feel like–"

Eyes turning from pained to scary-alert his head snapped to the side and he peered across the plain. Seeing nothing in the solid dark I started again, needing to confess everything, how I felt about him.

"Breandan, I–"

"Silence." He placed a finger to my lips and closed his eyes. He nodded, satisfied. "We are in a shield. We cannot be seen as long as we stay still." I peered into the gloom wondering what he hid us from. "A demon is close," he said into my ear as I curled against his chest.

Breathing in deeply I extended myself. Since I had become a fairy, what I could perceive had changed immensely. My consciousness could feel further than just a few feet. My mind could seek life forces miles away and that is what I did, pushing myself to the limit. I started. Someone two natured was nearby, a male. He was coming closer, curious and wary. He did not want to hurt us; it was his job to check we were friendly.

I opened my eyes and glanced around. My sight was keen and I had paid little attention to our surroundings other than how pretty it was at a glance. Now I focused, seeing a line of the grass moving in the opposite direction of the rest.

"The wind blows east and carries our scent into the Pride," Breandan explained and pointed to the grass. "It is not polite to run in another's territory without permission, even if you mean peace. Before we reveal ourselves I want to be sure he means us no harm."

The scream of a cat echoed across the Pride lands, and the soft stomping of heavy paws drawing closer found us through the silence. A panther raced into view. He weaved through the grass unerringly in our direction.

Oddly enough, I relaxed and my knees went weak with relief.

Breandan secured my waist and slid me behind him as the panther slid to a stop and exposed his sharp teeth in a vicious snarl and hissed menacingly.

Conall simply appeared from thin air, and held up his hands to both Breandan and the shifter; thank gods because it seemed like they would have torn into each other had he not. He shook his head, exasperated. "It is a good thing I decided not to scout too far ahead. Always are you in trouble, Rae."

I curled my lip at him. How unfair. Like this was in any way my fault.

Roaring, the panther leapt forward a bound. His ears were flat to his head and his claws scratched up the earth. He was huge, coal black, and I found myself wondering how the hell I had not seen him in the green grass. It was taller than him, coming up to just below my breast, but still. After his display of dominance, he turned his head to look at me, and blinked. His beautiful eyes were the trigger that revealed I did indeed have a memory of him.

I laughed and held out my hand. Breandan pushed it back. "Wait," he ordered and watched the cat carefully. He was not taking any more chances after our last encounter.

"Hai," I whispered to the panther. "It might sound crazy, but it's good to see you."

He padded over cautiously, whiskers quivering when Breandan hissed a warning. The panther slinked low, under Breandan's restraining arm. Keeping his eyes trained on my fairy-boy he pushed his head into my hand. His eyes slid closed and purred.

I was strangely touched that he remembered me too.

"You know this hunter?" Conall asked a hint of pride in his tone.

Breandan shifted and the panther's eyes shot open. He growled then settled on his haunches, tongue lolling to the side. I rubbed him behind the ears and he grumbled happily.

Breandan relaxed. His raised eyebrow was enough to tell me he was surprised, but then he pulled his face into a neutral expression, his thoughts hidden from me. "How did you know it was him?"

I shrugged. "He's unique. I just knew. He felt the same, y'know?" I glanced at Conall to let him know I had not forgotten his question. "We met in the forest yesterday when Breandan found me."

The words pulled me up short. Had it only been two days since I'd met Breandan and Conall? Had it been so short a time in which my life had been turned upside down and inside out? My mind shied away from it all. It would do me no good to dwell on such things. It would drive me mad and I was batty enough.

"Did you pick up the trail?" I asked Conall in a rush. "I want to keep moving. I'm rested now and I even slept."

Conall said nothing. He handed Breandan and I a cracker each and unhooked a small skin flask from his hip. Breandan ate the cracker dry in one bite and swigged from the flask.

I stared at what I had been given in my upturned palm. It did not look, smell, or feel appetising. Not that food ever did look interesting to me. I did not feel hungry, but sort of hollow and like food would be okay in my stomach, but not that it was an urgent need. Would it be rude to ask if he had a can of fizzy stashed in one of his pockets? Glancing at Conall I decided against it. Little human culture resided in the fairy way, so I simply kept my eyes low, and glanced at Breandan through my lashes.

He was already watching me. "Everything okay?" he asked politely.

Pushing my hair off my face, I plastered on a bright smile, and cupped my other hand under the one forced to hold the cracker. "Uh huh. I'm not much of an eater anyway, and I'm sure there is something else…." As I spoke I offered the cracker to him, but a glance at Conall showed more of the same kind of dry, mealy food in his hand. "Y'know, I can go days without eating anything."

Breandan grinned then bent down to bite half the

cracker from my palm. In a few moments, his rough tongue was licking crumbs and juices from my inner fingertips. Juices? I looked down to see a see-through golden fluid running down my palm.

Breandan smacked his lips then regarded me closely. "You don't like honey-nectar? It's sweet."

"Well to be honest I don't think I've ever tried it. We used to get given lots of bread, milk, water … and meat," I said thoughtfully. At the word 'meat', the oh, were-panther's whiskers twitched and his pink tongue flicked out to swipe over his maw. As I spoke, I grinned at him. "And drinks filled with sugar to keep us going, y'know. Like fizzy stuff."

"We have a much more varied diet," Conall said after a pause, eyeing Breandan and where he had licked my hand with a dour expression. "But our meat is mostly fish and small game. Red meat makes us sluggish, slow. We avoid it."

I nodded. "Makes sense. As a people we climb and live in the trees." My voice was reflective. "We're quick and light on our feet. It makes sense the food we should eat would be light in substance, but rich in goodness. And it explains why I never liked meat all that much."

Breandan nodded in agreement. I still held the oozing cracker in my hands and it was beginning to look odd. I nibbled on it and made an appreciative murmur at the firm, wheat biscuit, and its sweet sticky centre. I finished up and Breandan held out the flask. I felt positively doted on and I accepted it with a smile. I took a testing sip. Just water. I glugged it deeply and eyed Conall. "The trail?"

He rubbed the heels of his palms in his eyes and when he shook his head his ponytail swished behind him. "It is beyond me. Devlin has worked magics. Three different trails can be seen here, each is cold, and each carries his and Wasp's scent. Less than an hour ago, we were half a day away and gaining. Now, it seems we are days behind and losing more time. It is a trick, a spell, and I cannot see past it."

I took in a deep breath and handed him back the hip flask, wiping my hand over my mouth. Some sleep, something to eat and drink, and I did feel a little better. Sharper. "Then we follow of them. One trail each."

"No," Breandan said with forced evenness.

"Apart from the fact it would be most unwise to leave you alone, Rae," Conall said patiently, "what happens when one of us does find them? Or maybe we will find more false trails that we cannot navigate alone."

The were-panther – still seated comfortably on his haunches, tail swinging from side to side – leisurely turned his head each time one of us spoke. His emerald eyes were bright and aware and I knew he was taking in every word. His handsome feline face looked focused.

"Then we follow each one," I grated through my teeth. "We pick the most likely, follow for a while, and if we're wrong we'll backtrack and start again until we get it right."

"And what of the time we lose whilst doing this? What if we come across more trails that are false? We could spend days going in the wrong direction."

I opened my mouth to tell him I was ready to spend my lifetime hunting Devlin. Then I saw the stupidity in such words and my shoulders slumped. I burrowed the toe of my boot into the broken grasses strewn around me.

My voice was thick when I said, "There must be another way. We cannot just give up. Not just for my revenge. Lochlann needs the grimoire before he can start setting things right, doesn't he."

Even if Conall would not give in to a selfish endeavour – and such was the nature of revenge – he was the most loyal warrior I knew. He would do anything to secure Lochlann the fairy-lordship because he believed it was the right thing to do.

I looked up and found Breandan glaring at my brother, who sent him a short look of apology.

"Perhaps, there is something else we may consider. It is not without its dangers."

"It is not a good idea," Breandan said firmly.

Straightening, I cocked my head and tried to look attentive and brave, not desperate to crack some skulls. "Tell me and I'll do it."

Conall pointed a thick finger to the panther who had gotten bored just sitting and was purring and rubbing himself into my legs. "The shifters."

My nipped intake of breath was loud in the sudden silence. I gripped the fur at the base of the panther's neck and squeezed it. "Yes," I hissed, new possibilities opening up like a carnivorous black hole before me. "A Pack of were-cats could read each trail and save us time." I dropped to my knees in front of him. "Could you or your kind help us?" My head snapped up to Conall. "Which is the closest?"

"Byron's Pack is close and of the Alphas he is the most civilised. This panther must be of his Pride."

"You both forget I have already said no."

Breandan sent me a pointed look that told me he was serious. I returned it with some extra 'I'm doing this so back the hell off'. I won, of course. He would not dare deny me this.

"Alright," he said flatly.

His eyes were trained on the panther that looked rather smug to be weaving between my legs. I stumbled when he lay down, and rolled so he was pressed into my shins belly up begging for a tummy stroke.

I shuffled my feet from under him and accidentally stepped on his tail. He let out a strangled screech and jumped up.

Breandan laughed – his deeper baritone still managing to tinkle. It seemed the setting sun shone brighter and his smile made me blink. His silver eyes were breathtaking, and for a moment I was lost, falling into the gaze that swept over me lovingly. The moment changed, became charged, and I was acutely aware of his warm hands at my waist and his lips a short sway forward away from mine. I remembered the feel of his mouth and the heady scent of him, now on me marking me as his own.

The shifter nipped at my leg then buried his teeth in the material of my dress and tugged. The flimsy material tore a bit and I took the hint and moved forward.

"Will you lead us to Byron, hunter?" Conall asked politely.

The cat bobbed his head in agreement and plodded forward, back into the plain. He turned his head back and looked at me.

Breandan pushed me forward lightly. "It is an invitation."

I blinked, not understanding. "For what?" I asked mystified, joining the were-panther. I pulled at the fur on his spine playfully. He was so soft to touch I did not care that in reality I was intimately touching a being that was also a man when in human form.

He bunched his front and hind legs together and leapt forward, taking off at a speed that made my mouth drop.

"To run," said Breandan, winking at me a moment before he and Conall took off too.

After a beat, I laughed and started behind them. I

passed them quickly, and found myself following just behind the cat's tail. I tried to catch him up, but his tail winked in and out of sight between the tall grasses. My feet pounded the grass and I found myself going faster. The earth was soft and springy. Unlike the forest where you often had to jump and dodge, here the land was flat and flowed up and down in gentle hills. My wings fluttered and I extended them slightly and found my pace increasing. My tail whiplashed out to steady my balance when I thought I would tumble over and then I was by the cat's side, keeping up. I smiled and with a last push took the lead, laughing as I did so.

Breandan shouted – sounding terrified. I glanced behind me frowning. He panicked too much and too often.

Something brown and heavy crashed into me from the side and I went down, rolling over the spiky grass. Something sharp dragged at my hip. I smelt blood, and the stabbing pain across my side told me it was mine. I scrambled up and backed up a pace, hissing, the reaction instinctive.

A lynx stood fiercely before me, head down between her shoulder blades. Her luminous amber eyes locked on me and her whiskers trembled violently. The tufts on the top of her ears were jet black and the ruff under her neck bright white, the fur stretching down onto her underbelly. She jumped at me and I lurched out of the way, spinning round to meet her next attack. Growling, she crouched, ready to pounce, but the panther skidded to a stop between us and spun to face the lynx.

He roared at her, a series of deafening and commanding bleats. Pacing forward, he bit her on the neck, pushing her down onto the floor. She did not resist him and the change in her posture was instant. She lowered her head and whimpered. Her ears pressed against her skull in submission and her tail pointed down.

The panther shook her roughly and his jaw flexed around her neck. For a moment, I feared he would kill her.

He let go and I breathed out.

He plodded over to me and head butted me in the leg, hard. I got a distinct feeling of anger radiating from him.

Pressing a hand to my side, I brought it away to see a small smear of blood, but my side heated painfully and I knew I healed.

"Sorry," I said and knelt down to look him in the face. "It wasn't her fault, and I'm sorry."

"Good," Conall said. I had not heard him arrive. It was then I noticed he had Breandan restrained. He let my scowling life-mate go. "I know you wish to protect her, but you were not needed."

Anger flashed across Breandan's face before he composed himself. "You are right. It would have gone badly if I had interfered."

My face was flushed: a rush of colour that swept up my neck and spilled into my cheeks. What I had done was plain stupid. Of course the shifters would have many sentries posted across their borders. Lost in the joy of running I had forgotten we were drawing nearer to the heart of the Pride. The lynx would have smelled me coming and instantly reacted to what could be a hostile invader.

A bad thought came to me, "The Pack isn't going to be happy about the dead shifter are they?" I asked quietly. I gripped Breandan's arm, holding him to me like someone was trying to take him away. "Can't we hide the body? Like, throw it in a ditch somewhere and erase his scent from the place somehow?"

Nobody said anything for a long while and I knew my words had upset the fairy-boys. The were-cats stared at me like I was the most fascinating thing they had ever seen. I gave them a small smile in thanks. At least they understood where I was coming from. Conall and Breandan were honourable – to a fault – and though I knew they saw my idea as a cowardly one, I still thought it was the best one. It didn't matter who we were in the fairy world, the Pack we were visiting were not going to react well. They probably would have had an issue with us just being there in the first place but throw a dead one of their kind into the mix and things might get complicated. I did not want to have to persuade them we were not the enemy. The idea of going at it against powerful demons made my head hurt. My throat still ached, so shouting was not an option for me. My body felt beaten up and I resorted to a scowl.

Our assemblage stood still for a moment before the panther got bored, and with a low cat-like mewing sound signalled us to move. He took the lead again. The lynx slinking to his side, head still bowed in submission.

One look at Breandan's face had me all but pouting. "I guess you want to keep a hold on me now," I said gruffly and yanked on the end of my hair in irritation. I let my abused throat roughen my voice to remind him to be gentle with me.

A small smiled played on his lips. "For a little while."

Grumbling to myself, I did not hesitate to entwine my fingers with his. His skin glowed brighter and he smiled. I felt my muscles unclench and a troublesome anxiety that had gathered between my shoulder blades released. I relaxed and sighed. Breandan seemed to be experiencing similar sensations since he closed his eyes and rolled his shoulders.

"That is better," he said, satisfied, and tugged me along after him.

The were-cats travelled in front of us and soon the lynx pulled ahead leaving the panther close. Soon, I saw small house-like shapes up ahead and I caught a faint waft of cooking meat, sweat, and warm animal.

The moment came into sight of the Pack, Conall moved in front of me and become somewhat tense.

We drew closer to the heart of the shifter Pride and I sensed many more beings around us. Their auras were disquieted, some violent and unstable, as if they saw us as a threat. I found it upsetting. The shifters caught our scent, a mixture of fairy, shifter, fear, and blood.

We passed through unhindered and I wondered what would have happened if we had tried to come here un-chaperoned.

The panther came to a stop before a man and dipped his head low. He made a rumbling sound at the back of his throat and his tail hit the floor a few times.

Breandan shifted so he stood in front of me, shielding my body. I craned my head to peek around him.

I had thought Lochlann, Breandan's brother, was big. This guy was massive, and there was nothing delicate or soft about him. He towered over me and looked as solid as a tree. Muscles were packed upon muscle, and he wore two things; a strip of cloth around his waist that stopped mid-thigh and a leather braid necklace around his thick neck. He was missing one eye and a scar ran down from the top of his forehead to the tip of his cheek over the closed lid. His brown hair was cut close to his head, and his chin was strong, covered in a bushy beard.

The power and dominance radiating from him named him as the Pride Alpha.

And he looked pissed.

"Alec, shift," he commanded.

The were-panther lay down on its side and writhed in the dirt and patchy grass. I watched, morbidly fascinated by the Change. Soon, I wished I had not. There was no smoke, or graceful movements, no instant shift from animal to human. It was horrible and ugly. At one point, the panther was a deformed mass of quivering, convulsing flesh. Its jet-black fur seemed to shrink back into its skin, which smoothed out to become human like. The mess that had been the panther groaned; half human, half animal. I shuddered and cringed into Breandan who wrapped his arms around me. I pressed my eyes shut and buried my head into his solid chest. I could smell blood, sweat, and something floral but pungent to the point my nose burned. The heat coming from where the shifter was changing was immense, like a fire raged nearby. There was a thick, glooping sound, and a crack and snap of bone followed by the lush tearing of muscle.

I put my fingers in my ears and plugged my nose by holding my breath. A minute passed and I thought my lungs would burst. Breandan pulled one of my hands down and nudged my chin up with the other. I peeked an eye open and was rewarded with the sight of a muscular and naked boy crawling his way toward me.

He nudged his head into my hand. Flustered, I patted him twice, cringing as I did so then stepped back. He blinked up at me, and I recognised the colour of his irises, even if they were a different shape.

"Sorry," he said, raspy. "It takes a while for my brain to think human and not cat.

"Rae," I blurted. "Hai."

He smiled and stood, up. He wobbled for a moment, but once he had steadied his legs, he held out his hand. "Alec," he said.

I stared at the hand, then him.

"Oh right," he said and his eyes touched on my wings, ears, and tail. "I forget you fairies don't like touching much, do you. You seemed okay with me when I was a panther though."

I was having a hard time. I tried to speak but all that came out was a squawk resembling agreement. A young girl passed Alec a pair of trousers and he thanked her as he jumped into them.

"She is new to this life," Breandan said over the awkward silence.

The shifter-boy shrugged. "No problem. We do not Change in front of strangers often. I know it can be scary. I'm okay now, honest." He smiled at me and I relaxed.

Hesitantly, I smiled back. "It looked like it hurt."

He laughed a loud guffaw. "That's one way to put it."

"It wasn't like I thought…. I mean, I can take my glamour off now without any pain. Is it like that every time?"

"Yeah, sucks y'know."

I grinned at his use of slum speak. "You're a dwell?"

"I was," he said. "Until a full moon had me sprouting fur and a tail one season eight years ago. I can tell you, the neighbours were not pleased. Clerics came for me of course, but I was long gone."

I nodded gravely. "How did you get past the Wall?"

"Byron found me. He smelled me on a run and found me pacing the fence. What about you?"

Alec confirmed with his toss of the head that the man standing before us was the Alpha, Byron, not that any of the other shifters looked like they could match him. He watched us carefully, taking our measure. His nostrils flared, mouth pulled back in a grimace. He seemed almost to be fronting us, goading us on. I looked up at Breandan, who had been silent throughout this entire exchange; his gaze was locked with the Alpha's. Was he mad? We needed to get these shifters to help us, not put their backs up. I elbowed him in the ribs but he did not acknowledge me.

So I was distracted when I said without thinking, "I was a Disciple—" Alec's sharp intake of breath had me cringing at my careless words and shaking my head at the suspicion no doubt taking root in his mind. "No, I'm not here to hurt you. You see what I am." My tail flicked from side to side as proof I was like him, demon. "I was a Disciple who wandered too far into the forest. I got past the Wall and got lost. I saw—" I stopped there for Breandan squeezed me. I sighed, "The rest is a complicated story I don't think I have time to tell considering Breandan and your Alpha are having a non-blinking contest."

Alec looked between them. "Best we don't get involved." He reached to take my hand, but I flinched, which did reach Breandan through his focus since he hissed quietly.

Byron growled and it all got very tense.

Conall stepped forward and held up his palms. His presence was solid, calming, and he bobbed his head respectfully towards Byron.

"You know me, Alpha. We have crossed paths before and parted as friends. Why do you act so?"

The older man's face twisted briefly. "I remember you well, Conall. A fine talker you are, but also a fine warrior. If the fairies were to attack, would they not send the strongest of you to test us? Would they not sniff out our weakness?"

Conall seemed taken aback. "Why would you think such a thing? We have no quarrel with you."

Byron laughed; a big-bellied laugh that would have you think he had not a care in the world had his words not held such bitterness. It was then he took his eyes from Breandan and looked at my brother. "Do you not? Has that fairy-lord of yours stopped shooting bolts of fire at my kind if we dare enter the woods?"

"It is not what you think." Conall sounded tired. "We have broken, Byron. The High Lord has lost his mind and we are fighting him."

"Devlin is gone," I said before Conall could speak again. "He's gone and we're hunting him."

Byron ignored me. "You mean to kill him, Conall?"

I tossed my head. "No. I do."

There was a long-suffering sigh from the fairy-boy beside me.

Byron's eyes twitched to me, and he cocked his head. He smiled flashing teeth sharp and yellowed. He scratched at his greying beard. "You? Such a small thing."

"A small and fierce thing," Alec added and winked at me.

"Why are you here?" Byron asked Conall outright.

My brother looked at me and I shrugged. It seemed the Alpha had a hard time speaking to me.

"As Rae said, we hunt Devlin and his followers. He has taken something important and we need it back."

Byron picked up on what he did not say. "You have broken off your hunt to come here, meaning your own tracking has failed."

"Devlin worked a spell. I cannot see past it. We need your skills to find the right way."

Byron seemed to think this funny. "You fairies, so proud and bold to come here and ask for our help ... the felines who roll in the mud."

Conall's face was pained. "The words you echo are the

opinions of one fairy that is mad. Can you not see and accept that, Alpha? It seems for all your talk you want something from us. If you did not want us here you could have refused to speak and had your sentries escort us off your Pride. Speak quick and plainly. We do not have time for games."

Byron's face darkened. "You think such a speech will affect me?"

"Can we cut this out?" I asked, stepping forward. "We are literally travelling in circles. The day is wasting and if you won't help we need to go."

Though we could see in the dark, Breandan had told me fairies tracked better during the daylight hours, when we were strongest. We were wasting time batting words back and forth.

"Tell them, Bryon." Alec blurted unable to control himself. "They could help."

The Alpha's head whipped round, neck muscles bulging. "Silence, youngling."

Alec visibly snapped his jaw shut and seemed unable to open his mouth again. He made a small sound of repent and hung his head. I felt an inexplicable urge to stroke him to make him feel better.

"Alec is right," I said in the charged silence. "If you are in trouble, or need help of some kind I'm sure we could help."

I tentatively slanted a look at Breandan to check I was not speaking out of turn. His face was impassive and as readable as a stone slab.

The Alpha chose to ignore me, looking past me as if I was not even there.

"Come now, Alpha. You disrespect our female and behave sullen and you know I cannot allow it. Can we not move past this? You're making a small bargain difficult."

Byron suddenly looked old and weary. "You say I am sullen and difficult, but why should I be easy? I have no sons and my daughters have been taken. My line has ended and I have to remain strong for my Pride. You fairies and your squabbles have hurt my people. The vampires are simply mad, and goblins care for nothing and no one. We fight to keep the evils of the witches at bay, yet still they manage to curse us from afar. The humans hunt us like rabid beasts, and other shifter packs are hostile toward us. Tell me, why should I not be sullen and difficult?" His voice took on a sudden and intimidating edge. "And I smell you have spilled blood on my territory."

The reaction of the Pride rippled outward and soon there was a mixture of open distrust and calls for retribution for the fallen Pack mate. The shifters crowded around us and called for death. Some, so overcome with rage fell to the ground and Changed. The Pride was filled with heat and cries of agony as they morphed from human to animal.

These demons were like nothing I had experienced before. They were truly primitive and hungry for violence. Clutching Breandan by the waist, I glared at anyone bold enough to make eye contact.

Breandan was calm, silent, and simply held Byron's gaze. Conall buzzed beside me and only then did I realise Alec had left us and had a hand on his Alpha's shoulder. The muscles in his arms were taut and he murmured low in the man's ear the tone of his voice urgent.

Byron stamped his meaty foot and shouted, "Silence!"

The Pack immediately fell silent. Those in human form shied away, swelling away from him. Some of the were-cats whimpered and pressed their ears to their heads. This Pack knew to respect their Alpha.

"Speak, fairy," Byron said to Breandan. "I give you leave to move freely in my land and you draw blood. Enrage my Pack—"

"Kill the female," a reedy girl cried. "It is fair."

"I am in the middle of a bargaining, Sabine."

"My father is dead," she hissed. "Screw any pact."

Byron's head spun round and he fixed his eye on her. "Your father was half mad and more than likely invited his own demise." I was sure the pupil had changed shape to become a cat-like slit. "You will quiet yourself, youngling."

The skinny girl, Sabine, recoiled from the authority in his voice and backed up a pace. A few of the shifters next to her shifted away, dissociating themselves from the hot head.

"He laid hands on what is mine, Alpha," Breandan said calmly. He spoke in a low voice, but one that carried across the Pack to Byron and those in the inner circle. "If you had seen what I had you would have done the same."

Byron said nothing; he rubbed a large hand over his beard. "It is your word against a dead body. Fairies cannot lie, but you are a tricky sort, bending the truth until it breaks. Making a person hear one thing when it means another."

I untangled myself from Breandan, who immediately clamped a hand around my wrist when I stepped forward. Conall placed a hand on my shoulder, and I heard Alec growl low in his throat.

I wiggled. "Let go of me," I ordered. "I can hurt him as much as he can hurt me."

Conall released me, and so did Breandan, but not before giving my arm a warning squeeze. Alec tried to transmit 'be careful' with his eyes. I sent him a reassuring look then trotted over toward the Pack Alpha. Halfway across the space I doubted my plan. Gods, but he was huge. I stopped a pace away from him and slowly looked up, and up and up, until the back of my head touched my neck.

"Hai," I said, even though we had been introduced earlier I felt as if showing good manners could not hurt.

He stared down at me. "You are brave, little fairy. I could squash you like a bug, even in man form."

The brief yet ferocious urge to defend myself was swallowed by the logical thought that Breandan would never let anything of the sort happen to me. I shook my head. "No doubt you are powerful, Alpha, but I'm strong too."

I tried to push some of the gruffness I had heard in Conall's voice into mine and puffed my chest out. I do not think overall it was convincing.

He leaned back and rubbed at his beard some more. "I can believe it." Byron's eyes flashed with something I might have been able to mistake as admiration. "Feisty, aren't you."

"Damn straight. After all I've been through, speaking my mind is better than lying down and dying." My frustration bubbled over and had a familiar tide of stupid rising in me and blurting, "You shouldn't give up, the right to hope for a better future, I mean. You tell Conall how hard it is to keep your people safe, but it's a problem everyone has, not just you. If you give up, your enemies win. Your territory will be invaded and your Pride obliterated. Is that what you want? I am sure your daughters are waiting for you, hoping their Alpha is getting ready to save them. If they saw you now they would be ashamed."

The older man seemed to suck in enough air to fill the lungs of three men. His chest expanded, and his eyes changed shape. They glowed. "So be it, little fairy. You will help me get my daughters back and I will help you track down your rogue lord."

I blinked. Then my face creased in panic as I held my palms up. "Wait—"

"This fire in my belly was of your making. You had best prove you are as fierce as your words would have me believe."

I shot a look at Conall who bobbed his head. Breandan was exasperated, but he too inclined his head giving his support.

It seemed simple. Save the shifter-girls from the Temple and return them to their Pride. I could see no major downside to this deal. It would win us the best trackers nature had to provide. Devlin would be mine and I would have my revenge.

"Agreed," I said more confidently than I felt.

"A fairy's word is law," he announced satisfied. "You will help me get my girls back home safely, I feel it."

Grimacing, I thought now was not the time to mention I still had some wiggle room on that particular rule of magic.

"And now to deal with the blood spilled," Byron continued. "I understand why you have come so close. Do you know that unlike my Pack mates I can partially shift?"

Meaning was I aware that if he – a great hulk of a man – wanted to, he could turn his meaty hand into a paw, and scratch half my face off in one swipe? Yeah, I was all too aware of that and hoped that these shifters were politely ignoring the stench of my fear no doubt radiating off me in waves. In answer, I took a deep breath, and stepped forward.

"Your pack brother tried to mark me." I said. A surge

of anger rumbled down the bond, and a couple of rapid breaths helped to calm my nature's instant response. I lifted my head back to expose my throat to Byron. The gesture was simultaneously submissive and defiant. "I have been taught shifters are master trackers. No other being, human or demon, can match you. I can prove my life was in danger. Your brother tried to suffocate me and take my innocence. If you don't believe the bruises, which hurt like hell – thanks for asking – believe what your own senses tell you."

Byron did not waste any time. He wrapped his large hands around my upper arms and yanked me forward. He buried his nose in my hair, sniffed down my neck. Then, instead of bending down to smell my thigh where the shifter had straddled me, he simply lifted me up high above his head, and sniffed the spot.

Satisfied, he carefully set me down and stepped away.

"The male's scent lingers," he announced loudly in a voice that brooked no rebuttal. What fool would try to defy a proclamation from their Alpha anyway? Squirming, I felt in need of a hot bath. "From the marks on her body he tried to take what was not his. He attacked her from behind which is not behaviour worthy of a Pack Brother. The fairy is telling the truth. It was a fair kill."

I exhaled.

"But it was not his place."

I spun around. Seriously, there was a fool dumb enough to take it there? Sabine, whom I was fast recognising as troublemaker, piped up again. "Their laws are not our laws. You will let these demons from outside the Pack flaunt themselves and dishonour our way?"

A grumble of agreement rumbled from the watching Pack. Pressure - even I felt it. These people were his people and if they were unhappy, the Alpha must listen.

Byron nodded, if somewhat reluctantly.

"But you know Breandan was only trying to protect me," I said, frustrated with their narrow-mindedness. "I belong to him, of course he would react that way."

I struggled to think of another way to salvage this situation. I needed these shifters to help me track Devlin, and so there had to be a way to resolve this. I did not want Breandan and Conall to start killing them for that would achieve nothing and we would be back where we started. And I was starting to like it in the Pride.

"That is true, so I have made my decision. The fairy Breandan, shall fight a champion chosen by the fallen one's kin."

I started. "Uh, that's it?" If Byron wanted Breandan to kill another of his Pack that was fine by me.

"You look happy," the Alpha said to me, cocking his bushy eyebrow.

I shrugged. "Your loss, not mine."

"Oh?" He looked at me with pity when he called over his shoulder. "Sabine, I relinquish my right as Saul's Alpha to name the champion. This burden falls to you. Which male do you pick to champion your father?"

The skinny girl marched forward and grinned wickedly. "Alec," she said loudly. "I choose Alec our Omega as my champion."

"What?" I blurted, incredulous.

A thundering roar of the Pack hollering Alec's name barely registered in my mind.

I turned and darted back to where he, Conall and Breandan stood. They seemed calm, as if they had expected this.

Alec sent me a weary look and spun on his heel. As he walked his body twitched then he fell to his knees. I turned away, no longer in any way curious to see him

Change, but as with all gruesome things I couldn't help but keep turning until I faced him again to watch.

Face contorted in pain, Alec bowed, convulsed once then his spine cracked and a long length of bone jutted forth. Skin wrapped around the new appendage as a thick and dark sweep of hair sprung from the new pores. His hands thickened, wicked sharp claws snapped out, and his head whipped back. A feral snarl tore from his throat as his mouth and chin lengthened into a muzzle filled with dagger-like teeth. His nose flattened as his ears moved to the top of his lengthened head. Eyes wide and glowing with a pain and beastly fervour, he hunched over completely, his arms morphing into powerful forelegs ending in fat, heavy paws, even as his legs shorted and broadened, rippling with compact muscle. Torso bulging and waist shrinking he shuddered as his glossy coat covered his dark skin, ebony black and gleaming with perspiration.

His rolling eyes settled – the pain retreating to leave deadly focus and raw passion. He was focused now – focused on my fairy.

Breandan hissed, low and long, baring his own teeth. Rather than fearing him in such a dangerous state of mind, I stepped forward, the urge to grab his head and claim that proud mouth with my own the most compelling thing I had known.

Breandan stiffened under my touch and seemed surprised when I crushed my mouth to his, but he did not pull back. Instead, he met my ferocity with his own, his lips daring mine to take more. I started the kiss but he ended it, breaking away from my mouth to kiss my forehead.

Breathless and flushed I said, "You can't hurt him."

"That," he said faintly, "may be difficult. He certainly

will try to hurt me."

I glanced over at Alec who now paced back and forth in cat form. His sleek face was focused, in the zone. He growled, the hair on his back standing up in stiff clumps and paws scratching up clumps of earth.

"Say-so," I agreed. "Just don't kill him then."

I tugged his head down and lightly brushed my lips across his, blushing a deeper red all the while. I stared into his silver eyes and lost my train of thought. A small smile played on the corners of his mouth and he arched an eyebrow. I blinked and glowered at him, not impressed with his ability to confound me by just existing.

"Be careful," I begged.

The smile became a cheeky grin, a spectacular show of dazzling white teeth. "Alright."

A smile that lit his whole face up, and made him blaze with white light. How could I leave him when he looked at me like that? He seemed to sense my reluctance to leave his side since he handed me off to Conall who dragged me a few steps before picking me up and taking us both over to stand beside Byron. He set me down and I scowled, feeling all flustered and hot under the collar.

"I hope that fairy is strong," Byron sounded amused. "Alec is the best I have. My Omega, second-in-command."

"Breandan is a warlord, he was a Guardian of the Wylds. I hope your Omega has no dependents."

Byron opened his mouth to retort then his face paled at the look of rueful apology on Conall's face. My brother was certain my fairy-boy had this in the bag. Before I could tell them both to stop making light of the situation, Alec roared and leapt at Breandan's face, claws slashing.

CHAPTER THREE

I stood on the balls of my feet, ready to throw myself in there. Conall kept a restraining hand on my shoulder as I bounced up and down.

Alec lunged forward and Breandan sidestepped him easily. Twisting, Alec lifted up onto his hind legs to drag his paws across Breandan's torso. His claws ripped into flesh, drawing blood, and my fairy roared. When Alec jumped and sank his teeth into Breandan's shoulder, I snapped and spun around Conall to dart into the fray. I had zero idea what I was going to do to help in this situation, I only knew I could not stand by and watch these two boys tear each other apart.

Before I got two steps Conall was in front of me swinging his huge hand toward my face. I tried to block him, but the swing altered mid flow and jerked down to thump me in the stomach. Realistically, I knew if he wanted to hurt me, Conall could have hit me hard enough to break ribs. Instead, all the air left my lungs and my legs seemed to lock up. I staggered back and looked up at him wide eyed.

Breandan shot me a cursory glance out the corner of his eye. He made a low noise toward Conall and my brother rolled his eyes. He came at me again and I rolled back, gaining my feet to stand before him, hands fisted.

"What the hell are you doing," I hissed.

"Today you learn how to fight."

He came at me again with the deadly grace of a cobra. This time his foot flew toward my upper arm and I blocked him, barely. I still ended up being shunted two steps to the side from the impact.

Conall wrinkled his nose. "You have no technique, no instinct. You fight like a human. You must use all your senses; feel what I am going to do before I do it."

"Now is not the time for this lesson," I said seriously, trying to reason with him.

I pointed at Breandan and Alec who alternated between quick swipes and bites, rolling around, pulling away, regrouping then attacking again.

Breandan's torso was riddled with scratches and I swear my own skin itched in exactly the same places.

"Never will you have a greater distraction than a friend in danger," Conall said firmly. "You must remain calm and focused even in the face of losing everything you hold most dear."

"Fine," I said sweetly. "You asked for it." I reached to magic and it flooded me with white-hot rage.

Conall's eyebrows lifted in surprise. "You practiced as we ran."

"Hell, yes." I sent a blast of golden energy his way and followed it through with a smack to his gut with my fist. Before he could recover, I darted around to his back and kicked his leg out from beneath him. Conall fell, but he twisted around to land on the tips of his toes and the palms of his hands. His legs bunched up before he sprang, body curving into a perfect crescent moon before landing lightly on his feet and shooting me a quick grin.

I laughed. "You think that's good?"

He came at me, and I flipped backward, again and again, cutting through the middle of Breandan and Alec's fight, the amulets bouncing off my chest as I went. The world spun, but I was acutely aware of my surroundings. Before I was a fairy, had I executed this move, the world would have been a chaotic blur. Now I saw everything. I even saw the confusion flicker across Alec's face when I passed him, my legs up in the air and my back arching. It was odd because he was a cat in mid- snarl, but still clear as day, I saw how startled he was by catching his eye. As I flipped upright, making an odd square between the four of us, I thumbed my chin at Conall who looked mildly impressed.

Breandan's gaze locked on mine. Mischief flicked across his expression and he winked at me. At the playful gesture, my mouth dropped open.

My brother waved me forward the same time Breandan rushed to meet Alec's charge. Our faces came inches away from each other as I somersaulted over him, and his silver eyes twinkled at me before the love in them was replaced with hardness as his gaze twitched to lock on Alec.

I landed with my back to Conall, no longer caring that we were sparring and watched as Breandan finished his fight by grabbing Alec's jaw in his hands. He straddled the shifter's back and forced him to lie down.

The Pride fell silent.

And this was it, the horror they had brought upon themselves. Alec had lost; his life was Breandan's to claim.

My heart pumped double time in my chest. He would not do it. It was not in his nature. Oh gods, please. I knew I could not interfere this time. This was Pack law, not something I, Conall, or Breandan could override. The thought of leaving passed through my mind, because if we left right now this need not happen. We could try to track Devlin another way.

Was this boy's life worth my revenge?

I pressed my eyes together and waited for the sickening crunch.

There was a soft, warm pressure at my mouth. My entire body relaxed and I wound my arms around the boy who teased my lips open with his. I breathed him in. Sunlight and soil mixed with the faint tang of salty sweat. The firm skin of his back burned under my palms.

I heard a fierce roar and my eyes flickered open.

Breandan smiled down at me, and I pressed my fingertips to his cheek, reverent. Words could not express how proud I was of him.

His face was animated with mischief and he jerked his head to where Byron stood, clapping a panting and weakened, human Alec on the shoulder. "We dance," the Alpha roared.

His Pack took up the chant as I wondered if they had lost their minds.

Alec stumbled up to me with a dazed smile on his face. His dark hair stuck up in awkward bloodied clumps and his body was coated in a thick sheen of sweat. He looked as if he had enjoyed the tussle, invigorated. "You dance?" he asked me, breathless.

I scoffed, "No."

He looked at Breandan inquiringly. "A fairy that does not dance?" He sounded doubtful.

Taking my hand in his, Breandan followed behind the shifter-boy toward the bonfire in the centre of the Pride.

"Why do you think you cannot dance?" he asked.

Embarrassed, I wanted to tell him that I did not like to dance and that it was dumb, simply to save face. Instead,

I said, "Two left feet with no rhythm. And it's not like we had much chance. Most of my time was spent studying how to kill demons." I shrugged. "We did nothing but learn how to become the best at what we did."

He snorted. "The best? I have seen you throw a punch. And they do not come close to the best at hunting other beings." He slanted a look at me. "I will have fun showing you how to use your body."

That was how I came to be standing in front of the fire when the first drumbeat echoed into the night. A slow, leisurely pounding that had my entire body shivering. The sound seemed to sweep over my skin and ripple to the tip of my tail that flickered mischievously. The shifters danced, throwing themselves into the beat; ready to release the stress through laughter, music, and dance.

A hard hand caught my chin and turned my head. Breandan motioned me to watch him. Releasing me, he inclined his head and pointed downward to his feet. It was a simple thing, this dance. Booted feet a shoulder width apart, he rolled up onto the tips of his toes then back onto his heels.

The drums were loud, urgent, and insistent. Breandan rocked back on his heels then to his toes. He looked at me expectantly. I did the same. His lips twitched with the beginnings of a smile, and he matched the time of his movement to mine.

Conall was beside us doing something similar, and having one hell of a time considering the relaxed satisfaction dominating his usually stoic expression. One of the braver females stepped up to him, smiling coyly, and waved him forward. He joined her, accepting the invitation gracefully. They danced, but never did they touch. It was like they were connected in some other, unseen way. Eyes closed, heads flung back, lost in the beat.

Breandan's limbs entwined with mine, and continued to rock us back and forth. We pressed together in the writhing mêlée of bodies, and for a while, we swayed. Our bodies twisted slightly so we could stare into each other's eyes. A sigh of awe hitched in my chest at the sight of him. When I began to feel faint, I looked away, across the heart of the Pride to see the entire Pack lost in dance of passion and hunger. I was shocked to see some of the shifters in cat form, heads bobbing to the beat, tails curling around the air in loose, lazy patterns. They weaved through the crowd, backs arcing in pleasure as people stroked and petted them as they passed. Some rolled in the dirt playfully, purring up a storm.

I spotted Alec. He was near his Alpha, jumping in smooth, audacious movement.

The shifters danced differently than the fairies. The movement was bolder and slower in comparison to the liquid-like slink of Conall.

My view of the dance abruptly changed as I was lifted high into the air, Breandan's arms around my waist. Down I came, and remembered to rock back on my heels then up onto my tip-toes. Breandan pressed closer behind me, matching the curves of my body to his. I was tense now; my eyes wide and mouth parted.

"Let go," he murmured in my ear.

I sank my teeth into my bottom lip, feeling pain when the sharp tips sliced the delicate skin. Nervous at the suggestion of giving into the wildness of my nature, I licked up a sliver of blood as a flare of heat signalled my healing. Trusting in him, the one I was bonded to, I relaxed and closed my eyes. Again, he lifted me up and instinct took over. My arms rose up above my head; I arched my back causing my wings to flutter, and gently kicked my legs forward. Down below the crowd rejoiced.

It was a jubilant crush of bodies. The ground became damp with sweat as we danced. The floor beneath my feet shook. Everything I was hummed, joining in the collective ecstasy of being outside. Free. Alive. Smoke hung heavy in the air, mixing with the smell of wet grass and warm bodies. The drums beat on. Louder, harder, and forcing us to move with wild abandon.

A tingle of pleasure ran across my lower stomach as Breandan's hands drifted down to my hips and coaxed me into rolling in time with the beat. I let my head loll back and opened my eyes lazily to look up into the sky. Stars already twinkled above in the dusk.

The tempo increased, driving us ever higher, and I was off the floor again, swinging my head to the side. My arms flew up, legs thrashing. The breathless wail torn from my throat was crystalline. A melodic cry infused with power. It seemed to come alive and shoot sparks across the sky. As I fell, the air whistling past cooled my heated skin, but the moment my feet touched back down I was enveloped in heat. Breandan spun me around to lift me up so I could lock my legs around his solid waist. He ran his hand up my back and kissed my neck, then nipped it roughly. My pulse leaped as I nipped him back and felt his chest rumble with approval.

He set me down and jumped high in the air, landing silently. For a moment, I worried my bite and his lust had driven him crazy. Then I saw the shifter males did the same thing. Unsure of what to do, I watched the females. I matched the strange patterns of their limbs with my own. As the males stomped the floor, the torsos of the females rippled, their chests rose and fell, hips bucked. As they daringly ran their hands over the shoulders of their dance partners, they smiled seductively, sensually trawling their fingers through their hair before spinning away, faces turned upward to watch their men soar into sight with powerful leaps. Their bodies beckoned their chosen ones to come back down to touch and play.

My hazy focus was drawn back to my own partner, and when Breandan came down for a third time I caught surprise flitting across his face when I placed my hands on his chest. Face hot, I stroked down over the smooth hardness of him as my body moved in soft undulations I had not thought possible. His hesitation in returning my touch was brief. His arms wound around me as he accepted my offer to join closer.

Over his shoulder, I noticed the younger shifters, the cubs, were being guided away by their mothers. Conall was no longer dancing, but glaring at us. My eyes flicked to Alec who was avoiding the advances of several young shifter-girls trying to coax him into the dance. Byron stood slightly in the shadows, arms crossed over his broad chest. He nodded once at each young couple that slowly left the light of the fire, consumed in each other. They stroked and kissed as they faded into the coming darkness.

It seemed odd, almost ritualistic. What dance would mothers not want their cubs to see, that Conall or Alec refused to partake in with the female younglings? … couplings the Alfa must approve of?... Breandan's arms tightened around me, and I was distracted by how close he was. I felt his chest expand, drawing an intake of breath that carried the scent of me.

The drumbeat changed, slowing into singular thumps.

We were the only two left dancing. I followed my fairy around the circle in a series of simple, but beautiful steps that had me forgetting my confusion, and smiling shyly at him. I ducked my head down so my hair covered my face when he smiled back. He was so handsome. Not even the scar that ran across his cheek lessened his silver-kissed beauty.

The fire deepened to rich violet. I glanced at the horizon, easy to do from the flat grassland the heart of the shifter Pride rested upon. I saw the sun, a slender arc of shady orange visible in the distance that had yet to set completely. My fairy eyesight – which transformed the world into a vision of electric blue and purple at night – was not what had changed the colour of the fire. The longer I looked I was sure I could see naked forms dance among the flames. A warm wind wrapped round my body and swept around me playfully.

He used magics for me.

I laughed and danced on. For only the second time, I was truly, blissfully happy. Aware that both times I had been in the presence of my fairy.

Breandan's hand reached for mine and I took it without thinking. The brilliant glow of his skin astounded me. He was a beacon of light brighter than the purple bonfire that raged before us. He pulled me into him and rather than hurting my eyes, his light merely accented the glory of his face.

"So beautiful," he said quietly as he gazed down on me.

My gaze flicked from his into the crowd watching us. Many shielded their eyes, but still snuck glances our way. Intrigued as to what they stared at, I cocked my head, and looked down at myself. My legs, arms, feet, and hands glowed. Pulsing like a golden star against the ebony sheath I wore. My tail coiled into a tight ball at the base of my spine, and my heart started to race. I jerked at Breandan's gentle touch, the tips of his fingers brushing my hair off my neck and over my shoulder which he gripped.

He saw the fear in my eyes as he shook his head. "You will accept this," he said firmly.

His mouth captured mine and the crowd yelled in delight, stamping their feet in joy. Screams from were-cats rose in a rising crescendo, and a fierce roar cut above them all.

Like a ray of clarity through the smoke and passion, I knew what I was doing and what I was feeling. It was the bond, heightening our attraction to each other and our attractiveness to those around us.

I gasped and as Breandan tried to lean away, I pulled his lips down to meet mine once more. I stared up at him, daring him to accept me as I was, complicated and strange, indecisive and selfish. His face softened and his eyes shone with warmth. Breandan's hands slipped under the hem of my dress to stroke the sensitive skin of my hip. I breathed him in, the scent of sunlight and rain, and pressed myself closer, whimpering when he crushed me to him. I wanted him. He was mine, and I wanted him. Possessiveness washed over me like a poisonous cloud, and I dug my fingertips into his upper arm and back. Mine. I could hear his heart echo the claim as it thumped against my chest. Mine. Breandan walked us out of the firelight into the grasslands of the Pride, and I said nothing. I wanted this, wanted him. I knew that once this was done he would be insanely possessive, but my body screamed a need I could no longer ignore.

The feeling that burned in the pit of my stomach crawled through my veins and possessed me. I'd never felt anything remotely like it. His hands rubbed up and down my body, fingers delving in and out of curves rhythmically. I lay on the cool grass, his glorious weight pressed into me, the skin of his chest hot and smooth against my skin.

Breandan pushed up to kneel over me, gazing down, and from his intense expression, trying to bore a hole through my clothes. Not that he had to; the hem of my skirt was rumpled and hitched up around my waist. His gaze wandered up and locked with mine. He was just as lost as me – ensnared in a trance and fixated on touching. Fingering the seams of my dress he abruptly yanked it upwards, realising it covered my body from him.

He lent down to kiss my collarbone then stiffened and groaned. "You are mine," he growled.

"No," I said, breathless, and laced my hands together at the nape of his neck to pull him down. "You're mine."

The way his tongue felt when it slid over mine was amazing. He kissed me hard then sprung up, pulling me up after him. He cupped my face, silvery eyes luminous, and a smile kicked back one corner of his mouth. "I have something that belongs to you."

My eyes drifted closed and I breathed in deeply. I placed my hands over his, rubbing my face against one of his hands, but his light hearted tone had my brows furrowing distrustfully. Nothing Breandan said was light hearted. He was a serious demon who had bouts of mania. That was his fairy nature and I was becoming accustomed to it.

Sighing at how wonderful it felt for him to touch me this way, I cricked an eye open, sensing his restless excitement. "Say-say?" I asked, still suspicious.

His hand slipped into his pocket and his fingers came up with a chain of flat, gold links. It was short, the length of one of my hands, and as slender as my baby finger. On each elliptical segment was engraved a rune of power. It was simple, caught the lunar light, and sparkled – a bracelet, perhaps?

Mesmerised, I touched it with the tip of my finger and was gifted with a zap. That should have been my first clue. But it was so appealing and shiny I forgot I was wary of him and this pretty ornament and hovered my finger over it, mouth parted in awe. "Beautiful," I breathed.

"I know you are, but this is no trinket. It is a sign of your birthright."

He blurred into movement, and before I could object, he pressed the links into my forehead.

I jolted as the metal warmed, biting into my skin. I scrabbled to yank it from my face but still the ... the ... teeth sank into my forehead over my brow, temple to temple. I shrieked and jumped about, using my nails to try to find an edge to pick under. I only managed to dig myself in the face. It hurt, so I stopped and stood still, trembling as the links fused to my head and got hotter and hotter until it felt like my forehead burned.

The fire stopped, cooling until the metal was blessedly cold against my skin. My eyes rolled back as far as they could go and I could see a faint glimmering where the links sparkled. At least it had not sunken into my head entirely. Little by little, I raised my hand in hesitant jerks and touched it. My fingers slid across velvety gold, so slick it felt slippery. But then I noticed faint scratches, ah, the symbols of power. I rubbed it at the edges, amazed at how the metal changed to smooth skin and back again. My hand fell to my side and I heaved a sigh, praying for patience. I looked at Breandan trying to decide the best course of action. I could try and pound on him. The important word being 'try'. I had only tried, and failed, to hit him once before, and I would never come close. I could scream and rail at him, possibly throw a few sharp rocks. But could I be bothered? Should I calmly ask him what this thing merged to my forehead was, and what it meant?

"What the hell are you playing at?" I planted my palms on his stomach and shoved him. He shunted back a pace and fought what looked suspiciously like a smirk. "You can't just push these things on me and expect me to accept them."

"If I had told you what it meant and what would happen you never would have taken it."

"Why can't you see this was not your choice to make?"

His jaw clenched, all light heartedness gone. "You need to come to terms with who you are."

I stomped my foot. "You can't railroad me into being something I'm not."

"If I don't push you won't move," he said with an icy veneer of calm. "You need to be strong for what's ahead, yet you bury yourself in doubt and hide behind this façade of a simple girl when you have been born a warrior, born a leader."

I looked away, gritting my teeth and forcing down the tears that welled in my eyes. It would not cut so deep if he was wrong about everything. I kept trying to make him see my point of view but he had so much evidence to fall back on. All I had was a general feeling of doom.

"Can you explain it to me?" he asked. "Tell me why you're fighting this."

Rubbing my nose, my gaze fell from his perfect face, and I sighed deeply. "You know yourself, what you are capable of, and what is beyond you, right? I mean, you would never try to move a mountain with your magic because you know trying to would take more magic that you can handle." He was quiet, allowing me the time to order my thoughts and explain what I was feeling. "Well, for the last few days everyone has been telling me I'm destined to be the next Priestess, that I'm going to lead the fairy race into a new era and stop all the strife between the demons and the humans." I paused, struggling once again to come to terms with how I felt and what it meant. Saying it out loud had my heart thumping painfully and my stomach doing back flips. Just the thought of all that responsibility made me uncomfortably hot.

Breandan pushed my hair aside and placed a warm, soothing palm on the nape of my neck. "Whatever you say will be okay with me."

Breathing out in a rush, I splayed my hands out in front of me in a purposeful manner. "I know myself. I know what I am capable of and my limits. I believe that I can help the demons and humans come together. I feel that." I pressed a hand to my chest. "That feels real and obtainable to me. But beyond that ... becoming the fairies' spiritual guide...." I looked him in the eye. "I don't love them like you do. When I look into the future, I see nothing but you. I am not who I used to be, and I do believe I have a purpose, but it's not what you and Conall think it is."

"You will grow to love them?"

"That is not true and that is why you phrased it as a question."

A muscle in his cheek twitched and he clenched his jaw. "Why can you not move past this? Accept all of who you are."

"Because I know the road you're trying to lead me down is wrong. I'm not the wisest of people, or the bravest, but recently I have come to trust in my instincts and the more I listen to them, the more everything makes sense to me." His face was stubbornly set and I placed my hand on his chest. "Tell me, has there ever been a

Priestess before who was not mated to the High Lord?" Breandan shook his head. "Does this not tell you everything you need to know about what my future holds? Why has magic allowed me to form such a bond with a male other than the High Lord? Does that not seem wrong to you? Besides, how can I hope to rule alongside Lochlann when I can barely stand him?"

"He is difficult but he has a good heart. We can work around it. Find a way to—"

"Do you want me to go to your brother?"

His brows lowered and his eyes blazed. "No. Never. You are mine."

"Then listen to what I am saying. The Priestess is always the mate of the High Lord. Always."

"I have no desire to be High Lord," Breandan said carefully, weighing his words. "I do not wish any harm to come to my family."

My mouth fell open. "I wasn't suggesting we ... no you have me wrong." I waved my hands about. "I didn't mean you should be High Lord, though I'm sure you'd be great at it." I gave him a weak smile. "I was trying to point out that you and Conall keep drumming it into me that there are rules that must be followed. This keeps everything in check, in balance. Why am I being allowed to break those rules?"

His finger ran down the bridge of my nose and a feeling of peace washed over me. "You are special."

Nothing I said was going to get through to him. Pushing my hair back from my face, knuckling my forehead, and somehow already used to the feel of cold metal, I exhaled sharply. "I can't take this thing off, can I?"

Still cautious, watching to see how I would try to hurt him, he shook his head. "No. Not until death."

Well hell, I was pretty much stuck with it then. Slanting him a look under my lashes I curled my lip at him. "Can I at least know what it is?"

"The circlet announces you to be the Priestess. No demon can look on you now and not know who you are. All will know your importance and authority over them."

"Why didn't you give this to me before?"

"You had not accepted who you were. You were barely able to hear about your mother. Conall picked it up before we left Orchard and I swore I would give it to you."

I plucked at my bottom lip as I thought on this, then could not help but touch it again. I was in awe of ... of what? Myself? "Why now? Does it matter?"

"This is important. If I am dead you will be protected."

"You will never die," I said confidently.

His expression shifted from defensive to indulgent. "Hmm."

He took my hand and towed me after him. I followed happily, poking and prodding at this new part of me. It was true what he said; this thing was never coming off. Those teeth I had felt biting into my skin had anchored themselves in deep. Noticing he seemed to have a specific direction in mind rather than a random walk, I began to take an interest in our direction.

Since I had become fairy, my sense of direction had improved vastly. I could tell when the land climbed or when it sloped. I knew where there was a rocky place or one that was dense with flora humming with life. I had even become accustomed to the nagging buzz that was constantly on the edge of my mind. When I had first closed my eyes and stretched my influence beyond myself, I had touched on other receptive minds by accident, not realising that I was drawn to them by the buzz. When I closed my eyes now, I could sense live things and that was probably why my sense of direction was so good.

With Breandan beside me, it was a tad overwhelming. The bond was a pulsing thing that had settled over my skin, content for the time being since I had skin-to-skin contact with Breandan. Couple that with my sense of his aura and just his being there … next to me … it was a troublesome thing in itself … he was distracting.

Pursing my lips, I stopped, rocked back on one heel and smiled when he turned to question the hold up.

I let my gaze drift over his face. He'd not pulled his glamour on, not now I was used to seeing him in his true form. I myself had not glamoured myself human since Breandan had been injured. His hair was short and dark, a strong jaw and firm lips. And always his eyes, captivating silver-blue irises that shone like stars under his heavy brow, which cast a shadow that stopped at the tip of his bold nose. His skin —lustrous cream to my dusky hue — was covered with black ink tattoos. I still caught myself being shocked when I glanced at him or took my time to study their meaning. His arms and chest were covered in swirling intricate designs and incantations, some in languages I had never seen before. Creatures and flowers were sprawled across his chest and ancient patterns seemed to shimmer and shift the longer I stared. I had never seen the like. Would they truly protect him from witchcraft and darker magics?

My eyes slipped down, taking all of him in. It was so easy to get hung up on his face or the presence of him that I forgot to appreciate his body. He was solid, and radiated heat and life. His legs were long and strong. His posture faultless, but instead of looking stoic and uncomfortable, he looked infallible and mighty.

Belonging to him felt easier by the moment.

I flushed and bit my lip, ignoring his quirked eyebrow and knowing gaze. His thumb rubbed small circles on my wrist as he waited. He never seemed to mind when I ogled him, which was often a lengthy and meticulous practice I thoroughly enjoyed.

I cleared my throat and asked, "Where are we going?"

"Oh, there is a lake nearby. I want to share it with you."

This caught my attention. "A lake? I've seen the river and a few ponds, but I've never seen a lake … or the sea." However, I had seen pictures.

"One day I will take you. You would love the open water. It is soothing and smells like salt. The waves crash into the beach and make soft foam about your toes. The water is cold, but refreshing. Cleansing."

"You'd really take me wouldn't you?" I marvelled at how so simple a promise could make me feel so warm inside. "I mean, you're not just saying that to be nice."

He did not answer, but I was filled with warmth and affection, an impression of positivity. My ears strained to hear the 'yes' I expected after the feeling. How strange. I shook the feeling off and blinked when I took in Breandan's expectant gaze.

It was the way he stood, waiting, watching, and almost on the verge of asking me to react.

"Did you just say 'yes'?" I asked slowly. My eyes widened as I thought on the odd reactions or feelings I had been having. "Have you been telling me things like that for a while?"

He swept me up into a crushing hug and swung me around, beaming a huge smile that had me feeling dizzy. "Only since the first time I knew you belonged to me. At last you can feel it." He set me down still smiling broadly. "Our bond grows."

He seemed so completely happy there was no way for me to get prissy about this or think up a reason to be upset.

"You can send me messages through the bond?"

"Faint ones. Never will we be able to say more than a few words, and then only if we are deep in meditation. But we will be able to sense each other's moods and feelings and be able to send each other impressions of what we desire or need."

My fairy-boy was not one for gushing sentences, so listening to him rhapsodise over this new aspect to our connection had me as excited as he was.

"Can I try?"

"Oh yes." He nodded so sharply it bordered on enthusiastic. "Try."

Shrugging out my shoulders, I gripped his hand tighter and focused on the idea for a kiss. Sending him a thought was like trying to hiccup and speak at the same time. My tummy was clenched so tight and my face so squished I couldn't see any more.

There was a faint pressure on my lips. My face relaxed and my eyes widened. I flung my arms around his neck and pressed myself into him.

"It worked," I crowed, delighted.

He frowned then chuckled, face strained as he tried to hide his disappointment. "No."

Crestfallen, I released him and rubbed my nose, unhappy that I could not tap into the bond for something so simple when Breandan could send me waves of love and an answer to a question clear enough for me to understand it.

"Give it time," he soothed, stroking a fingertip down

the bridge of my nose and across my lips. My heart fluttered. "You may find you can only use it in times of great need, not that I will ever be so far that you need to rely on the bond." He paused but then shook off whatever dark thought had cast a brief shadow across his face. "Alright?"

Mollified, I let him tug me on, but kept trying to send him messages until my head hurt from trying to push thoughts through nothing but bloody air.

I saw a flicker of light ahead and noticed the air had changed. A musty tang of rotting wood and leaves saturated the atmosphere. A wispy mist crept along the ground and rose higher the further we moved until minuscule water droplets speckled my face and cooled my cheeks. The grass got lower, moving from our waists to our knees until it was a flat and chunky carpet of blunted blades the colour of ash. The grass became lumps of rock, pastel-coloured pebbles then, abruptly, murky water. It seemed to go on forever, a big puddle in the middle of nowhere surrounded by ferns and other plant life that liked the wet. I squinted. Were those dark, darting shadows under the placid surface schools of fish? At the edges I could see the pebbles continued down, curving into a steep slope that disappeared into a sapphire mirror overshadowed by fog.

I took a conscious step back. The last time I had looked into water I had seen my reflection. I was used to the feel of my fairy form now. I had no choice. No amount of hard thought was going to make the end of my spine drop off, or my wings shrivel up. But maybe I would not feel so different, so alien, if I could see others who looked more like me. Breandan said there were many variations in fairy colouring and form. Maeve was one extreme and I was the other. I guess I should be glad I was not green.

I swallowed, still not wanting to see myself and said, "It looks cold."

He looked at me oddly before his expression creased with amusement. "You have magic." He said this as if it was some big thing I had forgotten.

He kicked off his boots and unbuckled the leather strap across his chest.

"And…."

"You have the power to tear the sky asunder and shake the earth into a tumult yet you are bested by some chilly water?"

He threw his head back and laughed. It was not the usual chuckle or mirthless snort of delight that he usually reserved for me, but a loud, boisterous hoot of glee. I was too ensnared by the sound to be upset that he was laughing at me rather than with me. Wanting to share in the joke, I giggled, but it soon became a strangled squawk as he undid his pant laces and pulled them down. He chucked the garment onto his boots. I looked away, blushing furiously.

My fingers curled under into fists as I fought the urge to jump him. I would not shame myself by succumbing to such a base instinct.

"Would you look at me?"

I choked on my own breath. "I can't."

He grasped my chin and deliberately turned my face to his. "Look at me."

My eyes wandered down of their own accord, over his broad shoulders, hard pectorals, and well defined abdominals. Lower, over his hip and hovering at his navel. I wavered, enjoying how much the strong strip of muscle that tapered inward from his outer hip to groin … my eyes boggled. Ah, yes, he was naked. My breath quickened and my hands trembled. Gods help me I could not help but stare. Was it meant to be so alluring? Should I not be frightened, feel all shy and retiring?

Swallowing loudly, I made a point of studying an interesting moss-covered rock that rested on the edge of the riverbank by his foot. Moss, what an interesting ... plant-like-thing?

Chuckling softly, he let me go and his foot slipped from view. I heard him enter the water. Rubbing my hands on my hips, I struggled to bring my ferocious lust under control. He seemed to be managing just fine, and so would I.

In a dream world, I would have been fiercely proud of my body, revelling in how perfectly my limbs were shaped and how they affected him. I would have swept the dress off in one smooth, leisurely move, slowly shaking out my hair as I did, watching him with slumberous eyes. Then I would gracefully step into the pool, running my fingers through the water that warmed to my touch until I was immersed waist deep, confidently and proudly waiting for him.

With that completely unrealistic and unachievable scenario firmly in place, I whipped the dress off in one toss, chucking it somewhere behind me. I stomped over to the pool edge, the lapping water sliding over my toes confirming the temperature was a few degrees shy of freezing. My control over magic was so temperamental I was afraid that if I tried to warm it up, I would turn the pool into a bubbling cauldron. Acutely aware Breandan was seated comfortably in the centre, I decided the risk was not worth it.

Cursing my foolish pride, I splashed my way into the frigid water, shrieking mentally as each move caused the icy water to lap higher over my naked skin before dunking down till only my neck, head, and wing tips showed. My tail coiled into a tight ball at the base of my spine, trying to conserve heat.

Shivering, sending large ripples across the pool, I crossed my arms over my chest and glared at him defiantly.

"I am not prudish nor afraid," I said through chattering teeth, lifting my chin.

"No," he replied. "You have courage." He was quiet. "We could stay a while."

I turned my head, tilted it up to watch him. His jaw was relaxed and from this angle, I could only see a glimmer from his silver eyes as he watched me. Though the turn in conversation was abrupt, I knew exactly what he meant.

I clutched my arms tighter around me. "But … what about Devlin and the grimoire?"

We watched each other in the water. Somehow, a huge distance had sprung up between us though we stood a few paces away. Something broke the water's surface drawing my gaze. I missed what it was, but watched the ripples fan out and disturb the placid water. It was just jumping fish, right? It wouldn't be anything slimy or a small beast with many teeth….

A sloshing noise had me swallowing loudly. Breandan stood much closer now, waiting for me to look at him. I did, and he shrugged. "It can wait," he said simply. He motioned to me then himself. "This is more important."

"Uh, I don't think Conall will agree with you."

He stroked my hair, wound a thick lock around his palm, and rubbed it absentmindedly. "We need to think of a plan to retrieve the Alpha's daughters from the Temple without being seen, without creating uproar. This needs to be handled with care. Should the humans catch us they would use it as an excuse to declare war."

"We can do it easily enough. You know we can."

"Oh?"

I counted off the reasons why this would be straightforward on my fingers which was awkward, since I was still keeping my chest covered. "We can pass the Wall without detection. We can move fast enough that they wouldn't see us. I've seen that freaky 'blending into the shadows' thing Conall pulls, and I know you could do it too, even with all your glowing and pulsing." I pointed to myself with my thumb. "I've been trained in Subterfuge. I can manage a rescue mission and with you at my side there's no way we would be seen. We just need to find where they're being held."

I looked back to gage his reaction. He pursed his lips. "You seem to have become quite invincible."

I glowered at him and slapped him on the back with my tail. The tap I'd planned landed lower than intended, on his upper thigh. He hissed in my ear and I squirmed, the tip of my tail tingling.

"Sorry," I mumbled, blushing.

Letting out a long, protracted breath he placed his hands on my shoulders, and pulled me closer. I came to him reluctantly and focused on the pointed tip of his left ear. My wings flexed and rustled behind me restlessly, and rather than have my arms trapped uselessly between us, I unwound them to have them dither in the air. I had no choice but to place them at his sides, at the bottom of his ribcage. My head just reached his shoulder. He bent his knees, and in this half seated position my inner thighs slid over his outer legs until I sat on his lap. I stopped breathing and held still. Not sure what to do or what this meant, I decided the best course of action was none. I waited, still staring at his shoulder as if the silvery skin had all the answers to every unanswered question in the universe locked in its pores. His hands slid down from my upper arms to lace together on my lower back.

After a minute or so of barely breathing, I relaxed, one muscle at a time.

"Better," he concluded and his thumbs stroked circles into my skin.

My eyes drifted closed. "So you get antsy when we get frisky on the grass, yet naked frolicking in lakes is allowed?" I asked breathless and fidgety.

"Oh yes. We are not doing anything that would compromise your virtue. So calm down." When my face got pouty, he spoke again and I heard a smile in his voice, but I was too mortified to open my eyes and see it. "I guess you're wondering why I brought you here." I nodded repeatedly because I was majorly confused. "You need to get used to being around me. This way there are fewer barriers between us."

I couldn't stand it ... not seeing his expression as he spoke. My eyes opened long enough to send him a dry, assessing look. "At what point did clothes become insurmountable barriers to be defeated?"

"When you feel ashamed or scared you twist your hands into your pockets to stop yourself touching me." He frowned. "Always you should be touching me. It feels good and it makes us stronger."

Gods above strike me down the boy had me worked out.

"But ... you avoid me. Sometimes."

He stared at me. "I am an outcast. I have no Tribe. And you are a highborn fairy. It would be a dishonour to treat you so in public when we are not mated. But you can always touch me."

I was not sure I got it entirely. How could love be a

dishonour? Why could I touch him and he not touch me? It hadn't been an issue before. I knew Lochlann wanted us to be discreet, but Conall knew how we felt about each other. He may be a bit over-protective, but surely after a while he would just get over it.

Breandan moved off the topic. "We should stay here for a few days. Rest and be together."

His hands were so warm, so hard and gentle. They distracted me from trying to figure out why he was so careful all of a sudden. "Hmm, say-say?" I mumbled. It was more a moan than anything resembling agreement.

"I told you when Lochlann returned I would spend more time just being with you."

He was determined to keep on talking so I peeked an eye open. "You want us to stay with the Pride?"

"Byron, Conall, and I shall plan the rescue, and you can learn more about our ways. Who and what you are. No hovel is big enough for Devlin to hide in that we cannot find him. We have time."

I blinked at the suggestion of the arrogant fairy High Lord staying anywhere that was remotely 'hovel' like. Devlin was an extrovert character, someone who played games and played them well. He had infiltrated the human Temple, posing as a Sect Disciple for an entire month, to gain my trust before trying to trick me into joining him. He was beautiful and handsome, of course; most fairies were in their own way. Devlin had hair so blonde it was white, and mesmerising green eyes that sparkled even in the absence of light. His features were sharp and pristine, and his gait assured, confident. But he was also cruel and hard of heart towards all apart from his life-mate, Wasp. His flair for manipulation was bone deep, and I knew he would not give up the High Lordship to Lochlann easily.

We had a hard road ahead of us so what Breandan was suggesting was beyond tempting. He was saying I needed time to accept and adjust, to think about what I wanted to do next and allow myself to shape the future rather than be swept into it by what was happening right then. Possibly I could plan a little rather than just reacting to the explosion that seemed to happen after every decision I made. To spend a few days tucked in Breandan's arms seemed too good to be true. But then again sometimes good, normal things did happen to people. I could just have fun. Learn about the shifters, and get to know Alec more. He was so kind and he felt like a friend, something I had few of.

My heart squeezed painfully. No, I had no friends. My only friend was dead.

I looked down into the water's surface and saw us. Our skin glowed. My ear tips were elongated to slender points and peeked through a tangle of hair that cascaded down my bare back and over Breandan's fair arm that clutched me tightly. My tail weaved through the air over my shoulder, and my golden wings rustled. Pinions the width of my wrist supported the gauzy, multifaceted membrane that made up the main body of my wings, four ovals of shimmering segments, the upper two broader than the lower, that twinkled in the gloaming. I opened my mouth and saw the brilliance of my teeth, fang-like. My eyes sparkled like wells of light, even more so as tears pooled above my bottom lashes.

How strange and odd I looked to my own eyes.

Breandan, a silver sheen beside me, cupped my cheek, bringing my eyes to lock with his. There was sympathy and compassion there. Could he see my pain? His other hand moved to rest over my chest, fingers shifting gently as he closed his eyes, feeling my heartbeat pound against his palm. Could he feel my pain?

He leaned his head against mine then tilted his chin to kiss me. I sighed and brushed my lips against his, breathing in the scent of sunlight and rain. The water sloshed as I snuggled closer, into the warmth and comfort. My leg muscles tightened as my arms snaked around his neck to bring him closer.

He watched me out the corner of his eye as I rubbed my cheek against his, like he was afraid I was not real or something. His hands moved up under my wing pinions until he smoothed over where they joined to my back. His hands swept over my lower wings and I made a strangled noise. They tingled at his touch. Stiffening, he stopped and brought his hands to rest low on my hips instead; long, powerful fingers playing across my skin applying pressure.

"So we stay?" he asked.

He was trying hard to protect me. His protection extended beyond the physical, he wanted me to heal emotionally before the cracks I knew were already there broke open and obliterated me from the inside out.

I cupped his face in both my hands and looked deep into his eyes. He was my home, my light in the dark. Already I felt my heart healing. I paused, then placed a kiss to his clenched jaw.

"We stay," I agreed softly and smiled.

My dreams were filled with dark and wicked things but the silver light that surrounded me always kept me safe. The darkness could not have me and wrapped in my cocoon it was easy for my mind to become quiet and sink into a deep blissful sleep.

I woke before the dawn, overly warm, and tucked safely in Breandan's arms, my head pillowed on his chest. We had curled up together on the bank of the river and talked long into the night. Dew was heavy in the air and the horizon was awash with dense pastel colours, announcing the sun's imminent arrival.

A soft whistle over by the ferns revealed Alec standing in the gloom, jerking his head at me, beckoning. I cocked my head in question and he smiled cheekily before tugging on his pants. I leaned up onto my forearms then became painfully aware of the fact I had no clothes on. It wasn't like before, when it was just Breandan and I. After a while, I had become relatively confident in my own skin as we talked. Now I just felt exposed. Dropping back down I wiggled further into Breandan's side and crossed my arms over my chest. Managing to merge a blush with a scowl, I looked up to see Alec clamping a hand over his mouth hide his laughter. He held up his palms when I hissed quietly then turned on his heel, tapping his foot impatiently.

Jumping into a crouch, I breathed in the crisp morning and let the cool air refresh my damp body. I scanned the lake bank and found my dress in a crumpled pile a few paces away. Picking it up, a few spiders and ants fell onto my leg and I slapped at them, batting at the dress with my hands to make sure there were no more crawlies. Slipping it over my head, I itched at my neck and trawled my fingers through my hair which cascaded down my shoulders in dark waves. Since I had embraced my fairy nature it was growing ridiculously fast, and I wondered when it would stop.

Hearing a lusty sigh, I turned to find Breandan awake, sitting up with his forearms resting on his knees, watching me battle with the tangle on my head. My fingers stilled. There was something … different. His permanently clouded expression and guarded eyes shone with warmth and happiness. He looked peaceful rather than serious and plagued. He closed his eyes and breathed in deeply before standing to find his trousers. "I will come with you," he said.

I looked away as he pulled his pants on and heard the leather strings rub against each other as he knotted the tie, I walked over to him and pushed him down. "No. Stay here and rest." I kissed him briefly on the lips and then again, because the first was so sweet and it made me tremble. We both sighed. "You need to rest and Alec is protection enough. Besides we're on Pride territory, no wandering demon will come here." He did not look convinced. I laced my hands behind the nape of his neck. "I'll be fine."

"Come on, Rae! Gods, what are you doing?" Alec stomped over to us and tugged on the end of my hair. I slapped his hand away when he tried again.

"Bring the fairy with you if you must. We're going back to the Pride Heart anyway."

I untangled myself from Breandan, who stood gracefully and took my hand.

The three of us wandered back to the centre of Pride land and I enjoyed the peace of such a moment. Alec had a habit of talking until he ran out of breath. He'd heave in a gulp of air then start again, chattering on about how they ran the borders of the Pride at sunrise and sunset, and how the Alpha's daughters were taken.

"So you were with them?" I interrupted when his face turned a ruddy pink from talking so much. "You saw who took them?"

"No. The twins were running together in the morning,

but when they did not return by nightfall Byron knew something was wrong. He sent me to find them. I caught their scent quickly and with it human and silver. I found a pool of blood too. Not enough to suggest the wound it came from was fatal, but enough for concern." He looked toward the east, in the direction of Temple. "There may be two of them, but to get both under your thumb all you have to do is threaten the other. Even if one of them was able to get away, she would not. They would never leave each other, even if it meant dying."

"How long ago were they taken?" Breandan asked.

"Four days," Alec whispered and hung his head.

"And you haven't tried to break them out before now?" I questioned incredulously.

When Maeve had been taken by the Clerics she had been gone less than a day. She had suffered at their hands and I dreaded to think what the shifters Alec referred to were being put through. I did not like thinking the Sect capable of such horrors, but my eyes had been opened to the real world around me. I had to accept certain things, no matter how much I disliked them.

Both Alec and Breandan raised an eyebrow at me. "We tried to breach the Wall a few days ago but didn't come close. Humans have guns and silver bullets to the chest will kill. We lost two males trying to dig our way under."

With a flash, I remembered the screams of were-cats earlier in the morning before I had run in the forest and met Breandan. How odd something I had brushed off as demons battling over territory was something much simpler and purer. I felt ashamed. So much of what I had been taught by the Sect was wrong.

The Sect was the single greatest authority the survivors of humankind looked to for guidance and protection.

During the Rupture so many were slaughtered and only those who were strong were able to defend themselves. Many fled the inner cities, knowing it was only a matter of time before a shifter sniffed you out or a vampire caught the smell of your female's menstrual cycle. Nowhere with a dense population was safe – until the three men and five women, the Priests who had founded the Sect, erected the Wall and set the strongest survivors they could find as guardians. They had become determined to fight off any threat to their continued survival. Many sought sanctuary with these brave few who seemed to be able to hold their own and after a while that was simply the way it was. The Priests told us what to do and we did it. They told us what to think, what to eat, what to say, and in return they kept us safe from the demons beyond the Wall.

That had all changed for me, my eyes had been opened and nothing was ever as black and white as it seemed.

"I heard you," I confessed "I would wake up and hear you calling to them."

Alec gave me a half-hearted smile. "Wherever they are they're underground and more than likely in human form. They would have returned the call if they had heard us, if they could have responded." He sounded desolate so I touched his arm briefly.

"Is that why you were in the forest when I first met you? So close to the Wall?"

He nodded. "We've been trying to find a weakness in their defences for days. When I saw you two I was curious, but couldn't hang around to talk since I was supposed to be monitoring Cleric activity." He grinned. "Had I known who you were I would have tailed you until I was sure you'd help us." He clicked his fingers. "Oh, and I almost forgot. A vampire has been scented several times. Do you know anything about that? Byron was worried about us running the territory alone if we had a bloodsucker to worry about."

Awkward.

Breandan did not say a word, and neither did I.

"I had more than enough problems yesterday," I said, strained. "I think if anything else had happened I would have gone crazy." Yes, I had completely ignored his question about Tomas, but really, how would I explain it?

Breandan snorted. "Pure blooded fairies do not go 'crazy'."

"One word; Devlin."

"He is evil not insane."

"Say-so," I mumbled. "Black magic and human sacrifice seems pretty crazy to me."

His ears twitched and he rubbed a small circle into my palm with his thumb. "Not everything is as black and white as it seems."

"I second that," Alec added before turning his attention to the path ahead of us. Though it was still dark, I saw many figures moving about. The shifters were awake to greet the dawn.

Conall appeared and stood in front of us, his eyes flicking between Breandan and me curiously. After a moments inspection he seemed satisfied and his scowl smoothed when he noted the circlet on my brow.

Breandan said, "Today we discuss how to help Byron."

My brother crossed his arms over his chest and tilted his chin up. "Agreed."

I looked between them as they eyed each other up and down. Okay…. Why were they acting so twitchy around each other? Bloody melodramatic fairies. "I'm going with Alec." I took off when Breandan opened his mouth to object.

Brawling tiger cubs bumbled past me, growling at each other, and a few shifter-kids in human form darted past, heckling wildly and egging them on. A petite lynx the colour of honey-gold darted between my legs, and I tripped, trying not to step on any tails including my own. I clutched mine in my palm and trod lightly, keeping my wings tight to my back.

"Watch out," Alec warned from behind me and yanked on the end of my hair to pull me out the way as two much older tigers lunged past. They had half a deer carcass clamped in their jaws and they swiped at each other with paws the circumference of my face.

Bewildered, I looked up at him with wide eyes. "Can I hang with you today?" I asked and pointed over my shoulder in the direction I knew Breandan was in. "They're acting weird and I'm not into it." I scratched my knee where the hem of my skirt rested. "And if you could show me where I could bargain for some decent clothes I'd owe you big time."

"Bargain?"

"Well, I don't have any coin; it doesn't work like that at Temple. Everything I needed was provided for me by the Sect. And I have no idea if Conall has any."

I rubbed my nose, self-conscious about the sudden realisation I had no way to feed or clothe myself. Where would I sleep? When I was at the fairy Wyld everything had been done for me, but I'd been so out of it I hadn't thought to ask if anything belonged to me. Where did Breandan sleep when he was there? After all, it was his home.

"I guess it would be Conall I ask – since he's the head of my family," I said slowly. "But like I said, he's acting weird and I've had enough of the intense conversations he loves dragging me into. For now."

Alec laughed. "I can get you some new clothes. We don't use coin here either so do not worry about that. It's community labour we value, and I'll pick up your tab." I went to protest, but he shook his head with finality. "I've got to make sure none of the women need anything and run the territory, but you can tag along if you like and help. That would be payment enough." He jerked his head toward the clothes stalls and I fell into step beside him, walking down the gentle slope. "To be honest I'm surprised you guys are willing to wait around here for so long. When you first arrived it seemed like you were in a rush."

My attention was rapt on the community around me. Shifters prowled past and I roughly pegged the Pride population at no more than two hundred. It was amazing how much bustle such a small number of people could make. The smell of cooking meat had my stomach rolling dangerously. Did they eat nothing else?

"We decided to stay for a while," I replied, pressing a hand to my stomach and praying I did not start to retch. "Breandan wants time to plan the rescue of Byron's daughters, and well, I just want some time to breathe. Things have been crazy these past two days, and a few more to get things straight would do me the world of good."

"You're not doing badly. When I shifted for the first time I thought I'd lost my mind. Didn't take me long to figure out what I was." Alec became reflective, stopping us in front of a stall piled high with leathers and fabrics. "Only the gods know what would have happened to me if Byron hadn't taken me in. Between the Clerics, fairies, and vampires I wouldn't have lasted long." He shook himself up head to toe, like a cat coming out of the rain.

His dark hair flapped about a bit and he scrubbed his hands through it agitatedly, sending me a rueful look. "Morbid, yeah I know. So, you are staying on Pride land? It's not like fairies to spend so much time in the presence of other demons."

He pointed to a pair of plain russet leather pants and I nodded, rummaging through the piles to find a size that would fit me.

"No?" I asked, feigning nonchalance, picking up a pair, I pulled on them to make sure they were tough enough, Alec plucked them from my hands and motioned to the tunics.

I gazed over the selection not seeing any tops that took my fancy. I missed my tee shirts and jeans, but I had to get out of this dress. It was disgusting, crumpled, and covered in mud, blood, and sweat. Not a good look for me.

"By nature your kind are secretive and proud. Well, most of you are. I've never met any like you before."

Though my hands were on the scratchy fabric of the tunics, my eye had snagged on something else. I shot Alec a quick grin. "And you never will again."

I wasn't much into clothes, as a Disciple I was given tokens that allowed me to collect what I needed, the basics, once every six months or so from the seamstress. Unlike the other girls, I had never altered my wardrobe, slashing the tops and jeans to show more skin. I just did not care how I looked. But since I'd met Breandan.... Well, not looking a complete mess had become something of a priority.

The tops I could not stop staring at were no more than bras with all kinds of buckles and leather straps hanging off them. Alec caught my preoccupation and I hastily turned my attention to the sensible tunics on display, finding the beige and grey shades less than delightful. Alec took the scandalous top down and waggled it on the tip of his finger. It looked like a scrap of spare material in his big hands. He nodded his head toward the lace up boots, looking at my dirty, bare feet pointedly.

Refusing to be distracted, I shook my head and leaned in closer. "I can't wear that." I made to snatch it from him, but he bunched it up with the trousers under one armpit, and snagged my elbow to push me in front of the boot selection.

"It'll look good on you. Now how big are your feet?" He ducked down to catch my ankle and pull my foot up. Head swinging from side to side he selected a pair of soft-sole boots.

Picking the shoes up and hugging them to my chest, I glowered at him. "I'm not wearing it." I spun on my heel to go look at the belts.

Jogging up beside me, he laughed. "Don't you want to look pretty?"

"That's not the point. You do not need to show the whole world your entire hide to be pretty. I don't need to prance around half naked for people to notice me…. Not that I want them to … in fact, the less people notice me the better."

"Then why didn't you pick up a tunic?"

I stopped and cursed, ready to go back. He grabbed my hand and pulled me on. Fumbling to keep hold of the boots with one hand, I followed him, grumbling to myself.

His hut was small and a bloody mess. The walls were covered in scratch marks and the bedding looked like it had been attacked by a pack of, well, cats.

Alec dropped all my clothes on the floor and winked,

stepping outside to give me privacy.

I ripped a hole in the trousers above the seat; they were pocket-less, which made things easier. I sighed; it was a shame to vandalise such good workmanship but a necessity.

I dressed quickly, my eyes taking in the wooden beams, rumpled sheets, and mish-mash of personal belongings. It was simple, but homely too. Shiny rocks and dried leaves were scattered everywhere: on the windowsill, propped up against the wall. Each was so lovingly displayed it was clear Alec had chosen them for a reason.

Finished, I clutched the dress loosely in my hands. With a quick thought it went up in flames and turned to ash. I dusted my hands off.

In honesty, my new outfit was the most comfortable I had ever worn. My wings were free to move without restraint or the irritation of fabric rubbing at the base of my pinions. The air on my back, stomach, and shoulders was delightfully refreshing, I'd always run hot, a fairy trait it seemed. The leather trousers moulded to my curves like a second skin and hugged my ankles, tucked into the soft-soled boots that felt like they were made for me, which strapped up to the middle of my calf. The waist of the trousers rode my hips dangerously low and though I tried to yank them up the problem was a lack of material rather than the fit. Even the leather straps on the top were practical, criss-crossing over my front with a sheath for a dagger. Taking a deep breath, rubbing my circlet anxiously, I looked down. Skin, lots and lots of skin. Heat climbed up my neck and I scratched my throat like I was breaking out in a rash. I was embarrassed because I was surprised and proud that my body made such an impressive showing in the revealing outfit.

"I can't wear this," I muttered and yanked on the boning that nestled above the centre of my ribcage.

The door swung open making me whirl in fright, letting in a gust of grass-scented air, and slamming into the wall. Alec – fingers still splayed on the door – blinked at me owlishly.

He groaned. "If I were a lesser animal…." He leaned forward to grab my hand and pull me out the hut before I could voice my numerous protests.

As we stalked across the Pride, I felt heated eyes on me, both human and cat. Slowly, I straightened my back, under the influence of a fierce surge of female pride. Hell, my hips swayed and my tail waved from side to side with flirty flicks. Allowing a smile to brighten my face, I finally paid attention to where Alec was headed.

I dug my heels into the earth.

"Uh, what are you doing?" He kept going and I scrapped two divots in the floor. Not wanting to ruin my new boots, I let up and stumbled forward. "I'm only letting you pull me because I don't want to show you up in front of your Pack brothers, but by the gods, Alec," my voice lowered to a furious hiss, "if you take me over there dressed like this I will not forgive you." He smirked and kept walking, keeping me with him. I tried to distract him. "You seem interested in fairies."

He slid a considering look at me. "It's my job. As the pack's protector I have to be aware of danger."

I stopped. My booted foot burrowed into the hard packed dirt floor again. This time for entirely non-selfish reasons. "Things are changing, Alec." Gathering some confidence I looked him in the eye. "You don't have to be afraid to go into the forest any more or worry about what a fairy might do should they find you. And our being here isn't some undercover attempt to learn your weaknesses. Okay?"

He smiled. "You're something special, y'know. But you can't divert me."

I scrunched my face up and whacked his shoulder. "You're embarrassing us both." Determined he walked on and stayed quiet. I tried again. "Um, so ... why do shifter packs segregate like you do? I mean, there are were-wolves, were-bears, were-birds, but you live separately. Why is there no mix?"

He shrugged. "We've heard of mixed packs, but I can't see how they could possibly live together without the constant threat of the stronger killing the weaker."

"You have no control over your animal nature?"

"Yes, but it's easy to be overcome by instinct."

A woman holding a woven basket to her hip swayed past, her slinky movement screaming of effortless feline sexuality. Seeing the sensual way she moved, I was conscious of my own somewhat heavy stomp. It also reminded me of the dance the night before.

"Uh, so, the females are protected from the males by Byron?" Alec cocked an eyebrow in question. I cleared my throat and felt heat crawl up my neck to spill onto my cheeks. "Last night with the dancing ... he was nodding at the couples...."

"Oh. The Alpha always agrees to the mating. It is tradition. I find it a bit of a passion killer, but most are too ... involved to mind. They're basically asking permission to go screw each other's brains out." My mouth dropped open. Alec seemed perturbed by my reaction. He watched me carefully and his eyes flicked over to where Breandan and Conall sat in their council. His eyes came back to me. "His scent is all over you, but you and your fairy have not—"

"If you know what's good for you you'll end that

sentence right there."

I blushed furiously. I would not be called out so blatantly. It was none of his business.

He held his hands up, laughing. "The irritation and tension speaks for itself. I won't say a word." He mimed closing his mouth. I nodded once, feeling my face cool down. "Is there a reason you have not mated him yet?"

"Alec!"

At the sound of my voice, Breandan's head whipped round to stare at me. He made to rise, but Conall said something that made him freeze, and return to his cross-legged position. He turned away, but not before I felt the intensity of his mind upon mine, looking for any fear or concern. Finding none the pressure of his mind left mine and I scowled. Alec had seen the exchange and scratched the back of his head, expression mystified.

Still not happy with the fact the shifter led me over there I squeezed his hand until he grunted. By the time we reached the trio, the tendons in his arm had popped out and his face was strained. I applied more pressure and heard a satisfying crack muted by a short bark of pain. I let him go and he shook out his hand, glaring at me.

Rubbing my sweaty palms on my hips, I looked everywhere but at Breandan's face. My chest heaved, my breath coming short with nerves.

I made an impatient noise at Alec to get on with it.

"I am going to run the territory," Alec told Breandan. "Rae wants to come with me. I ask permission to guard your mate until I bring her back to you."

"As her Elder, I agree that Rae may accompany you," Conall replied easily.

I started and looked at my brother, cocking my head. Why had he answered? Alec simply nodded slowly and paused, waiting.

My face got hotter and hotter. Tears pricked my eyes because I wanted Breandan to say something, to object. How crazy was that. When Tomas made to touch me Breandan's jealousy was plain, the stress of it had given my stomach cramps. But was I secretly pleased? After years of being ignored and seen as weird, was I happy to have two boys fighting over me? Maybe that's why I felt an irrational urge now to smack him in the face to get him to look at me. I stared at him now, waiting for him to acknowledge me.

His gaze flicked to me and his eyes burned. Then he glanced at Conall and his lips pressed together in acute frustration.

The silence became charged. Byron and Alec shared a baffled look.

I turned and walked away.

After fewer than three steps, a hot and thick wave of lust gushed over me. My fourth step faltered before I gathered myself. Swallowing hard, stunned by the ferocity of the desire he had sent to me, and unable to help myself, I snuck a look over my shoulder.

Breandan winked before turning his attention back to the conversation Conall and Byron were deeply immersed in.

Alec skipped up beside me and I slanted him a pleased look under my lashes. "Shut up," I mumbled, but could not help the smile that tugged up the corner of my mouth.

Both palms shot up in innocence. "I knew he'd let you know somehow." At my puzzled look he said, "I see now that your culture is different to ours. Conall guards your honour, and Breandan cannot openly speak for you. 'Why?' is the riddle though."

Alec led the way out of the shifter's camp and into the

tall grass. As I walked I let my palms brush over the prickly tips.

"He has before," I murmured to myself.

"Conall seems to like him, but won't give his blessing on your mating. Why?"

My mouth opened to deny this then snapped closed. Breandan had openly defended me when Lochlann had considered trading me over to Devlin for a month of peace.

And he'd…. It was like a mental slap.

That was the only time he had openly spoken for me, and the result of that had been his oath breaking. Did that remove the fear of having to choose between his brother and me? The trust and devotion in that one action was mind-boggling. Was there more to it than I had initially understood? Gods, I had not thought much about anything because stuff happened so fast, but Breandan had turned his back on everything he had known to protect me. Fairies were tradition conscious and had a high concept of honour. If Breandan had broken away from his family, did that mean he was no longer able to lay a claim on me? No, that made no sense. He believed we were destined to be, that he was born for me, even if by fairy law Lochlann should be the one courting me. Breandan was no coward. He would fight for me, regardless if his older brother needed my power to bring back the balance, and keep to the favour of the fairy people. Could Lochlann have ordered Breandan to step aside if he'd remained oath sworn? Lochlann had plainly revealed he expected me and him to mate, despite what I felt towards his brother. These thoughts shone a new light on my first encounter with Breandan. He'd been upset that he had seen me first and that the bond sparked between us. I could understand his hesitation to openly proclaim me if our chance meeting had been as unexpected to him as it was me, but he'd known a month before we met what was going to happen. The white witch Ana had told him. He had been subdued and resigned that we bonded, but not unhappy. I hoped. Well, just because he wasn't unhappy did not mean he wanted to remain tied to me. Was he fighting the bond? Was that the real reason why he stopped himself getting closer to me? Did he expect it to be broken so Lochlann could claim me as fairy law required? Then why ask for Lochlann to release him if he wanted to get rid of me? Why did he defend our connection when Devlin had suggested it broken?

I stopped dead. Alec walked out of sight before he came crashing back, looking panicked. Seeing me frozen with a thunderstruck expression he did not speak.

Is that what Lochlann and Conall thought too? That the bond between Breandan and I could be broken? Was this why Lochlann asked me to be discreet, and why Conall was so hell bent on ensuring we were? My tie with Tomas made it clear that Breandan and I could still be separated, though I got the impression it would be emotional and physical torture. No! Breandan wouldn't let that happen. He'd broken his oath so he could have me. It was his only choice. He could not stay sworn to his brother and mate me when it was his Elder's right to have me. Conall thinking this way, I could understand to some degree. He was Lochlann's right hand man, and loyal to a fault. Despite my love for Breandan, he would try to save me for his chosen lord. Were Breandan and my Elder doing some secret power play behind my back? Was Breandan trying to strengthen our bond and get to know me, whilst steadfastly keeping to the rules, and giving Conall no option but to accept our time together because

Breandan was not actually overstepping any lines? Uh, I was confusing myself. I thought about what Breandan had told me at the lake. Of course, in public he could not stake his claim. I could show him favour, but he could not show it to me. Oh. Perhaps Conall hadn't voiced his disapproval before because he was unsure of what he felt between Breandan and I. When we had first met, Conall had told me he sensed something odd around me, but he did not know what it was. When he had found out, because Devlin opened his big stupid mouth trying to trade me for a month of peace, Conall had said nothing to oppose our bond. Then again, I guess it wasn't really the time for him to talk to me about such things. When he had tried to broach the subject yesterday I'd refused to listen, too wrapped up in Breandan. And my fairy was more than happy to get in the way of such a conversation. After all, I could apparently still turn my back on him and leave him with nothing.

How did I not see this? The tension between the two boys made perfect sense now. So did Conall's magic appearing act every time Breandan came closer than two feet from me. He thought he was protecting me.

But what was Breandan's plan to make this okay? He had been honest in the beginning, and on Lochlann's return he had told me his brother was not happy. But he had been sure he could make him understand, make him accept us.

That did not seem to be happening, in fact, quite the opposite.

The idea of being with Lochlann was horrifying. He didn't care for me at all. He had openly admitted my heart belonged to Breandan. Would he really condemn himself to an unhappy mating for the sake of the High Lordship? Would he hurt his younger brother that way? I knew him to be stuffy and cold, but even he could not be that cruel.

I waved Alec on, not wanting to share my revelations until I had worked it through a few more times.

We'd reached the edge of the grasslands and were light heartedly jumping over the low-grown shrubs and bushes that surrounded the young trees at the edge of the forest. Alec seemed to be following a specific trail since he took us in a curving, zigzagging path that went deeper into the forest then back out again into the grass.

"You going to Change?" I asked absentmindedly.

"I'll stay human for a while. My senses aren't as good, but I want to enjoy what's on show for a while longer." He wiggled his eyebrows.

I did not get it. "Can't you see as a cat?"

"Can't see colour and you are extraordinarily colourful."

He leered at me and I snorted. It was relaxing to muck around with someone.

"Where are we going?" I asked grumpily.

He pointed across the grass in no particular direction I could see, only that we would be entering the forest again and that was good enough for me. I breathed in deeply, enjoying the rich smell of soil and green things.

Alec himself smelled nice too, sort of like sweet grass and warm animal. With his dark hair and green eyes, he was not ugly either; quite the opposite, judging by the way the shifter-females reacted. He had a pleasantly square head and was unshaven. His body hair was raven black, like his cat form, and he was long of torso and short of leg. Byron said he was the Pack Omega, second-in-command, and I understood why. Despite his youth he had a commanding air about him. An innate calm. He was pleasant to be around and I was glad I was here, even if my body was already beginning to miss Breandan's touch.

So far the bond had not become annoying, but I wondered if one day always needing my fairy close would upset me.

"You and the fairy are so strange. I've never seen your like," Alec said.

I huffed a sigh even as I felt a pang of hurt. "Being different is not so bad."

"Your love is cold, awkward. So odd. Yet I would say the Claim between you two is stronger than anything I've ever felt, and I am not even of your species."

"I've never heard of this before." My brows furrowed. "The Claim?"

"It is what we call the urge to mark our mate. A sign to others that you are mated to another." He shook his head as he walked, muttering to himself. "A cold love."

"Because we don't cuddle and sigh in each other's ear in front of others – that makes us cold? The connection between us goes deeper than words or touch. I am bound to him, and he belongs to me."

I straightened and looked down, incredulous at myself. Did I really say that out loud?

"I never meant to offend you," Alec said. "I didn't understand. As cats we're open in our affection. We see no shame in nudity or excessive displays of courting or passion." He blushed. "If I felt half as passionate about any female as you seem to feel for him I would not be able to take my hands off her. His gaze rarely leaves you, but I thought it was more to do with protection than passion." He took my hand in his and held it solemnly. "I didn't understand it was that complicated."

I shrugged, feigning nonchalance. Neither did I until a few moments before. "Breandan is exercising control. It's not that he doesn't want to touch me, he mustn't, to

make sure that Conall … his brother needs me to be …
uh, it's messed up. He's different when we are alone."
From the dubious expression on Alec's face I was not
explaining myself well. "We're bonded. A rare
connection, and–" I hesitated, remembering the warning
from both Ana and Conall about speaking of the bond
freely. That and the fact I had told Lochlann I would be
discreet about my relationship with his brother. If Alec
ever spoke openly about this to my Elder.… "You can't
tell anyone about this. If you do–"

He tightened his grip on my hand. "I swear."

I breathed out and with it came a torrent of words.
"It's magic. Pure power. When we don't touch it starts to
build, and we do touch it explodes between us." I could
hear the excitement in my voice. "It's not so bad when
he's close, a few paces away, but any further and my skin
starts to itch, and my mind can't focus on anything for
more than a few moments before it seeks him out. It's
frustrating and exhilarating all at the same time." I felt a
rush of relief. It was good to talk to someone.

Alec chuckled. "Had we met in any other circumstance
I fear I would have fallen quite in love with you."

His eyes became distant, wistful.

"Who is she?" I asked. His eyes became hooded, his
expression clouded. I scowled at him, crossing my hands
over my stomach. "I bared my soul to you, time to
exercise some faith." When he said nothing, I rolled my
eyes. "I swear I won't tell." A ripple of wind passed over
me, I shivered. So creepy. "Happy now? You have an iron
clad promise sealed by magic. Spill."

"She is.…" He seemed at a loss for words. "She is the
sun, the light of my heart. When I run the forest I feel
closer to her."

Well, I was confused. "She's not Pack?"

He avoided my eyes. "No."

"Is there any reason other than this why you can't be with her?"

"She's never seen me, I've never let her," he said in a low confession. "She will reject me."

I held up my palm. "Please tell me you're not stalking some poor shifter-girl as a panther." His silence told me everything I needed to know. "Gods, Alec! Stalking is not sexy. Breandan tried that crap with me, and I ended up taking a tumble down a cliff, and getting lost, and–" I was getting myself angry. I took a deep breath. "Stop tormenting the girl and man up."

Avoiding my eyes he mumbled, "I've never actually, well, seen her."

I stared at him. "What are you talking about? How can you be in love with someone but never laid eyes on them?"

"Her scent is everywhere," he blurted. "In my head and my heart. But you see, I cannot simply look at her. I would not survive it. I would want to Claim her and she would reject me."

"Surely you can mate with a shifter from another Pack?"

He sighed and looked away. "It doesn't matter. No one will understand."

I shut up. He did not want to talk about it and I was in no mood to push him. He inhaled deeply, chest rising and expanding. Not liking the silence I blurted, "I wish I could see the world you do."

Alec's eyes bulged and he shook his head at me, baffled. "You are fairy, Rae. Other demons cannot experience the world as your kind can. You are connected to everything."

I burrowed my toe into the undergrowth. "No I'm

not," I confessed in a whisper. "I feel better in the forest or when I am near green things, yes, but I don't feel them. I know that Conall and Breandan do, they almost speak to the land. It sings to them, not to me." I shook my head. "I don't think I'm this Priestess they claim I am. I keep trying to make them see that I bring nothing but trouble. But they laugh and smile as they throw themselves into mortal peril for me." I thumped my chest. "I'm going to get everybody killed. And y'know what, I will say I told you so. They have made a mistake and they are so stubborn they can't see it."

"Horseshit." Alec gripped both my shoulders as I wrinkled my nose at his language. The visual it brought to mind was not pleasant. "I know you. The first time we met, you didn't run, hide, or snarl. You stood and faced me, a big stalking cat, even when your entire body was trembling. You touched me, you petted me for gods' sake. Why did you do that?"

I beamed at him. "You were cute."

His lip curled in disgust. "I choose to forget you said that. You touched me because you knew I meant you no harm. I know this because when you did it was like a flash across my skin, a wave of ... of ... knowing. A crisp clarity that allowed me to be certain I would be safe with you." He shrugged. "I have never felt such a kinship with anyone but my Alpha, and probably never will again until I Claim my mate. And I'm not the only one. I spoke to Byron last night and he said if you'd not have been present there was no way he would've agreed to align himself with the fairies. I, we, the whole Pack feel like we need to protect you. And as much as I would love to say it was all down to your sparkling personality and likeability..." I scowled and he laughed. "Your brother is right. You are their missing Priestess. Our reaction alone would suggest there is more to you than a girl with wings and a tail."

I harrumphed. "I still wish I could see the world better. Sense things better."

"It's only a lack of focus, Rae. You are a bit of a scatterbrain. Flaky."

My mouth dropped. "I am not flaky."

"Close your eyes."

I did as he asked. "What next?"

"Quiet yourself and be still."

Okay, I could do that. Be quiet and still. It is not like it was hard to stand and be. I made a small noise of annoyance. They treated me like a baby. I was not dumb. I rubbed my hands on my legs where the slash of my jeans used to be, anxiously. How long was I supposed to stand still for? My tail thumped my shoulder and I flexed my wings, enjoying the light stretch. I peeked an eye open and flushed.

"How the hell was that quiet or still, Rae?" Alec rubbed the bridge of his nose with his thumb and forefinger. "Your tail and wings were everywhere. Your hands could not stay in one place. And whilst I'm sure Breandan gets a kick out of watching you rub your own body I would suggest not doing that in front of other males. You made odd humming noises and you ... well ... twitched. A lot." He pursed his lips, shaking his head incredulously. "No wonder you have trouble controlling your magic. Isn't it all about focus and patience? If you cannot stand totally still and quiet for less than a minute, how do you plan to cast spells? Or be still enough to track a mouse through the undergrowth in a storm."

I was bright red and flustered. He was right, of course, but still it was embarrassing.

"Twitchy seems a bit harsh." He prodded me in the

side then in my shoulder, laughing. I slapped his hands away, giggling. "Okay fine, maybe I'm twitchy. Stop making fun of me and help me."

"I already have," he said proudly. "When you can learn to be still in your mind and body you will learn how to control your mind and body."

"Gods you demons suck. You never give me anything decent. Always I have to go away and work on control, or patience, or awareness." I yanked at my hair. "I think I may scream if I don't learn something I can use soon."

Alec stopped laughing and eyed me in disappointment. "Have you considered you aren't improving as fast as you could because you're resisting what you're being told? What if you stopped and listened? If you tried what you had been taught you'd learn more and faster." He nodded at his own words. "Fairies learn fast."

"Unguh, whatever," I grumped bad naturedly and stomped off.

Yes, he was right, but it was galling he felt the need to say that to me. Did I really not listen to what I was told?

My boots fared well in the forest, and I was able to move with surprising ease. Hearing Alec behind me, I moved into a jog, which in a flash became a run. Hearing him pull behind, I slowed, knowing he would not be as fast in human form.

It was easy to forget that shifters were essentially humans who had evolved differently, like witches.

"You like to run," Alec panted at my elbow, bent over with his hands to his knees. "That was a flat out sprint, impressive, and as much as I want to give you time to cool down, my head would get torn off if anything happened to you." His hand landed on my shoulder and spun me round. He looked deadly serious even with the colour high on his cheeks making him look boyish. "So don't do that again, okay?"

Opening my mouth to lash him with words, I took a moment to think on it. I gritted my teeth because he was right. Damn it to hell. I nodded sharply.

Alec returned the nod, went to speak but his mouth opened, and stayed there, his whole body locked up tight. His fingers dug painfully into my shoulder and he closed his eyes. His head snapped round and he wrapped his hand around my upper arm to hold me still. I shifted, crunching leaves under foot and he snarled at me quietly, eyes glowing, the pupils became slitted. His canines lengthened as I watched. His nose flattened even as his chin lengthened and his ears pulled back, smoothly curving to triangles. He snarled again, crouching.

He did not need to tell me trouble was close because I heard a sharp intake of breath on the wind and dropped to the ground myself. Instinctively I reached to the Source, a sun of brilliant light and heat that seemed nowhere and everywhere, a power that was mine to grasp despite how foolishly I had used it in the past.

Alec sniffed deeply, tasting the air and shuddered. "How did they get so close? Sentries are posted across the Pride border."

A hoof fall was within normal human hearing distance, and the warm smell of hay and horse curled into my nostrils. I listened carefully and heard the steady clomp, clomp, clomp of horse hooves.

My heart rate pumped double time and I struggled to come to terms with what was happening.

Clerics were on Pride land.

I stilled, my mouth dry and heart heavy, "Unless they died before they could raise the alarm."

The rumble that thundered from Alec's chest was not human. "I'm going to Change," he rasped and hunched over, stripping off his trousers and leaving them in a crumpled heap.

The shrubbery crackled, and through the tree line, I saw them. They were too close. I glanced at Alec, back already snapping, and joints popping. His spine exploded out with the extra vertebrae of his tail, and was quickly covered over with a sweep of skin and hair. His mouth was closed and he quivered with the effort of not crying out.

They could not find him here like this. If they did....

In a burst of speed, I darted forward quickly locating the two Clerics trawling the undergrowth from the backs of two freakishly large stallions. Snuffling the floor at their feet were bloodhounds. None of them reacted to me. I had moved so fast they hadn't seen me, nor had their dogs scented me yet.

Behind the backside of one horse – entangled in a net and dragged carelessly across the floor – was the body of a young shifter, a tiger. The bubble of disgust and anguish started in my stomach, rolled up my torso, forced its way out my throat, and exploded in my mouth. I screamed, long and loud. I was so horrified by the dead shifter youngling it was easy to project the fear and terror into my voice.

The Clerics' heads snapped to me, guns coming up to point in my direction. I bolted. The dogs sprang at me, barking and jaws snapping.

I kept my speed fast enough to avoid capture, but slow enough so they would be tempted to give chase. Hearing them urge their steeds into a gallop, I kept going, knowing I was headed somewhere high, somewhere near water.

Damn it, yet again I was running from the Clerics, and yet again I was terrified, but gods help me I would not let them take Alec like they had taken Maeve.

Leaving the forest treeline, I sped out of the tall grass, smelling the lake up ahead. Chest heaving from panic rather than physical exertion, I scowled when I saw Clerics were posted along the opposite bank. I careened to a stop, spinning round. The crimson red of the blazers were visible behind me, bouncing up and down wildly, so I changed direction and darted back into the grass.

A fierce growl pierced the morning air; Alec calling for help.

Fuelled by the need to get to him and ensure his safety, I ran faster, no longer worried those pursuing me would not be able to see me let alone catch me.

Alec launched himself on a Cleric, ivory teeth bared until they disappeared into the man's exposed throat. The horse pranced madly as the Cleric rolled from his saddle and was dead before he hit the floor. Alec was already a pace away, leaping on the next trespasser who was a woman, mounted on a huge black stallion. Her hood was up and cast a shadow over her profile. She raised her gun as the horse danced beneath her, neighing loudly and kicking his forelegs when Alec pounced back and forth, snapping at his fetlocks.

There was a loud crack and the smell of gunpowder. Alec screamed – the sound oddly human.

"No!"

I threw myself toward them as the horse kicked Alec away and sent his body hurtling through the air. He twisted and landed on his paws, but his legs buckled and his brawny body hit the floor. He scrunched his eyes shut and shuddered, blood pooling on the ground from his wounded side.

Falling to my knees, I clasped his head in my hand and patted him softly. I was relieved when his eyes slitted open then focused, jewelled irises trained on the Cleric behind me.

I shot a glare over my shoulder and the Lady Cleric pulled on the reigns so the horse backed up, her gun pointed at Alec's face. I froze, but my tail thrashed behind me like a whip.

"Back away from him and get down on the ground," she said calmly.

I did not move, trying to think fast but coming up with blank spaces and images of Alec's brain splattered all over the floor. I let go of his head and pushed him down when he struggled to stand. He whined, fearful for me, and I rubbed him behind the ear.

"Don't worry," I muttered in a voice too low for the Cleric to hear, but by the way his ears swivelled forward I knew Alec heard. "I'm thinking of a plan."

Standing, I stepped away from Alec, eyeing her distrustfully. "I'm not your enemy."

Another horse trotted up behind me with a haughty-faced Cleric. Neither of them looked familiar to me, nor particularly memorable in any way.

"Leave Brother Ryan's body, it'll just slow us down," he said tonelessly. "Leave the shifter, the tiger specimen is enough for now. And we have the other two. Take the fairy."

I feinted to the left then darted right, vowing to come back for Alec as soon as I had gotten help.

I'd taken no more than three running steps when something whizzed past my face, and something else slammed into my lower back. Pain lanced through my body and my muscles seized up. My limbs left my control and I dropped like a stone. The pressure and pain increased until it seemed my whole world was made of electric fire.

Everything went black.

CHAPTER FOUR

I was cold, I was groggy, and I was mad. A sharp, metallic aftertaste stained my mouth, and the smell of urine and dead things clogged my nose. Opening my eyes I was relieved - and infuriated - to meet two sets of adorable brown eyes set in sun-browned, heart-shaped faces.

"She's waking up," one of the faces said. "Give her some room to breathe."

The girl was pretty. She had a button nose, wide eyes, and a cute crop of dark brown hair. She crouched close by me, almost protective. A purple bruise decorated the side of her face and her pouty mouth looked swollen.

I tried to move my arms to crawl back, but I winced. My body was not fit to do much but lie still. Nevertheless, I did not want to lie there like a dead thing. I shifted up onto my elbows but a chain connected to the wall and a rusty manacle at my throat hindered further movement. My skin was swollen from the contact.

Uncomfortable on the hard ground, I scooted a little more before settling. Then I took in my surroundings.

The ceiling was low and dirty and the room wide, built of crumbling red brick. Candles cast glowing arcs of light and spilled sticky wax onto the wall. Rows of manacles and snaking chains were nailed into wooden panels on the floor and walls. Dark, shiny patches of red stained the grey concrete I sat on, and explained the dead smell. The gloomy corners made the walls seem curved. It was a room of death and shadows.

I shuddered and my eyes settled on the brown eyed girl again. Oh hell. I was seeing double.

"What?– Where?–" I made a rude noise and squeezed my eyes shut to hold back the tears.

Panicking would get me nowhere. I had to remain calm and not see double. Whatever had happened, the Priests would find me and save me from this… this… place.

I opened my eyes but little had changed, except one of the brown-eyed girls was grinning broadly.

"You're not going mad, fairy. There are two of us." She nodded her head to the second brown-eyed girl, "That is Nimah, my younger and spoilt twin. I'm Amelia."

I blinked and shook my head. I could have sworn she said fairy. "Hai," I said, relieved at least I was not seeing things even if I was hearing things.

"Why can we smell our Alpha on you?" Nimah asked and tilted her head back proudly, as if she expected nothing less than a full and immediate answer from me.

I'd knocked something important loose in my brain, I was sure of it. "Where are we?" I asked. I directed the question at Amelia.

She beamed at me, happy I had chosen to finish our exchange before indulging her sister. "We're in the humans' dungeon under the place they train the Hoods."

Biting my lip, I cocked my head. "Hoods?"

"The humans who wear the red hoods," she said and trembled. "The ones who protect the Wall."

Why did she speak as if human was something foreign to her? "We're at Temple?" I said, beyond relieved. I mean, I had never heard of or seen this place before, but it meant I had made it back alive.

That was the last time *I* ran in demon territory.

Thank gods I was safe!

Judging by the lack of light and the shape of the walls, we were deep underground. Perhaps a Cleric had found me and not wanted to alarm the other Disciples by taking me to Sanctuary. Intuition told me that was unlikely, since I was manacled. Maybe they were being on the safe side? After all I was a human, but maybe they were afraid a vampire had glamoured me, or something.

"What is going on exactly?" I asked, failing to keep panic from my voice.

The tight ball of fear in my gut was painful. Movement close by in the shadows made me tense. I squinted and then there was a hitch in my breathing.

A small, gangly figure was curled up in the corner staring at us with huge eyes with black holes for pupils that swallowed the whites of his eyes. His lips were small and pouty, and his bone structure delicate. He was clothed in a threadbare tunic. Stained and torn, it hung loosely from his shoulders and was bunched up in his fisted hands. He was bald and frighteningly skinny. Hunched over as he was, I could see the vertebrae in his back jut out from beneath his sallow skin. His fingers were bony and his cheeks sunken. He stared at me. But gods his eyes were huge, dominating the top half of his face. Cuffed to the wall, his manacle chain was coiled by his legs.

"Fairy?"

I frowned, shifting my attention back to the girls. "Why do you keep saying that?" I lowered my voice.

"And is that … is that a…."

"Goblin, yes. A half-breed I think. We call him Runt." She beckoned to him. "Come here, cutie. C'mon."

If such a thing was possible, the goblin-child's eyes widened to perfect circles, and he shuffled closer to the wall, turning his head into his shoulder to hide his face. He made a faint whimper followed by a snuffling noise.

Amelia shrugged. "He doesn't talk. They have zapped him one too many times I think. He is afraid of his own shadow. He won't even let us try to treat his sores. He just eats and drinks once a day then sits in his corner. It is sad really. It would be nice to have someone else to talk to. My sister can be a total bitch."

Nimah whacked her on the arm, scowling. "Bite me, I'm sitting right here."

"I know you think the whole world revolves around you, but believe it or not even though your name was mentioned, I wasn't talking to you."

"Why are you horrible to me? Even when we were cubs you were mean to me."

"What part of 'not talking to you' don't you understand?"

I cleared my throat. "Uh, girls…."

"What?" they said and turned to me simultaneously.

My head swam and I blinked a few times before squinting. "You called me a fairy…."

They shot strange looks at each other. The younger sister made a sweeping motion with her hand to her twin. "Go ahead. I know how you love to baby the broken ones."

"Touch your ears," Amelia said.

Frowning, I did as she said, confused as to what she was getting at. My fingers twitched over the tip of my ear. That was decidedly … pointy. Then I was suddenly aware of the two limbs that rested across my back. The tail curled about my waist. My heart pounded and I squeezed my eyes shut. "I– I feel sick–" I gasped. Memories hit me in the gut and bombarded my mind. My eyes shot open. "Alec!" I shouted and shifted into a crouch. I launched myself at the door, a moment after I remembered the iron manacle. I jerked to a stop, choked, and lost my footing. I fell hard and smacked my head on the floor. The skin at my temple split and I bit my own tongue, the blood sour at the back of my throat.

"Be still, fairy. If you make too much noise they'll come." Amelia touched my shoulder and I shrugged her off violently.

Surging up to my knees, I crawled away from them and put my back against the wall.

I remembered everything. I had been protecting Alec and been tagged by the Clerics. Me, dropped by taser probes ... how could I be so stupid? Why was I not focusing on what was going on around me? How the hell did they get so far into the Pride? Something was not right here and I needed to find out what.

"I need out of this hole," I growled.

"Oh, don't worry," Nimah said. "No doubt they'll be back for you soon. You're the new plaything." She shot me a dirty look and tipped her nose up. "Now you seem to have returned to yourself, answer my question. Why is the scent of our Alpha on you?" She crossed her sinewy arms over her chest tightly. Unlike Amelia, she had a heavy fringe that fell into her eyes. "I thought I scented Alec, and you seem to know him, but that's just crazy talk. Why would his scent linger on you? For it to be so strong there would need to be prolonged skin-to-skin contact." She glared at me. Was this shifter-girl the one Alec confessed he wished to Claim? But he had told me that girl didn't know he existed.

"Oh, shut up, Ni. Leave the poor girl alone."

A startling thought occurred to me. "I'm a demon... trapped at Temple," I said and blinked. I was still struggling to adjust. And though these girls seemed to need some answers from me, I was still running a few things through my clouded mind. Where was Alec now? Was Breandan looking for me? And how long had I been down here? Oh gods. How long had I been down here? Conall would be going nuts. And as for Breandan.... Yeah, I was in big trouble.

"Yes," Nimah promoted, jarring me out of my horrified thoughts. "You're a...." I said nothing, still shocked and confused. Witheringly, she looked at Amelia.

I looked too. I could use some direction.

"Fairy," she said.

At the expression that twisted my face, they both tensed and shuffled closer together. They waited for my shriek or yell, but it never happened. The twins watched me, heads cocked together. It was like there was a mirror but the reflections differed slightly. Amelia's face was a smidge rounder and Nimah's, eyes a fraction darker.

"They must have hit you with a high voltage to screw with your memory so badly," Amelia said after a short pause. "Don't worry, it'll get clearer soon."

"She's still hasn't explained why she smells like members of our pack," the young twin said bluntly.

Running a hand down her sister's hunched back in comfort, Amelia's voice was hard. "Give her time. She has been through a lot. Remember how you were when we first got here?"

The younger twin wiggled to get her sister to back off, but Amelia kept stroking so she stilled.

My hands flew up and out. "Unguh, they did hit me

too hard." I smacked myself on the forehead. "You're Byron's missing daughters, aren't you?"

"So you do know our father." Amelia shifted forward, a light coming on in her eyes. "He's coming for us?"

I nodded. "Yes. We had a deal. I'm going to rescue you." As I said the words, I flushed. "I mean, uh, I was going to rescue you before I was caught, of course."

Nimah was watching me, distrust plain on her face. "I don't believe you. Our father would never ask the fairylord for help. And involve one of his concubines? I don't think so."

I spluttered, "Concubine? Give me a break. I'm not Devlin's concubine. My name is Rae, and I'm—"

The door shuddered.

Nimah and Amelia instinctively slid closer together. Both turned their gaze upon me and I saw panic in their eyes. Even Runt had turned to look at me, and if possible, his face was even paler than before.

The door swung open and slammed against the back wall. Three figures in crimson blazers with black tails stood in the doorway, hoods pulled over their heads. Even in the poor light my eyesight was enough for me to make them out. All were much older than us. Men. One had sunken eyes and a crooked nose. The other was fair and stunningly handsome, for a human. The last was stockier in build and rougher in appearance; stubble was visible on his jaw and his blazer looked wrinkled. I thought I saw a faint trace of guilt flitter across his expression, but then it was gone and his expression was blank.

Amelia shuffled forward and crouched in front of me. She arched her back and hissed, sounding like a cat; a cat that was pissed. Nimah came up on my other side.

"Good thinking, Melia," she muttered. "Throw our lot

in with the fairy stupid enough to get caught."

The Clerics stepped forward and I figured out my next move. The iron had drained my strength, no doubt. I was weak, disoriented, and the stench of the metal made me retch, but I had been trained in combat by these Clerics. I knew how they would move and fight. If we could overwhelm them, we could escape. I may not get another chance. I had to try.

They needed to come closer. Close enough so that they were in punching distance. Close enough so that I could snap their necks in one of the three ways I had been taught in Martial Arts. Damn, close enough so that I could bite and scratch the crap out of them if needs be. I had never killed anyone before and I did not want to start now. But hell would freeze over if they thought I was going to die without taking at least one of them with me.

The Cleric with the crooked nose pulled something out from behind him. A silver blade. Nimah and Amelia recoiled then both growled, seeming to fill the dungeon with the noise of an entire shifter Pack.

Runt wailed in the corner. It sounded different from his usual sounds. A warning?

The Cleric brandishing the silver knife stepped forward and the shifter twins recoiled again, both taking hold of my shoulders to keep me with them. The touch was like a full body hiccup and I shrugged them off. I hated strangers touching me. The moment their hands left me, the two other Clerics grabbed hold of my feet and dragged me toward the door. Amelia made a high, strangled sound, enraged.

Still, they dragged me, and I dug my hands into the earth around me, snarling. I kicked my legs, and had I not been iron drained and bound, they would have flown with such a force that my captors would have been dead.

As it was, I was like a child struggling under the hands of her stronger parents.

I heard the clink of chains, the twist of a key in the lock, and I felt my irons give. I was no longer tethered to the floor. The Clerics let go of my feet and I flipped around, planning to attack the lone Cleric first then face these two with Nimah and Amelia at my side, but I moved a hell of a lot slower than I'd thought I would. By the gods, I was tired. I had no speed, no strength, but I refused to believe I had no hope.

Two pairs of heavy hands landed on my shoulders and dragged me back.

Runt hurled himself onto the lone Cleric's back and buried his teeth into his ear. The Cleric howled and spun, trying to shake him off but the goblin-child attached himself like a barnacle to the Cleric's back and would not let go. Blood splashed against the walls as the Cleric yelled and shook, trying to slash him with the knife.

Free from the fear of being cut with silver, Nimah and Amelia flew at me, clinging onto my arms. The Clerics' well-aimed kicks hit their backs and arms, but they held on to me. I caught the fear in Amelia's eyes. Not for herself, but for me.

Runt flew through the air and smashed into a wall. He twitched on the floor, his arm and leg bent at funny angles. His orb-like eyes filled with tears as he watched me. He opened his mouth and a lump of bloody flesh fell out. An ear. Moving quicker than I thought possible he was back in his corner, cradling his arm and leg.

The knife-wielding Cleric staggered forward, swinging the silver at the shifter twins. Their instinct took over and they let go. The Cleric with a crooked nose backhanded Nimah in the face and sent her sprawling across the floor. She smacked her head and was still. Amelia went crazy.

Eyes wild, she lunged at him but he unhooked the taser baton from his belt and rammed it into her chest. The girl convulsed and fell to the floor, spasming. The Cleric kept at it, prodding her with the taser until her body was contorted and twisted almost beyond recognition. The Cleric kicked her in the gut then he drew back his booted foot and brought it crashing into her face. She, too, was still.

Runt keened loudly, rocking back and forth in his corner, arms around his legs and eyes staring at me glassily.

The shifter twins were motionless, but I could see they were breathing by the dust that stirred by their mouths.

I was dragged up, but I fought. I twisted and turned. I bit with my teeth and yelled as they wrapped the chain around my neck and yanked. I resisted, knowing if I was dragged out that door something terrible would happen to me. They heaved on the chain and my feet slid forward. Again they pulled, and I stumbled forward out the door.

I was half carried and half dragged down a narrow passageway that was no more than a dirt tunnel. It smelt musky, and the oppression of it had me feeling claustrophobic. My Cleric guard said nothing directly to me, though the crooked nose Cleric behind me grumbled about his lost ear.

I stopped fighting, realising I was getting nowhere. My strength waned the more I fought, and I was not affecting them at all. I needed to be calm and plan my next move. I was weaker and slower than I had first thought. I had no magic in the iron-drenched hell, just my wits – which were thin and frayed from stress.

After a moment's deep breathing, I tried to feel through the bond for Breandan. Almost nothing; a faint sense of despair and anger. Why was he not coming for me? Fear gripped me. What if he was in trouble? What if he needed me, my power? Here I was chained and manacled, held by the Sect.

I concentrated on the bond again, trying to feel for fear and pain. No, he was not wounded I would feel that.

As I tried to seek answers through a bond I did not understand across a vast expanse of land, I noticed a darkness wobbling on the edge of my consciousness. It was familiar to me and the boy it connected me to was trying to reach me through it: calling, searching.

"Tomas," I whispered.

A heavy boot landed between my shoulder blades and I pitched over into the passageway. Dirt rammed into my mouth and my head spun.

"Quiet," barked the crooked nosed Cleric.

He pulled me up to set me on my feet then pushed me on.

I saw a soft light up ahead. My senses were dulled, but I knew we were no closer to the earth's surface. From what I could tell, we were headed deeper underground. Soon it was clear that the glow ahead was candlelight bouncing off blank, white walls and a bare concrete floor.

The room before me was empty apart from a single metal chair with a small table beside it. When my eyes landed on what was on the table I froze. Then my gaze drifted across the floor.

Blood.

I stepped back, shaking my head, trembling from head to toe. The Clerics grabbed my upper arms when I tried to plant my feet. I screamed. A wad of stinking cloth was stuffed into my mouth, forcing my jaw open, then another tied over to keep it put when I tried to spit it out. Within moments, my jaw was dry and aching from my muffled shrieks.

I was thrown into the chair and the iron shackles hooked into iron rings on the floor. The metallic smell of blood wafted off the instruments beside me and I consciously leaned away, pressing my head into my shoulder. I was strapped in with leather belts across my waist, chest and legs. The iron chains were arranged in a way that kept my hands lashed down to the chair arms, palm up.

Oh gods, this was bad. I'd fallen into ghastly situations before, but this was really bad.

I tried to look brave. Tried to look unaffected and bold, but the rise and fall of my chest gave away the fact I was completely terrified.

A figure stepped into the low doorway. His face was shadowed, but I could see he had big arms and calves. Wisps of curly hair had drifted out from beneath his crimson cloak, which flapped with each step against the back of his thighs. His black boots were buckled up to his knees, and his funnel-like sleeves fell over his hands. He stepped forward and I met the familiar but cold stare trained on me, flinching when anger sparked in their depths.

"You may not fear us now," he murmured, voice thick with emotion. "But you will. You may think you will not give up the rest of … your kind, but you will. You may think because you heal that our cuts," he hissed the word, "won't hurt so badly."

My eyes drifted closed. He would not see me cry. I had once thought this man to be the best of humanity, thought him kind, honourable, and good. Now as I looked into his face, I saw nothing but death. So I closed my eyes and thought of Breandan. I would focus on the good, clean things.

A sharp slap to my face had my eyelids slamming open.

"Pay attention, demon," Cleric Tu spat.

I flushed in anger, feeling welts stinging my cheek where he had slapped me. I fought the reaction to burst into tears; so derogatory was the blow. Instead, I glared at him and let loathing twist my expression into something inhuman.

"Yes. That's right." He leaned down and placed his hands on my forearms, squeezing me painfully. "Show us the creature beneath the magic. It makes my job a whole lot easier. Do you know our slashes, our stabs, never used to do much good? They never did hurt you fairies for long." He picked up a pair of pincers. Blood and bits of flesh crusted the tips. "Yes, I know what you are. The wings make it a bit obvious," he finished dryly. He brought the instrument inches from my face until it was all I could see. So strong was the smell I could almost taste the rotting skin stuck to the clamping end and beneath it the sharp scent of iron had my stomach crunching painfully. "Well let me tell you that in the last century of survival we've gotten extremely gifted at making our cuts hurt like hell."

A Cleric out of my line of sight slammed the door closed.

I wish I could say it was dark from then. In honesty, I had hoped I would black out from panic then repress any memories too painful to recall.

But I was conscious and aware throughout the entire ordeal. Surely, I screamed for days down in that white box? But no matter how hard I screamed his name, no matter how hard I tried to call him to me, he never came. Then I screamed for somebody, anybody, to save me. Each time I thought my pain had reached its peak, they would do something that would have my heart stuttering and my mind buckling under the strain. They knew how to cause maximum damage whilst keeping me conscious.

When I almost passed out they shot me with adrenaline. I had thought it was the end, was convinced the needle was full of poison that would burn me from the inside out. They jammed the thin tube of metal into my chest and my body convulsed.

When it was no longer safe to keep jump-starting my heart they would make me pop slammers until I was high, laughing as they stripped the flesh from my knuckles then brought me crashing back down with blows from fists and tasers.

My body healed, but soon it chose its wounds more carefully.

At one point, they tried to remove the circlet from my brow, but it zapped a Cleric with magic until he collapsed and they stopped trying.

The first time they sliced me open – a shallow cut to the forearm – it had healed instantly, the skin fresh and new, pinker than the rest of my skin with a faint scar where the wound had been. It was as if my body mocked them. The Clerics merely grunted and started hacking, slicing and ripping away at me until my body gave up and my blood ran over my wrists and the seat, like a waterfall, to pool on the floor about my bare feet.

I had broken bones in my body before, as a Disciple - it came with the territory of training. But it had always been accidental and a broken wrist healed fast, even if you were human. Legs, fingers, and toes broken in such a way as to cause excruciating pain were a different matter.

Always I healed, a fresh canvas for them to mutilate over and over again.

I remember thinking with a kind of horror that this

would be my fate. They would keep me in that room for an eternity and beat me senseless. Then when my body could no longer heal, its reserves used up and unable to draw power from the Source, they would kill me. The thought had brought with it a great sense of relief. I would die. They could not torment me indefinitely without giving my body sustenance. I would die, and right then I was thankful for it.

But they stopped, bringing the torture session to an end, and I was thrown back into the dungeon.

I did not realise it was over, even when iron door was slammed back into place. I noticed the absence of new pain first. Then suffered the searing agony of the wounds inflicted upon me as my weakened body tried to repair the damage.

Whimpering into the floor, I tried to feel through the bond. I was tied to Breandan in a way that defied the laws of nature. He would be able to feel my distress and he would follow me here – wherever here was – and rescue me.

I whimpered and it hurt my chest. Still he was so far.

The energy I'd gathered dissipated and I stifled a sob. Why so far? Why was he not much closer? Surely he would have realised I was gone and would feel the absence of me. Already the bond was telling me to go find him. It felt like an insatiable itch beneath my skin, a habit I needed to feed. He would feel it too, so why was he not on his way?

"Damn the gods," a tearful voice said. I heard the shifter twins' feet pad over to where I lay. I did not open my eyes; they were mostly swollen shut. "Help me get her up. Bring me that water there. Oh! Ta, Runt."

I felt my head being propped up and stale water trickled into my mouth. Swallowing was painful and after a while, I stopped and let it run down the back of my throat until my gag reflex choked me.

Amelia touched a hand to my neck, checking the strength of my pulse. "Can you move?" she asked and brushed the hair back from my face. "We don't even have a blanket to wrap you in or spare water to wipe the blood away. Your beautiful face—" her voice cut off and her breath hitched. "Your wings," she whispered.

I scrunched my eyes closed at the mention. The burning centred between my shoulder blades was reminder enough of what had been done to my wings.

There was a scratching noise and a faint shuffling, as if feet were reluctantly dragging. Then it morphed into the slap of footsteps as the person drew nearer.

I felt light pressure on my back as if someone had poked me. I felt the mildest irritation overwhelmed by fear. My eyelids jerked open and I found a last surge of energy to recoil from the figure hovering over me. The shadow squeaked and scuttled back. Runt watched me with a fear in his expression that mirrored my own.

After a moment his trembling stopped. I groped behind me until my hand connected with the curved wall. I dragged my aching body back and leaned against it. I lay my head in my knees, wrapped my arms around my shins, and bit my lip in pain as my wings curled over to cocoon me. Pockets of light seeped in through the ragged holes in the thin membrane, damage from the Clerics' knives. Rather than shining gold they looked dull brown, torn and tattered like crumpled paper.

There were no tears. My eyes were dry, but they were so itchy they burned, and my breath was raspy. A sob choked from my throat and echoed through the dungeon. I felt so pitiful and broken I didn't think I had enough strength to care that there was a strong chance the end was dreadfully near for me.

I would not have moved had he not stroked me so gently. It was as if a light breeze had disturbed my hair. I looked up and saw Runt's huge, orb-like eyes blinking at me. When I saw his long lashes were spiked, wet with tears, in an instant I held out my arms and he crawled into them to cry on my shoulder. This bony thing in my arms was more comfort that I could have imagined possible. Even so, he was like chicken wire digging into me, and I shifted a few times before I found a position that was comfortable enough to hold him.

I cleared my throat and announced to the darkness, "I know he's coming for me. Whatever's holding Breandan up is only temporary, but I can't wait. We need to think up a plan to get out of here."

"You don't think we've tried?" Nimah scoffed.

"Obviously you weren't trying hard enough," I shot back, tearfully. "We can't stay here. I can't go through … that again."

Amelia whispered, "I don't think any of us can."

We were all quiet for a long time after that. Hours passed, and we bounced ideas half-heartedly off each other, but never did our plans get us further than calling the Clerics in and fighting them. Each time we got excited, one of us would remember how easily they had subdued us before they had taken me. We couldn't get the manacles off our necks because of the iron and silver draining our strength, and picking the locks was out of the question. What were we picking them with? We would have to fight hindered by chains and with less strength than we were used to. It wouldn't work, we all knew it.

It was … strange to go from knowing I had the potential to be an unbeatable demon, to being unable to hold a one-on-one fight with a human because of some metal.

I knew in the core of me that Breandan would come for me. I simply had to survive until then.

Most of the day passed in silence.

My body healed, fixed the damage to the point where I only ached a little, but soon I stopped checking the places they had cut me. My fingers kept finding lumps and bumps of new flesh. Scars. Lots of scars riddled my skin. Feeling tears well in my eyes, my breath hitching, I stopped thinking about it.

I was alive wasn't I?

I suppose I should have been grateful for the rest, but my mind was in turmoil. Was this where they had kept Maeve when they had taken her? I would ask the twins when they woke, for now Amelia and Nimah slept, curled together, comforting each other.

Runt stayed by my side, snuffling occasionally, but was otherwise quiet. I tried to coax him into a conversation several times, but whilst it was clear he understood me, he did not talk back.

If the Clerics had tortured him like they had tortured me, I could understand that he might be mentally damaged. As far as I was aware, goblins did not heal fast, but were exceptionally strong and beast-like. Most were horribly disfigured, but Runt looked human for the most part. His ears were a little too pointy and his features a little too spacious, but passable. His lack of speech became frustrating, as I knew nothing about him, but had many questions. I remembered vaguely that Ro, a fellow Disciple and Lex's steady, had said he caught a goblin-child hiding out near a church in the slums the day before I had met Breandan. Was this the goblin he had caught? Amelia had said Runt was a half-breed. Half-human?

What was a half-human goblin doing in the middle of the slum dwells? Did he get lost? Even then, how on earth would he have gotten past the Wall? Was he left there by his demon family? How did they go undetected by the Sect?

All of these questions went unanswered since Runt would not speak to me.

Again the door to our prison was shoved open, and three Clerics filed in. Three of them ... could we manage it?

The shifter-twins shot up, instantly wide awake, alert. Runt scooted closer to me, his hand slipping into mine. My heart hammered in my chest, wondering for whom they had come.

They did not attack us this time, but the Cleric I had thought handsome did speak. "We are going outside," he said firmly then unshackled my manacle and tugged on the chain until I stood. "We're just going outside," he repeated when he did the same to the shifters.

They left Runt chained, and I opened my mouth to ask why but closed it again. We were being taken outside, but why? Intuition told me that whatever the reason, the goblin would be safer here. I swallowed hard. If staying in here was safer, what did that mean for Amelia, Nimah, and I?

When we left the dungeon, we turned and walked in the opposite direction to the white room. I consciously relaxed a tad. We were moving upward, closer to the earth's surface, I could tell. In my excitement I sped up, ignoring when the chain about my neck tugged.

Reaching the end of the passageway, the Clerics unbolted the heavy steel door and swung it open.

I hurriedly stepped through it and a cool breeze blew into my face and through the strands of my hair. I sighed in pleasure. The sun was hidden behind the clouds, and I was disappointed. Somehow, the sunlight had become stronger than the dark in my mind. I needed it to chase away the fear and pain, but even now I could not reach it.

As if the sky above was mine to command, the clouds parted and a ray of light streamed down to caress my face softly and warm me. I gasped and let my eyes flutter closed, basking in the heat and purity of it. It was dusk, the sun slowly setting, and yet I felt it had never shone brighter.

So lost in this comforting moment was I, I did not feel the clump to the back of my head until the dull throb registered.

The light cut off and for a moment it was utterly dark. But that was because my eyes were pressed closed, my body hunched, waiting for the next blow to land. I was not hit again, but pushed forward to catch up with the other two.

Sputtering fire drums were set alongside the pathway that snaked round Temple. Each one flickered, coming to life as the sun puttered out for the day. Electricity was hard to generate, and the Sect used it only when every other option was exhausted. Most light came from candles and burning wood in the fire drums. The electricity generated from the wind turbines spotted across human land kept the Wall charged.

As the Clerics led us through the main gate, my eyes darted over the Temple grounds and I felt a pang of longing for the life I had been forced to leave behind. The Wall was visible in the distance, peeking out from the forest that called to me. Outside – demon territory – was a place that had once held nothing but terror but was now, and forever, my home.

The Clerics stopped and took black hoods out from

their pockets. Nimah and Amelia glanced at each other, their hands fisted ... ready to go down fighting. I remembered that Maeve had been hooded when Devlin and I freed her after she had been taken by the Clerics. Perhaps they were going to take us through the forest like they had her? My heart tripped. It would be the perfect place and time to escape.

"It's okay," I said to the shifter twins, and ducked my own head in submission.

The handsome Cleric looked surprised, but placed the hood gently over my head. I couldn't see anything through the thick material. After a slight pause my chain was tugged gently and I moved forward carefully, planting my feet so as not to fall and choke myself. We walked up stairs, over what felt like marble floor and then down steps, across patchy grass.

I frowned, becoming somewhat alarmed.

Okay ... we were at Temple. Not outside it, or next to it, or beneath it ... but standing in the main courtyard in the centre of the main building. I had grown up in this place and I knew its layout like the back of my hand. Oh! We climbed wooden steps. This was new. I remembered the courtyard had a path through it that divided to pass around five huge boulders in the centre, before it rejoined to lead to the other side. From the dull thuds of my footsteps, I assumed we stood on a wooden platform.

The hood was pulled off my head and I blinked and scowled. Being the shortest person in the group, I couldn't see past the Clerics' broad backs. I stood on my tiptoes to see over their shoulders. I blinked again, repeatedly, stunned.

Several hundred pairs of young human eyes stared at me, and I stared back.

The Sect Disciples looked terrified and confused.

Some of the girls choked back sobs, their fear getting the better of them. They stood in formation, a sea of green blazers and heaving chests. Boy Disciples tended to leave their chests bare under the green blazers, but most wore jumpers now the days were getting colder. The girls were wrapped up too, but still rocked their blazers shorn at the elbow or tied around the waist to show off their lower stomach and back tattoos; protective marks stolen from defeated witches.

"Rae?" Ro's voice was a razor across my eardrums. I heard no hate in his voice, only pain and loss.

Skin milky-brown, his ebony hair was plaited back in thick cornrows. His black-rimmed eyes always looked over large in his lean face, and his blazer hung open to show his naked chest, belly piercing, and slum-tribe marks. His jeans were worn and slashed at the knee, boots scuffed and unlaced.

He looked confused.

Cleric Tu paced in front of the Disciples. "The best lessons are those learnt in action. There is only so much the Sect can teach from behind a desk." He pointed to a clear box behind him. "This is the cage."

It stood twenty feet tall and thirty wide on the wooden platform we stood on. There was a small panel with buttons fixed to one side and wires trailing down into the floor. I squinted; I could see a faint outline of a door. A door powered by electricity, why? And, well, that was it. It was just a box of glass. Okay....

"Here you will learn what you must face Outside. Once a month, on Demon Day, you will face our greatest enemies. You will learn exactly how terrifying it can be to fight these creatures." He spun and jerked his chin toward the shifter twins. "We'll use one of them first."

The crooked nosed Cleric dragged Amelia by her

chain. He punched a code into the keypad and the glass door smoothly slid up. I knew in the past humans had made wondrous mechanical things, and I had to admit I was grudgingly fascinated. The Cleric pushed a hesitant Amelia into the glass box, and made quick work of shackling her in the centre. She shot worried looks around her, not quite sure what was going on. The Cleric left the box but the door remained open.

"Change, demon," Cleric Tu barked.

Amelia bared her teeth and launched herself at him, only to come to the end of her chain and bounce back. She strained forward, and I could see the frisson of fear and panic in her actions. Sighing, the crooked nosed Cleric unhooked his baton from his belt.

Cleric Tu motioned to her with his hand. "Change," he repeated.

I wanted to yell at her to do what they said, but I saw the resolution in her eyes and watched as her jaw set in determination. She stepped back and crossed her arms, daring him to make her.

Nimah was going ballistic beside me, but the silver stopped her from getting far or doing more than growling and cussing. The Cleric jabbed Amelia in the back and she jolted. The second blow stunned the back of her legs and she stumbled, but held her ground. The Cleric glanced back at Tu who nodded his head solemnly. The Cleric set to work, jabbing her in the back, thighs, and arms. Amelia tried to out-manoeuvre him. She pummelled her fists on the wall, shrieking. She raced around the box, looking for an out as he chased after her.

Gasps of horror from the watching crowd drifted over the sound of Amelia's pain, and a few Disciples openly sobbed.

Ro's eyes were locked on me, considering, vacant. In

discreet bouts, his eyes roamed the space around me, but when he did not find who he was looking for they came back to me. I knew who he looked for and it killed me that he would never see her again.

A shrill cry snapped my attention back to Amelia. She hunched over, limbs and muscles quivering. The Cleric backed away, his job done.

"No!" Nimah cried.

Amelia screamed, not mentally prepared for her shift, and her scream turned into the piercing yowl of a cat as her mouth lengthened into a maw and her arms and legs shortened, spine popping and rippling. Her clothes tore to ribbons as her body grew in mass and density. There was a petrified screech from the crowd as Amelia grew a tail and sprouted ochre fur. Fully shifted into her cougar form, she snarled.

Though she was larger than some of the shifters I had seen on the Pride, her face most resembled the smaller felines that humans kept as pets. Scratching at the glass, her patchy white underbelly pressed into the cage as she drew herself up on her back legs, large rear paws prancing to keep her balanced. Repeatedly she pounded on the glass with her heavy forepaws from a higher level. She was enraged, half mad, as she paced the box and threw herself bodily into the walls. Each time she tried to leap out of the open door, her chain stopped her. Her tail, covered in short fur – dark as if dipped in ink, thrashed back and forth.

I could feel how pissed she was.

Cleric Tu turned round to face the shaken Disciples. "See. Do you see the monsters they are?"

"Stop it," I said. "You're scaring them."

Despite the softness of the plea, the whole courtyard fell silent. Cleric Tu's shoulders hunched but he quickly straightened and barrelled into the silence. "I have spoken to the Priests," he said in a jarringly calm voice. "They have agreed these sessions will benefit you in the weeks to come."

"You can't do this," I choked, horrified.

"I need a volunteer," he said. "I need one of you to come up here and show this abomination," his finger jerked to the cage, "exactly who the superior species is." There was silence, no movement. "I know you're frightened, and I know it seems barbaric—"

"That's because it is," I said through my teeth.

He ignored me. "This needs to be done. You have been protected at the cost of lives." His voice broke and I knew he thought of the Lady Cleric who Tomas drained because he was hungry after waiting for me in Bayou dorms. Maybe I would have felt bad about that if she hadn't been on a mission to kill me for just existing. "You have forgotten that every day we have to fight to stay alive, that we are trapped behind a fence that no longer keeps the danger away. These monsters have even managed to infiltrate the Temple." His finger swung to point at me accusingly. "This demon hid in plain sight for years. Had the gall to leech off our resources as she plotted to kill us one by one."

I made a noise that crossed a snarl with a groan. It was an odd sound I was mildly embarrassed to have made. "That's a lie." My hands fisted in anger. "If I had wanted to kill you, you'd be dead. In your case, I'm looking forward to rectifying that mistake."

My words were nothing but the truth. I had never meant to hurt anybody. I wanted to protect them.

His hands beat on his chest. "Even now she stands there and threatens me."

"Because you're a fool. You're trying to brainwash

them into thinking they have no choice but to be murderers."

"Who are you going to believe? The lies of a demon, one of them? Or me, your teacher, your protector."

"More like a rambling madman," I snapped, trying to get my point across. "Gods, can't you see you don't have to listen to him."

I realised then what they saw: wild hair, talons for fingers, the wings of a dragonfly fluttering at my back as my tail thrashed from side to side in agitation. They were not seeing me, Rae. They saw a demon, something to fear and mistrust. I pulled on my glamour, making myself look human, but it was a foolish thing to do. They had already seen the true me.

"See!" Cleric Tu screeched and pointed at me. "See how they deceive us."

Uneasy murmurs rippled through the crowd.

A Disciple I recognised, Jono, stepped forward aggressively, pushing his glasses up the bridge of his nose, but Ro's beefy arm shot out to halt him.

His expression was cold, hard. "I'll do it," he said quietly.

With slow deliberate steps, Ro walked up to Cleric Tu. His low-slung jeans showed a strip of boxer. Ro always had been ripped, but the idea of him going against a were-cougar was ridiculous. He passed by me, and I clasped his upper arm. I felt a prick of disgust; after all he was a human and I had no connection to him other than I knew my best friend had once loved him. But there was something else too, something darker lurking beneath the surface.

"You're making a mistake." I looked him in the eye, pleading with him to see reason. "This won't end well."

Ro tugged his arm from my grasp and got up in my

face. "You need to keep your hands off me, freak."

Shocked, I stepped back, truly taken aback by the hate in his gaze.

Turning his head he spat in disgust then turned away to look at Cleric Tu, who offered him a baton and a gun. "The demon is chained with silver. End this threat."

I blanched.

Ro pushed the weapons aside. "Don't need them to put the hurt on her."

He flexed, rolling his head round. He walked round the glass box, checking Amelia out. Still chained by the neck she did nothing but sit silent and still, her eyes filled with crisp intelligence, watching him as he watched her.

Was there a way I could stop this? I was outnumbered, and to be honest, I was afraid. The crowd looked at me with open fear and distrust. I had never been popular, had always been the oddball, but never had such loathing been directed my way. My being was sensitive to the hostile vibe pulsing from the crowd. The smell of fear was pungent, upsetting. My nature cried out, nudging me to make it right even as my mind sought out Breandan again, seeking the comfort of him. He was still far away, still closed from me, though I knew he was unharmed… wherever he was. I pulled myself back to the now.

I had to do something, not just for Amelia but for Ro too. He may not want my help but he was going to get it. I owed Lex that much at least. I may die a prisoner, unable to avenge her life, but I could at least ensure that someone she cared about was kept safe.

Ro was led into the box. Amelia did not move though I saw a tightening of her muscles. Ro bent his knees, keeping himself on the balls of his feet, his gaze locked on the demon before him. Ro was not a small boy. Easily topping six foot, he was well built and probably weighed four of me. He knew how to handle himself. Not only did the Disciples naturally have stronger, faster, and more resilient bodies and minds, training at the Temple was designed to hone these skills, to turn them into hunters and stalkers that could go toe to toe with demons in a fair fight.

Even so, the Sect had not seen the true might of the demons they so feared.

In reality, I knew if I were in a fight with Ro, I could eviscerate him with my hands, or simply end him with magic, should I be so inclined. I snorted. If I could touch the Source or focus for long enough, that was. In my iron-poisoned state it would be a fair fight. Likewise, Amelia was drained by silver and her reactions would be sluggish, slower than normal.

Shifters possessed the same strength and mental capabilities as a human, and when Changed they had the same power as their animal form. I had no doubt that Amelia or Nimah could meet other cougars in the wild and beat them, but it would be a case of higher intelligence rather than strength. If they ever came head to head with a bear, say, they may have a hard time of it.

But what I was looking at was not a cougar, but a young girl who had been beaten, humiliated, publicly flogged, poisoned, and now was being forced to fight a boy who was blinded by hate.

"Stop this." It was a command. I was done being nice. "Now."

Cleric Tu smirked. "And what are you going to do?"

"You have no idea what I am capable of."

"We captured you easily enough." His eyes flicked over my circlet thoughtfully. "You're important to them, aren't you? They'll come for you."

Knowing he was after information, I gritted my teeth

and said nothing.

He sneered and crossed his hands over his chest. "I'll take your silence as a 'yes', shall I? Good. I want them to come. It is long past time we rid ourselves of your kind."

"It's people like you that make it difficult to defend the human race," I spat. "You're pathetic. Let them out of that cage, now."

Tu paced forward and pressed his nose to mine. "Or what?" His eyes were wild, glazed. His hand snaked out grab my throat and tugged me closer. My entire body shuddered in disgust and I jerked my head away. He tipped his head to whisper in my ear. "You should be more concerned about what will happen to you once you're thrown back in your hole. I wonder how long it would take before I got you to show me your wings again."

Icy-cold fear clutched my heart before it was replaced by a burst of rage, hot, blinding rage that whiplashed across my frayed emotions.

"What's this?" There was a heavy pressure at the back of my neck then a snap. Cleric Tu held my amulets in his fist, frowning at them.

I reacted before any thoughts of caution had been formed.

A trickle of my magic, gathered from being outside in the sun, released in a punch of light and heat. The chains unravelled from my hands and my neck, and coiled on the floor. My glamour dropped as I lunged forward, and a powerful beat of my wings added crushing force to the impact as I pushed Cleric Tu off the platform, flat on his back. Someone screamed. Straddling him high on the chest, my hands found his neck a moment later and I squeezed.

"My binds, Rae,' Nimah ordered. "Quick, before

they...."

I refused to hear her. I had no other thought than to rip this man's head from his shoulders.

I lifted his head a fraction from the floor and bashed it down.

His hands scrabbled at mine as his lips turning blue. I sank my fingers in, satisfied when my talons pierced his skin and warm blood trickled over my fingers. I found it difficult to keep him down since I was still weak from the iron, but my rage and the reviving flare of magic was enough so that we were evenly matched.

The blow to my head knocked me sideways and sent me sprawling. Recovering, I rolled up onto all fours and shook my head, hissing when a boot slammed into my side. Another landed on the middle of my back, forcing me down to the ground and pushing my face into the cold concrete.

"That's enough for today," Cleric Tu said jumping up, a hand on the back of his head, face red. "Separate her from the others and call the Priests. We have work to do."

CHAPTER FIVE

Chained, I was dragged kicking and screaming back down into the tunnel, feeling my strength being leeched away by the hostile environment.

The humiliation didn't stop there; they took my clothes. Embarrassed, I pulled my glamour on and felt less exposed.

I still had some magic left and I tested it unsuccessfully on the objects around me. It seemed I could heal and use my glamour, but I could not make my magic work on anything else tainted by iron. I tried to get my manacle to fall from my neck again but nothing happened, my magic dissipated the moment it touched the iron. My stomach sank. I had wasted my one shot on Cleric Tu.

Thrown into an even smaller hovel than before, my chains were clipped onto iron rings on the floor. As the Two Clerics set to guard me worked, I saw Amelia – still in cat form – being forced down the passageway too, the Clerics jabbing at her with batons. Nimah was behind her cussing and swearing at them, dragging her twin back by the scruff of the neck so she wouldn't be hurt.

"Tell him what he wants to know."

Startled, I jumped back into a defensive crouch.

The handsome Lord Cleric I remembered from before

peered at the wall with a hard expression. The other one had left and it was just him … how brave. He tugged off his wide-brimmed hood revealing dirty blonde curls and a neatly trimmed beard. His eyes – plain brown and wholesome – darted to me then back to the wall. He cleared his throat, hands behind his back. "He won't stop hurting you until he's heard whatever answer he is looking for, so just tell him."

I eyed him distrustfully then muttered, "What do you care?"

His face creased in pain, turning to me a fraction. "You think I like being ordered to torture young women? I don't."

I blinked. It had not occurred to me that some of the Clerics might object to our treatment here. Still wary, I made no move to approach him but relaxed, seeing he was not going to strike me. "Then why are you following him?"

"To survive," he replied simply.

Glancing over his shoulder, he slipped a hand into his crimson blazer and pulled out a bread roll. He placed it on the floor and stepped back, pointing at it. Scooting forward, I plucked it from the floor then skipped back.

He gave me a small smile. "What's your name?"

"Rae," I croaked, choking up at his kindness.

He nodded. "My name is Samuel." He sighed. "Look, I'm not much of a thinker, and there's nothing special about me apart from the fact I fight well, but I like to think I am a good judge of character." He paused. "I don't think you're evil, or out to get me. I just think…." He smiled. "Well, thinking is not my strength so I'm going to stop now, but you need to understand that you're in a bad situation here, Rae. I know you used to be a Disciple, I remember seeing you, and honestly, I can't tell if you were planted here to spy on us or not." He shrugged. "But somehow I don't think so. He glanced over his shoulder again. "I better go. Tu has called the Priests to Council, and I need to be there."

My head snapped up. The Priests only assembled in Council in times of great danger. "Why?" I demanded.

He watched me carefully, shrugging, as if thinking it couldn't hurt to tell me. "To persuade them to evacuate the Temple. He believes that more of your kind are coming for you, that you're special."

Looking away, I rubbed my nose and tore into the bread roll. Here our conversation stalled, because I could no longer lie.

Samuel left without another word.

Exhaling, I moved into a corner and sat down. I was tired, irritable, and even worse I was dying to pee, so I crossed my legs and thought of all the horrible things I would do to Cleric Tu once I was free of this awful place.

Feeling the empty space around my neck, I stifled a sob. I had lost the amulets, the key to the grimoire. The thing I was supposed to protect above all. Resting my head on my knees, I wallowed. I can't say how long I sat there wallowing, but there was a sound at the door, and for what seemed like the millionth time, I struggled with the chain at my throat. I was naked, filthy, and covered in bruises, but if I could get this damn thing off, I could try to get past them. Maybe Samuel had come back to talk. Perhaps, I could tell him everything and persuade him to help me, to show me how to escape.

The door opened and a faint light spilled in, lighting a patch of the cold floor.

Helpless, I curled into the corner and rested my forehead on my knees, refusing to look up. I would not give them the satisfaction of seeing me cry or wail. I felt the person step closer, the pent up anger inside me threatening to lash out, so I shied away, hugging the wall. My chains clinked. I would show no emotion.

A blanket was draped over my shoulders and the manacle around my neck fell to the floor.

I started, then curled myself tighter. It was a trick. They were trying to show me kindness to learn something. I would not be fooled. I was wrapped up tightly, scooped up, and carried away.

We moved from the room of nothing into the narrow passage that was lit with candlelight.

Gah, I bet I looked like hell.

I did not recognise the scent of the person carrying me, nor his bouncy gait.

My eyes were still closed and with a measure of terrible hope, I realised I was no longer bound with iron. My feet and hands were free and my senses were already stretching. Slowly, my body was repairing itself, though I knew it would be some time before I was ready to exert any real effort.

My eyes flickered open and I gasped.

Ro only faltered one step when he saw I was watching him. I had not spoken or made any other noise, but possibly it was because I had stopped breathing and my face was turning blue that he looked concerned.

Gently, he set me down on the floor and quickly turned to drag an unconscious Cleric by the dirty boot heels into the dungeon. He shouldered the door closed, bolted it, and breathed out in a breathy rush with a hollow chuckle.

He picked me back up and continued on.

After a minute of heavy silence, he asked, "You right, Rae?" He did not look at me, just kept his eyes on the tunnel up ahead. Twice he looked over his shoulder into the shadowy passage behind.

I did not say a word. I wanted to, of course, but more than likely, my mouth would get me into trouble. It seemed – from his shifty eyes, uneasy disposition, and Cleric-stashing escapade – that Ro was in the middle of some kind of rescue attempt. But how did he know where I was being hidden? And why was he rescuing me in the first place? I was a demon, and to him that meant I was bad. The enemy. When I had tried to reach out to him before he'd called me a freak.

"I won't hurt you. I'm here to help, read me?" He patted my back soothingly.

I tried hard to be sensible, but my mouth won. "Why are you doing this?" I asked in barely a whisper. My throat was raw and my mouth parched.

"Because it's the right thing to do. And I always liked you, Rae. You freaky, and that's nothing but truth, but Lex is right when she say you have a good heart."

Gods be damned. He had said her name, and my tears were instant.

"Don't cry," Ro said, panicked. "You be safe now. I hate when a female cries. Rips at my insides, eh."

I sobbed in heaving gasps. The gods knew I did not need to waste any more body fluids, but I could not stop. Hearing the way he spoke had thoughts of Lex hammering at my heart. It was too much. I had not saved her, I had not avenged her, and now I was putting the boy she loved in danger. There could not be a worse friend than me.

Ro kicked the metal door ahead of us fully open. It was already bent back and swinging off its hinges and we came out into the forest just beyond the Wall. Who had done that to the door? There was more than one exit to the passageway? It was sunset, yet the fading light was enough to have my nature wiggle in joy.

I breathed in deeply, enjoying the smell of earth and green things. Ro trotted forward and fell into a brisk jog.

I closed my eyes and looked for Breandan. He was still far away, closer than before, but still far. I could not understand it. Why had he not come for me?

There was no point trying to feel for my vampire-boy. The darkness and blood tie we shared seemed to work a lot differently to the bond I had going with Breandan. When we were close I could perceive him better, understand him. When I dreamed, the darkness took me to him, allowed me to be with him even as I rested. But once he had died for the day the connection was almost totally silent. Dead, like he was, unless he sought me out. I had two demon-boys who claimed to want me, yet neither of them had come to save me. The steady of my best friend who died by my foolish actions was the only one who had risked it all.

Clearly, the gods were laughing at me.

"Do you want me to take her?" asked a hushed voice at Ro's side.

"I'm cool."

"Say-so," she whispered. A pause. "What happened to her skin? Why is she covered in–"

Heartbeat kicking into overdrive, my eyes popped open and darted to where the well-known voice spoke.

My heart stopped.

Shrieking in fear, I launched myself out of Ro's arms and landed crouched in front of them, unable to process what I saw. Scuttling back, I dropped my glamour and my wings jack-knifed out. I blinked rapidly and shook my head, my hands out in front of me to warn them back. The world had a slightly purple hue, and some things were difficult for me to see but I knew my eyesight was not deceiving me.

I could smell Ro, a boyish mixture of sweat and cotton. The she-being watching me with a steady, unblinking gaze was scentless. Seeing a look he did not like on my face, Ro drifted in front of her protectively.

Rolling her eyes, she pushed him out the way and he had to fight not to topple over from the force of it. "Hai, Rae," she said so softly my ears twitched and strained to hear her. "You call and I come."

Dominating her flawless oval face, sad eyes over-scored by thin eyebrows locked on me. The colourless tumble of hair waving around her shoulders – the strands translucent – was wild and bristled. Her hair was the most animated thing about her, everything else was stone still, unmoving. Her body was bare apart from some clever concealment with large green leaves and lashings of green vine. Her toes and fingers were tipped with crystal-clear ovals for nails. Her skin was immaculate, white like a stick of chalk and devoid of a single imperfection, as if someone had bleached all colour from her skin. When I said nothing she stuck her sapphire tongue out and her lips pouted. Such lips. Plump and sharply dipping at the cupids bow, the cold blue was striking. On a human, it would be the blue of death. Water droplets glistened on her exposed skin and adorned her hair like diamonds. Her body emitted no warmth so water simply rested on her.

What freaked me was that in fairy form I could sense another demon's consciousness, rather their auras, especially this close, but I got nothing from the being in front of me. Nothing, simply a blank space where my eyes told me something ought to be. My ears strained to hear her, a heartbeat, an intake of breath. There was nothing. She was empty space encased by lifeless flesh.

She stepped forward, gliding as if on invisible wheels. I

sucked in a series of gasps, but did not move, glued to the spot. She stopped and leaned over slowly, her eyes watching me carefully, and pressed her lips to my cheek. I touched the spot in shock. She was so cold, colder than a vampire, and that was saying something.

"You won't say hai to me?" she whispered and her eyes welled with blood. The intense colour was rich and vivid against the starkness of her colourless expression. Her face scrunched up oddly as she tried to stem the flow, but streaks of red ran down her cheeks, contrasting with the blue runes that prettily decorated her cheekbones. Those tattoos used to look sky blue, but now against her washed-out skin they looked electric.

"Alex?" I asked quietly, not trusting my voice. "Lex is that you?"

"Whom else you make a zombie?" she replied quietly, laughing faintly, hiccupping half way through as she controlled herself.

I was horrified, yet already a bubble of happiness exploded in my chest, and had me choking back a sob of joy. "Oh my gods, it worked? I mean, it worked."

Her lips twitched then pulled up into a smile. "I was surprised too. The last thing I remembered was demons chanting then a pain at my throat." Her hand wandered to the area where a faded maroon-coloured scar marred her chalk-white skin. "Then it was dark and warm. Peaceful. But I ... I jolted and fell for forever until I hit the floor." She smacked her palms together and I flinched. "I opened my eyes and was me again," she paused, looking lost, "but not me. I didn't have a body to move anymore." She shook and her face twisted with madness. "Then I swear, Rae, I have memories of things that I've seen and done. But, I couldn't have because ... I was dead, you feel me?" Her eyes glowed red, angry. "I don't know what they are, but they aren't mine, these memories."

Ro placed a hand on her cheek, on her shoulder to draw her away from me. He hushed her and whispered calming things in her ear. She relaxed against him and stopped shaking.

"Lex I–"

"I woke up in a coffin of dirt and leaves," she said over me. "Demons were close, but I was afraid. I did the only thing I could. I ran away and I ... I answered the call."

"What call?" I asked, confused.

She shrugged. "You called me. I woke up, this time in my body, and clear as a bell in my head I hear you asking me to save you. I wasn't sure what I was doing at first." She frowned deeply, her face darkening. "Everything was confused, and I was tired. I wandered, avoided living things, but I could not understand why. Then I came to the Wall and had no way around. I climbed over it–"

I spluttered, "You– You climbed...."

"That's when I knew I be dead, and that I was zombie. My mama told me the only thing that could touch the Wall and not be harmed was the Trapped."

Head spinning, I struggled to understand. "But when you didn't wake up I thought I'd failed. I thought ... Breandan thought he stopped me in time."

In a move that blurred in quickness, she trawled her fingers through her hair in agitation, her movements abruptly jerky and restless. "These memories ... they are not mine. They be yours. And it's not just memories, but feelings. When you said Breandan's name, my heart just–" Her gaze flicked to Ro who smiled broadly.

"This be the boy we saw outside Demon Theory, yeah? Nice."

I scowled at him.

Lex rolled her eyes, but spoke to me. "I think you had my soul, Rae. You carried it with you. And when the Sect caught you and started to … experiment … you released me somehow." She shrugged. "I woke up then and followed your call. Maybe you called other people too."

I looked at Ro. "How did you get involved?"

He bumped his two fists together repeatedly and frowned. "She was wandering around the Temple, looking for you. When I found her I didn't know…." He shook his head and made a funny noise, clucking his tongue to the roof of his mouth. "So many lies. I'm not who you think I am." He looked me in the eye and smiled half-heartedly. "I am Vodoun, and when I found her I knew what she was, what she had become. I didn't know who'd done it to her … she wouldn't talk to me at first. She just stared like she was trying to work out why she wasn't putting the hurt on me. I hid her in North House basement and was planning to take her back to the slums when night fell. Then the Clerics dragged you out in front of the Disciples." He smirked. "Didn't need to think on it much after that to figure it out. I was terrified she would try to help you and get caught. So … I agreed to fight the shifter thinking I could knock her out and save her. Then I told Lex what happened and she spoke to me." He looked at her. "When I told her you were at Temple, alive, the light flickered on behind her eyes and she whispered all quiet like, 'Fairy'." He chuckled. "Then she started ordering me about, and I couldn't get her to shut up or be calm until I agreed to go get you."

Rubbing my circlet then pushing the hair off my face, I breathed out. "That is one messed up story, Ro. Do you realise what might have happened if Amelia had managed to get your neck between her jaws, or if she'd swiped a claw too deep into your stomach? Do you not have the faintest clue of the risk you took coming to get me?"

He punched my shoulder. "I got your back."

I yanked on a clump of my hair, convinced I was going to scream in the face of how nonchalant he was about risking his life.

"We must keep moving," Lex said tonelessly and walked off in that strange fluid glide.

I hesitated, looking back over my shoulder. "I have friends back there. People I have to help."

She drifted on. "They will be rescued by the fairies when they come looking for you."

"Uh, but Breandan can feel where I am. If he senses I have moved on, he won't wait to check. We can't abandon them."

She stopped and spun to face me. I blinked because her features blurred together she moved so fast. "I don't want to fight," she replied stiffly. "I want to go far away from that place. It feels bad now. I want us to survive."

"It's just Temple."

A flash of something close to rage flitted across her doll-like face. "It feels bad now, something evil is happening there and I don't want to go back."

I hissed. "Well, I am."

Lex shrieked, the sound high, jarring, and deranged. I jumped, my mouth dropping wide even as her hands flew to her cheeks. Her face crumpled and her eyes welled with blood again. Gods, she was creepier than Tomas.

Ro approached her with care. "It's all good," he said soothingly.

"You'll take care of me?" she whispered and walked into his arms. It was beautiful to see, her chalky skin against the milky brown of his.

He hugged her to him. "I promise."

The sun winked out of sight and I jolted as Tomas awakened. He was close. Dreadfully close. I could almost imagine him crawling out of his resting place and coughing up dirt.

But one thing I didn't have to imagine was the distinct feeling of him getting closer, the darkness swelled.

He was coming for me.

"Uh, guys," I said not sure how to put this delicately. "How do you feel about vampires?"

Ro made a noise of disgust and derision.

Lex straightened. "Tomas is coming?" she asked with a shadow of a naughty grin on her face.

It was so like how she used to be, I smiled back as I asked, "How?–"

"I told you, memories and feelings. This thing you have with him is dark and complicated," she said solemnly. "And really weird, just saying. You should be careful the darkness doesn't– " Cutting off, both she and Ro took a step back, their gazes fixed over my shoulder.

Cold lips pressed onto the back of my neck. My hair was pushed aside to fall over my shoulder as Tomas ran his mouth up the side of my neck, breathing in. His hands slid under the folds of the blanket I was wrapped in and travelled gently over the bruises covering my hips and sides.

"How much do you hurt?" he asked.

"It's bearable," I replied breathlessly. "I'm healing."

He turned me in his arms so I faced him. I stared hard at his chin, avoiding his eyes, not wanting to see my reflection in them, afraid to connect.

He waited patiently.

The silence deepened and stretched on. Instead of becoming comfortable, it rubbed me up and unsettled me to the point tears threatened to fall.

I noted he wore all black again, right down to his boots.

"Do you take your clothes off when you sleep?" I blurted then blushed and stammered to apologise. "I mean, I just thought … it makes sense you'd be naked since your clothes would get muddy, and yours aren't. But don't answer." I waved my hands; still I had not looked past the smooth column of his neck. "I'm sorry."

Soon, my gaze drifted up, over his strong square jaw, firm, wide lips, and sharp cheekbones. I paused at his crooked nose that should have been repulsive, but instead was dear to me. His skin was ashy, pale, and cold-soaked. I could feel the frosty temperature seeping through the blanket, and I shivered at the contrast to my natural heat. Finally, I reached his eyes that glinted beneath his jutting brow and broad eyebrows. His coal black hair was swept back off his high forehead and was cut close at the neck.

He swallowed hard, and I watched his throat bob. "When I sleep in the ground … yes it is more comfortable and practical to sleep without any clothes. I simply hide these nearby until I need them." A strange expression flittered across his face. I would have said it was embarrassment but he was a vampire, and they were beyond such petty emotion. So I will say he looked enamoured of the idea of feeling bashfully discomfited. "Sleeping in the earth is an experience I would like to share with you," he said formally.

Unable to find a suitable response, I cleared my throat, and rubbed my nose.

Tomas slowly unwrapped the roughly woven blanket, and, without taking his eyes from mine, wrapped it tighter around my torso. He tugged off his shirt, ruffling his hair and making him shake his head to smooth it down, then handed the thin, black material to me wordlessly.

I took it from him, my fingers brushing his. "Ta," I murmured.

His head tilted with the slightest inclination as he stepped around me. "Turn around," he said to Lex and Ro, whom I assume did so without question, as I heard no argument from either of them.

I dropped the blanket, glad to be rid of its itchy confines, and paused, realising how ridiculous it was to be stark naked in a forest at night. But instead of feeling abashed, I felt outlandishly liberated. Pulling on my glamour, my hearing, sense of smell, and range of vision were muted as a blanket of magic transformed me into human form. I scrunched up my nose; never had I thought I would miss my tail and wings.

Leaves crunched underfoot as Tomas walked back round to stare at my face. "Rae?"

I was simply not bold enough not to blush, and I clutched the shirt to my chest. "Turn around."

"No."

I blinked, fighting a smile. "Uh, turn around please?"

"I find I like looking at you." His eyes flicked down and he grinned, all toothy, his fangs somewhat extended.

I glanced behind me and found Ro and Lex were steadily walking through the trees back towards Temple. Lex looked like a floating ghost as she passed in and out of sight behind the broad trunks.

Tomas touched my collarbone. My heart kicked and sped up. I tried hard to slow it down, but it was a useless task when his hands were on me, and I fidgeted when his smooth palm travelled over my stomach, traced my waist, and settled on my hip.

Being with Tomas wasn't like being with Breandan, not at all. I felt bold and confident when he looked at or touched me. I could relate to him. He wasn't perfect like

Breandan was … he was flawed, like me.

He pulled me closer and leaned over to murmur in my ear, "Do you remember how you felt when I held you like this before?" His hands were busy, and my mouth went dry remembering how I had felt the first time he kissed me in my dorm at Temple.

I dragged in a shuddering breath, experiencing tunnel vision. "I will never forget." The tunnel suddenly glowed silver and where the edges of the world had gone blurry, everything snapped back into focus. "But Brean—"

With a snarl, I was shoved back until I hit the dirt, Tomas over me. He was furious and I felt a prickle of fear quickly replaced with a surge of lust as his hand swept over my stomach.

"Do not say his name." He kissed me, full of fire and anger. I felt a sharp prick on my tongue and he sucked. He pulled away, quivering, and his fangs ran out. "You know you want me not him."

As I looked into his eyes, I felt something within me stir. It resisted the passion I felt and prickled my insides as if hands with sharp nails scored my heart. I wanted him? Yes, I wanted him, but did I feel for him enough to turn my back on Breandan? I knew it was a possibility, but my mind shied away from it. No … I knew what I wanted. The prickling at the back of my mind became a sharp pain as I pushed him away.

He resisted, frowning. "What is the matter?"

"Get off me." I wriggled from beneath him and snatched at the shirt. It pulled taut, the end caught underneath his frozen form. "Do you mind?" I yanked on it until he shifted his weight.

Hands shaking, I pulled the shirt on to cover myself. I wrapped my hands around my stomach, and took a deep breath. My body was going haywire but I did not want it to be like this. I did not want the fear of making the wrong choice to spoil my first time. I wanted to have a clear heart and conscience when I bedded the one I loved. Tomas had this way of making me forget myself. Ungh. I did not do things like this, so why when this vampire came near me did I lose all sense of self?

"You don't want me," Tomas said slowly peering up at me, his hands open on his lap. His voice was remote, cautious, but there was a trace of a question, hope.

Pushing the hair from my face, I exhaled sharply. "Gods, I'm sorry. It's just I touch you and think–"

"That you should be with him," he cut in. Well, he said it so I didn't have to. Tomas sighed and stood smoothly. Careful not to touch me he forced me to look into his bottomless eyes. "And when you are with him you think no thoughts of me." It was not a question.

I stumbled over my words, unable to lie. "That's … not true." Not entirely.

His cold fingers brushed along the outside of my arms causing the skin to goose-pimple. "Not in the way I wish you to think of me."

My instinct was to lie, but I couldn't physically bring myself to do it. I twisted my hands into the ends of his shirt and winced when it ripped a little under the strain. It was already threadbare and it smelt like freshwater and minerals. It smelt like Tomas. I fingered the fabric. "You washed your clothes?"

He nodded. "In the river."

Standing there, half dressed, in the presence of my vampire was suddenly awkward. In the time we had been apart I had taken the chance to think about my actions, and I had seen just how wrong my behaviour had been. When I had first met Tomas I'd been nothing but wary of him. Yet the spark of lust I had experienced in Bayou dorms had shown me an exciting and dangerous side to our relationship. After spending time with Breandan, I knew it was a side I no longer wished to pursue. Oh, there was desire, but what we want is not always what is good for us.

I couldn't be his girl, but I could be his friend.

Patting his chest, I kissed him on the cheek. "We will talk," I said and kissed him again before stepping back. "We'll learn everything there is to know about each other. I will help you, Tomas. I swore I would."

He did not move, blink, or speak. He became still, and I felt him withdraw from me entirely.

"Tomas?"

With a gasp, he stumbled back. His fangs were still down and his chest heaved – disturbing since Tomas didn't breathe. He placed a hand over where his heart might beat and shook violently.

"Tomas!" I was concerned now.

Not that it should have been possible, but his skin looked paler and a stain of darkness spilled from his pupils to blot the whites of his eyes black.

I hesitated, unsure why he was reacting so strangely. The darkness was no longer there in the corner of my mind for me to tug on or glean a better understanding. It was still inside me, I could feel the blood tie, but it was hidden from me. Should it be able to do that – hide away in my own consciousness?

I might have focused on how wrong that was, had Tomas not cried out and fallen to his knees.

In two steps, I was right there with him, ignoring the damp and dirt. His hands wrapped around my wrists and I did not know if he was going to crush me to him or throw me away. As it was, he simply held me then collapsed forward, his dark head resting on my lap as his entire body shuddered under the strain of his emotion.

"You choose him," he groaned and rocked back, seemingly unable to stay still.

He let his head fall back, the pale column of his throat taut with tension, moonlight streaming across his tormented expression.

His hands slipped away from me and slammed into the earth. Roaring his aggression, he beat at the ground causing the earth to shift and split open, creating shallow depressions where he pounded. My cool and rational vampire was mad with jealousy, and his resentment and hurt were palpable. When delivering blows to the ground did not ease his pain, he turned his fingers into rakes and scraped finger-wide gouges into the earth. Gutturally screaming languages and foul noises I prayed to the gods I would never hear uttered again – so evil and malignant they sounded as they rasped across my ears and tore into my soul – I trembled as he raged around me.

In the midst of his frenzy, I placed my palms on his cheeks and slowly moved my head from side to side.

"I need you to understand." I let my hand move over his head, ran my fingers through his soft hair, then gripped two fistfuls tightly. "Please."

"Why?"

I let my head drop, unable to meet his gaze as I mumbled, "It was one kiss, Tomas. It shouldn't have happened, and I'll never be sorry it did as it probably saved your life." I looked him in the eye. "If you hadn't taken my blood I probably would have let Lochlann kill you. So no, I'll never regret it, but I'm rational enough to see that whatever this is between us," I motioned to him then me, "would never work. Not when I–"

"A bond with magic is not love," he bit out harshly.

"And a bond enraptured by bloodlust is better?" I

pressed my fingers to his jaw, not trusting myself to touch him any other way. "The first moment I saw Breandan he ensnared me. I was lost before he touched me and the bond was made. Do you remember the first time we met? How terrified I was? The first time I met you I felt nothing but fear. Can't you see? Our blood tie was made from succumbing to desire not love." He tried to pull away from me, but I grabbed his hair and tugged his head back. "I am your friend, and I trust you. So don't ruin what we have by forcing me to explore a side to our relationship that is destined to fail."

Regaining some calm, he watched me silently. His fangs slid up and his eyes cleared. "Then what do you ask of me, friend?"

I winced at the coldness of his words. "I could use your help. I made a pact with an Alpha to save his daughters. They're still beneath Temple."

He blinked at me, and I could never say what passed through his mind. Taking a series of short breaths, he grunted and rose from his knees. He offered his hand.

"Come then." I curled my fingers around his and stood. I flushed when he paused and did not let go. "May I hold your hand as we catch your allies up?" he asked so politely I found myself nodding.

I was faster than him but reined my speed in so we could run side by side. It seemed my vampire could move faster than me, but only for short periods of time. I wondered why that was. Was it to do with how their bodies moved and how much blood was left in their systems? Did a lack of blood tire him like a lack of sleep and food would tire me?

"Have you eaten?" I blurted.

Tomas slanted me a look out of the corner of his eye. A felled log was in our path and instead of zipping round it like I had planned, he yanked on my hand, swept me up into his arms, and jumped over it. My heart thumped as I remembered the similar jolting sensations from when he had first carried me. He did not let me go when we touched down on the other side. He did pull me closer and look down on me with the saddest expression on his face. I used both my hands to smooth away the lines the troubled look caused, letting my fingers linger on his bold and objectionable features. How had I ever thought him ugly? He had character, and an aura of charming imperfection that only those tied to the dark could acquire.

He made a rumbling noise low in his throat and leaned down to slide his nose along my neck, inhaling deeply. I bit my lip and my eyelids fluttered.

"Rae?" Lex's voice was soft and apologetic.

Tomas set me down on my own two feet. He moved away to stand before the Wall and waited, staring at the wires with rapt attention, making me think he was not actually seeing the Wall.

My palms dampened with sweat even as my mouth went dry. I had done this before, so I could do it again. The klaxon had only gone off last time because my power had whiplashed out unexpectedly, a side effect of my exhaustion and emotional turmoil.

Lex rolled her eyes and walked over to the wires red hot with electric current. Like a spider scuttling up a web, she scaled the Wall as if it wasn't sending high-voltage bolts of electricity into her body. She vaulted over and climbed down head first, her arms and legs moving in a liquid crawl. Her colourless hair fell forward and obscured her face. When Lex reached the bottom of the steel web she walked forward on her hands, legs stiff in the air and toes pointed. With an odd jerk, her back bent and she lowered her feet to the floor. Bowed in a rigid arch on all fours, stomach facing the sky, she rolled her torso upright. She turned on her heel and waited for us, hair still covering her face like a veil until she flicked her head back.

Ro shrugged. "Whatever." He jerked his head to the wires to remind me that I was supposed to be creating us an opening.

"Can't we go through a gate again?" I asked.

Ro shook his head. "They might know we used it. They'll patrol the entry points in case we try to use one again."

It made sense. The Clerics would not risk our getting back so easily. Since our exit hadn't been scheduled no doubt they would have posted guards anyway, but with my disappearance they would also know I had inside help and would leave nothing to chance.

Without thinking about it too much, I focused my energies and sent my magic to the wires. They unravelled and pinged apart leaving a small tear big enough for us to crawl through. The edges cooled but the colour slowly faded back to deep red confirming the current still flowed. Had I ripped the entire fence in half no doubt the klaxon would go off – I would have broken the circuit completely – but this way the electricity still had a path to flow through, and the surrounding area remained blessedly silent. Ro went first, then Tomas, and I shimmied under last. I closed the tear with an easy thought tossed over my shoulder.

Between Ro and Lex's knowledge of the slums, and mine of the upper dwellings, we managed to plot an obscure path back through the human city that steered clear of the Sect Temple. We raced through the upper dwells, holding our breath and praying we would not be seen. The well-maintained homes abruptly became dilapidated huts as we crossed over into the slums.

Ro visibly relaxed the deeper into his childhood home we travelled.

The shacks were predominantly built from wonky wooden frames, filled by breeze blocks, and covered in plastic. Piles of rubbish clumped together under huge, overflowing dumpsters every twenty paces or so, and the rats that squeaked and scuttled across the floor made me grimace. Bats darted overhead and I shivered, they were worse than ravens. I was not sure when bats had been introduced to this region, but I knew they were not native. They had adapted to the climate and were bloody huge, bigger than crows, and incredibly intelligent creatures.

A young girl rummaging around in a pile of junk paused, peered at us, then grabbed a three-legged chair and trotted off, clutching it to her like a lifeline. Scavenging was the slum lifestyle, and if you were not good at it you wouldn't survive. No doubt the young girl had plans to trade the smooth wood and seat fabric for food. She had looked painfully thin and I hoped she was able to barter for enough to keep her going for a few weeks.

The slum dwellings held a mish-mash of old and new human cultures, and several colourful walls of art caught my eye as we briskly walked down the main street. It was busier here than the upper dwells, and running would draw too much attention. Most people who saw us had their own troubles, and turned their back when their eyes landed on Ro. His broad shoulders and confident gait were intimidating, and the hard expression on his young face – evaluating every dark shadow for danger – was warning enough that he was not be to messed with.

Tomas kept his head down. Lex was wedged between Ro and me, arms wrapped around her middle and back hunched. With my glamour on I looked human, horrifically scarred, but human nonetheless, and my scant clothing was nothing out of the ordinary here.

It was quiet. The darkness shielded us, and we kept close to the walls, avoiding passing too close to the fire drums that spat ash and small specks of burnt wood.

An old man, dressed in rags and crouched on the pavement, bony hands shovelling noodles into his mouth, happened to glance up. His wooden bowl clattered to the ground. His eyes went wide as he took in Lex's inhuman appearance, and his toothless mouth gaped.

Humans born here were a creamy tan in skin colour, and generally had hazel eyes and dark hair, like Ro. A tall, chalk-white girl with translucent hair and electric blue face marks was something outlandish to behold.

The old man heckled at us, and a quick look over my shoulder showed him hobbling after us, craning his neck trying to get a better look.

Tomas cursed and stopped. He spun on his heel and sped faster than the human eye could see back to the old man. He clamped a hand over his mouth and dragged him into the shadow of a building. It was quiet again. Tomas ran back to us and motioned us on. I considered asking him if the old man lived, but I didn't think I could stomach the truth.

Ro stopped at a self-contained hut with large white handprints across the fencing cutting it off from the street. Ravens circled overhead and I frowned. It was late for them to be flying, and why over this shack?

A malnourished goat was tied to a wooden post, and a wire cage was stuffed with clucking hens. The place felt wrong and I noticed mice scurrying as far away as possible to avoid passing too close. A wild cat, fur glossy and black, meowed at us from on top of the fence, and leaped over our heads to land silently on the ground, disappearing into an alleyway opposite.

I was wholly disturbed. "Where the hell are we?" I demanded.

Magic slid over my skin in an odd way. Usually I reached out to magic and called it to me, but here magics literally hung in the air, waiting to be absorbed. I took another step toward the shack and tendrils of power slipped through my body, cold fingers pushing through me, peering at who, and what I was. The invasion was nasty and I hissed.

Tomas muttered under his breath and took a step back.

Ro slid a good-humoured look at the vampire, fighting a smile. "Papa Obe is tied to the Loa. He can help us."

I had heard the name before, but like so many other people, had brushed it off. The Sect was supposed to have eradicated the Vodoun years before.

"He's a Bokor," I said, swallowing hard.

Ro chuckled darkly. "No. He's more than that."

"He calls on the spirits of the dead," I continued. "I didn't understand how that could be possible before I knew about the Source, but I've heard Voodoo is different to normal magics." I felt panicky. My nature did not like this at all. The space around me felt wrong, unnatural. I turned to Ro accusingly. "Why did you bring us here? This isn't how it's meant to be."

"And how is it meant to be, child?" The voice made me jump a mile, and I blushed, feeling heat creep up my neck and spill into my cheeks.

My vampire snarled and he reached forward to wrap his fingers tightly around my wrist.

"Ah, well, I mean, it's just that I...." I was having serious difficulty stringing a sentence together, intimidated by the person in front of us.

The man in front of me was not young nor was he particularly beautiful, but power radiated off him in waves. His face was nut brown and his hair a shock of white, eyebrows a slash of grey, His beard was neatly shaved to cover his chin and upper lip. He was dressed in a ratty black tunic and tattered jeans. His feet were bare. He was old yet had a spritely bearing. In one hand, he clutched what looked like a cane of human bone, but I could not be sure.

"I am a Houngan." He shook his open palms at the sky and the beaded bracelets on his wrists clinked and jangled together. "I serve the Loa with both hands girl. One must walk the path of light and dark to find balance. It may feel wrong to you but that is because you hold strongly to the light and see the dark as something wicked to defeat." He looked at Tomas. "Though I suspect you know something of darkness and its attractions."

My lips pressed together and I ignored that loaded observation. "The Loa?" I asked. "You speak as if there is more than one god of this name."

He made a strange clicking sound, his tongue hitting the roof of his mouth once, giving an impression of annoyance. "Even the oldest beings forget the old ways. You think in straight lines and disregard how many commune with and serve the Creator in their own way. The Loa are our link to the Great Deity, girl. Each have sacred symbols and rituals that we follow." He pointed at me. "You fairies used to have one individual who was marked with the symbols of all races and creeds. Does such a one no longer exist?"

I thought of Breandan and his marks. I had always

wondered why he had so many and what they meant. He had told me they helped him see the truth and were protection … from witchcraft and black magics.

The Houngan focused on me then smiled toothily. "I see you claimed some of what was lost." His eyes were on my chest, but then he cocked his head, as if someone had spoken in his ear. "But you have misplaced it again … oh … it has been taken?"

I touched my neck, missing the heavy weight of the amulets. "The amulets are mine now, yes. I know where they are and I'll get them back."

"And the grimoire is safe with the High Lord?"

It could not have surprised me more if he had sprouted wings. I sucked in a breath. "You know about the grimoire?"

He leaned forward face kindly now. "Of course. You fairies needed a way to keep it out of the witches' hands. My ancestor and the Mambo of that time gave you the solution, and gave it gladly. The Grand Bois – Loa of the forest – helped us craft the key, and fine work it was. The power of my people is effective against witchcraft because we dabble in the darkness witches feed from and use it against them. Who you think make the grimoire key? Fairy magics come from your connection to nature, by drawing from the Source created by the gods in the name of the Creator. You cannot hold that power indefinitely or store it in talismans. That is not how your power works." He held a hand to his chest where many chains and baubles hung. Some were pretty and others looked simply odd, made up of animal feet and bones wound together with twine and leather. "I use magic too, child, magic gifted to me by the Loa. But unlike you I cannot hold it at all. I must transfer it to objects or into spells. I am merely a conduit. That is how my power works." His head turned to Ro, and he held out his arms. "Boy, come here and greet me."

Ro broke out into a grin and slouched forward. Skipping up the steps he slung his arms around the man and thumped him on the back. "Hai, Papa Obe."

The man hugged him back and smiled broadly showing pink gums. "My boy, what you bring to me door, eh?"

Ro stood back and looked the older man in the face. "I need help." He stopped and looked over his shoulder. "And I need you to swear you won't hurt my steady."

Papa Obe rubbed his chin and eyed him thoughtfully. Though his expression was serious there was a wicked gleam in his milky orbs. "No good, Ro. There be no future with this one. Her time has come and gone. What remains belongs to that fairy there." He pointed his stick at me and I jolted as if he'd poked me with it. "It was you who call on the Loa, was it not?"

I bit my lip, nodding. "I didn't realise it was a 'them'. I just … I'd heard a rumour that Lex's Mother–"

"Mama Odette," the Houngan supplied. "She was a friend of mine. A mighty Mambo and a great force against the witches."

I shrugged. "I don't know about any of that. Lex was dying and I knew my magic couldn't save her … so I – I … looked elsewhere."

The Houngan tapped his stick onto the ground; hand tight around the knobby top. "I know, child. And the Loa answered you – a rare thing indeed. Her ancestral blood is no doubt the reason why. I hear whispers from the other side it was a gift to her mother." He looked past me into the alleyway beyond. "Won't you come out and greet an old man, girl?"

Ro started and shot Papa Obe a frustrated look. He

jumped down off the porch and jogged along to the alleyway, disappearing into the shadows. He and Lex had a short, heated conversation before he appeared again, her pale hand in his dark one. Her head was tucked into her chest, long hair covering her face, and her movement was stiff. I frowned. Usually she moved so gracefully, but now it was like she had planks of wood for limbs. She reached my side and breathed out, looking daggers at me under her colourless lashes.

I leaned closer and from the corner of my mouth whispered, "S'up with you?"

"She'll find it hard around me," Papa Obe answered. "You did not bind her to you, leaving her open to the influence of others." He tutted. "Dangerous."

I looked at Lex, took in her submissive posture and terrified expression. "You won't do anything to her will you?" Feeling less and less happy about the nefarious expression flickering across his face I stepped in front of Lex protectively. "Let's be clear from the beginning, it's not okay for you to control her, do you understand?"

The sinister look that had warred over his face was swept away by sheer delight. He laughed boomingly. "It's not me you must fear girl, but her. And them nasty witches. They could mess with your girl's mind until she loses it." He tapped his temple. "Twist her into something evil, you hear me?"

The thought of a witch using Lex for evil left me cold. My friend was in danger yet again because of my mistakes. It was bad enough I had to live with what I had done to her, that she had died simply for knowing me, but still my bad choices came back to haunt her. She had to live as a monster and now must face the fear of one day being controlled by others.

I inhaled sharply. I would not let that happen.

"Then show me how to protect her," I said fiercely. "Teach me how to use magics like you do."

He shook his head. "Too late, nothing you can do. She must guard herself."

I pulled my brows together and ran my top teeth over my bottom lip, considering what he was saying. "She is the last of her kind, a Mambo," I muttered.

"And a zombie," Ro added thoughtfully.

Papa Obe nodded. "She has the power, but I cannot teach her how to use it. I am a Houngan. The male does not teach the female." He motioned to himself then her and sighed. "Look how I run my mouth. All this talk, yet we avoid that which be most important. Why you come here, Priestess? What you want from me?"

I wanted exactly squat from this man. I looked to Ro since it was his idea.

He straightened and lopped his thumps into his jeans pockets. "I tell you I need help. We need help." He jerked his head at me. "A hideaway until her man come get her."

The Houngan laughed throatily. "You choose to come here instead of hide up inside Temple. Them Clerics figure out you are the Bokor they hunted all these years?"

Ro's lips twisted. "They know enough now."

"You come to me with the lost fairy Priestess, her vampire lover, and the dead daughter of Mama Odette?" His eyebrows rose. "You think I should let you in my home."

Ro pouted. "Had little choice, Papa."

"I know. I hear and see many things, boy." He stepped back and pointed through the door, into the darkness of his shack.

Tomas stepped forward.

"Stop!" Papa Obe's voice boomed. His hair lifted, crackling with electricity, and magic slid over my skin making me shiver. "You may not step here, vampire." His eyes rolled into the back of his head leaving white orbs with fine red webs of veins at the edges. "Something about you stinks of witchcraft."

An unexpected glint of steel appeared in Tomas' eye. "Calm yourself, Houngan."

Papa Obe's eyes rolled forward and his milky gaze switched to me. "I want to help, but you must understand that I cannot let him enter. I sense witches' darkness."

"Why?" I asked, truly at a loss. "Tomas won't hurt you, I swear it."

"Your word is your oath, but his is not." Papa Obe's head dipped down to peer at us from under his thick and short lashes. "Vampires are tricky, selfish things." He jerked his chin toward Tomas. "He cannot enter."

"He won't harm you," I said.

"No dead one can harm a servant of those who have power over life itself, child. The Loa keep me safe from their kind."

Tomas squared up to the man. "I'm here to help Rae. It is as simple as that."

"It's never that simple when it comes to your kind," Papa Obe replied evenly.

This was ridiculous. It seemed every demon had issues with any not of their kind and it was beginning to frustrate me. "Enough," I huffed, and placed my hand on Tomas' chest to firmly push him back a step while keeping my eyes on Papa Obe. "We need to get off the street. Ro brought us here because he thought we could trust you and that you could help. I want to stay, but I won't if I have to worry about Tomas roaming around out here."

The Houngan said nothing. He lowered his chin, expression dark, and slinked aside to make way.

Tomas nodded once and moved passed him through the doorway. His shoulders relaxed and he sent the older man an impatient look. "I told you I mean you no harm."

"And there was no harm in being sure," he replied. Confused, I looked between them. "No one that means me ill can enter," Obe explained and waved me forward.

Inside, magic hung in the air. It was like a constant itch between the shoulder blades you could not scratch because although you could use your arms you did not have a particular type of hand to scratch that specific itch.

The air smelt herby. Sniffing, I followed my nose and nodded in satisfaction at the fresh and dried herbs stuffed into a woven basket hanging from the ceiling. The wood floor was covered in dark sand. The grains were rough against the soles of my feet, and oddly warm.

Ro tapped my shoulder and handed me a pair of boots, dark trousers, and a sleeveless muslin tunic. Nodding my thanks, I ducked behind a woven screen in the corner and quickly got dressed. The clothes fit fine, better than Tomas' shirt, but the footwear made me unexpectedly tearful. The boots Alec had gotten me were quite lovely and these could not compare. Walking back out, I tugged at the tunic to get it to fall properly around my wings and handed Tomas back his top. I couldn't keep my glamour on any longer, I felt too constricted and weak.

The shack was one of the larger I had seen in the slums and one of the best kept. Not that it meant much when it came to the slums. Tattered, yet colourful tapestries covered every available space and were pinned onto the walls. Every flat surface or shelf was crammed with dirty glass jars and bottles cloudy with age. I leaned over to stare into the murky grey water of an open-topped jug and recoiled when I realised the white bulbous things floating in it were eyeballs. On closer inspection, all the pots held some kind of body part or other, and I began to feel faint.

Tomas looked repulsed and stood stiff as a pillar in the centre of the room, hands tight by his sides.

There were aged wooden faces, masks, tacked onto the ceiling. With gaping mouths and narrowed eyes, they were faces condemning us from above. Their eyebrows and beards were painted in garish colours. Clumps of straw lashed together with twine sprouted out of the rounded heads in the imitation of hair. Shuddering, I tore my eyes away from them. Threadbare blankets and pillows were piled in a corner. A low table was placed beside them. Abandoned dirty cups and plates had me thinking that was also where he slept and ate.

My eyes settled on the far wall. I stepped forward, my mouth parting in wonder at the beauty of it. With another step, I caught an odd vibration and stopped dead in my tracks even before Tomas reached for me. He clasped my tail and yanked it once forcing me to stumble back. He wrapped his arm around my shoulders, and there was nothing romantic about the gesture, it was born of fear.

A wide drum was by my side, its rim decorated in interesting runes. Unable to help myself I slapped my palm onto the taut surface. The sound boomed and echoed in the tiny shack. My hand stilled before it beat the dried skin again. I retracted it slowly feeling rather than hearing Tomas' snarl, and rubbed my now sweaty palm on my thigh.

"The Tamboulas won't hurt you," Ro said after a pause and leaned round me to thump it again. The sound seemed different. It still echoed, but was less powerful. Crestfallen, he shrugged his big shoulders and knelt in front of the colourful wall.

"Ro will be a fine Houngan one day." Papa Obe wagged his stick of bleached bone at him, voice accusatory in tone. "He would be already if he came home more often."

I looked again at the shrine that covered the entire back wall, though I was careful not to get too close. My nature did not like the feel of it. No matter how pleasing it was to my eye.

"What is that?" I asked quietly feeling that shouting would somehow desecrate the sanctity of it.

"The Hounfour, my place of worship. I miss the old days, when we had whole temples dedicated to veneration of Bondaye, the Creator. We honoured the gods in style." Papa Obe sighed and paused in whatever he was drawing on the floor. "But in times like these we do what we can to commune with the spirits. I pray they understand and forgive us." He bowed his head then went back to his task of scratching a pattern on the floor with his rough piece of chalk.

Lex and Ro seemed to take comfort from bending down by the Hounfour to help him. Well, it gave me the creeps so I steered clear of it, as did Tomas.

Papa Obe chucked the chalk into the corner and dusted off his hands. He plucked one of the bulging bags hanging from his neck and handed it to me with a flourish.

I bounced it in my palm. It was weighty for something so small. "What's this?" I asked curiously.

"My blood, chicken bone, cat spit, a shifter claw, and twice-burnt wood."

Horror struck, I tried to hand it back to him. "Ta, but I don't think I need this."

He smiled showing pink gums and missing teeth. "I want it back. You need to hold it for the blessing,

Priestess."

I attempted a grateful smile, but considering the sly chuckle from Ro I don't think I pulled it off.

Lex stood to one side of the shrine, her head flung back, and Papa Obe motioned Ro to stand behind me.

Tomas needed no prompting to let me go and slide out the way. He plastered himself to the wall and glowered at Papa Obe. I did not like seeing him so uncomfortable but letting him roam outside when he was so moody was not the best idea.

The Vodoun surrounded me and I felt a dart of apprehension. "Uh, what are you going to do?"

Papa Obe grinned and my skin crawled. "We're going to ask the Loa to watch over you."

The magic in the air thickened and the smell of the herbs became sharp and pungent. The hanging basket exploded into flames and dark blue smoke gathered then snaked through the air, moving like it was alive. It twisted around Papa Obe and caressed his skin. I waved away tendrils of sapphire smoke licking my neck and shoulders.

"Y'know, I'm good," I squeaked, and flapped my hands with an air of panic. "Don't, ah, bother them."

Ro thumped the drum behind me. I jumped and spun round. Lex beat another drum, and I spun again, my heart pounding erratically.

Papa Obe's eyes rolled into the back of his head and he muttered into his cupped hands, breathing in the smoke then blowing it toward me. A vine of smoke darted into my mouth. Back bowing, my head filled with empty space even as all my limbs became weighty. The smoke curled out my mouth and circled me, sliding over every inch of my skin.

The drums steadily increased in tempo. Obe opened his hands wide and wailed something in a language I did not understand. His words hammered against my ears painfully, and the increasing drumbeats had me shaking my head.

"Stop," I mumbled as I fell to my knees, but the pounding continued.

A gust of wind stirred my hair; blue smoke swirled against my legs and brushed my face.

The wooden slats of the shack rattled and the roof squeaked and clattered against the foundations. I glanced up and I swear the masks on the ceiling had changed expressions; lips curving into evil smiles and eyes becoming swirling vortexes.

I freaked out big time, and staggered across the shack with every intention of leaving. Surely, the floorboards should not look like brown snakes? Swells of sand slid in between the writing serpents and a few grains flicked into my eyes. It stung and I pressed my fingers into the corners by my nose, covering my mouth. I kept moving toward the door.

Ro jumped in my path. "Don't break the circle," he panted, then closed his eyes and chanted with Obe.

Lex was not saying anything. She stood there and stared at me with red eyes and a blank expression, beating her drum in repetitive thumps.

My mouth dried with fear and I shot a terrified look at Tomas whose fangs had run out and who was darting suspicious looks between the Vodoun.

As abruptly as the ruckus had started, it stopped, and a sudden pulse of dark energy slid across my skin. I quivered, my limbs twitching uncontrollably before I was left panting, my eyes stinging. I shuddered, realising I was clutching the bag of bones and blood to my chest.

I thrust it out to Obe who took it and retied it to his chest. "That should provide you with some protection."

He cupped a hand to his ear. "The whispers tell me you need it."

I said nothing. I turned to Ro. "I'd like to leave, please. Now."

He set his drum down and wiped the sweat beading his brow. The beads on the end of his cornrows clinked together as he shook his head. "And go where? You need to rest up, Rae."

I wrapped my arms around my middle and sent an apologetic look at Papa Obe. After all, in his own creepy way he was being hospitable. "I can't stay here. We can go back to Temple tonight. Amelia, Nimah, and Runt need my help. The thought of leaving them in that horrible prison turns my stomach to rot. My nature does not like it here. I won't be able to sleep. Please, I'm fine, I just want to go."

Ro studied me. "Them demons worth it, eh?"

I bobbed my head. "I made a bargain with their Alpha. We have a real shot at getting them out alive and unseen through the tunnel if we act fast. They might not even have found the Cleric you stashed in the dungeon in my place yet."

He shared a look with Papa Obe who inclined his head. Ro knuckled his head then shrugged. "Say-so. If going back is what you want then I'm with you."

"I'm sorry. I don't mean to put you in any more danger, but I have to do this. You guys can stay here, safe."

"No. We stay with you," Lex said from beside me and I jumped, pressing a hand to my heart.

"It is decided," Tomas said, already half way out the crooked door.

Ro hugged his mentor and murmured his thanks. Obe clasped the back of his head and muttered a prayer, pushing his fingers into Ro's forehead. Lex bowed her head at the Houngan in a show of respect then left without a backward glance.

Papa Obe slid in front of me when I tried to leave.

Hearing my startled gasp, Tomas was back up the steps in a blur and grabbed the man by throat. Papa Obe's eyes rolled back in his head and the masks on the ceiling rattled. Tomas' knees gave out and he dropped like a stone.

Infuriated, I turned on the Houngan but he held up his palm.

"Hear me. I have a message from the other side for you," he said calmly. "It is not something that happens often so I suggest you listen."

I jutted my chin out and nodded stiffly, my eyes darting from his face to Tomas' rigid form.

The tenor of his voice changed radically. It became gentler and more ancient. "Love your family and all will be well," he said.

Well that was helpful. I did love my family; Conall was most dear to me.

"Ta," I mumbled and slipped past him.

Tomas' stiff body relaxed when Obe slammed the door. Eyes flying open he sprung up and dusted himself off, sending a look of hate at the shack then an accusing one at me. With a shrug, I reminded him, "You did grab him." He sniffed and walked away. I followed behind, biting back a smile.

Passing the goat I paused and chewed my lip. He watched me with such gullibility I melted inside. I looked left, I looked right, then untied the rope around his neck and stamped my foot until he trotted off. Hopefully, he would have a small taste of freedom before he found himself inside some hungry slum dwell's cook pot. My gaze drifted back to Papa Obe's shack … better the goat feed a starving family than die under a ceremonial knife in the name of black magics.

We made it back to Temple with no problems and I was so excited about getting the shifters out I barely thought about how odd that was – to make it back without seeing any Clerics on guard. I knew they couldn't exactly publicise my escape lest they cause mass hysteria, but still. Nothing?

Under cover of darkness we gathered at the opening in the compound wall that led to the rooms beneath the Sect Temple.

Without slowing and without a word, Tomas ducked into the tunnel and was gone.

I pressed my back into the wall and crossed my arms over my chest. I sank down onto my ass, and smiled tightly. "Lex, you got this?"

She took a long look at me then nodded. "It won't take long. They must be in a room further down." She ducked down into the tunnel and her slender form was swallowed into the gloom in moments.

Ro stepped one foot in and paused, cocking his head at me questioningly.

I shook my head. "The iron," I explained, thankful there were two reasons why I could not go down that tunnel. "The walls and doors are brushed with it. It'll weaken me and I'll be more a threat than help. Get them out and come back. I'll keep anyone from coming in here after you."

Ro snorted then was gone.

Sitting with my back against the wall, I kept my senses open in case of patrolling Clerics. The smell of iron wafting out of the tunnel truly made me ill, and I scooted further away from the opening to turn my nose into the breeze.

Being scared of going back down into a small cramped place was stupid. I couldn't have such a fear, what if Lex or Tomas hadn't have been here? I would have had to go in myself and deal with it. I looked up at the sky. We still had most of the night to work with. When we got them out we could hide in the forest until we figured out where to go. No doubt Amelia and Nimah would want to go home, but Breandan's location had shifted. Whatever was holding him up before was gone now, for he drew closer to me at tremendous speed.

Left alone with my thoughts, the creeping doubts returned. Things were starting to make far too much sense to me. The more I learnt the more I began to believe I was meant to lead these demons from the darkness. As impossible as it was, they listened to me and respected my opinion. No matter how many times I messed up or said something stupid they still turned to me and trusted my word. Even more worrisome, though I could fight for them and be the warrior they needed me to be, I still did not think that I was meant to be their Priestess. Being a voice of reason when others damned the human race was one thing. Leading an entire race for millennia was another.

A crunching noise caught my attention and I slipped into a crouch and spread my wings. There was a soft curse, more snapping twigs, and I relaxed.

I knew that voice. I straightened, and crossed my arms over my chest, my unease dissipating. Ana came out of the bushes and froze when she saw me. Her blonde hair was plaited into an intricate braid and a few wisps framed her elfin face. Ana was short, shorter than me, and petite in frame. She had eyes a funny shade of blue and high cheekbones.

Ana the white witch was young and powerful, extremely powerful. She could see the possible futures of people she looked at or touched, and was often simply referred to by the fairies as the Seer.

Even now her eyes glazed over as she looked at me. Ana had told me Breandan and I were overwhelming to look at, and that we had many futures, each more dangerous than the last. Whatever she saw when she looked at me now troubled her.

"You shouldn't be here," she muttered.

I arched my eyebrow at this. "What the hell are you doing here, Ana?" I narrowed my eyes. "I know you live in the upper dwells, but you're off track to be at Temple."

She untangled herself from the branches caught in her clothes, and stomped up to me. She hesitantly brushed her fingertips over the Temple wall and shuddered. "I was following the pull of black magic. Believe me when I say I'm more than surprised to see you here." She pursued her lips and spread her hands out in front of her. "I'm here because someone is working a spell. Someone powerful."

"Someone you know?" I questioned, curious.

Her eyes flickered, unfocused, and she grimaced. "Possibly, but superior practitioners of witchcraft don't leave a signature in their castings, and the amount of power being thrown here is immense." She shrugged and her hand dropped. "Old members of my Coven had as much power as this." She focused on me abruptly and her hand lifted once more to feel the air, but this time around me. "You reek of death and your futures are hazy to my Sight. What have you been doing?"

I remembered the blessing ceremony with a quiver of revulsion. "You don't want to know." Pushing the hair out of my face, I raked my top teeth over my bottom lip thoughtfully. "Uh, I never realised you belonged to a Coven."

"I don't," she said smoothly. "I used to, of course, but I left. Didn't I tell you this?"

I jerked my shoulders not bothered. "Maybe."

"So you're here for … shifters … I thought for sure you would carry on for Devlin when you reached this far. What happened to the grim–" She looked troubled and rubbed her temples focusing. "It's so strange…. I can't see him anymore. His path is no longer entangled with yours. He's just … gone." She shot a puzzled look at me.

"What does that mean?"

She gave me an irritated look. "We've had this discussion before. I can't tell you reasons why. Only what is and what isn't. I don't like repeating myself."

"Helpful," I said dryly. "Maybe Breandan will know."

"Whatever. I'm not here to toss theories around with you. I'm here to–" She stopped and cocked her head, staring through me.

I rolled my eyes down to look at her and my brows furrowed. "You're here to…." I clapped my hands in front of her face.

She twitched then her head snapped to the tunnel opening. "I came to stop the witchcraft, but since you're here…." Ana backed up, shaking her head. "The vampire is down there." She took another step back. "I shouldn't have come."

"Stay," I begged and listened to the sounds down in the tunnel. A strangled yell cut off mid-way. Soft grunts were almost drowned out by half bellowed cries of terror. When she took yet another step I pinned her with a glare. "You say there is witchcraft here and I don't know if I will be able to handle it on my own without Breandan." I took in a deep breath. "So please stay with me."

The noise down the tunnel got louder. I listened carefully to the sound of many people coming toward us at speed. I could hear Lex's fluid footfalls, her two separate feet almost indistinguishable. Ro's heavier thuds were a few paces behind. I could also hear what may be claws scraping along the floor. Paws?

Yellow eyes glinted in the gloom before a cougar burst out the tunnel a moment later, sailing overhead. Amelia. She turned to scream at us in triumph, blood-stained jaw opened wide to show four dagger-like canines curving inward.

Nimah tumbled out behind her sister. "Oh," she said dryly. "You again."

Lex glided into view next and her chest was drenched with blood. Gasping, I stared at her. She roughly swiped the back of her hand across her mouth, wiped her other hand down her front, but it just made matters worse, especially when she sucked a bloodied finger into her mouth and groaned, "Mmmm."

Ro staggered out the tunnel next looking bewildered, a pale goblin-child attached to his back. "Not so easy this time," he grumbled. Blood ran down his temple and his movement was sluggish.

"Where is Tomas?" I asked and stepped forward into the mouth of the tunnel then stopped. All the walls closed in around me and I gasped and stumbled back. I couldn't go in there … I couldn't. "Tomas," I called and my voice echoed down into the dank dark.

An answering snarl and the sound of boots scraping along the floor echoed from the passageway. Tomas appeared from the gloom a moment later, his movement silent and deadly. He dragged a Cleric by the throat behind him, legs flailing as he scratched at Tomas' hand.

A gust of wind blew the Clerics crimson hood back,

and my stomach rolled. "Jono?"

This boy – who a mere few days ago was my fellow Disciple – started at his name and gazed up at me. Taking in my tail and wings, he sneered before his eyes bulged. Tomas' grip on his throat tightened as he lifted him one handed high into the air and stared in his face, daring him to sneer again.

Overcoming my shock, I placed my hand on Tomas's cold arm. "Don't kill him. We've gotten what we came for, so just drop him, and let's get out of here."

My vampire's eyes blackened out, the darkness of his pupils spilling over to stain the whites. His fangs shot down and buried into Jono's neck.

Covering my mouth with my hand, tears welled in my eyes and I shook my head.

Lex crouched and made a keening noise, slapping at Jono's spasming body. When Tomas was done he threw the twitching body at her. She half caught him and fell, rolling out of sight behind some shrubbery. Then the tearing and guzzling sounds started. Jono screamed, but it was cut off by a sickening crunch. Squelching, and greedy murmurs of appreciation came before a sucking noise that drifted over the sound of my horrified gasps. The wet sound of flesh tearing had my stomach rolling.

I plugged my nose and ears at the horrible smells and sounds.

Ro looked ill. Bashing the back of his head with his palm, he shook his head. Swallowing hard, his hazel eyes fell to the floor.

Lex stumbled out of the bushes, her chalk white skin soaked in blood. Looking between Ro and me guiltily, she tried to wipe away most of it, her expression pleading. Again, in her attempts to clean up, she smeared more gore over herself. Most upsetting was the faint rosiness of her skin and the relaxed set of her shoulders … the look of fulfilment on her face.

Tomas watched me blankly then his gaze switched to Ana. He regarded her dispassionately for a while then looked away his mouth pressed into a thin line. The witch looked horrified, and seemed to have shrunken in on herself. She turned her wide eyes to me and opened her mouth to speak.

The klaxon blared.

My hands flew to my ears, as did Nimah's, and Tomas'. Amelia grumbled and rubbed her head into her twin's legs, irritated. The alarm was bloody loud, and I was not the only one squinting in pain.

"We can't leave. Breandan is coming," I yelled.

Ana shot a cautious look at Tomas then shook her head. "Rae, whatever is happening inside those walls is one of the foulest things I've ever felt. We should not be here. Trust me. Breandan won't come here if he can feel you're gone."

"But he knows the Clerics took me, and he knows that I wouldn't leave without the shifters. He's coming here."

"The bond—"

"It's fuzzy. I can't pinpoint him like I usually can, the pressure is too great. It's like trying to grasp a single drop of rain in a downpour. I just know it's the same for him. He can't feel where I am, just the direction, and he'll pass straight through whatever danger is lurking inside Temple. I can't risk not being here. What if he needs me and my power?"

She pressed the heels of her palms to her eye sockets. "Rae…."

"I agree with the witch," Tomas said. "We should not linger."

"We're staying," I said loudly with finality, resisting the

urge to stomp my foot. "He's coming here. I can't leave."
I don't think they understood that physically I could not
leave. It hurt to even think about going in any direction
that was not toward him. "Besides, if something bad is
happening we have to help the Disciples."

"The same people who would hunt you down and put
a bullet in you?" Ro pointed out angrily.

I sent him a cold look. "They're not all like that and
you know it. You're not like that."

His chest puffed out. "I'm Vodoun, not the same
thing."

I inhaled deeply, praying for patience. "They're worth
saving," I argued vehemently. "We can't abandon them."

Ana's hands flew up in the air. "Perfect timing for you
to grow a backbone," she spat sarcastically. "Really, just
perfect. What do you have in mind?"

"Well, uh, it would be useful to know what kind of
spell was being cast."

"It feels like a summoning. The power here is being
fed from afar and poured into someone," she paused, "or
lots of someones. That would explain why the
reverberation is so vast." She made a frustrated noise.
"Why isn't clear. Why are the witches looking down here
now? It's like they're looking for something."

"Or someone," Tomas murmured.

Despite their seeming dislike of each other they shared
an alarmed look. Then all eyes turned to me.

"They know," Ana whispered. "Somehow the witches
know about you, and where you are. It's the only thing
that makes sense." She turned to Tomas accusingly.
"What have you done?"

"Nothing," he hissed back.

I held up both my palms. "Well, this isn't my fault.
The only witch I've been near is you, Ana, and why blame

Tomas for this? He's been down here the whole time."

Ana lifted her chin. "Do not presume to know everything about him, Rae."

"Don't push me, witch," Tomas snarled.

Ro took a bracing breath then held out his hand to Lex who grabbed onto it and pressed it to her face. He grimaced, but did not pull away. "Listen, we need to move. We be exposed here and they will search the wall perimeter and the prisons. The Clerics we killed will be found in a few minutes at best." He looked at me pointedly. "You know how it works, Rae."

I kind of yelped an agreement at him, my emotions suddenly clutching my airways in a vice like grip. My head snapped round in the direction of the siren call, and I gasped and trembled.

"Rae?" Ana called over the klaxon sounding worried.

I breathed out and flushed. My skin felt too small for my body. I ran a hand over my lower stomach, letting my fingers slowly brush the soft fabric. My breathing increased until I panted. I pushed my hair back and remembered the feeling of Breandan running his hands through my hair.

Amelia's nose lifted and she sniffed the air a few times. Her eyes roamed before they settled on me and she purred.

Nimah stuck her nose up and sniffed too then she watched me strangely. "I thought only my kind had mating cycles ... but she smells like she's in heat."

Hearing this, my hands dropped to my sides and my mouth swung open, but my attention was diverted yet again. My heart pounded and my knees shook. My wings uncoiled. My tail wound round my legs, sliding up and down. I whimpered and my eyelids drooped as I focused on the tingly buzz that drew closer.

"Rae," Ana said slowly, her eyes unfocused. "Is Breandan coming? Can you feel him through the bond?"

I nodded weakly, sighing at his name. "He's coming." The irresistible tug had my whole body swinging to the direction he was coming from.

"What's wrong with her?" Nimah asked. "She's more twitchy than usual."

"Her lack of awareness is a side effect of the bond," Ana explained. "She and Breandan are two halves of a whole. As they draw closer the urge to touch each other will increase until they, well, crash together and blow up. He's coming for her and she can sense him. That level of emotion must be distracting."

I swear, just thinking of Breandan's body beneath my hands had heat pooling low in my belly. Had I been in my normal frame of mind I would have been shamed by my body's reaction. I felt sensitive, like the air merely brushing my skin would cause me to– I swallowed loudly.

"Is this normal?" I shook my hands, trying to physically shake the feeling off my fingertips. "It feels like I'll combust unless he's…. I want him, right now. Here on the ground and I'll–" cutting myself off I blushed furiously.

"Please go on," Nimah said dryly, clearly enjoying the spectacle I was making of myself.

Ro snickered, Lex looked perplexed, and Ana's cheeks were pink – she could not meet my eye.

Tomas, stood silently taking this all in and looked supremely pissed off.

"I told you," Ana said shaking her head. "I told you what it would be like."

I spun round and jabbed a finger at her. "You never said it would be like this. You never said I would want him to … to just … Unguh. I want him."

"You need to calm down," she ordered. "You're no good to us like this."

Running my hands down my body I shuddered, thinking of Breandan's lips on mine, his hand on my waist, my lower back. His hips grinding.... My eyes landed on the Temple wall then drifted up....

Ana followed my gaze then cried, "Wait!"

Too late, I jumped and beat my wings, clearing it in one bound and landing silently the other side. Not that my impressively quiet landing mattered.

I dropped down right in front of two Clerics.

They kind of jumped, glanced at each other, baffled, then drew their weapons and took up warrior stances. An immediate hail went up and the edges of the courtyard filled with Clerics.

"...so we need to catch her." I heard Ana's agitated voice from the other side of the wall as I paused, trying to decide what was best here. I did not want to hurt them, but the way they paced forward made it clear they had every intention of hurting me.

Lex landed on one Cleric's back, digging her thumbs into his eyes. Tomas appeared behind the other and snapped his neck. The shout to tell them not to kill died on my lips. I was way too late. Amelia and Nimah landed at my sides; both human, and took hold of my arms.

"Real clever, fairy," Nimah sighed shaking her head.

I itched to smack the smirk off her pretty face, but punching her would be like smacking Amelia, of whom I was fond.

Ro scrambled over the wall, unlaced boots kicking wildly, Runt still hanging on his back. He jumped onto a nearby tree, grabbing hold of a branch to shimmy down. Runt fell off him as he hit the floor but was back up on his feet in a flash.

Ana followed, her face red from the exertion of climbing. Both feet back on solid ground, she calmly walked up beside me and put her hands on her hips, frowning at the dead Clerics. Rather, she frowned at Tomas who was latched onto a neck, slurping. We all watched him for a moment or so then looked away.

Vampires were quite terrifying. I would hate to have to deal with more than one at a time; I don't think my heart would survive it.

"Rae, when you and Breandan touch none of us must be in the immediate area," Ana said.

I tore my eyes from the horizon. I knew Breandan was coming from that direction. Each step he took heightened my awareness of him. It was like moving closer to a bonfire; with each step the temperature increased. Right now, the heat was a balm across my skin, getting warmer, and soon it would burn me up. I needed to touch him, to hold him, to lick–

Fingers snapped in front of my face. "Rae, focus." I blinked repeatedly and looked at Ana. Her face was right up in mine and I took half a step back before she grabbed my shoulder to shake me. Gods, the way she behaved reminded me of myself sometimes. "You must wait before you touch. You'll want to rip his clothes off, but you have to wait."

At these words, I bared my teeth, anger bubbling forth. "Why? We've been apart too long. He's mine." My voice was a growl.

She sighed. "Would you listen to yourself? Does anything you are doing right now seem logical and sane? You have to give us time to get away before you touch. Don't let the bond control you. You control it and you must...."

Not really listening any more, I nodded ardently, my

eyes roving across the courtyard, over the gathering Clerics heads. "Can't you feel it?" I groaned and reached out. "It's all hot and fidgety, growing stronger inside me."

Ana stomped a large circle muttering curses.

Tomas dropped the body of the Cleric he had been drinking onto the ground then snatched up the wrist of the other and bit down. Lex watched him hungrily, but Ro had a tight grip on her, his expression stony.

"What's the big deal," Nimah asked eyeing me. "She and lover boy bump uglies and she'll mellow out. All the females go nutty once a season on the Pride; soon as they are mated they're fine."

"For how long have she and Breandan been apart?"

Amelia looked up and to the left, "I don't know. Probably too long if I'm understanding what you're saying."

Ana frowned. "The build-up of power starts from the moment they stop touching. It's not so bad if they separate and keep the physical distance relatively small. Say, if they're a few minutes from each other for half a day, you may see a spark when they touch, nothing to be alarmed about. Across such a distance we're looking at a blast radius of about a mile."

"Blast radius?" Amelia echoed, startled.

"And, the bond reacts to their emotional state. If they were happy and only separated under pleasant circumstances the effect wouldn't be so powerful. But with Rae's mind under such strain…. And you can bet Breandan is almost chewing his fingers off for lack of touching her…." She let the sentence drop. "Based on what I saw mere days ago they can't control their bond yet. A nexus will open and since they'll probably be focused on slaking their need for each other, their entire focus will be absorbed in sensation, not on the magic exploding around them. With practice they will be able to manipulate the connection to achieve wondrous works. But that takes self-control. When the pressure is on, Rae's not big on self-control." She pointed to me and her voice was shrill. "Does she look in control? Right now all they'll manage is an explosion of raw energy that we'll all be caught in."

Some of what she said filtered through to me. "Are you trying to say that if Breandan touches me," in spite of everything I trembled in anticipation of such a touch, "when you guys are near, that—"

"We could die? Yeah, pretty much. I'm seeing a few paths where you collide without warning and I can tell you it's not pretty ... for anybody other than you. All I see is blackness, and roughly translated that means I'm dead."

"Leave then," I muttered.

Amelia and Nimah simultaneously took a step back, eyes wide. They looked at each other and I saw the instinct to get the hell away from me warring with their instinct to stand by the one who had rescued them.

At least forty Clerics were scattered across the opposite side of the courtyard now, watching us suspiciously.

Amelia spun to me, gripping my arm in a death grip. "Why did you come back for us?"

I managed to tear my eyes away from the sea of crimson, and frowned at her. "I made an oath." I shrugged. "I had to keep it."

"Father says fairies are bound by magic to keep their word," Nimah told her sister, but even she did not sound convinced.

Amelia was struggling. She let go of my arm and looked at the Clerics whose numbers still increased. "The chances of your surviving this…. Why did you come back?" She was truly astounded. "You could have run to your mate."

Runt blinked up at me too.

I swallowed hard. I heard the lies ringing in my ears, proclamations this somehow benefitted me, but in truth, nothing about this situation had ever been good for me. Yes, I had made a bargain, but I could have left them there and gone back to the Pride. But, I knew in my heart that the Sect would have moved them, and then how would we have found them again? I could not have left knowing what horrible things they would endure … possibly worse since Tu would be enraged by my escape.

"It was my responsibility. I feel…." I sighed. "I feel responsible for you."

She watched my blank face carefully. Her own smoothed out as if she had just found the answer to a complex question. "So you're the Priestess the fairies have been looking for." She rubbed her own forehead. "Is that what the gold on your head means? I've never seen that before."

I hesitated. "Why would you think that?"

"We shifters try to stay out of the mess that demonkind created for itself, but you are legend. Every learned demon knows about you. That, and Conall the fairy has been searching for you for a long time.

"You know my brother," I whispered.

She smiled. "My great grandmother was my age the first time he came to our Pride searching for word of you."

There was no time to dwell on what I had just learned. My past was key to my future, but every time I drummed up the strength and courage to look back, I found nothing but death, horror, and pain.

The shifters reached a decision and nodded to each other once. Amelia said. "We're with you, Rae. By coming back to save us you have earned our loyalty. Our Alpha would approve of this alliance."

Nimah did not blink an eyelid at Amelia's swift decision. She acknowledged and respected her sister's words without question, which was interesting since Nimah did not seem one to follow others without causing trouble.

"I'm sorry we have to fight," I said, "but please try not to kill anybody, especially the Disciples. They just don't understand."

"I'm going cat." Amelia finished firmly and crouched down, her face already contorting into a grimace.

"Crazy fairy going to get us all killed," Nimah muttered and watched her sister initiate her Change. Her gaze drifted to me. "If she wasn't Alpha female this would have gone down differently. I want you know that."

I shrugged, my attention already focused elsewhere. Hell, I was barely aware of the scorching heat that emanated from Amelia's quivering body. Her shrill cry as her bones popped and muscles tore did not even puncture my lust-induced haze.

A frozen hand landed on my shoulder and I jumped. Lex smiled, the runes on her cheek crinkling. She had snuck up on me again. Her zombie movement was so creepy. I could not feel, hear, or smell her at all. She was a void. If ever she turned on me, she would be a force to be reckoned with.

Her hand slipped from my shoulder and she glided forward to go stand beside Ro. Jumping up and down on the spot, Ro punched his fists in a way that showed he knew how to use them and tipped his chin defiantly toward the line of Clerics that advanced.

I offered my hand to Runt and placed his cool palm in mine. He was so small and skinny, yet he clutched at me with a strength that defied his fragile appearance.

I looked deep into his eyes and in a serious voice said, "If I die, you run, understand?" His huge eyes blinked up at me then he nodded. Satisfied, I let him go. I was not worried; he knew how to protect himself. I just hoped that he would be able to escape unscathed if this went sour.

Amelia had finished shifting and slinked back and forth before our odd defensive line. She was a tad stockier than her twin as human, and in cat form, this revealed itself in greater muscle definition. Nimah remained human, her wiry arms crossed over her chest and eyes slitted as she took in the advancing line of red. Briefly, I wondered what she would look like in cat form, and why, out of the two, Amelia always shifted.

Tomas simply inclined his head at me then disappeared into the shadows at the edge of the courtyard.

The Clerics drew their weapons; the first few paced forward, boots stomping across the concrete. Disturbingly, Disciples now watched from the shadows, faces ashen and wild with anticipation of the fight. If they decided to take up arms and fight the numbers would be uncontrollable. Magic or no magic, there were too many, and I had not the stomach to wield magic with the intention of killing them.

"He won't make it in time," I said quietly, tears pricking my eyes.

Ana patted my arm and I shrugged her off. Gods, these people, and the touching.

"Have faith, Rae," she said. "He'll get here soon. He'll

find you."

Taking a deep, bracing breath I set my two feet apart. I drew strength from Ana's unwavering confidence my mate would make it here in time to save me so I could save him. Hmm. This was not one of my more intelligent moves.

Then why did it feel like I needed to be here, right now?

I sensed him draw nearer, moving impossibly fast across the earth to reach my side. I could feel the determination, his single-minded goal to reach me.

My tail cracked like a whip and my wings, fully healed, spread to reflect a brilliant gold light onto the ground before us. I took hold of the Source, bared my teeth, and hissed menacingly.

Like a punch to the gut I felt a panicked command slam into my mind.

Be still.

CHAPTER SIX

E yes wide, I spun looking for the source of the command. I knew his voice, his presence, but had never felt him so strongly in my mind before.

A screaming Cleric fell from the sky and hit the floor in the centre of the courtyard with a loud thump, arms and legs sprawled. This in itself would have caused a stunned reaction, but the uproar was heightened since Conall was crouched on his chest. He'd ridden the Cleric to the dirt like a sled.

Broad chest bare, Conall's dark hair flowed across his shoulders. His brawny legs were covered with dark leather plates engraved with leaves, and a thick strap of leather latched his sword to his back.

A Cleric, half mad with rage, bounded toward him and a small ball of fire appeared in Conall's hand. He sent it at the man with a wide throwing motion and it collided with his face in a shower of sparks and blood. Conall calmly unsheathed his sword and sounded an ululating wail to the sky. Then he set his legs apart and braced himself.

The wall of Clerics roared in fury and surged forward.

A swirl of fiery hair and green limbs dropped down to stand behind my brother. Maeve, with a bow in hand, dressed in armour sleeker and darker than Conall's, hissed at the line of Clerics. She notched her bow and sent an arrow flying in one smooth fluent move, then ducked as a taser probe went flying overhead from a Cleric's gun even as her arrow impaled him.

Alec, Changed into his panther with long white whiskers, leapt down beside her and brushed his boxy head across the back of her calves.

A cougar male, his entire body rippling with muscle under mottled yellow-gold fur, followed him. The were-cat – missing one eye – had fluffy tufts sticking out of his pointed ears and his mouth opened wide to release a loud string of enraged growls.

Amelia tipped her head back and screamed. She bunched her fore and hind paws together, short, sharp rumblings breaking from her throat. Nimah looked fierce beside her swaying from side to side her fingers curled into claws. The shifter twins took one glance at each other, back at the male cougar, and leapt forward toward their Alpha.

Lex darted behind them – a white streak of death. Ro followed a moment later.

The demons launched themselves on the outer line of Clerics, determined to fight and protect me.

A Cleric drifted too close to the shadows and was yanked back into the darkness. He did not appear again.

I was appalled by it, by them – all of them – protecting me. Wasn't it supposed to be the other way around?

Even as I fretted for the safety of those who fought for me, it was the fairy darting between the Clerics on the Sanctuary roof that captured my total and immediate attention.

Men draped in red cloaks were flung screaming from the rooftop by a blur of black and silver, to land hard on the concrete with a sickening crunch, twitching before they were still.

He leaped down and landed protectively in front of the others.

Breandan.

I opened my mouth to call to him but magic thickened the air and was practically shoved down my throat. It was disgusting, vile, and I retched. I wasn't the only one affected. Ana's hand covered her mouth and clutched her stomach.

Unable to take hold of me the magic swirled away.

The Disciples freaked, batting their clothes and clawing at their faces. In eerie synchronicity they fell silent and still. At some hidden signal they stepped forward as one, small knives and batons unhooked from their belts. Their faces were vacant, like the personalities that animated them weren't there anymore.

"Gods help us," I breathed.

"The spell," Ana supplied helpfully. "At least we know what all that black magic was about now."

I darted looks from the Disciples to the Clerics, over the demons, then back to Ana. I set my jaw. Truthfully, from the moment I saw the Disciples standing on the outskirts of the courtyard I'd decided what I was going to do. I rocked back on my heels.

"Oh, thank the gods. You're going to stay out of harm's way." Ana sounded beyond relieved. "Would you like to try meditating with me to prepare for Breandan's touch? In some futures that helps—" Her eyes became unfocused. "Aw, Rae. Really?"

Grabbing her hand, I dragged her with me back a few paces so we were against the wall to stop anything coming up behind us.

Crouching down I took my worry out on my lip. I wasn't going to dive into the fight and make a nuisance of myself, but that didn't mean I couldn't help another way. "I'm going to save them, Ana. I know I am."

She pointed at the Disciple nearest to us who was trying to slash at Nimah with a stubby blade. "Rae, face facts. They're here to kill us," she argued.

The shifter-girl took him down with one heavy backhand and moved on.

I scrunched up my nose and shook my head. "Black magic aside, I think they're in over their heads. They don't understand what is really happening. I just need to show them we're not the enemy they've been told we are."

Nimah ran back up to us then in two swift moves yanked off her tunic and pushed down her trousers.

I flushed and focused on her face.

Buck naked and quivering, she motioned to me forcefully. "I knew your sappy 'don't hurt any Disciples' plan was stupid," she hissed. "Look at Melia's coat. She's been sliced a dozen times trying to maim instead of kill."

I winced as Amelia grabbed one half of a Cleric as her Alpha grabbed the other and they both yanked. Blood spurted like a fountain.

"And please refrain from taking any more limbs," I added.

She glared at me.

"Why have you taken your clothes off?" Ana asked curiously with pink cheeks.

Nimah slid her a sly look. "Melia's going to Change back to human to spare her energy. She's too injured to carry on much longer. She'll need clothes. And I'm going to shift and take her place." Her voice took a smoother tone. "Ana, will your magic be enough to get the young humans to back down?"

The white-witch smiled at her and felt the air with her

palms. "The magic here is strong – a powerful dark. We'll be lucky if they survive this - being pulled in two directions at once would be strenuous even for a fairy mind." She looked at me expectantly. "Is there any chance the bond has eased a bit?"

I closed my eyes and bit my lips. "No," I breathed and touched a hand to my lips thinking of his.

"Well aren't you a whole bowl of crazy?" Nimah muttered.

I glowered at her, but my attention came back to what Ana said. "This spell. Something isn't right about it. Only the Disciples have been affected, but it hasn't ensnared me, Lex, or Ro, and we're Disciples too."

"You're not human, sworn to none but yourself, and those old ties have broken. And your friend reeks of weeds and black magics meaning he can only be a–"

Her gaze slipped out of focus. Flinching, she stared at the ground by my feet in horror. She came back to herself. Ana rammed herself into me and sent us tumbling down. Nimah was already on all fours. I landed hard on my back, crushing a wingtip beneath me and feeling my tail become trapped under my shoulder blade. I yelped in pain and surprise.

Three wicked sharp daggers sliced the air overhead.

Wide eyed, I stared up at the night sky then cricked my head to see down the length of my body. I spotted the Cleric who'd almost stabbed me and tried not to feel satisfaction as Amelia's maw clamped around his neck and ripped into his jugular as her front paws dug into his chest.

I turned to Ana who trembled. "So close," she whispered.

Death no longer scared me. I had prayed for it, so now I viewed it as a friend I had yet to meet. My voice was calm as I said, "You were saying?"

She shot me a hard look and breathed out slowly. "The spell is targeting Disciples loyal to the Sect."

I stood and scanned over the carnage before me.

Nimah dragged Ana up by the arm then looked over to where Amelia was limping away from the fight with her Alpha hovering by her protectively, taking down anyone who got too close.

"I have to go," Nimah threw over her shoulder running off toward them.

Ana and I measured each other silently.

"It's a spell, you're a witch. Break it," I said.

"I don't think I have that kind of power," Ana countered.

Scowling, I spotted Zoe from the corner of my eye. The girl was a bitch to me when I was a Disciple, and she'd be worse now I was named a demon. Purple hair and blue eyes wild, she clambered her way across the bodies of Clerics to get me. Keeping my eyes on her, I reminded Ana firmly, "Using my magic right now would be dangerous and you know it. So no."

"You're the fairy Priestess, Rae. No one is your match for raw power. You just have to focus." She paused, wavering at the dark expression on my face. Her eyes flicked to Zoe and impatience twisted her lips.

"Well, I'm about to be busy so can you please do it?"

"I'll need time to focus my energies," she grumped with the air of a martyr. This will take everything I have."

I nodded sharply, not once taking my eyes of Zoe. It was amazing. My eyes were on her, my ears were on Ana, but my other senses had stretched out across Sanctuary courtyard.

I could feel everyone I cared about. There was the stubborn spark of Maeve, wounded, but whole, and a bubbly fizz of gold that was Alec close beside her. A blank spot indicated Lex, and a pleasant buzz tinged with darkness close by that was Ro. I could even feel the shifter twins, identical bright spots of determination, and Byron, the sheen of orange surrounding and protecting them. A brilliant white light blazed a trail in the centre indicating none other than my brother, Conall. Runt was a smear of warm brown darting here and there. My attention lingered on the heavy cloud of pulsing darkness that was Tomas, but I pushed it away. Dearer than the dark was the blush of silver, a shimmer that weaved through the masses and encircled all. I could sense others, the hazy, clouded, and confused consciousnesses of Clerics and Disciples, but none as dear as the demons that fought them. My extra sense gave me the peace of mind to focus all my energies on the one approaching me.

Ana knelt down and turned her face to the sky. She raised her palms upward and chanted something.

Pulling a rusted dagger from the waistband of her jeans, Zoe smiled cruelly, making her face somewhat animated, but the smile did not meet her eyes. They had a glazed look. She felt wrong. I bared my teeth at her in warning, hissing when she stepped closer.

Ana's voice got louder, "Purge the dark and hold to the light!"

Zoe twitched.

All the Disciples twitched, and their eyes wobbled as if someone had conked them on the back of their heads. The brief interlude passed and they fought on.

Shaking it off Zoe started after me again.

"Ana?" I barked over my shoulder.

"Not strong enough," she panted. "I'll try again."

Zoe lunged for me, wild and uncoordinated. It was too easy. I smashed my fist into her face and she dropped like a stone. Shuddering as I did, I dragged her limp body over to where Ana knelt.

"Keep an eye on her," I ordered and spun round at the sound of boot falls coming closer on the concrete.

Before I could step away Ana grabbed my ankle. "It's not a spell," she breathed. She let go of me and thumbed back Zoe's eyelid. The pupils were contracted to pin pricks. "Look at her eyes. It's a hex. He's hexed the entire Temple. I think I can break it."

I narrowed my eyes at her. "He?" I asked sharply.

She shot me a cool look. "Give me time, Rae."

Holding Zoe's arms down with her knees, she leaned up and slid a knife from inside her boot. She pulled herbs, bones, and runes from a pouch about her waist and set them on the ground beside her. Lifting Zoe's hand, she pricked her with a blade and squeezed some of her blood out.

A Cleric ran at us and I skipped forward to block him from where Ana dealt with Zoe.

The Cleric swiped his baton at my head and I dropped and rolled. The entire length of the steel sparked and crackled with electricity.

One brush of that on my skin and it was over for me.

He lunged again and missed. I spun, kicking his leg out from beneath him. As his weight shifted abruptly, I grabbed his shoulders and pushed him down so he smacked his head on the cold ground.

Another three spotted us and broke away from the main fight.

"For gods' sake, Ana," I screeched. "Hurry up."

The girl saw our attackers and started flinging rather than placing the herbs together. "I call on the powers of light and creation…." Ana's voice rang strong across the sounds of death and violence.

I pushed off the ground with my leading foot to propel me into the air. My hind leg rotated around to the front and lashed forward. My heel impacted the wall of a chest and I used it as a platform to push, twirl, and throw my body like a battering ram into my other attacker. We landed hard, him on his back. Hands of steel yanked me upright and constricted around my chest. My wings were squished awkwardly onto my back and I yelped. A fist slammed into the side of my head and I swear I saw stars. A streak of white flashed past and I heard a crack. I was free. I turned but the Cleric was already dropping like a stone as I staggered forward rubbing my head, the world going wonky. I turned to thank Lex but she was already gone. A blade that was on target to impale my chest missed by inches, but the slash drew blood from my shoulder to inner elbow. I sucked in a gasp of air through my teeth at the sting. I brought my knee up to connect with the soft flesh between his legs and the Cleric crumpled in agony.

Again, I went to thank Lex, but the words died on my lips. She was dominating two Clerics. Gripping a bloody clump of hair that had been ripped from the root in one hand, her other arm was elegantly positioned across her chest for balance. She perfectly composed and preening like a deadly bird. Her lifted leg hyper-extended and cracked back to front, smashing one oncoming Cleric with enough force to make his feet leave the floor. It caught another on the return journey. She jumped and landed on top of him. Dazed, he tried to stand but her weight kept him down. I watched with horror as she prowled over him, legs and arms moving like a spider, snuffling his chest before she reared back and darted forward to snap his neck. Then she buried her teeth into his cheek and tore into his flesh.

I retched and fell to my knees. "I didn't see," I whispered. "I didn't see it."

Breathing in deeply, I gagged mid-inhale and dry heaved until I had to press my eyes closed.

"…. And find me the darkness that binds these people." Ana's voice was calm and steady as she worked her incantation. "Show it to me and dispel it from this place. By my power, by my right…."

Slightly off to the side the fight was shifting. The Clerics were losing.

I sought out Breandan. When I found him I gasped aloud and trembled. The speed, the strength, was incredible. He danced his forms with a face of death. Four already lay broken at his feet. He stepped aside and thrust the heel of his palm up, smashing a nose. Spurts of blood accompanied the sound of bone breaking. The Cleric fell, dead before he hit the floor. He closed the gap between him and another. He could have been embracing a lover as his arms wrapped around his enemy. His hands found purchase and a quick twist shifted the Cleric off centre and he flung the man through a wall across the courtyard. The last Cleric standing nearby feinted for a few moments and Breandan drew himself up to his full height. Power hummed from his being and the air crackled. Face dark and withdrawn, he was the scariest thing I'd ever seen. The Cleric fled. A flicker of annoyance crossed Breandan's face and the Cleric was plucked up by an unseen force and slammed head first into a building before being dumped unceremoniously on the floor.

Just as I had looked for him he looked for me. His eyes followed the stream of blood down my side and dripping off my fingertips and his languid body stiffened. His eyes snapped to my face.

I reached out to him but an unexpected tug pulled me in the other direction. My eyes skipped over the courtyard and there, in the centre, was Cleric Tu. He stood on the platform by the cage and shouted for the Disciples to keep pushing forward. Had he not realised they were out of control? Was he so blinded by hate he could not see the true evil afoot?

Around his neck hung the key – my amulets.

Following the hum of power I ignored those who rolled around me and crashed down in front of me. Ignoring Breandan's yell I leapt up onto the barricade, jumping past all the hands reaching for me, to land in front of Tu, snarling.

I ripped the amulet from around his neck. "This belongs to me."

I was positively ready to tear him apart. I was not bloodthirsty, it was not in my nature, but some people had it coming.

I jumped on him.

He rolled with me and kicked me off. I took the blow to my stomach and slammed against a wall. It stung, but I barely registered how odd that was – for a wall to sting. I was focused, my eyes never leaving the Cleric.

Twisting so I was on my stomach, I surged up onto my feet and fisted my hands. I hissed at him, watching as he stood slowly, smiling. I narrowed my eyes. Not the reaction I was expecting. I re-tied the amulet around my neck, happy at how it sighed and readjusted its ripples of power to cover me. Yet, the ripples felt unstable, and they faltered, leaving me wide open. I had no time to dwell on this worrisome oddity, for Cleric Tu kept his steady walk.

I shifted from side to side, ready for him. When I had been stuck in the forsaken white room, I had dreamed of this moment, a time when I would be free to beat him into submission. No. I did not want to kill him. I was beyond that, superior to such crude thinking. I wanted him to kneel and look up at me with terror and reverence. For him to see that I was his better and to hear him acknowledge he was wrong about my kind. He took a final step then stopped.

Smirking, he pressed his hand to a pane of glass and stepped into the cage as the door slid down and locked us in.

I straightened fully, my heart crashing in my chest. I was in the cage. Cut off from everything and everyone.

No, no, no!

I needed to get out. I wanted out.

I spun and launched myself at the wall I had been thrown into. I beat at it, ignoring the blood that smeared the glass as I did so. The edges of my palms bled and sizzled.

Wordless with rage, my scream was a wail. I pummelled the glass. I needed to get out, free of this place. My throat was tight and sweat popped out on my brow to trickle down my neck. Chest heaving, I sank to my knees and scrambled to scratch out a hole at the bottom. The solid wood crumbled under my talons, but the deeper I dug, the more glass I saw.

Panicked I kept up this frantic burrowing until Breandan slammed into the other side of the cage. He splayed his hand on the glass and spoke. I could not hear him; it was quiet apart from the deep breaths of the monster behind me.

Calm.

The feeling was an instruction. Hell, no. Hell. No. I would not – could not – be calm in here. Tears streamed down my face, blurring everything as I blubbered.

He punched the glass, catching me off guard. He tilted

his head, his expression fierce and resolute. He speared
me with his eyes, lifting his chin. I knew what he was
saying; crying would not help. Writhing on the floor
keening and begging to be set free would not help. I
needed to pick myself up and fight.

Hiccupping, I sucked it up. My bottom lip trembled
but I controlled the fear, repressing it until it was a bubble
of pain low in my chest. I could become a hysterical mess
later, when I was safe and out of sight.

Breandan's eyes darted over my shoulder and his face
went white.

I stiffened and turned slowly.

Cleric Tu stood legs apart and face twisted in disgust.
His crimson blazer was spattered in blood and singed at
the edges. One of the black tails was missing and an
entire sleeve had been ripped off, revealing a slashed arm.

I twisted around to press my back to the wall, taking
slow measured breaths.

The instinct to hurl myself at him and bite and scratch
warred with the debilitating fear that this man had locked
me in a hole and cut me over and over again. He had
intravenously jacked me up so he could torture and
torment me. Everything was blocked out by the
overriding urge to run away. I was good at running, but
there was nowhere to run to.

I was trapped.

I couldn't get out.

I was back down there in the dark … all alone.

The bang on the glass behind me had my eyes
snapping open. I was not alone. Breandan was behind
me; he was there. I needed to get up, stand, and fight. I
tried to make my expression hard and unafraid. The effect
was probably ruined since I was cowering.

Cleric Tu's hand briefly slipped behind his back then

rested by his side. "I thought you'd gotten away from me," he said quietly, knuckles white where he now clutched a gun. He raised the barrel so it pointed at my face. "How mad I was. This time I'm not making the mistake of keeping you alive."

His finger squeezed the trigger, but I hauled ass, using a burst of speed to latch myself onto his back and bury my teeth into his neck. Vampires liked doing this? They craved the vile salty blood swilling in their mouth? It was thick, sticky, and bloody disgusting. I clamped my jaw down, going for maximum pain, and flexed my talons; resisting the urge to grin as they sank deeper into the flesh of his abdomen. Cleric Tu was not going down easy. He thumped me hard on the side. I grunted but held on, his blows not landing with enough force to hurt. He switched tactics and wound his hands into my hair, yanking with all his might.

I shrieked, my teeth coming out of his neck and ripping his flesh as I did. He tossed me off him and I landed hard on my back, spitting out a wad of blood and flesh as I did so, my stomach churning. Oh gods, now was not the time to be sick. I dry heaved once, twice, making a disgusting retching sound before I got it under control.

A knife flashed in his palm as he dived on top of me, roaring in anger. I jerked my head to avoid the tip spearing my eye. I rolled, taking him with me and we brawled on the floor. He rained punches and kicks down on me as I hissed, bit, and scratched, too wild to think about fighting properly. Screw graceful stances, I fought for my life; teeth and nails would do me just fine. Managing to pin me under his knees – squirming and cursing – he slashed the blade across my back. I screamed; the burn was instant and intense. He shifted off me and I scrambled up to crawl forward, only to get the blade brought down full force into my shoulder. Screaming did not describe the harsh cry torn from my throat as the tip of the blade punctured my skin then sank down. The edges radiated an intense heat through my arm and side. My arm buckled and my cheek hit the wood.

Breandan beat his fists on the glass, silently roaring his frustration. I watched as the iron that had stopped my own escape eroded his skin and left smears of blood.

Cleric Tu paced around me, eyes bloodshot and crazed, unfocused. His arm swung into view and I saw he had a new tattoo, a rune of power noting his new rank in the Sect hierarchy.

I shook my head in disbelief, mentally preparing myself for the next attack. I needed to focus and take him on as a Priestess not a rabid animal as I had been doing. Now if I could only stop my entire body trembling....

"Priest?" I asked with convincing calm.

"Those old fools have seen they need a warrior like me." He pointed a finger and spun it once in the air above his head. "Liking the cage? It was built with you demons in mind. Particles of silver and iron have been blasted onto the surface to weaken you." He shrugged. "I often wondered if we were wasting our time on such a thing but now ... its true value has been proven."

"You truly think this is worth something? You think because you trapped me here that you're a warrior?" I scoffed. The idea was laughable. I jerked my head toward Breandan, still trying to pound a hole through the glass. "That is a warrior. My brother, the Elder of my family, is a warrior. I am a warrior. Hell, Runt the goblin is more of a warrior than you are. You are a gods damned lunatic."

He lunged for me. I rolled out the way, but his heavy boot landed on my bad shoulder, knocking the breath out of me. Another kick to my stomach had me curling into a ball, tears in my eyes. Winded, I was dragged up. Cleric Tu twisted my arm behind my back and the stabbing pain was enough to make me cry out.

He snatched up the gun he had dropped and pressed the barrel to my cheek. The particles of iron around the rim made my skin sizzle where it touched.

Breandan dug at the glass wall with a dagger but was not getting far since the iron drained his fairy strength. He backed up and a swirling blue orb of fire appeared in front of him and hurled itself into the glass. It dissipated without leaving a scratch. Three balls of blue flames, each greater in size, thumped into the cage in quick succession but nothing happened. Breandan's face was dark with rage and he yelled at Ro who fumbled with the control panel to open the door.

I lifted my chin, refusing to be afraid. I turned my head, the iron gun barrel burning a trail along my cheekbone as I did, and locked my gaze with Breandan's.

Time halted, and I saw desperation in his eyes. *Fight.* His voice echoed in my head.

I was so tired, so weak. I couldn't do it anymore. I was not strong enough to keep fighting for a life I was not even sure I wanted. Something as big as being the fairy Priestess was too big for me … too big for Rae.

Ro stopped trying to open the box and shouted at Cleric Tu through the glass, banging his palm against it. He cocked his leg up to kick at the keypad in an attempt get the door to slide open.

My defeat, my acceptance of the end, had Breandan sinking to his knees. *Please.* He pressed his palm to the glass. *For him.*

My breath caught in my throat and I heard my own heart stop. Breandan tried in desperation to coax me into fighting again. He meant Tomas. How could Breandan not see, not know, how absolutely infatuated and devoted I was to him? My eyes almost closed but snapped open when the fear of dying in darkness instead of basking in silver light came to mind.

With death breathing down my neck, I acknowledged the truth I was too terrified to say aloud. I would live for him, and no other. No one else would ever hold as much appeal, and not because of the bond, but because of who he was. The boy who would risk his life to save a vampire he hated to make me happy. The one who would turn his back on everything he had ever known to have a chance at being with me.

"For you," whispered as my eyes drifted closed.

Cleric Tu breathed in deeply, I heard his finger slip onto the trigger to cradle it. The man was basking in my death before it had even happened. To think of all the respect I had once had for him.

Selfish!

Fight him.

It was not loud, but unfalteringly, and unreservedly present in the moment of my death. Invigorated and incensed by emotion fed through the bond, I stood, faster than light, and pivoted on the ball of my foot. Gasp. Tu looked down at the empty space between his hands. Thump. I twisted his hand back. Click. The gun exploded.

I did not see the bullet tear through his skin. I heard it. The flesh of his stomach caved in and blew out his back spattering his guts on the glass behind.

Eyes wide, face etched in shock, he staggered back.

The gun clattered to the floor.

I stumbled back, barely registering my own movement, my mind struggling to catch up with my body.

I knew the very last thought that passed through his

mind. This death was not meant to be his. He was so sure he had me; he had won. The good guys always won didn't they? Demon fairies couldn't defeat a paragon of virtue like him.

"You're wrong," I said. "I'm a better person than you are, and you were wrong."

He slipped on his own guts and hit the floor with a dull thud. He would not be getting back up again.

Tears threatened to fall and I forced them down. I had never taken a life before and it brought me no joy, but I could not deny I was grimly satisfied.

My shoulder flared in pain and I rotated it to help ease the mild hurt that soon smoothed out into nothing as my body healed. I was covered in aches and pains though none were as pressing as the one in my heart. I needed to get out of here.

I walked to the wall and lay my forehead and palms against it, hearing a tiny clink as my circlet hit the glass. Gods, I was tired, but stronger at his side, even with the iron seeping from the glass. Magics shot out from my fingertips, fed from the bond. I gave a mirthless laugh. So simple. If I had turned to the bond in the first place ... if I had understood what Breandan was really trying to say when I was spiralling into panic, I could have done this the first moment I'd been trapped. The glass chimed a high note of sound before it cracked, a spider web racing along the cloudy surface. The cage shattered, and glass rained down on us in sharp slivers that bounced off our skin and settled in our hair and clothes like deadly snowflakes.

The bond increased steeply in urgency until it was an acute pain. Lust had me panting in want. I trembled and bit my lip, knowing he was going to touch me, and knowing I was going to simply smash to pieces once he did.

Breandan groaned and reached out.

Distant, as if heard through fog, a fierce roar rang in my ears.

Conall leapt into view and rammed into Breandan. I felt the gush of shifted air as my fairy's fingers curled by my arm – sparks crackling between us as he almost touched me – before he was gone. Conall's attack carried them both away from me and hollowed out a crater of dirt as they smashed into the ground and skidded across it. He rolled with my brother trying to pin him down.

I stumbled forward. The bond was a steel chain tugging me closer, my own need pushing me to connect. But when Conall yanked Breandan's arm back, his shoulder buckled. Breandan's silent scream shunted his focus onto his own pain, shifting it from me, and allowing me enough distance to break the bond's overwhelming influence and reel myself in.

A prickle of energy rolled over my skin and magic swooped past to settle close by. I frowned. It felt weak, a pool of power I could wield without thinking.

I remembered.

Ana.

Her spell gathered force.

Conall had Breandan in a submissive headlock, and since I was able to cling to thoughts of helping my friends, I turned away and vaulted off the platform.

I ran back to where I had left Ana, and the Clerics attacking us stumbled back, their eyes fixed on the body inside the ring of glass that had been the cage. The closer to the witch I got, I noticed the smattering of Clerics were torn between being afraid of me, and whatever she was doing. Annoyed at how long it was taking me to reach her, I jumped, beat my wings twice, and sailed across the rest of the courtyard twenty feet in the air. Wind whistled in my ears and blew my hair back as I fell and landed in a silent crouch. My tail flicked about above my head and I tucked my wings neatly against my back.

Ana stood rigid, arms out wide and blonde tresses tossing about her face in the wind. Her body smouldered in black flames that licked the space around her and protected her like a shield.

Disciples surrounded her, faces twisted beyond recognition, but they held back, hesitating.

Tomas paced forward, his eyes locked on the Clerics surrounding me.

An eerie silence came upon the courtyard, as if everyone waited for something.

The dark magic suffocating the light reverted and crushed together until it formed into a tall, willowy silhouette. Each pulse of magic that flowed into it made it denser until I could make out the figure was male.

Tomas recoiled. He backed away into a shadow, crouching down and baring his fangs. His own darkness cloaked him until I saw nothing but his red-rimmed eyes gleaming faintly.

"Be gone, he-witch," Ana hissed as the herbs combusted into sickly green flames. "*A bheith imithe*," she cried and with a wave of her hand ordered a gust of wind to carry the be-spelled smoke into the face of the phantom figure.

The body of shadows steadily grew in power and potency until his blurry edges came sharply into focus. Transparent and shrouded in darkness, he ignored Ana and his cloaked head slowly turned until he stared straight at me. His head tilted in greeting and I took a step forward. A cloaked arm lifted until the shadow-cloth fell back, and a strong palm stopped me in my tracks.

The voice that greeted me was smooth and reverent in tone, *"Feicim tú, deirfiúr."* He turned his gaze back to Ana. "Daughter, you cannot banish me." The figure sighed. *"Gach gur éirigh idir linn go bhfuil dearmad a dhéanamh.* My child, come home. Your Coven misses you." The voice was melodic and rolled over me smoothly. I had not heard a voice so appealing unless it came from the lips of a fairy.

Ana blanched. *"Ní féidir liom ar ais.* I'm with my family," she whispered back.

The figure crackled with power and disapproval. "Move out of my way. I have no wish to harm you, but there is only so far you can push me."

I noticed Ana's hand bled, blood dripping off her limp fingertips onto her altar. The puddle of blood forming beneath the green flames boiled and turned black as I watched.

The white witch seemed unable to look away from the hooded figure.

Reaching out with my senses I was easily able to feel the link between her and the he-witch's dark power. Of course she couldn't banish him. It was blood, the life-force of all things that fed this he-witch. She had tried to banish one of her own kind, but instead of being overcome by her power, the figure fed off her to become stronger. I could see it, his power leeching on hers, making it weaker by the moment.

Ana had been right. It should not have been her to cast the counter spell.

In five strides, I came to her side and snatched the dagger from her loose fist. I sliced the curved blade across my forearm deeply, grunting at the pain. The blood flowed like a river and I felt a moment's light-headedness. Next time I would slice my palm that was for sure. I felt magic take hold of me in a vice-like grip and start to suck on my remaining energy. Without having released the pressure of the bond with Breandan, or recharged after my hellish experience with Cleric Tu, I was weak and getting weaker.

Holding my bleeding arm over the green flames I mumbled, "My blood," I grabbed Ana's hand to slice it open. "His blood." She shrieked and tried to pull away, but I dragged her down with me as my knees gave out. I sliced Zoe's shoulder, threw the dagger away, and placed our blood soaked hands over the cut. "Their blood."

Great, now what?

"By my power by my right," Ana muttered in my ear, her eyes locked defiantly on the he-witch.

"By my power! By my right, I–"

Black magic punched me in the face. I choked on my words, head snapping back.

Ana grabbed my shoulders and hauled me upright. Digging into the pouch at her waist she pulled out some of that green gunge she'd once made me eat before and forced it past my pressed lips. Knowing I needed the energy I swallowed and a wave of healing magic flowed over me.

The phantom quivered and the wide cowl was blown back to reveal an enthrallingly handsome man with dark hair streaked with honey-blonde. He had shimmering white orbs for eyes with striking gold irises, multifaceted like jewels. An amused smile curved his lips as his gaze rested on my wings. His expression was full of contempt and utter self-confidence.

I looked down at Ana who cowered at my side. She looked the spitting image of him, the same nose and soft brow, with a high forehead and distinct widow's peak. However, whilst Ana's face was covered in a sickly sheen of sweat, his was dry as ash, and contorted in rage when he looked upon her again.

Scrambling to gather my wits and deal with everything going on around me, I inhaled slowly, focusing on finishing the spell. What was I supposed to say next? I exhaled sharply and lifted my chin. Gathering magic to me, it thrust through the air in lances of bright light, cutting through the dark. It whirled around me like living twine, flickering and pulsing with energy.

Keeping it simple seemed to work for me and I simply hissed, "Leave!"

He screeched – hands flying out to the side – and imploded. The particles of slate grey left in his wake twisted into a whirlwind and took off into the sky.

As one, the Disciples screamed – a tortured, mewling cry – and clawed at their skin. First, one fell trembling, then another, arms and legs thrashing, and another convulsing, as vicious smoke seeped from their ears, eyes, and mouths to join into a cloud of poison above our heads.

"Rae," Ana's voice was strangled. "Burn it," she choked. She hunched down and placed her hands on her head. "Cleanse the sky with fire." She raised her voice and infused it with power so it rang loud and clear. She shouted, "Hold!"

Conall, Breandan, and Alec – Changed to his human form – dropped their opponents. They stopped. Stared at Ana. Then their eyes snapped to me.

My wings unfurled – shining a brilliant gold, a beacon in the raging madness surrounding us. Still the ropes of power snaked around me like a protective shield and glowed brighter.

Alec grabbed the shifter-twins by the scruff of the neck – both still in cat form with a twitchy Runt between them – and pushed them down flat. To my surprise, he shouted to Maeve who was busy with the Clerics, arrows from her bow flying at a speed I struggled to follow. One came up behind her as she slipped her bow across her back, the string resting across her chest, seemingly unaware of the danger approaching. The Cleric lifted his gun and Maeve reached behind her, grabbed him by the wrist, and flung herself forward sending him hurtling across the courtyard like a cannonball. He crashed into two of his crimson-shrouded allies on the way whilst Maeve nimbly rolled back up onto her feet. She was so focused she did not hear Alec yelling at her as she readied her bow again.

I swept my hands into a graceful oval – using the gathering and holding motion to help me focus. The ropes of power whipping around me rushed over my shoulders and between my legs to sweep into a ball. They twisted and coiled, merging into a glassy sphere that exploded into golden flames.

Alec took off across the courtyard toward Maeve.

Breandan powered toward me until Conall tackled him, wrapping his hands around his ankles so he lurched and fell. Conall smashed Breandan's head onto the ground and I felt his consciousness black out.

I drew on the Source. As if my entire body inhaled, the power was sucked into the pores of my skin and buzzed. The cloud bloated, doubling in size. Taking a deep breath – muttering prayers that I would not burn out – I drew deeper and deeper still, until if felt like I was dipped head first in molten lava. My skin was so hot the sweat that trickled down my back sizzled. My mouth went dry and the moisture in my eyes evaporated leaving them itchy.

With a shriek of rage, I flung my arms open and released my power in a blade of bright light that just missed Alec as he dived for Maeve and knocked her down then split the cloud in two. The broiling mist quivered – the reds and oranges writhing in a sycophantic harmony – then merged back together and deepened into a rich ruby that tainted the heavens. The land was bathed in a red glow making it seem we had all been dragged to hell and left there. The air churned and whipped past at ferocious speeds.

"Rae!"

I could not have told you who screamed my name. The wind was too loud.

Standing, I shielded my face with my hands and pushed forward, angling my body so I could cut through the wall of wind. I climbed up the stone barricade, my foot slipping only once as I scaled the dusty rock. I reached the top of the stones, and set my two feet shoulder-width apart.

I ducked when a screaming Cleric's flailing body flew past, and was sucked toward the spiral of wind. Seeing it was Samuel, I lurched forward and grabbed his ankle, channelling magic into the stone beneath me to ground us. Yanking him back down, I took his head in my hands and forced him to open his eyes and look at me.

"Climb down and run," I ordered in a calm voice. "Get the others away from here."

He nodded repeatedly, his blonde curls whipping in the wind. "Come with me."

I frowned; I did not have the time to see him down safely. "I can't. Trust me if I could go with you I would, but my place is here. Go."

He scrambled down without another word, and I watched him to make sure he reached the bottom.

The cloud above twisted around and around until it was the shape of a tapered spike. Lightning cracked the sky and thunder rolled. A freak spray of rain pelted my body. I staggered back, arms flapping in circles until I regained my balance.

I wiped my hands over my face, dragging the wet and heavy hair that lashed my neck and shoulders out the way so I could see.

The tunnel of wind swooped over my head and touched down on the ground, blocking everything and everyone from view. It became eerily quiet, the wind a distant roar in the background. I could hear my own panicked gasping as I stood, waiting, anxious.

I was trying to fight, I knew I should not give up ... I just could not see what I was supposed to fight.

There was a pulse of energy overhead. My head snapped up and I stared into the churning ruckus, searching.

"You cannot defeat me," a voice said behind me.

I spun on my heel and tried to step back, but the he-witch grabbed my throat in his hand and squeezed. I swung my fist in a punch, but my hand sailed straight through him. He was made of nothing but shadows and smoke.

"It is my power that holds you not my body." He cocked his head at me and frowned as if I should have understood this.

His eye sockets hollowed and his mouth opened to an unnaturally large size. He inhaled me, the essence of me, and I whimpered as the world spun and lurched.

"The High Lord had nothing on you, did he? *Ní fhéadfadh sé seasamh in aghaidh mo fhéadfadh.* But you ... you are powerful, Rae." He chuckled as he said my name and I could not help my eyes widening. He drew me closer and whispered in my ear. "Yes, I know your name, Priestess." He spat the word. "Do you know mine?" The hand of shadow at my throat tightened. Black spots danced across my vision. "Do you know who I am? I am the one who is going to destroy everything and everyone you love. Your time has ended, you just don't realise it yet." His power rolled over me, trying to scare me into submission. "And the one you're bonded to … hmm … would you like to know his fate?"

My eyes snapped fully open and my nature flared. Furious. Enraged. Whoever this man was he had just made a mistake. He almost had me. Almost. But he'd made the ultimate mistake in threatening the one person I would die for. When it came to protecting myself I would always hesitate, always think twice about taking a life. But nobody would be able to threaten Breandan without being annihilated. This witch was about to learn that. What I should and could do became all too clear.

I called magic to me and drew it through the amulet of power. I took hold of it so forcefully and quickly I thought my head might pop off from the pressure. Then I tapped into the amulet of protection, and felt his hold on me loosen as I focused my strength on the ever-present hum of energy from the amulet of wisdom. It was incomparable in its wonder, and I felt superior magics to rival the clout of the gods themselves come under my control. The amulet of wisdom gifted me with the ability to think in separate channels. I protected myself, channelled the Source, and became aware that Breandan was close, ready to help if I needed him. I shut that channel of thought down. I was strong enough to manage this task alone, and the longer I focused on our bond the more it sucked me in.

I reached out and grabbed the he-witch by the throat. My hand did not pass through him – this time it was able to take hold. It was as if I pulled more of his spirit from wherever it was into this form so I could touch him.

Then something strange happened. Recognition. I looked at myself but saw different features.

"I know you," I whispered.

The shock on his face reflected mine. He grunted then closed his eyes and disappeared.

He reappeared a few steps back and held up his hand. A smooth-edged beam of azure light grew in his palm. The light darted toward me and I sent a shield of magic to smother it, but before my spell could take effect, the light broke into a dozen forks. I screamed as they struck me in the chest and scorched the stone beneath me.

I staggered back, gasping for breath and trembling. There was no pain. I had expected my skin to sizzle off, but rather than an overwhelming agony it felt like butterflies danced on my chest, their wings fluttering across my skin.

The he-witch started, jerking back. Muttering an incantation, he watched me with rapt attention.

A bolt of lightning struck the ground beside me. My head flew back as another raced from the black sky to earth and struck me square in the forehead. The lightning glanced off me, hit the ground, and disintegrated. My hand flew to my circlet, now scalding hot and burning my brow. It cooled as I pushed my hair from my eyes with a shaking hand.

The he-witch pursed his lips. "Interesting," he murmured and his voice echoed deeply.

After several beats of my heart kicking my chest in fear, and adrenaline making my entire body quiver, it became clear there would be no aftershock of pain either.

The Vodoun shield protected me.

Setting my jaw, I lifted my chin and blazed determination. Pacing forward I raised both my hands, increasing my step into a skip as a rough fireball flared into being. I threw my remaining strength – physical and emotional – into hurling the flaming sphere at him as he swept his hand in a graceful arc and conjured a maelstrom of liquid fire.

Both orbs of magic collided and it sounded like a clash of boulders. The avalanche of power exploded with an earth-shattering bellow that resonated and expanded in a mushroom of dazzling violet light streaked with swirls of blue and slashes of green.

I was kicked back, flying head first off the barricade, through the eddy of wind and lightning as it collapsed into nothing.

The shadow figure lost shape and form; his darkness melting into the breeze and swirling away. "*Feicfidh mé thú go luath, deirfiúr,*" his alluring voice boomed in my ears then was gone.

Weightless, directionless, I sailed backward until I slammed into the dirt. My head smacked down, bounced, then cricked oddly as I tumbled over myself before I lay in a crumpled heap on my side.

I was motionless, staring up into the sky, watching as the clouds rolled away to reveal the gleaming moon.

The he-witch was gone. His darkness had left. I felt it.

My choke reflex kicked in and I coughed, my whole body shaking from the force of it. My head lolled to the side, and my wings stirred restlessly on my back.

"Ow," I muttered.

Already my nature was scratching my skin from the inside out, demanding that I get up and find him. He was close, so close. Lying in such proximity to him was like someone pressing hot coals into my pores.

I sat up looking around, searching. Wood chips, stones, and bits of rubble fell from my hair and clothes, but I did not care. I could not think or focus on anything else any more. My nature had grown in potency since we had first been separated, and now it demanded I find him, no more waiting.

Over the clearing smoke, Disciples dragged themselves up, looking around bewildered. Some still crouched on the floor looking up at the sky with horrified expressions on their faces.

I ignored them.

There were no more distractions. Nothing else I had to worry about or focus on.

I had done my part.

Cleric Tu was dead and his followers were retreating. I had defeated the he-witch and dispelled the black magic from the Temple. The shifter twins were free and no doubt reunited with their Alpha. My eyes drifted closed, there were no more distractions, no other dangers to face or fight.

I let my instincts guide me, feeling my pulse quicken as my gaze sought him out.

Close. He was close.

There.

My eyes locked with his, as he stood, victorious in his own battle. Conall struggled to pull himself onto all fours in front of him, body swaying.

I inhaled in a hiss, savouring his unique scent of earth and sunlight, and bared my teeth.

Mine.

I lurched up and lunged forward only to slam into something immovable. Seeing nothing, I tried to run around it but there was no end. I shrieked and whacked my fist against it. The barrier of air shuddered under the force of my might, but held, not letting me past. Not that I was concerned, Breandan had seen me and was already speeding over. A few more moments and he would be in my arms.

My entire focus was on my love when a golden spark shot in front of him and caught his shoulder. Planting his feet, Conall barely missed Breandan's swipe for his head. My fairy-boy snarled – trying to shake his hold – but Conall held firm.

"Wait, Rae," a pained voice said from behind me. Ana moved into my line of sight and there was a fierce look of concentration on her face.

She muttered something under her breath. An incantation. I hissed at her, and reached out with my own magics, knowing that if it came to brute force I could smash any spell she threw at me to pieces. Right now, she was my greatest enemy. She kept me from him.

Had I not done enough? Had I not been put through enough? Had I not yet earned the right to feel his hands on me?

I just wanted to hold him.

I pushed magic at the shield she had erected. It trembled, but held. Again, I threw magic at the wall, but still it held. Enraged, I hammered at it with my fists and mind. Cracks. I could feel them, and I hammered harder.

"Run!" Ana screeched collapsing. Her eyes rolled into the back of her head.

Conall looked at me, possibly hoping to reason with me. With one look at my face, he let Breandan go, and darted over to where the white witch shivered on the floor. He scooped Ana into his arms and blurred away. Three cougars were hot on his heels, one with a goblin-child clinging to her back.

Breandan slammed into whatever Ana had erected to hold me.

The Clerics backed off, alarmed by the immediate

demon evacuation, and sprinted away too, grabbing Disciples as they went.

Now two of us beat at the barrier, and it thinned, rippling under the strain. More cracks, huge cracks. I found the last knot in the spell Ana cast and tore it down.

Before I could order my own limbs to grab him, his hands were on me, in my hair, running down my back.

The bond steeply increased in urgency, and my heart stalled, my knees giving out. Tingles ran across my scalp, the back of my legs, and down my arms. A magical current running across my skin sparked against the same electric charge jumping off Breandan. Colliding, the power pinged back and forth between us growing in might until it reached breaking point. We clutched each other riding out the numbing pressure. I shivered uncontrollably then flung my head back and inhaled on a gasp. Breandan grunted as intense light blasted from his body and mine, so bright it seared my eyes. I scrunched them shut, crying out as the ground rumbled and pushed us aside.

Ripples of power which pulsed from me, slammed into swells of force radiating from Breandan. Both merged into crushing waves of energy strong enough to obliterate anything in its path.

My head snapped forward and I collapsed into Breandan's arms. I couldn't focus on anything but him. Not on what was happening, nor the terrifying magics exploding around us. My fingers dug into him, I was not letting go. Breandan ignored the chaos erupting around us and tugged me closer. My body jolted and pushed against his hands needing more. I gasped into his mouth as the light continued to flow from us in a devastating surge of heat.

My heart vibrated in my chest; the sensation rumbling

across my ribs and lower back. Frenzied blood rushed in my veins and the love pouring from him to me was rapturous. I strained to be closer, exhilarated by the need to fuse to him, wanting to mount him. It was odd and creepy, but gods, I just wanted to crawl into his skin.

His hands swept over my back, clasping my waist, and pulling me closer so our hips locked. He made me feel tiny, fragile, and precious. His fingers splayed across my skin tracing patterns. He traced my scars. Shame and self-loathing was a powerful thing. So powerful, it managed to separate me from the thing I wanted most.

I jerked away and stumbled back, tears stinging my eyes.

The light dimmed though the ground did not stop trembling.

Furious at myself, at my ugly scars, I glared at him and narrowed my eyes to slits. Breandan stood and stumbled with me, his hands still running down my sides. How could he still want me when I looked like this? The building at the edge of the courtyard halted my escape, and I covered my face with my hands, pressing my eyes closed to try to block out his light.

"Don't touch me," I mumbled. My voice shook and tears threatened to fall, "Don't look at me."

"Rae-love, you are beautiful." His voice was raspy as he struggled to focus.

My hands fell from my face in shock. How was it possible for him to lie?

His confusion at the look of horror on my face was clear. His glassy eyes dimmed as he fought for control, his dilated pupils contracting. All this evidence of his complete loss of control only served to enrage me more. He was lost in sensation and I was too self-conscious to stay in that place with him.

I punched his chest. "No, I'm not." I punched him again, the contact somehow soothing and irritating at the same time. He grunted. "I was before. I was beautiful before, but now I'm ... I'm ..."

I slapped him across the face. Four claw marks from cheek to chin had him hissing sharply. He stood still, not flinching under my blow, but his eyes blazed like shards of glinting crystal as the slashes healed leaving smooth skin. My eyes filled with tears. I was not vain, nor did I care before what I looked like, but I had never been ugly. Now my skin was covered in scars and I could not bear knowing he loved what I once was and never would be again.

"How could you let them do this to me?"

He flinched this time.

His head moved slowly back and forth as if he was saying no to a question I had not asked. "You will accept this. Accept us."

I stumbled over debris at my feet, lost my balance on the unsteady ground, and smacked the back of my head against something. The urge to hold Breandan was so fierce I had to fight to stay focused on moving my mouth to speak. "Go away."

"I belong to you." Breandan's jaw clenched as he too fought the urge to touch me. "Where you go, I follow. I will always follow you."

"Don't," I spat. "I want you to le–" I choked on my words.

"You want me." Back against the wall, I had nowhere to go and nowhere to hide. His hands slammed into the brick on either side of me. He ducked his head down, expression torn. His fingers dug into the dull red brick and gouged out deep grooves. "Accept us, Rae. Oh, enough of this. Just accept me."

"Do you not see me?" I whispered.

His eyes looked me over carefully. His thumb brushed over a mottled slash that ran from the middle of my cheek right down to my collarbone. He took me in, all of me, and I felt disgusting. I hung my head and failed to muffle a sob.

His nature beat upon my own like a drum, loud, bold, and relentless.

"You truly wish to know what I see?" he paused and I waited for the words that would crush me. "I see nothing … but the one I would die for. The one I would destroy the world for," he murmured. "I see nothing but my Rae."

He wanted me, unconditionally and without the slightest of hesitations.

My heart beat against my ribcage in bold and singular blows that made my chest ache. My eyes closed, but it only heightened my perception of him. He was a mere jerk of my body away. He wanted to hold me and his body screamed for the contact as loud as mine. My hands rubbed my thighs and drifted up to brush past my hips. The feeling grew, rolling around me until I fidgeted in my own skin.

All I had to say was… "Okay."

He became completely still. Then with a savage snarl of triumph, Breandan's mouth crashed down on mine.

My need for him escalated into frenzy and I wound my fingers in his hair, sighing in pleasure as the pressure shifted. It was no longer pressing down on me from every angle, but had surged inside to writhe under my skin. Now I had to appease the bond by joining with my mate.

I unfurled like a wildflower opening to the sunlight. His sunlight. My thoughts broke apart and scattered like whispers on the wind before they zapped together and pushed me higher, sending me unbidden thoughts of how we would look, bodies entwined, and hands greedily sliding over bared skin. Through our bond the slide of flesh on flesh, and each gasp of breath across wet lips, was intensified, feeling each other's reaction to each stroke, each mindless caress.

His lean body shimmered under my hands, his hard flesh pearlescent. He traced his strong hands over my curves as if I were delicate, then simply took hold of my wrists, pinned them to my side, and held me as I strained forward, offering everything.

My thunderous heartbeat raced faster with every touch and caress. Each breathless moan had our connection growing and increasing in poignancy.

The world was awash with translucent colour. Splashes of red clashed with violent blue and glossy purple. Sensation became a sound, the soft sigh of his hand as it left my wrist and grasped my waist. His thoughts a physical torment that battered my senses.

His eyes – usually silvery-blue and sparkly – were opaque, flat cobalt, and smouldering.

I embraced the madness, did not dwell on how outrageous it was that I could need him more than the air dragged into my lungs – which then was released in a shuddering breath as his teeth grazed over my neck.

The darkness within me throbbed, threatening to blot out the light. I pushed it away from me, turning away from its welcoming coolness, and threw myself into the hedonistic flames of Breandan's light.

His mouth skimmed my chin and hungrily latched onto mine. He pressed me into the wall. At this dominant display, my nature flared and responded by becoming submissive and malleable. My body went languid; muscles tense yet easily manipulated. His hand drifted down to brush my breast. I gasped and tugged on his hold. I equally wanted to cover myself and drag my clothes off.

He let me go, unconsciously offering me the choice. I laced my fingers around his neck.

In the end, his fervent kiss undid me. I could feel his hunger as his tongue lashed mine yet his hands ravaged me with such care I felt safety like I had never known.

Soon my trousers were pushed down over my hips. I kicked one pant leg off, too absorbed to bother with the other, and I fumbled with the laces at Breandan's waist. His mouth found mine again. He hoisted me up and I wrapped my legs around his waist. The friction between our bodies was maddening, torturous.

My breathing deepened and his eyes glazed over. Yet, his movement slowed, almost as if what was happening was only then dawning on him. I was too hungry for this to slow down. If it slowed, we would start to think. Thought was bad, very bad. In fact, if I could feel like this forever instead of ever having a single coherent thought ever again, that would be damn fine.

I grabbed his head and pulled him back to me. Our teeth smashed together painfully and he grunted but readjusted himself and took control. He deepened the kiss and gripped my hips, tearing away to lean back and look me in the eye. Ready? His voice in my mind was thick with desire. I responded with my body. I tightened my legs as my stomach clenched in fear and anticipation. Breandan kissed me and I cried out in pain and pleasure as he thrust forward. I jerked back, breaking the kiss and staring at him, eyes wide. It hurt. My hands fisted on his shoulders and I locked up. Damn. Tears pricked the corner of my eyes and I tried to breathe out but the air was caught in my throat. By gods, it hurt, but my love for him was enough to numb the pain, and stop me from attacking him in a panic. I was tense, dragged down from my lust-induced pedestal by the shock of it – the welcomed invasion of my body. Breandan shifted and his tongue flicked out to slide across my bottom lip. Then he kissed me, gently pressing his lips to mine as if he wanted to absorb all the pain and suffering for me. This simple gesture had me relaxing enough for a flare of heat to rack my body and turn my rigid muscles to jelly. The healing heat was swiftly followed by a ripple of pleasure.

The pain was gone. He fit beautifully, and a hot and deep sensation pushed me somewhere I had never dared to hope I would glimpse. Not until this fairy came into my life and changed everything.

I felt our bond expand, flutter, then contract, locking itself tightly in the core of me, chaining my soul to him for the rest of my life. It made me happy, content, and nothing could make the moment more perfect or wonderful.

Breandan's back rippled under my hands. Gasping, I jerked back. He groaned, and pressed his forehead to mine. His body quaked violently before surging forward as a loud ripping sound was almost drowned by the harsh cry he shouted into my shoulder.

I watched in utter shock and amazement when wings, a luminous grey so pale they matched the whitish silver of his eyes, unfolded from Breandan's back.

They uncoiled and fluttered behind him. Thick and wide, they were like mine, their many segments shimmering with light bluish veins webbed throughout. They were gossamer thin yet sucked up the moonlight, intensifying it, and threw it back in a prism of brilliant light. Breandan glowed like the sun. When his pinions had extended to their full length he faltered, and we slid down the wall some as he panted.

I clutched his face between my hands and peppered his face with kisses, tears in my eyes. My tail snaked around his thigh before coming into contact with ... his tail! I laughed in joy, tugging on its end playfully.

Breandan chuckled then pushed us back up the wall and bracketed me with his arms. He crushed his lips on mine, and I kissed him back as ferociously.

The pleasure warming my lower stomach grew and got hotter. It was harder to breathe, harder to think straight. His kiss swept away any doubt this was meant to be. The way he said my name as he moved inside me left me aching for his love.

Pained, delirious, and drunk on passion, I scored my nails down his sides. He bit my shoulder hard enough to draw blood and I moaned. Pinned between a rock and a damn hard place my body was under an assault of sound, touch, and taste. Mmmm, taste. I licked his shoulder and dragged in a lungful of his scent; sunlight, soil, and a native wildness that spoke to me in a hushed whisper. Everything was foreign. I was thrilled with the excitement of it. I knew what we did was breaking the rules, but it was happening regardless.

My fingertips tingled and my stomach clenched. He was in the zone, lost in me.

The pleasure took a steep and sudden ascent to the realm of the amazing. Eyes wide, my fingers flexed then my grip on his shoulders tightened even as my muscles contracted.

He paused and held himself taut, waiting. He took a series of short sharp breaths and his entire body quivered as he shifted. That small shift of his hips made everything urgent.

"Do it," I gasped. "I'm yours." I leaned forward to bite his bottom lip.

He thrust forward again then roared, pushing forward and sending my body shunting back. Grazing my cheek on the wall behind me, I shattered, and my shout was soundless.

The pressure exploded from under my skin, leaving my body blissfully weightless and tingly.

Though my eyes were wide, I saw nothing but a brilliant radiance. A colourful rainbow tinted with electric blue and purple, a violent explosion of glitter and sparkles, a rainbow cloud of power that sucked up the air to push it out in a mighty breath. I gasped. Coming back to myself, enough air in my lungs to carry the sound, I screamed, the crystalline sound infused with passion. Light. Heat. Colour. Sound. The crushing melody of snapping metal and crumbling stone was heard under the roar of his heart racing mine. Shaking, my entire body shook. Everything heaved and churned. The ground shook in a tumult, the building quaked, the wall behind me disappeared. A sudden jolt vibrated so forcefully my teeth chattered. Light exploded in front of my eyes. I swear the earth moved and groaned beneath us and everything shuddered.

The world fell apart around us and I did not care. I was warm in his arms – safe in his arms. We were together, our bodies at peace and entwined together.

I buried my head into Breandan's shoulder and rubbed my cheek across his chest as his wings closed around me.

The light cut out and it was utterly dark.

CHAPTER SEVEN

At first neither of us moved, chests heaving. The relief in such a reunion was too extraordinary to bear.

Face rapturous, Breandan clasped my neck and pulled my head forward to press his forehead to my own. My hands rested on his chest, balled up into fists. How easily I had been prepared to give this up in the cage.

"Everything you are belongs to me," he rasped, enveloping me in his arms to crush me to him. "You're mine."

His wings flexed behind him, and he glanced over his shoulder, eyeing them thoughtfully. His tail twisted around then flicked side to side purposefully. "Oh," he said and made an amused humming noise low in his throat.

I briefly remembered how I had reacted when I got my wings and tail. I'd screamed, and it had taken a sharp slap to calm me down. My fairy simply said, 'oh'.

He set me down on my feet, keeping a tight grip on my waist. His gaze was soft, caressing, and had returned to luminous silver. I gazed up at him, breathless and dazed.

Then my eyes wandered away from his face and I balked, my stomach plummeting.

The human Temple would now forever be only a memory. Devastation. The wall behind me was gone. Sanctuary was gone. The courtyard was … gone … nothing but piles of rubble remained, some chunks no bigger than my fist.

My mouth swung open as I peered through the settling dust to take in the ruin laid to waste around us. Is this what our love – our bond – had to offer the world, the complete annihilation of everything that dared to stand in its path?

As the haze cleared, my actions before our tryst returned to me. Suddenly, I cared again. With a sickening flash of clarity I saw myself, wild eyed and crazed, hurling my magic at Ana as she wavered on her knees, trying to protect people so they could run from us.

So, this was it? I was reduced to nothing more than a battering ram of need until I got my fix from the bond. How the hell were we supposed to control something like this? What would have happened if Ana, Conall, or anyone else had not managed to flee in time?

Oh gods. Such a bond should not be possible, especially when wielded by one such as I.

"We will destroy everything," I whispered.

Breandan breathed in deeply and seemed concerned as he looked out on what remained of the Temple. "This is not discreet," he muttered. "But we will deal with the consequences, together."

His grip on my waist tightened and I winced. Lochlann would be … mad. Breandan made a sound of frustration and knelt down to untwist my trousers and help me back into them. I rested my hands on his shoulders to steady myself.

I lifted my head, and the small smile teasing the corners of my mouth at the idea of us together, dropped.

Tomas stood on the edge of the courtyard staring at us. His hands were loose at his sides and had I not been able to see his face, frozen in an expression of wrath, I would have thought him relaxed. His eyes were black, brows drawn together, and his lips pulled back to show his fangs. Blood ran down his chin and his clothes were ripped where he had been fighting. He had lost the gaunt, starved look, and his cheeks were plump rather than caved in. He had fed well and looked better for it.

"He just arrived," Breandan murmured as he tugged my trousers over my hips. He pulled me in and kissed my brow. "He saw nothing."

"But still enough to cause him pain," I replied quietly.

Stepping around Breandan I took a step toward Tomas, but his look of anger turned to one of anguish and he shook his head. He walked off briskly until he turned and was hidden behind a collapsed outer building.

He was still close, I could feel the darkness comforting him, but his message to me was clear, so I respected his wishes and I did not run after him.

I entwined my fingers with my fairy and leaned my head on his shoulder, enjoying the feel of him. I did not feel guilty about Tomas, but sad it had come to this, and wretched that he had to see Breandan and I that way so soon after I had set him straight on the way I felt. I had told him exactly what Breandan meant to me and my conscience was clean. I cared for Tomas deeply, but not enough ever to consider turning my back on Breandan. Not again. Never in this lifetime would I put him through that uncertainty again.

From the rubble and smoke came more demons I knew and I exhaled so sharply my entire body slumped.

Oh gods, thank you.

It was the crouched figure ambling behind the shifter

twins – who still looked fierce, naked and in human form – that caught my attention first. Runt had a black eye, a split lip, and a few bruises across his ribs, but was otherwise unharmed. He started over to me in that odd lurching amble, but stopped abruptly when he focused on Breandan standing beside me holding my hand.

My fairy sighed. "Rae, must you befriend every stray demon you find?"

I blinked up at him innocently.

Giving me an exasperated look, Breandan extended his arm. Runt shied away, scooting around him to reach me. I picked him up and he touched his head to my shoulder. I patted his dusty crown fondly. I was so proud of him – he had fought like a demon.

Breandan swivelled on his heel nimbly and offered his arm again, managing to send me a reproachful look even as he softly said, "I won't hurt you, but if you're afraid of me this will not work. I'll have you sent away."

I scowled. "He's just–"

He held up his palm to silence me. "This is up to you, goblin. Only the strong can stand with us."

Runt took Breandan in slowly, wriggled out of my grasp, then straightened his back and lifted his chin. My eyes got wide when Runt had reached his full height – my height – and jerked his head in an odd bow at Breandan. He blinked his huge orb-like eyes at me and spread his thick lips in an ugly smile before his body curved back in on itself and he ambled off to go stand beside Amelia.

Byron had come to stand behind his daughters and a placed a hand on their shoulders. Lines of strain that had been around his mouth had eased somewhat. The scar that slashed through his eye crinkled as he cracked a brief but delighted smile to have his children safe.

Alec and Maeve wandered back next. He had her safe

in his arms, and jumped down off a high pile of bricks, landing heavily. She giggled, squeezing her eyes closed, and wrapped her arms around his neck to steady herself, legs kicking gently.

They both looked okay from what I could tell. Alec had a dark red sticky spot on the corner of his temple, and some of his hair and left shoulder were drenched in blood. Otherwise, he looked okay. Maeve looked better than fine to me, only flushed and missing some armour plates.

At least Alec had managed to find some trousers. Byron and the shifter twins were completely bare and I had to focus hard on their faces to keep myself from blushing. Nobody else seemed bothered. Clearly, the demons did not have the same issue with nakedness that I did, but I supposed that was down to my human nurturing.

The Omega's eyes were wide as they took in Maeve's green skin and fiery hair. Her lids fluttered open and her red irises locked with his amber ones that shone admiringly.

"Hell," I muttered. "How are we going to explain that to Lochlann?"

Breandan eyed me then his sister. He shrugged. "I do not understand."

I waved my hand to where Maeve and Alec were staring at each other – completely absorbed in nothing and no one, but each other.

Alec smiled and Maeve blushed prettily.

"Maeve?" I called and could not keep the smile from my face. "What are you doing here?"

She beamed at me and waved back, her small hand blurring she shook it so fast. "When Breandan and Conall knew you had been taken, they sent Alec to appeal to

Lochlann for followers to help rescue you. So here I am."

I was stunned. "Lochlann sent you?"

She shrugged and looked away. "You are important, Rae." She looked back at me, grinning evilly. "And you really needed rescuing."

Alec snorted and she elbowed him. "She's tricking you all." Maeve gave a breathy gasp. She scrambled in his arms and tried to put her hands over his mouth. "I didn't make it further than the outskirts before she cornered me and made me tell why I was on Wyld land." Alec shifted her about in his arms then tickled her sides. She squealed and kicked her legs, laughing. "I was coerced into telling all I knew. Once she had what she needed from me she was off, and I struggled to keep up." He pulled her into his chest, smiling, and she hugged him to her in return.

Nimah narrowed her eyes at them and moved forward. Amelia caught her shoulder, and the younger twin froze and pouted.

"I guessed as much," Breandan said. "Lochlann would not have sent our sister."

"I am old enough to make my own choices," Maeve said in her high chime abruptly serious. "It was better this way, Breandan. Lochlann is still upset with you both." Her gaze flicked between us, resting on Breandan's wings. "And now the bond is sealed he will feel betrayed." Her small hand waved at the damage around us. "This is not discreet."

Alec coughed into her hair, but I saw the grin he tried to hide.

I frowned. "We did try. I mean, Lochlann has to accept this now, right? I can understand he hoped I would choose to stand by his side as his mate, that I would break the bond. But the simple fact is I didn't want to." I looked at Breandan. "My heart was lost the moment I saw Breandan. Nothing and no one can change that. It is done."

And I was happy, content. I had no doubts this was how it was meant to be.

"Nothing I do will make him think well of me." Breandan sounded so sad I took his hand and our bond soothed him.

The fairy-girl was not the slightest bit swayed by how forlorn he looked. "Gods be damned, brother, you must swallow your pride and apologise. Always are you stubborn. You are in the wrong this time, not him."

Alec gasped and tickled Maeve again, making her break out into high-pitched giggles mid-lecture.

Breandan's eyes slitted as he focused on what flowed between the two young demons. "No," he said as if the word was an order to stop the affection growing between them that would be instantly obeyed.

He took a step forward and I dug my heels in to jerk him to a halt. "Uh, too late," I replied dryly and caught his hand with both of mine before he could pull away. "We're not the only ones stuck on each other."

I was delighted for them both. No doubt, Maeve was the mysterious forbidden love Alec had been referring to. It was easy to see that the Claiming was upon them both, and disrupting that would be wrong.

Breandan caught my gaze and his own warmed, it caressed my face even as his thumb rubbed the inside of my palm.

Stomping boots broke our moment of peace as Conall darted up to us to stand a few paces away. His gaze roamed over me in concern, mouth pulled down into a scowl. He was covered in patches of gore and long wisps of dark hair from his ponytail trailed down his face and neck.

I assured him wordlessly that I was okay, touching the back of his hand gently, an apology for scaring him so deeply evident in my eyes.

Pale faced and exhausted, Ana hung limply over his shoulder like a sack of grain. "Can I get down now?" she squeaked.

Breaking eye contact with me, he set her down carefully, and the first thing she did was stick her tongue out at him then me. She dusted herself off and crossed her arms over her chest, still looking hot, bothered, and embarrassed.

Before I could apologise, Lex stumbled into sight. Her chalk white skin was splattered with crimson from chin to waist and she held Ro up. One of his arms was flung over her shoulder and he looked like he'd been to hell and back. A deep gash over his eye seeped, and his shoulder looked dislocated judging by the funny angle he held his arm. With each step, he grunted in pain and gritted his teeth.

She set him down on a chunk of wall that had survived some of the blast, and he winced, eyes closing in pain. She shot me a bloodied smile over her shoulder then made Ro comfortable. When he was relatively settled she yanked on his arm and pushed his body back. There was a loud crunch and Ro howled in pain. As he cursed at her, Lex rolled back onto her heels then settled down to cross her legs. She calmly placed her chin in her upturned palm as he jumped up and down damning all manner of gods and creation.

Safe. All of my friends were safe and well. My eyes closed briefly and I sent up a small prayer of thanks. The gods had to be listening for us to have come through this relatively unscathed. We had removed a dangerous threat and were alive to fight another day. Yes, my prayers had been answered. The shifter twins were free and back with their father like I had, ah, planned, and we could get back to hunting Devlin, this time with the weight of an entire Pride behind us.

I jerked my chin toward the far corner of the courtyard. "What shall we do with them?" I asked Breandan.

The dust-covered Disciples had rallied together and cowered in a far corner. A few unconscious, or worse-for-wear Clerics had been dragged into their midst, and were being shaken or slapped awake. Squinting, I was relieved to see Samuel in their midst, seeing to his comrades' wounds. The Disciples were torn between staring at us demons, and the rubble that used to be their home.

I felt guilty all over again. Had the Temple been destroyed a few days ago and I was still clueless like them, I would have been devastated. My confusion would no doubt have turned to anger at the demons that had done it. How scared they must all be. The Priests and younger Disciples had already been evacuated by the order of Cleric Tu. The dead in this battle were those of the few who had remained and been unlucky enough to be gouged in the wrong place with a claw or blade. I did ask the demons to go easy, but Conall, Breandan, and Maeve had not heard me, and had released a whole world of pain upon them.

The Disciples watched me as if I was going to chomp their heads off at any moment. I sighed. Was it worth trying to talk to them as an equal? Maybe if I explained what was going on they would understand. They must have felt the hex settle then lift off them.

Breandan's eyes had clouded with confusion and concern. "Rae-love...."

"Are you going to murder us now demon," a pissed

voice called across the space. Zoe sat up clutching her shoulder and glared at me as if all her troubles were my solely fault.

And it wasn't fair.

I'd been through hell to protect the Disciples, her included.

By gods. I stomped my foot, and shrieked at her, "Okay, so I gave you a black eye. Yes, my fairy and vampire destroyed half of Bayou. Sure, I flattened Sanctuary," I paused. "Okay, fine, the entire Temple, but really, everything is not entirely my fault. Technically I saved your ungrateful ass," I held up two fingers, "twice!"

Zoe's heavily-freckled face looked anxious, but her eyes sparked with anger. Lex had dropped her hold on Ro, and the look she shot Zoe had the girl's complexion jumping from pink with anger to pale with fear.

The look of hunger on Lex's face had me drawing in a deep breath.

"No," I said and drew myself up tall, daring anybody to defy me. "Lex, we're letting them go."

"They wouldn't have left us alive," Ro wheezed.

"It doesn't matter. They shouldn't have been out here in the first place." My eyes roamed the Temple grounds. "Gods, what were the Priests thinking, allowing Cleric Tu to bring them here." I pushed my hair out of my eyes, and my tail thumped the floor once in finality. "We're sending them away."

Lex scowled at them, at me, but nodded then crouched down beside Ro, licking her lips. I shivered, nauseated. I was still having a hard time accepting her new bloodthirsty nature, and it was upsetting she could not extend sympathy for the Disciples. She used to be one. I sighed. I had done this to her and I still didn't know all the ways her transformation had affected her.

Breandan clasped my chin and made me look at him. It looked like he was the only one brave enough to challenge me. I knew all the arguments he could use. All the logic and battle strategy said that leaving enemies trained to hate us alive and well was reckless, risky. That it would cause more trouble later, and I would regret it in the end.

All these arguments, logical as they were, did not detract from the fact that killing them would be barbaric, something we needed to change.

As a human, I had been shunned and mocked for never blending in or being part of the 'in' crowd. Yet, I had been taken in and raised by these people. Living as a human shaped who I was, how I saw the world, and it always would. There was so much good in them, and holding on to thoughts of how Lex used to be, Samuel's kindness, and the Priest that had secured my future when I was a baby, I strengthened my resolve. I would protect them as my own.

I stared Breandan down until he nodded his acceptance.

Taking my hand, he turned to face them. "You may go," he bellowed, his voice amplified by magic into a melodious boom. "Remember the kindness you have been shown today." He motioned to me. "If not for her, you would be dead."

"Or eaten," Lex mumbled under her breath.

The Disciples did not need another word to be spoken. Blubbering between themselves, they scrambled up, and stumbled away in a tight knit group, jumping and shrieking at every shadow. Zoe held her head high and kept her back straight, moving with decisive slow steps. And she was not the only one. The truly hard and strong amongst them simply glared over their shoulders and calmly walked away. From those calm few would come the next hatemonger, but that was a worry for another day, and one I knew I could handle. The key to dealing with the humans was getting to the Priests. I knew they were simply full of fear and confused. I had to reach them somehow and make them hear me.

"We cannot stay here too long, Rae. They will come back to fight," Ro said.

I rubbed my head. "I know you all think I'm making a mistake letting them leave, but we're not the bloodthirsty demons they think us to be." Lex snickered and there was a honking laugh from Ro. I bit my lip to stop my answering smile; their inappropriate humour was infectious. "If we act like heartless creatures it will vindicate the lies of the true monsters like Cleric Tu."

"Well said. Once we have the grimoire everything will change for the better," Conall said firmly. "We use the spell, dispose of Devlin, and put you and Lochlann in your rightful places. The rest will follow."

"I don't know, Conall," Maeve said in her high chime. Alec smiled down on her and her flush of pleasure had a purple stain blooming across her cheeks. "After what we've seen here, do we still think using witchcraft is the right way to do this? At first I agreed wholeheartedly, but now … after seeing Rae struggling to deal with such darkness … no … I'm not so sure using the witches' grimoire is the right way."

I almost missed the meaning of what had been said, so focused had I been on the backs of the retreating Disciples. Samuel glanced over his shoulder at me, dipped his head then he was gone.

"Uh, wait," I butted in and frowned as I ran Maeve's words around in my head again. "The witches' grimoire … you mean the book was written by witches?"

The fairies fell silent.

Papa Obe had made me think more on the significance of the spell book since he explained the Vodoun had helped keep it from the witches, but I hadn't realised why the witches wanted it so badly. I was still looking at the grimoire as Lochlann's way of taking the High Lordship from Devlin whilst keeping within the rules of fairykind. Essentially, I saw the grimoire as a book of fairy magics, but that was not the case. The book had a bigger role to play, especially if the witches had written it. That made the magics it contained dark. It explained why the witches were interested in finding me, and why their attention had fallen on the Temple. They wanted their book back, and I had the key.

The look Conall gave me was apologetic and almost ashamed. I narrowed my eyes, looking at each of their faces slowly. Maeve looked discomfited, resolute, but ashamed. As always, the only one in the dark was me.

After a full minute of silence, I found my voice, and I yanked my hand from Breandan's to move away from him. "You have got to be out of your minds? You were going to try to depose Devlin from the throne by using *witchcraft*?" Conall winced at the power of my voice. Good. 'Cause I was pissed. "Why was I not told this?"

"We didn't want to frighten you," Breandan explained. "You only knew of witchcraft as an evil practice."

"That's because it is," I said furiously. "They feed off darkness and you want to use it to bring down the fairy High Lord?"

"The Vodoun use black magic, Rae." Breandan pointed to Lex, who started guiltily. "You stood in the way of natural order to save your friend. You called on the Loa and used the dark arts to bring her back. Were your intentions not good and noble?"

I shook my head. "You're twisting everything. What I did wasn't an accident, but it wasn't exactly intentional either. I reacted in a moment of grief."

Breandan glowered at me. "Our actions were intentional and carefully planned as what was considered best for the fairy people. You saw what Devlin was doing to us."

"One wrong does not cancel out the other," I said firmly. "Ana told me Devlin could be removed by a spell in the grimoire, but I didn't understand the implications of what she was saying." I looked at him pointedly. "You once told me Devlin could be removed by majority vote. I foolishly assumed the two were tied."

He was already shaking his head. "The people won't vote against him. They are too frightened, and the vote cannot be cast without him present. He has been a lord for over seven centuries Rae, and High Lord for two. Even if they fear him, they respect him. They won't vote against him."

"Just so I'm clear, your family," I started with Breandan then spun to Conall to include him in my damnation, "and mine, decided to lead a revolt against a rightfully appointed sovereign who is still in power because the people respect him even if they fear him?" They all looked away from me and I had my answer. I was besieged by anger. This was not what I had been led to believe was happening. "You lied to me."

"No," Breandan and Conall said as one.

I made an impatient movement with my hand. "Fine, but you twisted everything to make it seem like Devlin was this evil tyrant who needed dragging down lest he ruin the whole world."

Devlin's words came back to me; "Don't you see, Rae? The rebels are still part of my Tribe and they will be until the day I no longer rule … they may not agree with me, and encourage Lochlann's tantrum and defy me for a while, but so be it…. Breandan overstepped his place … turned his back on tradition thousands of years old…. Don't be foolish, you have a chance to save many of our kind…. Our ancestors' legacy flows strongly through your veins, and you could help bring us back together…. We are fairy and bound to keep our oath by magics … take your rightful place in my Tribe so we can put an end to this feud."

All the blood drained from my head and I swayed. Breandan stepped forward to help me, but I staggered back. If he touched me he would overwhelm me and make it too hard to think, make it hard to see past the web of half-truths they had told to manipulate me.

"He wanted the same things you did. He wanted me to help him bring the race back together. He told me himself, and we fairy cannot lie. He practically begged me to help and I didn't listen because you all had me convinced that he was evil."

Breandan cut the air with a bold swipe of his palm as if to erase the words and the feeling of distrust swelling between us. "You have seen what he has done. Do not make the mistake of seeing our actions as immoral. He is poison."

Balling up my fists, I shook them at him. "Being evil and being a hard-assed leader are two different bloody things. What I'm beginning to understand is that Lochlann decided he knew what was best for the fairy race and fractured it." I turned to Conall. "You told me our family had to fix the mess we made, but all we've done is make it worse."

Conall shook his head violently, ponytail flicking from side to side, his face anguished. "This must be done. He was making things unbearable. He became suspicious of everything and everyone."

"Clearly he had reason to be," I seethed.

"He withdrew from the other demons instead of using his influence to guide them into a new era," Conall objected. "He was killing us."

Even now, their words sounded reasonable, and could be nothing but truth, but I now knew it was only one side of the story.

I put my hands over my ears. "Stop it. Stop talking."

Breandan did touch me this time. He yanked my hands down and kept his long fingers wrapped round my wrists. "We had to resort to base measures to remove a base threat. What we did walked the line between what is right and what is wrong, but we never crossed it. It was my purpose to give my body to protect the people. I am covered with symbols and incantations of power that have been gathered for millennia and passed down from one chosen fairy to another. They help me see, guide my actions. I swear to you that we were doing what was right."

I wanted to push him away from me, but the moment my hand slapped against his bare chest, I felt so grounded, the rage flowed from my body and was replaced with eerie calm. Almost reverently, I traced the marks that flowed down his torso. He shuddered and turned his back to me as I glided the pads of my fingers over his skin, around his pinions, swirling and twisting with the ink drawn onto his skin in bold and frightfully sinister curves. I had wondered why some seemed evil to me and now I had my answer. Breandan was covered in tattoos that represented the light and the dark. My fairy-boy was a mix of both and I had thought him so virtuous and good. I flushed. Some of the things he had done were not virtuous indeed, and most of those concerned me.

I sucked in a breath, knowing the moment I let him go the clarity would fade and everything would become a confused scribble across the canvass of my understanding. It would be an unholy muddle and I did not know if I possessed the wisdom to see past it.

I stepped back and let my hands slide from his skin, immediately mourning the loss of connection. Breandan flexed his back and slanted a look over his shoulder before turning to face me fully. Pinning me to the spot with the intensity of his stare, he reached out to pull me into him. My eyes darted to Conall who stood off to the side, looking stressed and guilty but too distracted to say anything about how Breandan held me. His warm hand on my cheek had my gaze returning to his.

"Forgive me," he said humbly and bowed his head. "I should have shown more faith in you. I only wanted to do what was best."

I cupped one of my hands behind the nape of his neck, and let the other clasp the waist of his trousers to tug his body flush to mine. His eyes burned with silver flames and he swallowed loudly. For once, he did not seem worried about anybody else nearby. He was single-minded. Focused. This I could tell from the impression he sent down the bond – a glowing, golden light that represented me in his consciousness. All his attention was on me and it was an intense, breath taking thing.

Of course, I would forgive him, but other people would have to work harder for my forgiveness. I sensed there was another key to this mess.

"Ana," I called and jerked my head at her. "Get over here."

She hesitated, blue eyes suspiciously moist as she shuffled forward.

My wings jack-knifed out, fluttering in irritation. For the first time I noticed they were bigger than before. I could feel the velvety bottoms brush the middle of my thighs, and the tips climbed so high they were out of my line of sight.

Still, Ana dragged her small feet.

I hissed, "Now."

Breandan brushed his lips across my temple. "Be nice." He kissed me again and stepped back.

My lip twitched. Be nice?

The white witch's face was pink as she stopped before me. How different can a small piece of information make a relationship?

"You're the he-witch's kin, aren't you? And not just because he's Coven Father, you're his blood relation. You look far too alike so don't try and lie."

Her shoulders slumped. She nodded. "Yes," she whispered. "I am First Daughter of Cael. Father of Blackthorn Coven."

I stared at her. The names meant nothing to me but I got a distinct feeling from the way the others stiffened it was not a name to carry with pride. "Why didn't you tell me?" Her eyes clouded over and I snapped my fingers in her face. "Don't you dare. Stay focused on me and ignore everything else." She sent a frightened look at Breandan who started to speak, but I held up my hand. "You've said enough. I understand why you did what you did, and how in a twisted way you thought you were protecting me. But she can lie and she did."

He reached for my hand and I slapped him away. He sighed. "It's not her fault. I asked her not to tell you. Not to tell anyone who she was."

I kept my eyes on Ana. "Tell me what happened."

She rubbed her tummy. "You saw the scars." Her eyes

briefly flittered across mine and her face creased in sympathy. "The Tribe caught me and Wasp tortured me for information on Cael's plans."

"I've already heard this story." I paused. "An altered version but–"

"What I didn't tell you is the real reason why I've given my loyalty to the fairies."

"You told me you were from the upper dwells–"

Ana made an annoyed sound. "No, you assumed and I didn't correct you."

My tail cracked from side to side in irritation. Ana side-stepped to avoid getting lashed by the tip. I took a deep breath. "But you told me about demons hiding behind the Wall."

"Demons do hide in plain sight behind the Wall." She shrugged as if this was common knowledge. "There are many humans with goblin, witch, and shifter blood. Not enough to mark them as demon though. Many probably don't realise they're descendant from a supernatural. The fairies have always tended to stay within their own race, but recent events wouldn't be the first time a fairy had tied themselves to one outside their gene pool. Your own mother bred with a human."

Fisting my hands, I looked down at them as if they held all the answers. "Are you saying that I might have more family somewhere?"

This time Breandan did take my hand. He unfurled my fingers and stroked my palm. "I would ask that you forget any thought of more family. It will cause you nothing but pain. All right?"

As always, he was blunt and matter of fact. Not that it bothered me anymore. Better to flatten a silly hope then let it take root and grow. Even so, I struggled with this because I still fought to understand the timelines of when this all occurred.

I asked, "Why have I not aged? You believe what you're saying to be the truth, I get that, but shouldn't I have two hundred years worth of memory, or be physically older than I am?"

Breandan stroked one of my wing tips then followed the curve of my pinion down to my back. "Physically, you're still growing." His own wings flexed then and the corners of his mouth kicked back in a smile. "As am I. When we reach our prime our aging slows drastically. Combine this with our temperament and we begin to act matured yet remain … youthful in appearance. Our minds refresh themselves to stave away the apathy and ennui that comes with long life. Understand?" I nodded. Really, what else could I do? Burst into tears? Breandan smiled at me, and that was more than enough reward for sucking it up. "Do you remember what you did when we fought Devlin?"

My own smile slid from my face. A shudder rippled through me as I remembered the feeling of being stretched and yanked from one place to another. "Somehow I moved us from the forest into the old church."

Breandan nodded. "No other fairy would think of attempting such a thing. Generally we do not hold enough power, therefore it is not physically possible for us. Yet you managed to not only move yourself, but Devlin and me, purely on instinct."

From the look of awe on Conall's face, I could tell this was a big deal. I eyed Breandan speculatively. "You didn't seem shocked at the time."

His face creased with amusement. "When have I ever looked shocked to you? When has Conall, Devlin, or Maeve? It is not something we experience often. And when we are surprised, we adjust so quickly you'd be lucky to catch us suffering through it." He smoothed his hand down the space between my wings and I squirmed. "We suspect Sorcha did something similar when Devlin and the warriors chased her down after she split the amulets and took you. Only I don't think it worked the same way."

Conall reached to touch my shoulder, but then held back and looked down to his booted feet. "Our mother was powerful. Beautiful and powerful in ways not even her own family truly understood. When it happened, those of us sensitive to magic felt it rattle our bones." His eyes closed in memory. "Everything stopped and was quiet. A silence so loud it was deafening."

The way he stood, arm reaching and ears twitching, it was like he was back there, remembering. He had once told me that as a young boy he had peeked into my cradle. My eyes boggled as the implications of that became clear.

He smiled faintly, and when he opened his eyes, they were already trained on me. "I've been looking for you for a long time, little sister. It brings me joy to know that I did not fail you. I could not find you because you were not there to be found."

I floundered, shaking my head. Were they honestly trying to say my mother had used her magic to walk through an opening in time and leave me on a Temple Priest's doorstep?

No, impossible.

"I'm struggling to accept this," I admitted. "I mean, you can't be serious."

My brother touched my amulets briefly. "What are we Rae? What is the first thing I taught you about magic?"

"That it's energy."

He nodded. "Energy that flows and connects all things. When you and Breandan touch how does the nexus manifest itself to you?"

I swallowed. Was this a trick question so that he could scold me? "Light," I said tentatively. "Burning light."

He smiled, but it did not reach his eyes. I saw a great sadness there and knew then he would never fully accept that I had chosen Breandan over Lochlann. "And there is no power on this earth that moves faster than light," he explained. "Do you understand now?"

Ana had told me when the nexus fully opened, Breandan and I would become a Source in our own right and be able to wield insurmountable power. We had all seen a glimpse of its destructive capabilities by the obliterated Temple grounds. What if a smaller portion of that power was focused on moving as fast as light itself. Could you move so fast it seemed you shifted from one location to another on a blink, like I had? Moving so fast, your energy passed through, around, or over any stationary barrier. Was my magic that powerful? Inherited from my mother then amplified by my connection with Breandan? Ana could see the future … in a fashion. Ghost images played out over what she saw in her waking hours. Though she could only focus on one possible future at a time and often missed many, I did not get a feeling that she had ever lied or held back what she had seen. Could I use her Sight to an even greater advantage? Say she tells me a future path and I try to move fast enough to jump into it. Would I be able to jump back too?

I spoke slowly still reeling with the possibilities. "So if I focus enough I can move through–"

Breandan glared at me with such violence his eyes shifted from silver to black. He sent me a wave of caution so strong it hit me like a physical blow and I stumbled back. My ears rung and my stomach lurched dangerously.

Gods, at this rate there would be nothing left inside me.

"*Banish the thought*," Breandan roared and took hold of my arms to shake me roughly. "What one can achieve does not pass over to the other. Every fairy is unique and none do the same thing the same way." He lowered his voice and trembled as he struggled to control his reaction. "Should you try we cannot predict what would happen to you."

"Our mother died, Rae," Conall said softly as an explanation for Breandan's fearful anger. "She was found dead in a circle of burning grass and you were gone." My brother shrugged hopelessly. "Just … gone. Her magic had burnt out on the return journey. The only reason we knew you were still alive is that the years passed and no new Priestess was born."

When I had shifted us I had barely been able to stand or think straight. Attempting it again would have probably killed me ... like it had killed my mother.

Oh, Conall. My heart hurt for him. Everything and everyone he loved, the life he'd once had, simply disappeared overnight. My whole life I had thought my family had abandoned me, but it looked like I had been forced to abandon them. Amelia had told me Conall had visited her great grandmother searching for me. He had held onto the hope that I was alive and that he would bring me back to my rightful place amongst our people. He had shouldered the shame of our family, the burden of our legacy. Son to the murderess who broke the balance and sent away fairykind's one hope to restore order.

There could only be one Priestess and since I was still

alive, the fairy race lost their spiritual leader for two hundred years. No wonder we were so fractured and lost. Worse, when the Priestess was found, not only was she selfish, foolhardy, and scatter-brained, but she didn't mate with the rightful High Lord. She fell in love with someone else. And not just any mating, a dangerous bonding that had rocked the foundations of their race a millennia before.

How could *I* repair such damage? I needed time to learn and grow but they needed me now. Things were happening now and as always I was hesitant, or too afraid to throw myself into what I was, in fear I would lose myself.

Lochlann was an ass, but he did what he thought was best. Just like Conall. He had seen Lochlann as a leader who wanted to bring positive change. If I had been in his shoes wouldn't I have done the same?

"I'm sorry," I said to Conall quietly, and before I talked myself out of it, I wrapped my arms around his waist. He was so bulky and big it took some effort on my part. I rested my head lightly on his chest. "I'm sorry I left you and that we had to spend our childhoods alone."

Conall wrapped his bulging arms around me and buried his head in my hair. "All will be well," he said roughly.

There was a soft thump of boots trying to walk away quietly and my eyes snapped open.

"Ana," I said firmly and she froze, looking sheepishly over her shoulder.

"You and I are nowhere near done." I disentangled myself from Conall's arms and waited, arms loose by my side. My wings flexed and extended again and the witch swallowed loudly. "Did your father send you to spy on the fairies?"

Ana lifted her chin. "It was my job to get close to Devlin, yes. To use my Sight to convince him I was on his side. I was to return after one month and report all I knew." That month had come and gone yet still here she was. That spoke for itself. "I don't want to be like him, Rae. Surely you can understand that? Not wanting to be like your parents … I don't … fit in," her eyes welled with tears. "I don't bend to the darkness like they do."

"But that is where your magic comes from, isn't it," I said. "Humans were never supposed to be able to touch the Source and use magics. The Vodoun can use magics because their power does not come directly from the Source but from the Loa. They can only infuse other objects with magics and that's why they use charms and fetishes or the bodies of those who have passed on."

Everything came together. A clear understanding of how each race was connected and how they used the forces around us. I touched the amulets around my neck and glanced at Lex from the corner of my eye who nodded her head slowly.

"They can't manifest like we fairies and the witches can," I carried on, confident I was on the right track.

I had learnt a fairy's temperament had a depth that made it complex. We were ruled almost entirely by instinct and our nature. It helped us adjust to things quickly, but humankind didn't adjust well to sudden change that they had no control over. They were passionate, strong-willed, and resilient, yet stubborn and single-minded. Their collective nature couldn't handle the power, and always did they choose to walk the left hand path.

"But you're an exception," I blurted out loud, and my eyes widened. "Because of your Sight! You don't have to choose one path because in a way you walk them all.

You're able to choose your own destiny."

Triumphant, I beamed at her. Tears streamed down her cheeks, and my grin slid from my face. Ana dropped to her knees in front of me and bowed her head. Nimah started forward but Amelia held her twin back. I didn't quite understand what was passing between those three, but I really didn't have the time to worry about it.

Flustered, I waved my hands. "Well, don't cry," I squeaked, panicked.

I looked to Breandan for help and flushed harder. His face was a smug mix of pride and accomplishment. No doubt my bout of clarity helped prove to all present that no matter how much I proclaimed I didn't know what I was doing, I was born to do this ... that my wisdom was something that did not come from a passing of time but from whom I was.

"I've felt so alone and wicked for walking out on my family," Ana said. "And in one moment you make my choice worth it." She smiled up at me through her tears.

I opened my mouth to repeat my wish for her to stand the hell up, but something at the edge of the courtyard moving in the shadows over the rubble caught my attention.

My eyes slitted with resentment. Seriously, the crazy-assed fairy with snake hair, and a dangerously unnatural affinity with knives had come here? Wasp was Devlin's life mate, and completely loyal. Was he here? Why had Ana not seen this? My gaze darted past Wasp into the shadows from which she emerged. I narrowed my eyes further when no one appeared after her, and hissed, my hair crackling with the power I called to me, my wings unfurling.

Breandan side-stepped so he stood in front of me protectively, his wings springing out to shield me. I blinked at this and felt disgruntled. It had taken me hours to use my wings without falling over and I was still just getting the hang of them.

"I am alone," Wasp said in the gritty voice I remembered, stepping forward into pale beams of moonlight.

Breandan and Conall all looked at me, waiting for an answer. I shrugged. At my calm acceptance, the tension in the air wound down, but I was still taut. A memory of this girl pulling Lex's neck back flashed across my memory. But before I could say anything about binding her, a shriek of rage shattered the stillness.

A streak of white knocked Wasp over. She flipped up to land silently on her feet then spun and kicked Lex in the stomach when the zombie-girl lunged for her again. Lex landed in an ungainly sprawl as Wasp eased into a loose crouch. She cocked her head. "They made you a zombie," she laughed without mirth and without missing a beat her gaze flicked to me. "You are pathetic."

"Enough," Conall barked. He picked Lex's trembling body up and patted her on the head as one would a favourite pet. Ro came to her side and hovered, wary of the fairy. Conall left them and turned to face Wasp, crossing his huge arms across his torso and tilting his head, face displeased. "You are not among friends. You will show respect here."

Wasp narrowed her red eyes at him. She straightened. "By fairy law I am leader here." She tipped her head back in a queenly way, but I saw a flicker of doubt crack her untouchable facade. "You will not harm me. I am the mate of the High Lord."

I blew out a breath, fed up of her posturing, and stepped around Breandan. "You think that means anything to me?"

Her lip curled. "You are not my Priestess, you vapid excuse for a royal."

"And you are not my High Lady," I replied easily. She could not offend me with disrespecting a title I had no love for. "You're lucky you're still standing in one piece. The fairies may not hurt you but there are shifters here whom I'm sure want payback for how you and Devlin treated them." My eyes flicked to look over her shoulder and I pursed my lips thoughtfully. "That is ... if a witch doesn't get you first."

Breandan sighed and in a blink was behind Wasp, catching Ana's thin arm mid swing, and holding firm. Wasp stumbled back, eyes wide with shock, but kept her mouth shut. She nodded, stiff-necked, as thanks to Breandan who did not respond.

My fairy shot me a look of consternation and I stared back blankly. He fought a smile. "I will make a peacekeeper of you yet," he murmured. He plucked the knife from Ana's grip and shook his head at her. Handing back the knife hilt first he said, "This is not who you are."

She snatched the blade from him and slotted it back into her boot. "She hurt me." A rare glimpse of vulnerability claimed Ana's expression, and her eyes shone with tears. "She hurt me, and I want to hurt her."

Breandan's fingers brushed away a tear. "You know that is not the way."

She swallowed and surprisingly she looked at me for back up. I hesitated, but the silver-kissed pressure at the edge of my mind spoke to my sensibilities. I shook my head. "He's right. She'll pay for her crimes," my voice hardened, "and I promise her punishment will be more than suitable for the pain she's caused. But even I know, killing her will achieve nothing."

"Especially if you fools wish to try to finish your

nonsensical attempt at rebellion." Wasp rallied her courage and stood hand on hip, head lifted high. Her dreadlocks bristled and her scarlet eyes were cool as she locked gazes with Breandan. "The vampires have Devlin. I want him back and you, boy, you and your insipid mate are going to help me."

Ignoring her poisonous tongue, Breandan and Conall shared alarmed looks.

"The grimoire?" Conall asked. "Do they have the book?"

"Hidden," she replied then tutted at their expectant stares. She flicked her hands at us all with blatant derision. "Not by me, fools."

My fairy hissed. "Says one idiot enough to pass through a vampire city."

"We had no choice. We were trying to lose those who hunted us." She glared at him pointedly. "The vampires ambushed us as we passed the inner city and forced us into a corner." Her handsome face creased with pain and her forest-green skin paled. "I was separated from Devlin and the others were slaughtered. Only Gunarr and I made it out alive. Everyone else was drained dry. We went back during the day with the intention of freeing him but the Nest is … larger than we expected."

"How big?" Conall asked.

"Four hundred strong at least. That excludes those who went underground elsewhere in the city."

"Lies," Alec interjected and I started. I had forgotten he was there next to Byron, who still had his beefy arms around his daughters. Maeve was tucked under Alec's arm and smiled at me shyly before her gaze travelled up to the shifter again, not bothering to hide her adoration. Hell, when we fairies fell we fell hard. "No Nest is that big," Alec finished.

Wasp turned to glare at him. With a few flicks of her ruby irises she had his measure and sneered, ivory fangs glinting in the failing daylight. "I am a warrior, kitty-cat. I can infiltrate a Nest and steal something from those dead things with my eyes closed. I know what I saw." She turned her attention to Breandan and a cruel, seductive smile curled one side of her pouty lips. I resisted the urge to throw myself at her and gouge her eyes out. "You know I'm telling the truth. I swear it." The air thickened with magics as she said the words.

Conall sighed heavily, his big chest puffing out and collapsing, slumping his shoulders. "This is not good. The humans will regroup and there is no doubt they will declare open war. Our race is fractured, and we have lost the grimoire." Conall turned to Wasp and was sincerely apologetic. "There is no time for this. I would not wish Devlin's predicament on any being, but we cannot—"

"But we have our weapon," Wasp interjected irritably, and jerked her chin at me. "Useless as she seems she is all we need. We throw her power at them, scatter and confuse them. They'll be too busy fanging every shadow that moves and trying to work out how to get their lips on her pretty neck to worry about Devlin."

"No," Breandan said, eyes seemingly far away.

"Let me be plain." Wasp took a step forward and stood in the centre of the group as if addressing an assembly of her followers. "I am here because I have no other choice. Clearly Rae is the next Priestess, may the gods spare us from another of Sorcha's bloodline; as if they have not caused, and are not *still* causing, enough trouble. But this is not something you can say 'no' to. It is her purpose. The High Lord has been captured and she is the only one with enough power to get him out of there alive. Since you are no more than a mere rabble of children it's not surprising you're reluctant to march yourselves into reach of the vampires, and no doubt you can tell I do not give a damn whether or not you die if it means Devlin is returned to me and our people safely." She looked us each in the face, silently marking us all as expendable. "We go in there and we get him out. That is the end of it. No discussion, no questions, and no fawning over a silly weakling who is too fearful to place the needs of others above her own and lead." Her words were directed at me and I glowered at her. "The vampires cannot be allowed to keep our lord without swift and brutal retaliation."

Breandan simply … shrugged, unaffected by her outburst. "I will not condone starting a war for your mate."

"And I will not allow our race to dwindle and die as you foolishly try to shield yours. This is inevitable. The vampires are moving against us and you're too lust blinded to see it." Wasp shook her head, lips twisted in dislike. "I can't believe I have to be the one to point this out to you, but have you not considered that Devlin does not want to mate Rae? You two could be together, accepted as you are, and have a place in the tribe if he remains High Lord." She motioned to me. "Try to tell a lie and say that is not what you want." Wasp eyed us both speculatively then understanding dawned and her face smoothed out. She was beautiful when her face was not scowling. Her skin was darker than Maeve's, more like the leaves of the fir tree and her hair was richer and thicker. She was tall, nearly as tall as Breandan and her muscles were defined, hinting at speed and strength. "You no longer carry the word of your brother. You are outcast." She smiled, her green lips pulling back. "You did this for the Priestess, yes? Because by law she would have to be

Lochlann's, and if you'd remained oath-sworn you would have had to stand aside and watch him claim her." Breandan said nothing but flicked a troubled glance my way. Wasp laughed, a screeching warble that made more than once person wince. "I'll admit I am surprised Lochlann allowed this to go so far. He could have been powerful with her at his side." Her laugh puttered out to a chuckle. "Then I suppose he had no choice. We are all fools in love."

"No. Lochlann will never back down, it is not his way. I will not allow any harm to come to my family." Breandan's jaw clenched. "Lochlann will let us—" With a gasp he cut off. He took a few bracing breathes. Whatever he was going to say he did not believe it and that made it a lie.

I moved closer to him, worried. "What do we do?" I asked in the tense silence.

"By the gods, is she always this needy?" Wasp asked, incredulous. "How do you stand it?"

Breandan placed both his hands on the side of my neck and let his hands flow down, soothing. "We return to face my brother. In time we will get the grimoire back, and in the meantime we prepare for war." I jerked, looking up to stare at him anxiously. "The humans will not stop nor will they show mercy. It is us or them." His hands briefly brushed over the scars on my shoulders and arms. "And I choose us."

My brow crumpled, I was upset. "This can't be. You will erase not one species but two. The vampires will die out because … they need human blood don't they? I remember reading that human blood is their only natural food source. So if the human population becomes extinct…."

The collective silence told me all I needed to know

about what they thought of that potential risk.

"Many are in danger," Conall said to cover the awkwardness. "Lochlann needs to know about this. With Devlin gone, he is High Lord."

"He is not gone," Wasp said angrily. "He is captured and all we must do is save him. Your under lord does not hold the throne yet."

Wasp walked over to me, a steely glint in her eye. I kept my back straight and showed no fear though my heart was pounding. I knew she could hear it, they could all hear it, but I locked my joints and stiffened to stop myself trembling.

Her eyes flicked over me curiously. "Nice scars. Almost puts my work to shame. Who knew humans could be so skilled and inventive."

I wrapped my arms around my torso, holding myself together. There was a low rumble from Breandan but he did not move. I knew he was giving me space to stand my own ground, but right then I wouldn't have minded him smashing her face in because, from the churning and lurching in my stomach, I was not going to be fit for much more than bending over in a corner somewhere.

"So," Wasp continued casually, "did they use pincers on your wings or a branding iron?"

My stomach clenched painfully. Spinning around, I fell to my knees and retched. There was a small hand at my head, running a soothing hand down my back. Peering at me in concern, Maeve stroked my back. I looked away, nodded that I was okay. A wave of embarrassment had me ducking down and tears stinging my eyes. So not only was I clueless, a misfit, and scarred, I was weak-bellied and considered a coward for wanting us to find a non-violent way to end the feud between human and demon. I scrunched my fingers together in the hard packed dirt. I did not feel strong any more. Everything was so screwed up. I was looked to for guidance and strength and I could barely keep myself from jumping at my own shadow.

No matter how bad I felt, or how ashamed or self-conscious I was, I knew I had a job to do. One I had to be successful at. I would be brave until I felt brave. At the least I could show courage even if I felt hideous inside.

"Quiet," I said aloud.

The snarling ruckus behind me stopped dead. Heaving myself up I brushed dirt off my knees and hands.

"Ah, the delicate one speaks," Wasp spat.

"Hag," Lex shrieked and swiped at her with clawed fingers, but Ro quickly grabbed her wrist and yanked her back.

Amelia snarled and got in Wasp's face. Most surprising was that Nimah was there too – in-between her twin and Ana – looking the fiercest of the three.

Conall and Breandan seemed about to come to blows, as usual. My brother made calming gestures, cautioning Breandan to use restraint as he eyeballed Wasp balefully.

Alec looked pretty mad too, but was held back by Maeve, her slender green hand clasping his tightly. I had less than a moment to recognise the surprise in his expression and the longing in hers.

Runt was positively animated – darting around between their legs – not sure who to scratch or bite, but the way his eyes kept landing on Wasp told me he had a good idea of where to start.

These demons stood for me, were ready to fight for me. Rae the oddball, who was indecisive and scared of making the wrong move or saying the wrong thing. None of them had looked at me any differently when they saw the mutilation of my skin.

Breandan called me beautiful.

Yeah, I got picked on big time when I made a mistake, but they were always there to help me get back up. To help save me so I could save others. And I couldn't grow up and suck up my insecurities?

"I know at times I seem weak, or afraid. And you're right. I'm scared nearly all the time and I know I make mistakes." I cringed and rubbed my nose. "Lots of mistakes ... but I promise I am trying, and I'll get better." Gathering confidence, I blew out a breath. "What's happening here isn't all about me, so let's not make it all about me. There is something huge and world changing about to go off. What we decide here will shape our future, and that of all species, human and demon. Both are important." The entire group seemed stumped. Eyes got wide; breaths came harder as they widened their perspectives. They were listening to me. With all the attention, I blushed, and wound my hands into my tunic. "So, uh, we'd better ... um ... I mean...." I straightened and lifted my chin. "We need to make the right damn decisions the first time round." Silence. "Don't you agree?" I finished in a small voice.

"I could go get Kalcifer," Nimah offered. "We could use some muscle if we're seriously going to consider meeting up with the vampires."

Grateful for some of the attention to be shifted off me, I nodded enthusiastically then asked curiously, "Kalcifer is who?"

"A were-wolf," she clarified. "Though they'll only be useful for a couple of days. The moon cycle does mess them up big time. Damn witches and their curses. Just imagine it, being tied to the lunar cycle, unable to control your shift." Her head shook in sympathy. "Kal's pack is a two day run to the South. They hibernate at the tip of the region before the sea. Apparently there are fairies up there too that his Pack has been having troubles with. He'll be grumpy, but he'll forgive us."

Ro made a sound of confusion. "Wolves are solitary."

"Full wolves maybe, but for shifters the motto is safety in numbers. I know if we tell them of the human threat they'll help us."

"Kalcifer is temperamental," Byron advised, rubbing his beard. "Alec will go instead."

The shifter-boy stiffened, his gaze cutting from his Alpha to Maeve then to the floor. His lips twisted with the unsaid. He would not want to send Maeve back to Lochlann on her own. Not when humans were roaming around looking for vengeance, but he could not openly disobey his Alpha without making his reasons for wanting to go with her plain.

"I'm thinking...." I cleared my throat as Byron's stone-like stare turned on me. "Maeve shouldn't go on her own to get Lochlann." I lifted my chin. Any higher and I wouldn't be able to see past my own nose. "In fact, I say she is not."

"It's okay, Rae." Maeve gave me a small smile. "I am not afraid." I might have believed her if her voice didn't wobble.

"No. You need an escort and I'm sorry but your brother stays with me." I slid a look Breandan's way and flushed at the look of pleasure that flashed across his expression. "And I'm not ready to go back to either of the Wylds yet. I need to go get Devlin."

This was met with silence. Then Wasp said, "Finally, some loyalty."

Ana, eyes fixed on Wasp distrustfully said, "Devlin's future is no longer tied to yours, Rae. I cannot see him at all anymore, and I am pretty sure that means he's–" She cut a look at Wasp who stood rigid at her words. "Well, I don't think you should go. The vampire city will take you too close to my father's Coven."

Breandan drew me into him and rubbed his cheek on the top of my head, sighing. "You cannot go into a vampire city and crash about looking for a fairy High Lord who wants your power. It is little more than suicide. And Ana is right. I am not letting you out of my sight and I am going nowhere near that city." His high handedness annoyed me, but I let him keep up this rare public display of affection and possession. It felt good, and this was not the time or the place to argue with him.

Ignoring both him and the witch I said, "Alec will escort Maeve." I leaned around Breandan to pin Byron with my glare, showing him how serious I was. "After all I've done for you, I insist on it."

Byron went red, buffed out his ruddy cheeks and broad chest. "I don't have to do anything for you fairy."

"And what of the bargain?" Amelia asked. She went toe to toe with her father. "I thought the deal was Rae should save us and then you would help her track this fairy lord." She crossed her hands over her chest. "The fairy was found without Pack help. The debt we have incurred from this bargain has not been paid. The least we can do is give the young fairy-girl an escort home."

"Rae saved me," Alec added softly. "It would have been me the Clerics caught had she not...." He did not look at me, embarrassed. "Her scars are my fault and I ... she has suffered ... I owe her."

Byron levelled a quelling look at his second-in-command then turned his big head to regard his eldest daughter. His expression shifted into admiration. "You've spoken wisely, younglings. I am in agreement."

Alec breathed out and the radiant smile he and Maeve shared had my heart rolling over in my chest.

Nimah looked satisfied too. "I'm going to go get Kalicfer." Her eyes cut to Alec and Maeve briefly. "I'm not needed here. You can't leave the Pride Dad, and Amelia has business elsewhere."

Her twin blinked rapidly. "I do?"

Nimah smirked and bobbed her head in Runt's direction. "Second to Rae, you're the only one who can control the pest. We need to at least try to ask goblinkind for their help."

Amelia pursed her lips. "I see your point. They are strong." She cleared her throat and blushed. "I too would like an escort." Her eyes darted to Ana who now had pink in her waxy cheeks and was smiling at her shyly.

"I suppose," the witch began, her tiny hands twisting in front of her in agitation, "that I could go too. My Sight would keep us well out of harm's way."

"A good idea," Breandan said and shot a glance at me, his eyebrow quirked.

"What will you do?" Byron asked me curiously. "I doubt you will go to the vampire city. Your mate seems resolute."

I made a rude noise, but didn't disagree. I had no doubt that Breandan would rather die than let me go into the vampire city. "I know. I suppose I'm going to make myself useful by training. I need to get my magics under control to have any chance at defeating the he-witch I faced today."

I scrunched up my nose. The idea of facing Cael again did not appeal to me at all. The shield from Papa Obe had worked wonders on his black magics but I doubted it would hold for long, and a witch of his power would find a way around it. I needed to learn more about the Coven Father. Where did he fit into all of this? I had many questions to ask Breandan and Conall, but now was not the time or the place. I could confidently guess that since the grimoire was a book of witchcraft, that Cael wanted it for some evil end or another. Even though the book was almost in his grasp, he still needed the key, which hung around my neck. It was only a matter of time before I had to face him again ... or was there more to it than that? Unlike the fairies whose magic was structured around rules of engagement, I was certain a witch would have no problem simply taking the amulets from me. Cleric Tu had proved that. So why did the he-witch focus his mind on the Temple, announcing himself and his intentions, when he had the perfect element of surprise? He could have taken the amulets from me before I knew what was happening. More than this, why did I feel like I knew him? I still did not have the full story and it was beginning to bug me. There was a huge piece of the puzzle I was missing. I was so close, yet so far.

"I need to somehow figure out how to fight the effects of iron, or how to store magics within me," I said out loud. "Is that possible without an amulet or charm?" I had intended the question to be answered by Conall, but I realised he was not next to me. I scanned the rubble for my brother, my teacher, wondering why he had been so quiet for so long.

Alec whistled to catch my attention and threw a thumb over his shoulder.

Conall was asleep standing up. Head bowed, and leaned slightly to the side, his chest rose and fell in a steady rhythm. A snore rumbled from his throat.

A bubble of laughter from Ana had me in fits of giggles. Resting my head on Breandan's chest I was thrilled to feel his own body shaking with repressed laughter.

Wasp clapped her hands together in irritation. "What

about my mate? Or have you forgotten?"

My giggles stopped and were replaced with a grim smile. "No. I remember the problem of Devlin quite well. I have an idea."

Stepping away from Breandan I searched through the darkness. I looked inward, felt along the blood tie and called him to me. I wish I could have given him space but we simply didn't have the time. I turned the moment Tomas stepped from the shadows. Our circle swelled outward, openly distrustful of the vampire in their midst.

I stepped forward and jerked my head toward the other side of the courtyard which led into the desolate Temple. Tomas walked off and I followed behind.

Breandan caught my hand, eyes narrow and panicked.

"We need an ally with the vampires," I soothed. "You know this."

Dangerous.

The word came with a flood of emotion. Jealousy. It was a warning that had my nature twisting in discomfort. I sent back a wordless wave of reassurance. Tomas and I had so much between us. I would be fine and he had to see this.

Breandan let me go, fingers releasing their hold one by one with reluctance. "All right," he said flatly.

My eyes wandered to Conall. "Will you find him somewhere to sleep? Away from this place. We can't stay here."

"We all need to rest before we go our separate ways," he said thoughtfully. "I will find somewhere." Oh, my heart swelled at the sight of him. Trust. It was a beautiful thing. He smiled, showing his fang-like teeth, then yanked me back to him. "Kiss me," he demanded.

I gave him a timid look from under my lashes. "In front of everybody?"

He dipped his head down to flick the tip of his tongue over my lips. Inhaling in a rush, I fluttered my wings as he pulled me to him. I crushed my lips fiercely to his. Pulling away, his eyes were wide and burning with the silver-blue flames I loved. I flushed and gave him a challenging look, which he intensified and returned. He kissed me again and I clamped one arm around his back. The other fisted in the dark hair cresting his head.

There was a not so subtle throat clearing, giggles, and long-suffering sighs that became grumbling mutters about public displays of affection.

"Rae! Off!" Conall barked unexpectedly not sounding at all sleepy. Thunderous brow smoothing, he shrugged his shoulders helplessly, eyes darting every-which-way. "Perhaps, it does not even matter now the bond is sealed."

Jerking away from Breandan guiltily, I stumbled. My wings flexed straightening me out and I settled them neatly against my back. I had known Conall would not bestow his blessing on my mating with Breandan, but it was done now. Surprisingly, the blood tie with Tomas was still there. I knew Breandan had been sure it would break when we mated, but I had a feeling Tomas was bound to me till death. And since he was immortal, that meant pretty much for the rest of my life.

Breandan pressed a cracker into my hand. "Eat," he ordered then strode away, motioning the others to trail him.

I flicked my tail at Alec when he gave me a cheeky thumbs up and followed Maeve.

Trotting after Tomas, smiling and blushing furiously, I clutched that damn cracker like it was a gift from the gods.

CHAPTER EIGHT

We walked without speaking for a while and Tomas took my hand after a few steps. I bit my tongue when my mouth opened to tell him that I did not think it was a good idea. He was just holding my hand.

Nothing bad ever happened from someone holding your hand.

"Thank you for not taking off," I said quietly.

He stopped and stared at the empty street. At what, I cannot say, since he seemed look past it. "I can't leave. I need your help."

I nodded slowly. I found I was hurt by his cold admission that he stayed because he needed something from me. I slapped myself mentally. Hadn't that always been the case with Tomas? He had always needed something from me. When I thought of it objectively, so did Breandan … in the beginning. The difference was that now Breandan no longer needed a thing from me. He was guiding me to make the right choices, helping me to carry out my decisions. I sighed. But the comparison wasn't fair. Everyone wanted something from someone I guess.

Raking my bottom lip through my teeth, I glanced at Tomas then away. Peeked again, then looked at his chest. "You're bleeding?"

"I healed."

I nodded three times too many, feeling awkward. "Are you hungry? I mean, can you eat solid food at all? I have a cracker." I offered the mealy disk-shaped biscuit to him. "It has nectar in the middle. It's not awful; it's sweet in an earthy kind of way."

He grimaced uncomfortably. "Anything but blood makes me ill."

"Oh." I looked at my palm then shrugged and stuffed the cracker in my mouth and swallowed. Even with the liquid centre it made my tongue dry without water to follow it down. I guessed it was good to have something in my stomach. I did not feel hungry at all, but mentally I felt better for eating. I wiped crumbs from my mouth and felt rude for eating in front of him. "Sure you're okay?"

His grip on my other hand tightened. "Rae?" There was no patience in his tone.

"Okay, okay." I plucked at my bottom lip before placing my hand on his shoulder in what I hoped was a friendly, platonic way to still him. "I need you to bring the leader of your Nest back here." I paused and forced myself to look him in the eye. "Please."

He cocked his head and shifted so he faced me. "You wish to meet my Queen? Why?"

Queen? The vampires truly called their leader Queen? There was reverence in Tomas' voice when he had spoken so I swallowed my pithy remarks about the title. Just because I found being called 'Lady Priestess' awkward did not mean others would not approve of being addressed by the title their hierarchy afforded them.

"Well, we agreed that a meeting between demonkind would be best to decide what to do about the Sect and the witches. We should work together to find a peaceful solution to the mess we're in. If we remain divided everything will continue to spiral out of control."

"What of your promise to me?"

I stopped fidgeting and glared at him. "I am helping you, albeit not in the way you expected."

His brow furrowed, lips twisted in anger. "You gave me your word."

"Breandan does not want to go," I snapped. "I can't, okay?"

"You let him control you this way?"

I gritted my teeth and squashed the rebellious voice that yelled he was right. "I know you're anxious about what's happening to your kind, but you won't starve."

"No thanks to you."

Now I was mad. I tried to tug my hand from his but he held on. Trying to argue with someone whilst they clutched your hand like a lifeline was difficult, but I managed to keep my voice biting as I said, "Believe me when I say I've done more for you than I've ever done for another. Never has Breandan received the same blind faith as I've given you and he is bonded to me by magics. I've kept your secret about the fairy you drained two days ago." He jerked back and I got in his face. "Yeah, I know. I saw it. Felt it." I thumped my chest. "If I didn't care what happened to you I would have told Breandan or Conall, and not even I could have stopped what they would have done to you." I breathed in sharply through my nose, controlling the urges of what I wanted to do to him for taking the girl's life. "You keep killing people. And while I can forgive you once, even twice, I can't simply ignore it or pretend it isn't happening." My voice lowered dangerously. "If I didn't care, Tomas, I would have let you burn in the sun. I risked everything, everything, turning my back on my kind when I saved you. Don't you dare ignore or forget what I have done for you."

It was clear from the blank look on his face he was unmoved by my words. He made a fast movement with his free hand. "This is your choice."

"There never was one. This is who I am and I refuse to run from that anymore."

He regarded me silently. "You've grown."

His hand was cold as he stroked my cheek. His touch sent a shiver down my spine and I no longer knew if it was lust, fear, or my nature recoiling from him. Slowly and with great tenderness Tomas wrapped his arms around me and pulled me into his chest.

"I'm going back to my Nest, to whatever fate awaits me, but ... please," he whispered over my head. "Please do this for me. You know what I want, and what I need from you. To have you with me is something I never dared to dream. Two nights ago I did not want to wake to the reality where you had chosen him over me, but I understand. Now I only ask that you come to help me save my Nest, my family."

He sounded so forlorn and grief-stricken it made my heart wrench. My conviction wavered. "Gods, Tomas, what you do to me...."

Working my bottom lip in my mouth I tried to make the decision that would let me have Breandan as my mate, and Tomas as my friend ... the one that would mean I could go to his Nest on behalf of demonkind, and say the words that would make them help us.

Would making this situation work for everybody make me the Priestess they believed I was destined to be? My heart sunk. But I didn't truly believe I was destined to be the fairy High Priestess. Is that why this was so hard for me?

Was there a way to convince Breandan to let me travel

with Tomas to the vampire city? Would he believe my desire to destroy Devlin had been doused by my wish to help bring peace?

Devlin dying at my hand before Lochlann was named High Lord would throw the entire fairy race into turmoil, I saw that now, and I would not bring more harm to my race. But my behaviour in the past had been so mindless and self-absorbed, the chances of Breandan believing me were slim. I guess I could swear with magic…. No, no I could not go. It was too close to where Ana said the witches' Coven was located, and Breandan would have a fit at the idea of my walking into a vampire Nest without him. I doubted Tomas would agree to take my fairy with us, or protect him if things went wrong when we were there. More than this, I knew Breandan wanted to return to the fairy Wylds. He wanted to see his brother and be in the presence of the Tribe. I could understand that.

A secret part of me now yearned to see Wyld land too.

"Stay then," I blurted. "Stay with me. I'll keep you safe, and you can show everyone what you're really like. You would be a great help. We will find someone else to see the Queen. I know it's a lot to ask from you, but I think we could make it work."

His shoulders shook and a grizzly sound broke from his chest. "I cannot lurk beside you like a silent shadow and hide when your friends and mate try to kill me. It would not end well, Rae. There would come a time where your fairy and I would clash, and not even you could stop the end result."

The end result, one of them dead, stolen from me forever.

The thought of Breandan meeting his end at Tomas' hands was unconceivable. It went against everything I knew and wanted to know. When I imagined Breandan and Tomas meeting in anger, I saw the end of him – the end of my vampire.

I closed my eyes and twisted my hands into knots behind my back, letting him go physically as I knew I had to do emotionally.

Yet I whispered, "Don't leave."

"My Rae, my sunshine," he murmured and wrapped his arms around me tighter. "I must. There can be no middle ground."

My hands flitted up to rest on his sides. I gave him a squeeze then released him and made him release me by placing my hands on his chest and pushing him away. My decision was made and my heart throbbed in pain.

"I swear I will help the vampires as best I can, Tomas." I braced myself. "But I cannot go. He'll never forgive me if I abuse his trust this way, and I honestly don't think my going with you is the right thing to do. I feel like I'm needed here, and I have to start trusting myself, my own intuition. I admit it feels like I will go to your Nest someday, just not now. My own people need me now."

A raven crowed. The sound was loud and brash. There were always ravens around the Temple, vile carrion eaters.

I waited for Tomas to react with anger, but he became oh so still, and quiet. He looked away and nodded stiffly. "So be it." The words were uttered so softly my ears twitched and strained to catch them.

Tomas turned his infinite gaze upon me and the small smile that had lifted my lips at his composed acceptance faded. His cold hands came to rest on my cheeks, and at the contact I was sucked into the unending, falling into him. The darkness inside me squirmed, writhed, and twisted around my mind until I thought it would shatter. And I … I wanted to move … to move us somewhere else. I could not understand where he wanted me to take us. So the darkness guided me, showing me where I was to go. The familiar feeling of being stretched, of being pulled apart by magic, bombarded my senses. I frowned. This was wrong.... Faintly, I remembered it was easier than last time, and I slipped through the opening, pulling the darkness with me from one place to another. My stomach revolted, wanted to empty, but I breathed through it. Tomas tugged on my hand to make me walk forward.... But I didn't want to be here ... and I ... I wondered why he led me this way.

We passed the first of the dilapidated buildings and I felt a tremble of fear. The windows were blown out and I thought I could see glowing eyes peering at me from the gloom. An eerie fog crept along the concrete floor and lights flicked and died in odd spots in the distance.

The air had a funny, dry, ashy smell. Like something had gone mouldy and was so old and putrefied the smell had aged beyond any specific odour you could name or compare to anything else.

We walked further. I took in the burnt out cars, and smashed up pavements, and wondered why if the vampires wanted the world so badly did they let it go to hell? Why fight so fiercely for something to turn around and let it fall to ruin? Why had they backed off when the Rupture was over and retreated into the depths of abandoned cities like these to hunt scraps?

The devastation in this city was odd. There was little physical decay, but it had a sinister and unpleasant sort of look about it.

"I don't think we should go any further," I said without thinking. Literally without thinking. My mind was almost void, blank. Random memories and thoughts pinged around, but there was nothing underneath but a cloud of darkness.

I stopped walking, my thoughts becoming less muddled. There was a loud buzzing in my ear. Tugging my hand from his, I pressed my palms onto my head and pushed, hoping maybe the pressure would release whatever was causing this wrong feeling all over me.

Tomas brushed his hand across my forehead. The coolness was refreshing and I looked into his bottomless eyes, feeling such peace.

"How do you feel?" he asked compassionately and rubbed my shoulders.

I was being silly, so silly, and here he was being all brave and strong. I shook my head at myself. "Fine. I think today ... all the fighting and use of magics is catching up with me." Breathing out I let him take my hand again and squeezed his gently for being so thoughtful and considerate of my needs. "I know as a fairy I don't need much sleep, but it helps me keep things straight. Sometimes so much is happening around me I feel lost, y'know? I mean, I know I miss a lot of stuff ... and Breandan says I must start being more aware of...." Frowning, I fisted my other hand and knocked myself on the head. My hand knocked something hard, and I fingered the metal pressed into my skin. How odd. "Uh, everything is a muddle."

"Come. Once we reach the inner city you can rest." His voice was light but I thought I heard it crack at the end.

My senses told me dawn was hours away, but I checked the sky anyway. I wasn't exactly in a right state of mind – maybe my senses were off too? The sky was inky black.

"Are you okay?" I asked concerned. "You seem strained."

He smiled, fangs running out as he lifted my hand to kiss my wrist. He pressed a kiss to the veins he found there. "I will be," he murmured.

A dart of fear and disgust shot down my spine and I snatched my hand away, but at the startled look on his face, I instantly was contrite.

"I'm sorry. I...." I reached for him but stopped, somehow knowing, deep down, that I should not be touching him. Not with love. My love belonged to....

Biting my lip I started walking, not sure why my body trembled when Tomas fell into step beside me.

There was a soft scuttle to my left and I jumped, as Tomas quickened his pace and pulled me deeper into the city. My eyes darted across the flat-walled buildings and tried to pierce the dense shadows that hung over every surface. I could see in hues of blue and purple in the dark, but it was almost as if my gaze passed through anything that did not want to be seen in those shadows.

Were there really dozens of hungry red-rimmed eyes staring back at me through the dark from down the alleyways?

The deeper into the city we rushed, the more I felt my magic being pushed into me, compressed inside my body, and my heart sped up.

There was more scuttling from behind us and I shot a fearful look over my shoulder. I swallowed a scream seeing the hunched figures lumbering behind us. One grinned maniacally and I saw the glint of fang.

"There are vampires behind us," I whispered to Tomas, tugging on his hand to get his attention, which was focused on a point up ahead and had been for the last ten minutes.

"Do you trust me, Rae?" Tomas' voice was soothing, and the darkness inside me smoothed over my nature, which was agitated, spiky, and telling me something was wrong here.

Why was I here again? Coming here was probably the worst idea I had ever had. It was my idea to come here wasn't it? Where was Breandan and why was he not with me? Wait. He definitely did not want me to come here, but he would never have let me come here without his protection. Or maybe he thought Tomas' protection was enough to keep me safe?

I swallowed hard and looked over my shoulder.

More vampires - dozens of them - ambling behind us in liquid slinks. One darted past, whooping and shrieking as he did. They ran with a fluid yet cumbersome gait, zipping across the wide street maniacally and passing from shadow to shadow so all I saw was bare chests and ragged jeans. The slap of bare feet on the concrete had the hair rising on the back of my neck. The moon was bright and when one of the vampires passed through its light I saw a starved, emaciated body covered in grime and dirt.

Breathing hard, I stumbled but my wings fluttered and I was okay. This was not right. "I don't think I'm supposed to be here."

Tomas squeezed my hand. "Do you trust me?" he repeated with a firm undertone. He sounded like he was asking the question for the sake of it and that I should simply say yes.

I trusted him did I not? Why would I be here if I did not? I decided to come here with him didn't I?

"I–" A high-pitched squeal of delight pierced the night, and my eyes rolled seeking the mouth it pealed from. "I–"

Something icy brushed past the nape of my neck. A mad chuckle echoed in my ears before a gangly vampire appeared in front of me. I stopped dead, my hand slipping from Tomas' and I heard him curse as another slipped in behind the first, slobbering, pushing at him so as to get a better look at what might be his food … me.

Stumbling back, I remembered those behind me then spun round to see what they were doing, which was nothing. Well, they were collectively wiping the drool from their chins and licking their lips as they eyed me up and down hungrily, but other than that, they were still.

Backing up, I held my hands up and tried to step around the vampire. He feinted to block my way. Heart pounding, sweating, I tried to go the other way and he jerked to block my path. Terrified, I reached out to the Source and armed myself with energy. It buzzed at my fingertips. The vampire spread his arms out wide and swung his head from side to side once then smiled toothily at me, his fangs running out. I was used Tomas' extended fangs, but he had all his other teeth, unlike the one in front of me who smelt like he bathed in sewage. My stomach dropped as he chuckled oddly and jerked forward, making me jerk back. He did it again and I got the distinct sense he was playing with me, taunting me. Just like I had been told vampires liked to do when they were hunting.

There was a pained grunt and the littler vampire – who had been trying to get a better look at me –flew toward me and I ducked to let him sail overhead and crash into those behind me.

The vampire that was playing with me spun and got Tomas' fist in his face. He dropped to his knees and keened, then shrank back when Tomas raised his hand again and snarled. Crawling back, the feral vampire gave me a wide birth and quivered when Tomas took a step forward to offer me his hand. I took it and let him pull me into his arms.

I shook so hard I could barely stand. Vampires were not to be messed with. Even as a fairy I knew if a strong vampire got lucky it could take me out. They were powerful, horrendously strong, and nearly as fast as fairykind. These specimens were also completely insane, and insanity had a way of lending extra cunning to a hunter.

And I, a tasty blood bag, was standing in the middle of them, my heart beating wildly.

"Calm down," Tomas said quietly and stroked the back of my head. He inhaled deeply. "Release your hold on magic Rae, it will bring you nothing but pain here. It is okay, you are safe. They got carried away because you smell good."

Holding onto the calm tenor in his voice, I let my grasp on the Source go and instead clung to him. Only the pang that was quickly muted by the darkness had me wishing it was someone else. The one who bathed me in silver light ... but he was not here.

Why was he not here again?

"Did I mention that you vampires are creepy?" I shifted back so I could look at his face, my eyes still wide with fear. "You know them?"

He nodded then focused over his shoulder. "Come on. We are almost there."

He took my hand again, wrapping his fingers securely round mine, and sneered once more at the vampires trailing us.

The fog of uncertainty had thinned in the face of my fear, clarity coming on as an after effect of the adrenaline preparing me to fight or run. Okay.... None of my current situation made any sense. Rather than feeling indifferent about it this time, it made me uncomfortable, and concerned about what was going on.

"Tomas, I … I decided to come here with you, didn't I?"

"Yes."

"Why didn't Breandan come with us?" I looked down at our joined hands. I was confused and wary. "Why isn't he here with me? I think he should be here."

"No. Keep moving, Rae."

My brows furrowed, my head hurt so much. "But … where? Where are we going?" Tomas picked up the pace. "I mean, we spoke about coming to see your Nest because we need to talk to vampires. We need to be united." My words were right, we did need to be united, but why did I sound and feel unsure.

More of the fog cleared and I blinked even as the road opened out and ahead of us was a large, grey stone building. Dozens of shallow steps led up to the wooden doorway flanked by rounded pillars. Engraved into the stonework were small furry animals and flowers, and even those stone depictions looked creepy.

"Stop." I yanked my hand from Tomas' and rubbed my temples, keeping my eyes on him. "What is happening here Tomas? My mind is … not right. I am missing memories, like they're covered in smoke I can't see through." Even saying the words helped me dispel some of the shadows in my mind. "What are you doing?" I whispered. "Whatever you have done to my mind, stop."

Tomas' face creased in panic. "Rae–"

Where was Breandan, and why did the look in Tomas' eye make it feel like ugly, dark things were crawling over my skin? I sought out the bond and was rocked when my awareness of Breandan snapped like a coil and stretched, and I could identify that it was bad for him to be so far away.

My heart rate leapt and I hyperventilated. "Right now," I shrieked. "Get out of my head!"

Tomas caught my chin between his cold fingers. "Don't fight this."

He pulled me forward to kiss me roughly. At the contact, the fog thickened and swelled through my mind again. His fangs ran out and sliced my bottom lip open. Greedily his tongue lapped the blood that flowed, but even that was done distractedly, his focus was elsewhere. His influence tried to push me under again, tried to cloud my mind, but I resisted, realising that he was keeping me this way.

I shoved him away, my hand covering my mouth as he skidded back.

He made a sound of frustration. "This will be difficult for you to understand. I don't want you to feel any needless pain. Accept me back into your thoughts."

"Can you imagine if I was the jealous type? I would think you had replaced me, love."

The voice came from above and my eyes danced up the stone steps until they landed on a tall, curvy woman with dark brown ringlets that brushed her chin at the front and cascaded down to her shoulders at the back. Dressed in a sleeveless tunic, shredded jeans, and barefoot, she came down the steps toward us with an intense expression. Her pink-rimmed eyes never left my face and the intensity of her blinkless stare was the most probing and unbalanced I had ever felt on me. She inhaled deeply and her mouth parted as two broad fangs dropped.

"I sent you for a human, Tomas. You bring me a fairy." She did not sound angry, more considering anger and merely bothering with apathetic curiosity.

Tomas said nothing, but the tender expression that

had come over his face looking at the female vampire had me extremely anxious about my current situation.

"Gwendolyn," he murmured. "I am home."

"I missed you," she said without any real kind of emotion, still walking steadily toward me.

The space around her was disturbed, like the air surrounding her body did not want to get too close. I inched back, feeling my wings fit more snugly on my back and my tail curl up to whack my shoulder in agitation. The dark that wreathed round her was evil. The nasty, sticky kind. The dark that cloaked Tomas had never felt evil to me, his dark was clear, but hers was sinister and radiated malevolence.

My nature pushed at me to run, to attack. To do something, anything, but I just stood there. My shock was too great and, frankly, my limbs felt like they were glued to the floor. Whatever compulsion Tomas had forced on me had not yet left me. Even though I could recognise my reactions and memories were not as they should be, I could not bring myself to leave this place.

Tomas said, "Where is Daphne?"

Reaching him, her eyes left me. The corner of her mouth lifted as her attention switched solely to Tomas. "Your pet is around here somewhere. She has a habit of appearing at the oddest of times at the strangest of places. I think you set her to spy on me, no?" Her voice hardened at the end and Tomas' face took on an innocently blank look.

The darkness that surrounded him merged with hers, and they were one. She snaked her hand around his waist, and the other fisted in his hair, pulling his mouth to meet hers.

Stunned, I stood still and stared at the middle distance, my mind reeling, stomach sinking. I lifted my hand to ...

what? I was not sure, maybe hit her … but Tomas pulled out of their kiss, grabbed my wrist, slid his other round my waist, and pulled me to stand in front of him, as if offering me up for inspection. His head came to rest on my shoulder, as if in affection.

The vampire giggled, and her gaze roamed over me, curious. She gave Tomas a toothy smile filled with anticipation and excitement. "This is her … the one that I saw. I remember her gold eyes, but I thought she was supposed to be human."

"So was she until a few days ago."

It was surreal. They talked about me over my head as if I was not even there.

The vampire's eyes lit up and she looked me over. "She has a story to tell I see." Briefly, her eyes closed and she inhaled and exhaled with a lusty sigh. "Full blooded fairy, delicious." She stepped closer and took my head in her hands. I tugged once half-heartedly, not liking the contact, but she gazed deep into my eyes. "I am Queen here, tell me everything you know," she ordered and she was so close I could see her pupils contract.

I blinked, grabbed her skinny wrists, and yanked them off my face. "No. And don't touch me." I glanced over my shoulder. "Tomas? What. The. Hell. Is. Going. On?" I shook my head, still not understanding what I was seeing. "What … I don't get how … what are you doing?"

Gwendolyn looked from Tomas to me, and back again so many times, and so quickly, her face blurred. "She is breaking free of your compulsion, yes? But she does not bend to mine … why can you…?" The disgust on her face made her pointy nose screw up in an ugly way. "No. Tell me it is not true."

"I did not expect it to happen," Tomas grated and from the tension in his face, I could not tell if he was embarrassed or concerned. "And I am not sorry. The connection was the only reason my compulsion worked on her. Even now she fights it."

She narrowed her eyes at him. "Whether you expected it or not it does not explain how you forged a blood tie with this girl in the month you have been gone, when we have been together for the better part of a century. Our mating was not forced and we have never experienced…." Her head swung and she stripped me with a glare. "What passed between you and my mate, fairy?"

I looked at Tomas and his expression told me nothing. "A kiss," I said, stupidly.

Lips flattening to a taut line, he made a dismissing movement with his hand. "What has transpired between Rae and I does not concern you."

Gwendolyn's body shook with repressed rage and the darkness began to blot out the whites of her eyes. "Does … not…." She sounded like she was being strangled.

Chest rising and falling in tense jerks, her bone-white hands became claws. And even as I saw the thread of her calm snap and her lips curl back, Tomas slid in front of me. She grabbed his shoulder, digging her nails in, but he wrapped his hand around her throat.

"Calm yourself," he ordered. "It means nothing."

She snapped at him and he released his hold on her throat to pull her into him. Tomas murmured something soothing in Gwendolyn's ear as she completely freaked out, clawing at him so she could get to me. She made growling noises mixed with rabid shrieks and her dark eyes rolled madly.

Tomas struggled to keep her in his embrace, but managed to stroke her hair whilst he watched me tremble. The corners of his mouth pulled down when he read the fear in my face.

Well, what did he expect? I was no longer fully under his compulsion and this situation got scarier by the moment.

The whole time I had not moved, but I honestly had no idea what to do. I remembered bringing us here using magics, and I could tell we were not near a forest. Hungry vampires surrounded me so running like prey through the streets of an unknown city was not an option, and where was I running to? My senses were muddled from Tomas' compulsion, and I was not entirely sure I could move my feet yet. The bond between Breandan and I kept stretching into nothing then flowing over me in full force as if he drew nearer, but I ignored it as I couldn't trust what I felt. I swallowed loudly and forced my heart to stop trying to bash free through my chest, no doubt it sounded like a dinner bell to the demons that had me trapped.

The mad fire in Gwendolyn's eyes cooled and her rabid expression faded. Tomas let the Nest Queen go and without hesitation, she slinked over to me, taking my measure.

I ignored her as silent tears spilled over to run down my cheeks. The last vestiges of the compulsion were fading and freeing my emotions. They came tumbling back in full force – fear and complete betrayal. The darkness was everywhere, still writhing and wiggling through me because I was tied to Tomas by blood. But he had led me here to these starved and insane vampires.

Icy breath tickled my ear and cold fingers brushed the back of my neck. "Looking for someone?" Gwendolyn asked quietly.

She could sense my magic? My eyes closed, and I shook my head, not in answer to her question, but in denial of the entire situation.

The vampires that had followed Tomas here watched me openly with hunger and longing. Everywhere I looked, fangs dropped and tongues snaked over parched lips. A few were even salivating, and I looked away from the carnal pleasure I saw lurking in the depths of their bottomless eyes.

I found my voice, "Tomas, why have you done this?"

Gwendolyn giggled and tugged on a clump of my hair and I flinched, my hands flitting up to bat her away. Tomas did not answer me. He looked between us, and sighed, as if we troubled and bothered him.

My mind was still not coming to terms with what he had done. "But I trusted you." I turned to look him in the face, my confusion and horror plain. "I trust you, Tomas."

Gwendolyn smirked and came to stand in front of me blocking my view of him – twisting a lock of her hair around her middle finger. "Are you so desperate to believe you have done no wrong that you refuse to see what he is?"

I sucked in a breath. My heart crashed in my chest, which was painfully tight. "I don't believe it." I leaned around her to search Tomas' eyes. "I know you're mad about Breandan," I mumbled. "But there was no choice and you know that. There was no choice for me."

Tomas finally moved again. He shouldered past Gwendolyn who pushed him back playfully and slowly placed his cool hands on my face to cup it gently. His thumb stroked over my bottom lip. The corners of his eyes tightened. "I know you will never understand why I did this," he said earnestly. "I am sorry, for everything, but I had to get you here, Rae. I had to."

He let me go and I staggered back.

Gwendolyn bit her grubby fingertip coyly, giggling. "Silly fairy."

My legs gave way and I fell to my knees. Tears splashed on the grey concrete like rain, making a dark puddle beneath me. I pressed my forehead to the ground, wanting nothing more in that moment than to curl up and die

Deception. Everything Tomas had done was a trick, a ruse to get me here.

Gwendolyn's laughter and the laughter of her Nest burned me. It echoed through the cold, empty buildings to be magnified and thrown back at me, infuriating me.

I lurched up, filled with fire, determination, and an anger so consuming I feared it would choke me if I did not appease it with blood. I drew deeply on the Source until it filled my being with white-hot light then I–

Nothing!

I tried again to channel my power and manifest a fireball but nothing happened. Staggering back, a terrified squeal of horror was torn from my throat as I repeatedly tried to use my magic. I could not wield the energy gifted to me as my birthright. The breath whooshed from my lungs, and I looked down at my hands willing them to fill with fire. My head snapped up and I sent Tomas a hate-filled glare.

He raised a thick, dark eyebrow. "Do you remember what I told you, Rae? That some vampires used to be able to touch the Source before they turned," he said coolly, and inclined his head toward Gwendolyn who smiled sneakily.

"No magics for you," she chimed and waggled her finger.

Holding onto the Source was making me agitated, so I released it and focused on the vampire Queen. She had some power, this I could feel, but not enough to manage a spell great enough to hold me back.

"You are not powerful enough to cast this enchantment," I said. "Who did?"

The animated expression bled from her face until all that was left was the effortlessly blank look all vampires seemed so good at. "I think you should be more worried about what happens next." Her hand stroked the side of her throat and her tongue flicked over a fang.

The vampires surrounding us took a step forward and the anticipation became so thick in the air I could taste it.

I blinked and Gwendolyn was behind me, yanking my head to the side, fangs scraping my throat. Yet as the points of her fangs pricked my skin, I wrapped my hand in the ringlets that brushed my wrist and yanked, hard. There was no way in hell she was biting me. Her head jack-knifed back and I released her only to run at super speed right into Tomas' waiting hands.

At the contact, the darkness flared again and my body went limp, lethargic, and weightless. Tomas lifted me like a rag doll. "I promise it won't hurt," he whispered. "I'll take care of you."

I shivered and waited for the pain. I had no energy to fight. My mind was exhausted from fighting his compulsion and my body was simply confused from all the mixed signals it was receiving. Honestly, my spirit felt broken, and I could not bring myself to struggle.

All that would be left for Breandan was a promise of forever, that I had loved him, and would have loved him, always. Oh gods give him strength. I had to believe he would be fine. He would suffer, but in the end, Lochlann would give him a life worth living. Conall would be full of rage, but he was sensible enough to know I would want him to watch over my friends.

In a sick, twisted way, this end was of my making. Had I not acted like a fool and ended up tied to Tomas, he never would have been able to bring me here. I would die in the arms of my vampire-boy, and I tried not to feel ambivalent about it, but found fear lacking. Truth was I still felt as if death had been postponed for me. It was an inevitable conclusion, just one I would have to face sooner than some had thought.

I embraced death in the arms of one I could have loved … I was okay.

Tomas sank his teeth into my throat and I sucked a breath in between my teeth, but was otherwise still. I scrunched my eyes tight and fisted my hands in his shirt, trying to claw comfort from his embrace. He lowered me to the ground, and I saw the others crowd nearer, eager for a taste.

The moonlight drifted down and my wings fluttered as my eyes slid closed. A cool breeze carried the smell of green things, and Tomas' mineral scent.

Gently, with reverence and care, my vampire fed from me until my heart stuttered.

CHAPTER NINE

Opening my eyes, I sighed at the stone ceiling. My mind was clear, all too clear, and I knew I had been captured. Again. This time I had nothing but my own foolishness to thank.

Sniffing, I tried to sense where I was, up high or down low, and was relieved when I determined had not travelled far from the last place I was conscious. I scrunched my nose up. It smelt dreadful; so bad I could taste the decay.

Rolling onto my side, I ignored the figure I had sensed in the corner when I woke up, and touched a hand to my neck. The skin was tender but fully healed. I fingered the two raised lumps of skin and closed my eyes remembering how it felt to have fangs sink beneath your skin and your blood sucked from you. No, that part was not a dream either.

"Our bites leave scars." The voice from the corner was hesitant.

As if I needed more of those.

My sweaty palms slapped loudly on the hard floor "Why do I always find myself in these uncomfortable situations? Why don't holding dungeons come with warm blankets and cushions?"

Shifting onto my hands and knees I arched my back, working out the stiffness, then levered myself up onto my knees. I stood and rolled my shoulders. When I opened my eyes Tomas stood in front of me, eyes fathomless and deceptively filled with life.

I breathed out slowly. "Why are you here?"

"Protecting you."

I chewed my bottom lip. "From the vampire Queen?" He nodded once. I flushed angrily. "Why does it matter? I saw the way she looked at me when she realised we have a blood tie. It's only a matter of time before she drains me, right?"

Like hell it was, but I was curious. For all intents and purposes, he had betrayed me, but then why was he down here lurking in the shadows like a weirdo?

"None shall feed from you but me."

"Oh, don't you like to share." My eyes narrowed. "Unless you have something I would want to hear, I suggest you leave. Looking at you is making me feel ill."

His hand lifted as if to touch me, but he let it fall loosely to his side. "You hate me."

"What do you think," I snapped and moved around him to place my hands on the door. No iron, just wood. It had a locked rusty doorknob. I frowned and opened my senses. Okay, no iron close by. I furrowed my brows at him over my shoulder. "It's like you were expecting me to stay in here."

"Yes," the response was unassuming.

The rank odour of my prison had me retching again. "What is that sm–" My eyes landed on the body twisted in the corner. My heart sank to my feet and my face flushed in anger. "Oh gods." Swallowing hard, my eyes twitched to his. "Why have you done this?"

Tomas glanced at the body in the corner. "That was

not my doing. He and his followers entered the city and Gwendolyn defended her territory. No doubt she was hungry too."

My mouth swung open, and all I could see was a chain of events that had spiralled out of control and led me to this moment. Was this my fault? No … he had come here to escape his own mad actions. Knowing this made the sight in front of me no less easy to bear. "Do you have any idea what you've done?"

The body explained why Devlin had unexpectedly disappeared from my future, from everybody's future.

He simply did not have one anymore.

In this moment of pain, I did not think of the entire fairy race but of Wasp. She would be devastated. Hell, deranged would be a better description. I remembered Devlin speak of his life-mate. The way the insanity had drained from his eyes to be replaced with adoration. He would not have left her, anyone else but her. What if that had been Breandan lying there and I was her?

I spun on him with tears in my eyes. "You evil, heartless—"

Blurring into motion Tomas pressed his forehead to mine and backed me against the wall. My wrists were pinned to my side as one of his thighs slid between my legs until my feet lifted off the floor.

"No. No, I have a heart and it is yours. I even have a soul though you may question that as I willingly did this to you despite the tie we share. You put your trust in me, gifted me all faith, in the hope I was a clean dark. I have manipulated and pulled you. Twisted your mind until it was confused and pliant." I turned my head as the knife in my heart twisted at his words, but he simply pressed himself harder into me and spoke into my ear. "You should know I always meant to bring you here, but I could not have imagined losing the love that lingers inside me to one such as you." Stunned, my head snapped round so I could see his face. He peered into my eyes, his blinkless stare allowing my own unfaltering gaze to measure his. "Whatever you think of me, if you never dare trust another word that comes from my mouth, I beg you to believe that."

He released my wrists and eased back. My feet touched the ground and my heart thundered in my chest.

My hands lifted, fell. What did I feel? Not the same overwhelming need to connect that broke me down each time Breandan came too near. It was not the flare of need, and want, that attacked me before Breandan and I touched.

I reached up again, steeling myself, and my palms slid over his cool face and my eyes closed.

When my skin touched his, there was not a dual sense of completeness and breathless infatuation. Something was there. The same spark that allowed the blood tie to form between us. It was hot and bright, and when I tried to touch it or see it more clearly it burned me. Possibly such a thing is not to be understood or endured? How did it get there in the first place? Why did Tomas appeal to me so, but not enough to form an attachment over what I felt for Breandan? Why was I pulled to him? And then ultimately, here to this Nest where once again my life hung in the balance.

"I don't understand you," I whispered. Frustration gave way to anger for I simply could not figure out this thing between us. I knew I should hate him but I didn't. "I don't understand us."

He looked saddened when I took my hands away. "You don't have to. I will protect you, Rae. Believe it or not you were not brought here for blood. Gwendolyn has a plan, but the Nest is hungry and they will do everything they can to taste you. Few have any control and that situation would be … bad for you. So only I will feed from you and the others will feed from me until I manage to discover what Gwen has planned." He jerked his head toward Devlin's dry, mangled corpse. "That is more than I can say for him."

"Lucky me," I muttered and put my hands back on him. I let them slide down his neck to his chest. Keeping eye contact, I started at his collarbone and dragged my talons down his chest, ripping through the fabric of his top, and gouging deep groves that gushed with blood, my blood. I hissed and bared my teeth at him, as he snarled at me. "You will never taste me again. This I swear."

As expected, magic thickened in the air.

Tomas sniffed and his eyes darkened. "I don't want you to die."

I hissed. "How touching."

"Don't be like this." He touched my cheek and I turned my head away, disgusted that my heart still tripped at his touch. "We can make this work."

I snapped my head back around to glare at him. "You're delusional if you think Breandan is not on his way down here with an army to tear you apart."

The vampire's lips lifted with a hint of a smirk. "Will he? The last memory he has of you is you walking off into the dark, with me. The vampire with whom you share a blood tie." He leaned in to whisper in my ear, his cool breath tickling my neck. "You've mated your fairy but still your tie to me remains. Why do you think that is?"

My conviction wavered for less than a beat, and I ignored his barb about the blood tie's significance. "He won't be fooled. Breandan knows I'm his." I shook my head pityingly. "When he gets here this Nest is finished.

Hell, I'll help him stake you all in the sun with a smile." I snapped for his throat and he never even leaned back; he did not flinch.

His arms bracketed me and I bashed my head back against the wall, upset with the whole situation.

"Bold words, yet here we stand. You could kill me if you wanted to," his gaze flicked to the circlet that framed my face, "Priestess. So why don't you? Kill me, then walk out that door."

I lifted my chin. "Step back." His lips quirked but he did as I asked. Pushing the hair out of my eyes my hand trailed down to touch the gold upon my brow. "I expect more from myself. I won't be a mindless killer; I'm worth more than that." Pausing I made up my mind. "I understand that the Nest is starving and I sympathise, I always have, but you must not keep me here. You must let me leave peacefully. If I have to fight my way out there will be nothing I can do to stop the others coming here."

He regarded me thoughtfully, a pillar of darkness, arms loose at his sides and stance confident. "You truly have grown." His head turned to the door as it squeaked open.

I sniffed and screwed up my nose at the dry and mouldy smell that saturated everything.

A vampire-girl stepped into the room, her gaze flicking between us curiously. Her eyes were a murky brown colour and would have been unremarkable had they not had a most unusual shape – two slim ovals with ridiculously long and straight lashes the colour of dried wheat stared over at me. She had white-blonde slender braids, surprisingly tanned skin covered in freckles, and dark eyebrows. Dressed in cut-off jeans, boots, and a dark green plaid shirt, she had the same skinny, starved look all the vampires had, though there was a flush of colour in her cheeks.

She inhaled deeply, head falling back, and nose pointed in my direction. As her eyes opened, her fangs ran out, and I noticed a rather wide gap between her two front teeth. She started, and placed a hand over her mouth, shooting a guilty look at Tomas.

"It's okay Daphne," he said soothingly and smiled at her broadly, opening his arms.

The young girl darted another look at me before stepping fully into the room, shutting the door firmly behind her. She blurred over to Tomas and wrapped her arms around him, tucking her head under his.

"I missed you." Her voice was light, delicate, and if I was honest, lovely – soothing and husky.

But I was pissed off and feeling a twinge of jealousy, so I heard it as inappropriately breathy and weak.

"And you are?" I asked icily, boring holes into the back of her small skull.

She looked at me over her shoulder wincing daintily. She untangled herself from Tomas, and gave me a diminutive wave. "Gwendolyn said you had a mouth on you, but Tomas says you're nice when you're happy. He's told me all about you, and whilst Gwen is my Queen, I obey him above all others." Her head leaned to the side and her braids fell forward. "I'm going to excuse your unpleasantness as this is a less than hospitable situation you've found yourself in." Her calm rationale and amiable greeting grated on my nerves. Huffing, I crossed my arms tightly over my chest. She gave me a sincere and beautiful smile. "I'm not your enemy, Rae."

My tail coiled around my legs, whipping my lower thigh in irritation. I focused on keeping my wings snug against my back, refusing to let this girl trick me into liking her.

Tomas moved closer to me. "Daphne is like a sister to me," he said reassuringly and stroked a hand down my back.

I avoided a second stroke by taking a hasty side step and scowling at him. Rather than ordering him not to touch me I lashed him head to toe with my eyes, making sure disgust seeped from my every pore.

Daphne tittered behind her hand. "My, my, is she mad at you."

Tomas barked a laugh and pinched his brow. I stared at him. I'd never seen him like this. He almost seemed … happy. I turned my hate-filled gaze on Daphne, who smiled at me as if we were the best of blood friends.

I nodded to Devlin's body. When it came to telling Wasp what had happened, I had no doubt the fairy-woman would be eating out of the palm of my hand if it meant avenging him. "Can you get rid of that?" And it was a 'that'. Devlin was not there anymore – not in that rotten corpse. The High Lord was gone, and though I wished I felt grief, I felt nothing but a vague sense of regret. Despite the fact that the High Lord had not been the patron of evil as I had once believed, he had killed my friend, sacrificed her. Now I understood why he had needed a pure sacrifice to invoke dark magic. He had been trying to use the he-witch's source of magic against him. Devlin had known all along a great danger was gathering power … no wonder he had pursued me so stubbornly.

"Of course," Tomas replied, breaking my maudlin thoughts, and motioned to Daphne.

She hefted the stinking thing over her shoulder without question, and in a blink was out the door, closing it behind her.

"I am sorry." Tomas did not sound sorry at all, or

particularly bothered that he sounded false. "I didn't know that he was in here, and I didn't want to risk moving you with Gwendolyn so … disquieted."

"What?" I began sarcastically. "Was the appearance of Devlin not part of your master plan?"

"No, it was not. When I left here I was prepared. I knew you would not want to come with me. When I met you and realised you were so vulnerable, I thought it would be easy to persuade you to accompany me here. I never knew you were a demon, nor someone of such importance to fairykind. I had no idea I would find myself in the middle of a fairy uprising. How could I? This is a mess I have not planned for."

"Then why didn't you back off?" My hands rose to fall with slaps on my thighs. "I can't see where you're going with this, Tomas. It makes no sense. In fact it's plain stupid if you ask me. You've risked everything to get me here, and for what?"

"For them," he barked. "I told you we are dying out here. There is nothing to eat, and one by one my family goes insane – devoured from the inside by their bloodlust. They attack each other then become enraged when the blood does not satisfy their hunger. We cannot sustain each other; it must be the blood of another kind, or our minds break."

I watched him coolly. "So you travelled all that way to snag one human? How would I have changed anything? One human body does not hold enough blood to feed a Nest of hundreds."

"Gwendolyn had a vision. She saw that bringing you here would save us. I don't know how, but she was certain enough for me to want to try. She is never wrong."

"She's a hateful bitch who wants me dead. You've

brought me here to die." His shoulders hunched with every word I yelled at him. "You might as well have drained me and had done with it." My chest heaved and I fought tears. "Why did it have to be you? Why couldn't it have been Daphne or Gwendolyn that came for me? Why did you make me think you—" I choked off and refused to finish.

Tomas spun on me, face livid. "It had to be a male because that is what Gwen saw would sway your sympathies. It had to be me because the other males were not sane enough for the task. And it had to be done in secret in case Cael found out!" The moment the words were out of his mouth his face blanked.

I froze then tilted my head at him slowly. "The he-witch? You are working for the Blackthorn Coven?"

His shoulders slumped and his face took on a look of the beaten. "Cael's witchcraft has held our Nest under his thumb for some time now."

Scoffing a disbelieving laugh, I pushed the hair out of my eyes and my talons scraped my circlet reminding me of who I was. "How long is 'some time'?"

Tomas made a dismissive gesture with his hand. "Less than two hundred years. Cael is older than me yet how he has managed to prolong his life and keep his youth is unknown. Witches have a human lifespan. He is a mystery."

I took a step back, purely in shock. I fumbled for the wall behind me until my fingers pressed against the cool, damp stone. I leaned against it heavily and groaned.

Tomas was at my side in an instant but refrained from touching me.

"The Rupture," I gasped. The leaps of understanding taking place in my mind were immense and the room spun. "Vampirekind didn't start it."

"No. We were forced into a corner and had no choice but to do as we were told."

My head whipped up to pin him with a glare. "Ana told me—"

Tomas held up his hand and his expression rippled with what on a human face would have been mild displeasure. Since he was vampire it looked like a nervous twitch.

"The white witch can tell lies, Rae. You forget she is not fairy like you. She is a Blackthorn, a powerful being born of Cael's bloodline – the most influential Coven in this region. Though she's different from her kin the white witch will bow to his authority if he catches her in his snare. It is their way to follow the word of the Coven Father, instinctive. Unlike vampires where loyalty must be earned in blood." He paused thoughtfully. "No doubt when she saw me coming she would have warned Breandan and you. Even then she would have tried to turn you against me." He laughed without any real humour. "The fairy and I were destined to loathe each other."

I whimpered and pressed a hand to my throat, feeling physically sick. Could Ana have lied to me to protect her family? Was she swayed by a need to defend her Father even as she tried to fight for what was right and good? She had looked me in the eye and told me the vampires had started the Rupture; the global event in which everyone believed the vampires attacked the humans first, and the rest of demonkind were forced to fight since the humans turned on them too. Did she know the truth? That the vampires were under her Cael's influence? I knew she had kept things from me on Breandan's request, but surely, he could not know about this?

I dry heaved and bent over resting my hands on my

knees as I fought to regain my equilibrium.

More unanswered questions. Everything I learned took me one step closer to nothing. I was moving sideways, darting through shadows of half-truths and lies. How was I supposed to know what I was meant to do when I couldn't trust those closest to me? Was every action a cover for a nefarious end? No wonder Devlin had turned in desperation to black magic for protection. It seemed there were hidden daggers waiting to spear you at every turn.

Satisfied I was not going to toss up any nectar, I said, "This changes things." I stood and shook my hair back. It had finally stopped growing, and reached the middle of my back. It made my head feel heavy, but it smelt like the forest, a comfort in this dank place. Tomas' expression was curious. My tongue burned as I added, "This makes your kind worth fighting for." I looked him in the eye and squashed the knee-trembling pleasure I felt when I did, afraid he would see the way he made me feel. "Tell me everything."

The door burst open. Daphne bolted in and closed it behind her.

She spun and plastered herself against it, arms flung wide. "Gwendolyn," she whispered before the door was flung open pushing her with it until she and the door slapped into the wall.

The vampire Queen strutted into the room, ringlets bouncing, bare feet slapping the dirty floor. It was meant to be a casual entrance but it reeked of quiet desperation. Vampires had a liquid movement that went beyond mere grace. They didn't strut, they glided, so her flippant attitude looked forced. Her hands were in the back pockets of her ragged jeans and her collarbones jutted out painfully. Gwendolyn looked underfed. Her eye sockets were sunken and her skin ashy pale, even for a vampire. None of this diminished her breathtaking natural beauty, and it took a great deal of will not to pull my glamour on in a pitiful attempt to cover my scars.

Daphne grunted and slipped out from behind the door, rubbing her cheek.

Gwendolyn took in Tomas' closeness to me in a lingering gaze, her thin brows rising with exaggerated slowness even as a fire burned in the depths of her eyes.

Rather than step away from me, Tomas moved in front of me and cocked his head in a show of respect. "Love?" he asked with a hint of impatience.

She smiled and held out a grubby hand with nails bitten into ragged stumps. "We have a visitor," she purred.

Tomas went stiff and Daphne's head whipped round to stare at him. Her entire body shifted into battle mode, even her braids appeared rigid, but with the slightest motion of Tomas' hand, she relaxed her stance. She sent me a sorrowful look then looked away at the floor where Devlin's body had lain.

My blood ran cold. Was the he-witch here for me already? I lifted my chin. I had faced him before and I would again. No matter if I was tired, emotionally drained, unable to use magic, and struggling to hold myself upright. I had faced him before and come out alive. I ignored the voice in my head that whispered the fear I had not hurt the he-witch, but that he had left of his own accord with a parting message....

"*Feicfidh mé thú go luath, deirfiúr,*" I muttered.

I didn't know what it meant, but it felt like he meant me to think of it – of him – until our next meeting.

An odd slapping sound snagged my attention. Gwendolyn scuttled back on her heels away from me.

"*Labhraíonn sí an teanga ar an witches?*" Gwendolyn spat at Tomas. "*Dúirt tú liom go bhfuil sí eolas beag.*"

"*Níl sí ar Cael's Coven,*" Tomas replied in a soothing voice. "*Calma síos.*"

"You understood what I said?" I asked them both sharply.

"We have an alliance with the Blackthorn Coven," Gwendolyn said with an odd roundabout rolling of her eyes. "Of course we speak the tongue of their incantations."

"Alliance?" I echoed. "Tomas didn't make it sound as voluntary as that."

"Because it's not," Daphne confessed. "Cael's hold over us grows stronger by the day." She placed a hand on her stomach, which gurgled loudly. "I don't know if we could survive without him if we tried. He sends us blood, be-spelled blood, that keeps us full enough to do his grunt work. It's the only reason we're alive."

Gods, it kept getting worse. My hands fisted in anger. "Tell me what it means." The look Gwendolyn gave me was rude and self-satisfied. This vampire Queen was somewhat underwhelming now I had seen how insecure she was. I ground my back teeth together, understanding why Breandan succumbed to the habit so often. The pressure helped ease the anger and frustration building behind the eyeballs. "It's not that big a deal. Tell me you demented–"

"I will see you soon, sister," Daphne blurted. "That's what it means, Rae."

Gwendolyn slapped her.

I hissed and she snarled lurching forward, but Daphne was already in front of me, fangs bared, eyes flashing black.

"Enough," Tomas said in a hard voice.

Daphne straightened and bowed her head. Gwendolyn sniffed and crossed her arms. She leaned back on her heel as she fixed me with a glare.

Already over it, I frowned and looked to Tomas for confirmation of what had been said. He gave a small nod.

"That's it?' I muttered. But it makes no sense. I'm not part of his Coven, and—"

"And thank the gods for that," Gwendolyn butted in. Recovering fully from her sudden rage, she drew herself up tall. "Well, my consort and his loyal subordinate have spoken out of turn yet again, I see." She gave said mate a lethal look. "No matter, such things can be dealt with. Come along, he is waiting, and the night grows old."

Gwendolyn waited until Tomas clasped her extended hand. They left the room, but not before his dark gaze pinned Daphne for the briefest of moments, and she returned the unreadable look with a deep nod. She motioned me to walk and, since I had no choice, I did.

We climbed a steep and narrow staircase and exited into a long, high-ceilinged passage. The paint on the walls was flaking and the corners of yellowed wallpaper curled down almost to the floor in some places. The dry, mouldy smell was intense. It smelled like vampire and my nature recoiled, disgusted; for once, I didn't fight the feeling. The building was empty of life apart from us. Where was the rest of the Nest? There were no humans to hunt, so where had they all gone?

"Are we the only ones here?" I asked Daphne in a low murmur that still echoed loudly down the empty hallway.

Tomas glanced over his shoulder, his eyes two black pits, unreadable.

"Yes," Daphne spoke low in my ear, her cold lips so close they brushed across my earlobe. "The Nest has been sent to look for the grimoire. Cael discovered from the fairy High Lord that he had hidden it somewhere in the city." Her eyes darted forward to the back of Gwendolyn's dark head. "But they won't find it," she said with a hint of excitement. "They'll never find it."

We exited the building into the empty street where Tomas had fed from me.

Raindrops spattered on my face and I blinked, wiped them from my nose, and breathed in deeply.

I stopped mid-breath my heart soaring.

Sunlight. I could smell sunlight.

CHAPTER TEN

Breandan was alone. He stood at the base of the stone steps with his hands fisted together, head back, eyes closed. He was magnificent. Lean body taut, he burned with silver light. His black tattoos were outlined starkly against his pale skin, and the dark edges seemed to glow. His wings rested tightly against his back, and his tail wove lazily through the air. He breathed deeply, I watched the steady rise and fall of his chest. What he tasted in the air I could not say. The angry expression on his face was intense, and when his head snapped forward, he opened his eyes, and focused completely on our bond. His gaze became a weapon that flew through the air and speared Tomas, who stumbled half a step back.

Rain fell heavily and soaked our clothes. My hair plastered to my head in a matter of moments and ran from my fingertips in small streams, droplets flicking wildly as I trembled.

Delirious with relief I lurched forward then paused, wincing, expecting someone to grab me. No one stopped me. I shot a wide-eyed look at Daphne.

She tried to smile, but it tumbled from her face leaving behind a worried frown. Her eyes flicked to Tomas and squinted in pain. I too looked to my vampire and saw he watched Breandan with a look of resigned acceptance that he tried to hide with defiance. I took a more confident step, and when no one moved I rushed forward. As I passed Tomas, I ignored the frisson of longing that seemed to spark between us, and jumped down the steps of the house. The rainwater trickled ahead of me like a shallow river until I stilled on the last step, my heart thumping wildly.

Breandan's gaze was still fixed on Tomas, but I felt him greet me with joy. Through the bond, I felt how scared he had been for me and how glad he was now that I was near.

Turning my concentration from the demons at my back, I focused on him and him alone. I took a hold of my nature and reached out. His hand was already there, and our fingers laced together to clutch tightly. A pulse of light danced across our palms and lit the dark street briefly, but no more. It was nothing but a flash of harmless light. I breathed out; relieved we had managed some control over the bond. My eyes drifted closed and peace swept over me. His presence was a balm that revived and refreshed me. Sighing, I let my hand fall to my side and so did he.

Then his focus turned inward, and my perception of him completely winked out of existence.

Shocked by the unexpected disconnect, I lost my sense of direction since Breandan acted as my centre of being. I stumbled off the last step. He sidestepped me and I had to use my tail to steady my faltering movement. Straightening, I looked between him and those who stood above us. Somewhere in the haze of my consciousness, I glimpsed a forewarning. The death of one of my loves was upon me, and it was inescapable.

Lightning flashed above in a fork of bright light,

highlighting the vampires from behind so they seemed like malevolent shadows gilded with a gloom darker than the night. Thunder boomed and the ground shook, yet the profound reverberation did not cover Gwendolyn's sudden and creepy giggles.

"No, fairy. It will not happen," Tomas said apropos of nothing. "This is my territory. On this ground I decide how this will be resolved."

"We have a score to settle," Breandan replied.

The vampire's shoulders lifted in what could be passed as a shrug. "Your ways mean nothing to me."

The rain fell so hard the water on the concrete ran over the tops of my boots. My clothes stuck to me uncomfortably and I pushed my hair back off my face, wiping it roughly as I did so. The clouds flashed with a myriad of colours, and beneath my confusion, I felt a jolt of excitement at the weather. My nature buzzed, my skin goose pimpled, and I shivered.

"I see," Breandan said after a pause, and a flash of irritation down the bond was abruptly erased by the nothing. "Then only one thing can be done."

My fairy turned to face me and bowed low at the hip, one hand pressed to his heart.

Tomas moved forward. "No," he growled.

Gwendolyn blinked with a faked diffidence and put a hand on his arm. "Stop." Tomas' snarl cut off and his head dipped in submission to his Queen. Gwendolyn leaned on the rusted railings and snickered. "Priestess. We never got a chance to fight like the warriors we are, but I live in hope you will be victorious so we may yet meet on the battlefield." She paused, her gaze briefly switching to her mate who stood stiffly at her side. "That is if I ever persuade my consort to retract his claim on you as his plaything." She giggled madly, ringlets bouncing, and gods didn't I want to scratch her pouty face off.

Not that I ever fully understood what was happening around me, but right then, I was completely lost. I looked at Breandan for answers as to what the hell was going on and got none.

He watched Tomas with a fierce concentration like he was waiting for something. I tried reading the vampires' expressions but ended up more confused; Daphne looked horrified, Tomas anxious, and though I knew Gwendolyn was crazy, the twinkle in her eye looked anticipatory rather than manic. What the hell was the Queen talking about? What was going on? Breandan was here beside me, he had come to save me, and her lunatic subordinates were scattered across the city looking for the grimoire. I was about to escape so Tomas' reaction kind of made sense, Daphne seemed weird anyway, but my main worry was Gwendolyn. She seemed happy, jovial even.

I turned to Breandan to gauge his reaction and that was the only reason I saw his fist flying toward my face. I ducked – more like my legs gave out in shock – and I hit the ground with a frantic splash. His stamping foot came a moment later, cracking the concrete when it landed between my legs. I scrambled on all fours before I rolled backward and regained my feet.

I bent my knees and held out a hand, palm up. "Breandan!"

He paced; eyes measuring and stone cold. He took note of my movement – searching for a weakness. He was fighting me. He took a feinting step toward me, beautiful face etched with deadly intent, and I had no choice but to feint back.

Breandan came at me again, face blank of emotion.

I was terrified. Absolute, heart stopping, terror. It was all I could do to keep him from smashing into me.

Whirling on my heel, I turned to dart away.

Was I running away? Hell yes! I was running away. I was no match for him physically, and magic was no good to me here. I could grasp it, but nothing happened when I tried to use it.

Breandan dived over my head, spinning in an intricate tumble of flips to land with a soft splash ahead of me, expression contemptuous.

I shot a wild look at the vampires watching us. Tomas leaned forward apprehensively. The skin on his face seemed over-stretched as he stared at me.

Breandan lunged for me again and this time he clipped my arm as I shifted out of the way. I cried out, my arm wrenching in my socket, and crumpled.

I did not understand what was happening. What had I missed? Had he covertly signalled to me or tried to transmit his plan to me through the bond but I had missed it – too busy sneering at Gwendolyn?

Breandan slowly stalked over and picked me up. My heart stuttered in relief. Then he heaved me overhead, swung round, and tossed me. I hit the concrete steps with a loud thump, and it felt like my bones snapped, shuddered, and ground together trying to escape through my flesh. I lay there for a few beats before rolling onto my side. Only once my body flared with heat and healed – my blood returning to my extremities rather than rushing around my ears and blocking the painful rasp of my own breath – did instinct scream at me to pull myself together.

I hauled myself into a crouch, tail lashing from side to side causing the air to whistle. My wings lifted and sprung out. I straightened, raising my fists. Something akin to pride flickered in his expression, but I shook off the feeling that I had missed something. It did no good to hope when it was clear Breandan had made his choice and given up on me.

Before my fairy could lay his hands on me again, Tomas appeared, a phantom shrouded in a cloud of smoke. He grabbed my arm and spun, dismissing my body weight as if it were a feather, throwing me across the space out of harm's way.

Wings catching the wind I landed on my feet, skidded across the rain-slicked floor, pivoted, and careened to a stop.

Tomas snarled menacingly, fangs bared and eyes pitch black. "I am here, fairy. Do your worst." He crouched low to the floor, compact body lithely pacing to the side so he was not boxed in.

Breandan tilted his head almost imperceptibly, as if to say 'about time'. He had what he wanted. He had forced Tomas to fight to defend me.

Ancient vampire and youthful fairy circled each other. The heavens rumbled again and lightning streaked across the night in fiery rods of blue and purple. Why, when death approached, did the world hold its breath? Wariness. Mother Nature herself perceived the danger these demonic forces embodied. The air became still and after a final crash of thunder, it was quiet.

It came to me in a sickening bout of clarity. This was it. This fight determined my future. This was the crucial moment in time that would send me down one road or the other. I had thought that moment had already come and gone as I faced my own personal demon – Cleric Tu, a human who had come to represent everything hateful and wrong in the world. How wrong I was. Love, not hate, would define me, and there were none more dear than the demons before me.

Breandan moved first – lashing out to curve a hook at

Tomas' cheek. The vampire dodged and slipped around his back to snap for the nape of his neck.

With a deep breath in, hands fisted, I took three long strides and dived in with a roundhouse kick that Breandan took to the side of the head. My leg snapped back to slam my heel into the soft flesh at Tomas' throat. It was hard to control my body since everything was wet and there was little grip, but still I managed to execute my moves with enough speed and force to do damage.

I skipped back, swaying on the spot, ready to end this. I threw myself into the fight, parried and kicked, knowing I had no choice but to keep up. Both boys pushed me back, flung me away, and slid me behind them as they landed strike after strike on the other.

, I slipped back into the melee, doing my best to make them stop, make them see it did not have to end like this.

It should not have been possible. I should have been pummelled, but I was there and in a flurry of stances, I forced them to acknowledge I was an equal contender in this clash. They had to fight me back and that complicated things. They had to be mindful of not hurting me whilst trying to inflict fatal damage on each other.

My sense of self-preservation was obliterated by feral anger. I wanted to tear them both apart. Smash their heads into the wall and beat them senseless. I was done watching these to fools snipe at each other, and I was over this jealous foolishness in a big way.

Even as I thumped him in the stomach, Breandan jabbed right around me then swung left – raining blows down on Tomas.

The vampire changed his tactics. He kept low. His punches alternated between uppercuts and loose-handed swipes. But then he sprung up, entire body lengthening, and brought down an overhead swing that landed square on Breandan's forehead. Stunned, he stumbled. Tomas followed the move through by going for his neck – fangs glinting, fists flying.

Grabbing Tomas' wrist as it sailed past my torso, I dealt my vampire a blow that had him shunting sideways; his arm bent too far the wrong way and snapped. He fell to his knees with a scream of pain.

I spun round to Breandan, unsteady on his feet, and launched myself at him with a shriek of rage. My ankles locked behind his neck and I threw myself backward. My hands hit the ground, and with all my might, I pulled my knees into my stomach. His weight smoothly shifted from my calves to my thigh and stomach muscles then released completely as gravity took over. He flipped over and slammed onto his back. My body bowed, elbows jarring as I landed hard on my chest, my butt sticking up in the air. I unlocked my ankles and slid my feet apart to keep my balance.

It had taken me an entire month of Disciple training to learn that move and never did I think I would find use for it.

I leapfrogged backward and straddled him, but he twisted his hips to unseat me. Breandan pushed forward so I fell back and smacked the back of my head on the concrete, softened by nothing but rainwater. We rolled in an indistinguishable haze so fast was our movement. Mid-tumble he gained the advantage, his combat dexterity superior to mine, which was nothing more than frenzied instinct. He grabbed my wrist and yanked my arm high up my back. I howled in pain and jerked my head. There was a loud crunch and my wrist was released. The back of my head throbbed, but as I scrambled up, I saw his hurt was worse than mine. His nose was crooked and bloodied. It jerked oddly and healed as he swiped his forearm over his lips to clean away the blood. Not giving him a moment's breather I boxed his ears, kneed him in the gut, and brought my foot down hard on the back of his knee, feeling the joint shudder under the strain.

All this was accomplished at inhuman speed that I had thought only warriors like Conall possessed.

Gasping for air, I backed a step away, and opened my mouth to speak.

Breandan darted past me and collided with the vampire, whose broken arm had locked back into place and who was already springing forward to meet him half way.

I was half a step behind.

I punched Breandan in the neck causing him to gurgle oddly, then twisted round to plant myself in front of him protectively when Tomas tried to manoeuvre him into a chokehold. Grabbing the vampire by his coal-black hair, I rammed my fist into his solar plexus. I pivoted on the ball of my foot and with my back to him, snapped my elbow into his nose then again into his stomach. The double tap was done with a speed and sharpness beyond my own comprehension. His feet left the ground and he flew back. He rode his own darkness like a wave, somersaulting in the air, and landing silently. He snarled at me – his entire body trembling in rage.

I tugged on the darkness trying to appeal to his better nature. It was a thick broiling cloud. It swelled, the edges blurry but more present than I had ever felt. It called to me, the sinister depth alluring.

Breandan tried to use my pause to his advantage and sped past. I beat my wings twice and lifted from the floor. I kicked him in the stomach and again higher up on the chest with the other foot – running up his body – using the powerful impacts to flip over and land in a crouch with my left leg sliding out to expel the spare momentum. My fairy staggered back and glared at me balefully.

Chest heaving, I held my hand out to him and pleaded with my eyes. Words could not to convey the sentiments I felt, so I sent a plea with a wave of love. Please. The entreaty hit a wall and dissipated.

Breandan was done letting me sway his decision when it came to my vampire.

Reason had fled this place.

The air crackled with the intensity radiating from the three of us – elemental power, pure and potent. Neither boy looked ready to quit and I was long past rational. I buzzed with anger. Strength and speed were physical burdens racing through my veins.

Breandan pulled his gaze from the vampire to flick over my face. His jaw worked, but never did the tension in his body lessen. He saw in my eyes that I was in this to the end like he was. He understood. I would not back down, not now, not ever. Apprehension flickered in his eyes when he glanced at me, quickly repressed by cold calculation. I focused my mental abilities on the barrier he had erected to keep me out of his mind.

I tuned in to our bond, throwing myself into it like I never had before. Reaching out with mental fingers I tried to slip past the barricades and trenches he'd created across his psyche to keep me out. I was sucked down a channel of emotion. A flash of knowledge burned into my mind's eye as the jealousy and hatred he felt for Tomas poured into me. My nature panted in approval.

Dragging myself back, I saw the world with my own eyes once more and understood Breandan with a lucidity that defied logic.

My feet slid apart, boots making a soft scraping. My

knees bent and I bounced from side to side. I was hyperaware of everything. The low growl from Tomas that hung on his lips rang loud in my ears. Breandan's heart thumped into his ribcage – racing with the thrill of the chance to rid himself of this rival for my heart.

The three of us measured each other and acknowledged that this fight would take everything.

If Breandan got the upper hand, Tomas was dead. If the vampire managed to get his fangs into the fairy's neck, he could drain him in seconds.

The blood rushed in my ears as the finality of this moment swept over me. Neither of them would back down so I had to win this. If not, one would be lost to me forever. Oh gods. A bubble of panic had tears threatening to fall. No. I needed to stay calm and focus. I had to use what I had seen and manipulate it to my advantage.

Breandan favoured his left fist and would always swing left if presented with a choice. Tomas' fangs and his ability to cloak his next moves in darkness were his greatest weapons. Breandan had difficulty in anticipating his next strike so he had to take the blows and deliver his own with enough force to wind the vampire. Both were blinded by the fact they hated each other, and were sloppy in executing their defensive blocks. They wanted to attack, advance, and cause pain. Both focused their energies on the offensive rather than defending their vital spots.

Breandan stepped closer, as did Tomas. I had no choice but to move forward too. Our circle closed step by step until we were a mere leap away.

"Rae," Tomas growled. "You must leave this place."

"Agreed," Breandan said simply. His eyes were opaque, grey, pupils dilated.

My chin lifted as a sudden gust of wind whipped my hair into my face. "I will not."

We stood tense and aware. Silence. Who would make the first move? Who would be the one to start the beginning of the end?

Tomas broke first – a flurried lunge and swipe. In slow motion, I watched as Breandan's foot shoot out and clipped him in the jaw. The fairy's fist swung toward me and I reacted – realising a fraction of a second too late that his other arm was headed for my torso. His open palm connected with my upper body even as his left fist sailed past my head as I jerked to avoid it.

I had trusted my instincts and my instincts had been wrong. My mind reeled as the end of this fight became horribly clear to me.

By the gods, it was impossible. No one, *nothing*, could move *that fast*.

The blow to my chest vibrated my whole body. The force behind it sent me airborne, soaring back until I hit the steps with such momentum they buckled inward. With immeasurable speed and unbeatable grace – even as I flew through the air – Breandan's legs shot out in a double kick that jerked Tomas to the left then instantly to the right. Tomas crumpled to the ground in a tangled sprawl of limbs. My fairy was on him and rained blows upon his limp body; a left hook to the ribs, a straight jab to the face. Finally, he gripped the vampire's head in both hands and slammed their foreheads together. Tomas' head bounced off the floor and there was a hollow sounding crunch. Blood spattered. Beaten beyond recognition, he spasmed.

Hissing, Gwendolyn landed in front of me. Before her clawed fingers could grab my throat Daphne jumped on her back. She sank her teeth into her Queen's throat, long braids jiggling madly as she buried her fangs deeper. Snarling, they fell backward entwined. Gwendolyn tried to scratch Daphne's face, but the girl threw her head back gasping, blood dribbling down the corners of her mouth and throat. Even as her eyes fluttered in pleasure, she rammed Gwendolyn's head into the concrete in a powerful push that cracked the pavement. She sprung up and dragged the vampire Queen back up the stone steps by those dark ringlets she was so fond of – smacking her head on every ledge as she went for maximum damage. Gwendolyn's legs flailed and she shrieked in high-pitched squeals of rage.

My heart skipped a beat before pounding erratically. The balance of power shifted and Breandan filled the street with the influence over magics I lacked. I fought him, trying to claw the power back to me, but it was done. His power had grown to fill the void mine had briefly vacated.

Fisting his hands in Tomas' shirt, Breandan hauled the limp vampire onto his knees. He swayed and Breandan wrapped his large hands around his head, fingers pressed into his skin. His wings unfurled, gleaming silver, until they fully extended from his body. My fairy-boy glowed like the sun, a spectre of light.

I was afraid – terrified – of what would happen next.

Dragging myself up I tottered on my toes. My body screamed at me to lie back down, but I gritted my teeth and took an unsteady step. Already the bond tugged on me, the urge to touch my other half flaring to become a desperate thing. No! I would fight it. I would not be overcome this time.

Tomas' face healed, revealing the bold and unusual features that had stunned me the first time I had met him.

I clutched my chest and applied pressure to the

stabbing, wrenching agony I swear was more than my heart could handle.

"Please," I mumbled so quietly my lips may have not moved. My head swung sluggishly from left to right. "Don't do this." Breandan's eyes were riotous. His nature was wild and aggravated – ready to destroy. "Wait," I held my hands up and drew in a ragged breath. "Just wait. Let him go. We will leave this place and never look back." He shook his head causing my heart to thump and quiver. A tear rolled down my cheek, slid across my lips, then dropped from my chin. It was lost in the cold rain streaming down my face. "Don't. Don't do this. Wait."

"No," he roared. "I am done being patient. I no longer understand nor do I care to. You belong to me. We are bonded and that is the end of it."

Behind me Gwendolyn's grip on the stair railing tightened until the metal groaned and warped.

Daphne held her by the hair and the strain on her face was horrible to see. Her eyes were locked on Tomas and they filled with sorrow and acceptance. The Nest Queen tried to crawl forward, but Daphne tightened her grip in the fistfuls of ringlets she held and yanked her head back.

Gwendolyn had no choice but to stay crouched as she was. The railing buckled as she wrung her hands. "Leave him, fairy," she rasped in panic. Her eyes pinged from my fairy to her vampire consort. "I'll let you leave. I'll let you both leave."

Breandan's nostrils flared, but not once did his eyes stray from me. "This has to happen because he will never stop. Do you understand, Rae? He will never stop wanting you. I will not live in fear that he may take you from me. You are mine and there can be no other. The blood tie will leave you open to him for the rest of your life. I let you save him once, and still he pursued you, brought you closer to danger. At one point your light winked out completely and I thought he had–" He choked up. "You nearly died. I cannot let this go. I will not." Abruptly, Breandan's mind touched mine. He twitched when he felt the darkness that connected me to what he saw as an enemy. He openly recoiled when it twisted inside me, whispering for me to embrace wicked things, for me to save my vampire.

"Rae, you remember what I told you?" Tomas asked urgently. "I never knew it would happen. I didn't know I would love you." He stared hard at me, eyes begging forgiveness. "Believe me." He reached out and his pale fingers curled in the air as if he stroked my face.

Opening my mouth to give him what he needed, my words caught in my throat. I ran forward and clasped his hand, pressing it to my chest over my heart. "I can't say it," I sobbed. "I can't give you a lie."

I cried, unable to express what I felt for him, knowing that it was not enough, not what he needed to hear. Breaking. My heart was breaking, and the sound that choked from my throat was inhuman. No, I could not give this demon my heart because it did not belong to me anymore. It never would again. And I could not give him a lie to give him peace.

However, I could give him a truth. "But I believe you," I whispered.

From Tomas' red-rimmed eyes – bottomless puddles of black ink – flowed contentment. He was saying farewell; that I would be safe and that this was the end of him. "Quiet now," he murmured and brushed away a tear. I memorised the feel of his cool hand, knowing this would be the last time he touched me.

Standing, I let his hand slip from mine. I locked eyes with Breandan who worked his jaw, expression stony. He would not relent, nor would he back down while there was breath left in his body. Breandan's life for Tomas'. It was a trade ... one I was not willing to make.

This time I could not be the one to save my vampire. It was over.

Backing away from them both, I kept Breandan's gaze. I summoned the last of my strength to endure the finality of those steps, to turn and look away, but in the last moment, I broke and watched it happen.

I watched, as my fairy gripped Tomas' head in hands that glowed with silver light.

Then ripped it off.

EPILOGUE

I remember flashes. Pain. Screams. Blood-curdling shrieks razing across my eardrums and drowning my cries of terror. My heart took stabs of emotion, splinters of pain. I had been braced, prepared, yet still my world rocked, trembled, and crashed down. Then I was sprawled on the ground as my legs failed me and buckled, the strength knocked away by shock. It did not matter how hard I screamed, how wildly I shook my head, or how quickly my wings fluttered.

Breandan's bellow as he dropped Tomas' head was savage and triumphant. Once again the lightning silhouetted him. Thunder rumbled across the sky and he roared back, but the end was tinged with misery and sorrow.

Gwendolyn's grief-stricken wail seemed endless and hollow as she crawled to Tomas' side. She grabbed at his clothes and pulled his headless body toward her, draping herself over him. Her body shook as she extended a hand to the head that lay face down a few paces away.

Daphne stood still, head bowed, lips moving in silent prayer.

Breandan stepped over the vampire Queen and crossed the distance to loom over me. He scooped me up and cuddled me close. His nature was sated and rolled over mine in comfort.

I stopped screaming, and stared into his face, still struggling … no … unable to comprehend what I had witnessed.

The absence of Tomas' darkness was stark. The cold clarity of his demise reached me and I shook. My eyes landed on the headless body sprawled beneath Gwendolyn. She stared at nothing, face slack and dazed.

Tears blurred my vision and I gasped, choking on the air and on my own tears. I could not breathe. I could not think. The darkness on the edge of my vision was ebbing away. Like clear water washing a stain, a silver-blue glow bloomed. I shook my head to try to stop the purge. I sobbed, but it caught in my chest, a bubble of pain that bloated and pressed down on my heart, restricting its erratic beat. It hurt. Oh, Tomas. A numbing disbelief crept through my legs and arms, sucking away all feeling, all hope. My eyes burned so I clenched them tight and tucked my fisted hands into my stomach – holding myself together.

"The Queen," Breandan muttered, weary. "I must–"

"No," Daphne murmured. "She's no danger to us right now, and besides, Cael won't let her live long once he discovers Rae was here. Is she all right?" She asked and it sounded as if she spoke from down a long, windy tunnel. "I'm out of practice with this kind of thing, being immortal and all, but she looks feverish."

"We should not have lingered here," Breandan said quietly. Sighing, his chest heaved against my body. "It is too much for her. Let me pass."

There was a faint and cool pressure on my forehead. "She's burning up."

"It is how we grieve." His arms tightened around me.

"Her body and mind are fighting to accept the loss. She will bear the pain and live. Now let us pass."

"I'm coming with you."

Breandan was quiet before saying in a curious voice, "You stopped the Nest Queen from hurting my Rae. Why?"

"Saw that, did you?" she asked dryly.

"Why?"

"Tomas told me all about her as she slept off the effect of his feeding." Her dainty hand pressed against my forehead again, trying to cool me down. "She is special, isn't she? Even if he had not explained who she was, I would still feel the need to help you. He told me it was likely you would follow her here, and that you would challenge him. He knew the chances of facing you and surviving were slim. He wanted to try to protect her as best he could, so, he gave her me." Daphne sighed heavily and I could imagine her white-blonde braids falling over her shoulder as she tilted her head. "And as for why I am not attacking you … I understand what has happened here. I accept it. Tomas knew, despite Rae's promise, that when the blood tie formed it was likely the end of him. She had a high fairy mate; of course, it was over for him. He brought her here to try … to just … try to see if there was even the slightest chance he could make it work. But you and I know it was nothing but a matter of time before Gwendolyn killed her. Even with Tomas' protection added to my own we could never hold back an entire Nest, and Rae can't use magic in this city because of Cael's enchantments. It was best you came for her."

Breandan was quiet for a long time. I slipped deeper into the darkness. "I am her protector," he said.

"Yes, and I am not trying to steal that from you, but I

swore that I would guard her body with my own. Tomas is…. Tomas is gone but I will honour my promise. I have never been one to believe in destiny, but I think it might be my calling to protect her. And that is what I'm going to do whether you like it or not."

"I have no quarrel with you."

"Despite what you think, I have none with you because she doesn't." Daphne touched my cheek softly.

"The day she does?" Was that humour in his tone? Breandan talking to a vampire and sounding amused?

"On that day I hope you're ready to see how a warrior of my kind fights. But the way Rae feels about you … I don't think I'll have to hurt you for a long while yet."

"If you betray her—"

"Never," Daphne replied fiercely then urged in the same breath, "but I don't have time to convince you of that. We must go. We cannot be here when the Nest returns. We must get Rae out of the city. Cael will be furious when he discovers she was here and Gwendolyn kept her from him. He'll send the Nest to find her, and we must be far from the city. Safe, so she can rest. We don't have much time, and I'll need to find somewhere to rest for the day."

"Her safety is my main concern but I—" Breandan cursed the gods under his breath. "I must find the grimoire. My brother needs it."

Daphne breathed out sharply. "I have the grimoire."

His body tensed. "How did that happen?"

"Who do you think captured the High Lord?" Daphne sounded proud, fierce. "I am the Nest hunter. No other of my kind can match me in a fair fight."

Breandan was quiet for what seemed an age. "He gave her your protection. He gave her his immortal life." The hold he had on me tightened as he burrowed his face in my neck and breathed in deeply. "He loved her." It was not a question, but a sadly spoken statement of fact.

"Yes. Yes he did."

Breandan rubbed his cheek on my temple. "I tried to warn her," he murmured. "I didn't want her to see him … he left me no choice."

Daphne's cool hand swept my hair back from my face. Shuddering at the cold, I scrunched my eyes tighter together and curled myself into Breandan's warmth.

"Words will never make what you did less painful for her," Daphne said sharply. "Remember that."

My fairy cupped my face with his hand and pressed kisses to my eyelids, my cheeks, and forehead. I gripped his wrists, feeling his pulse beat steady and strong beneath my fingertips.

Tomas had loved and betrayed me. He lured me to his Nest so his family could feed from me – to become revived as I faded. The demon had broken my heart in two. He tied himself to me in blood then turned his back on the trust I gifted to him. He was a vampire, a dark predator who was never mine, he had always belonged to another. No matter what he felt for me, he had made his choice.

In the end he had chosen them, his family, and … rightly so.

I cannot keep you with me, Tomas. Should you stay it would end me. I would not be able to breathe through the pain of your loss. I cannot hide in shadows of your dark. And I choose not to.

The darkness dissipated with a sigh.

The glow pulsed; filling me with warmth and love so luminous, it threatened to blind me. For the briefest of moments, my eyes fluttered open and I glimpsed eyes of liquid silver.

"I am with you," I breathed.

Breandan's mouth brushed across my jaw and the tip of his tongue gathered my tears, as if losing them to another caused him pain. "Beyond forever," he murmured and pressed his lips to mine.

The sound of vampire shrieks drawing nearer had my heart thumping erratically.

After that there was only a memory of darkness.

Find out more about Penelope Fletcher and her novels at PenelopeFletcher.com.

Made in the USA
Charleston, SC
30 October 2014